BASTION

THE COLLEGIUM CHRONICLES
BOOK FIVE

MERCEDES LACKEY

DAW BOOKS, INC.
DONALD A. WOLLHEIM, FOUNDER
375 Hudson Street, New York, NY 10014

ELIZABETH R. WOLLHEIM
SHEILA E. GILBERT
PUBLISHERS
www.dawbooks.com

First Printing, October 2013

1 2 3 4 5 6 7 8 9

DAW TRADEMARK REGISTERED
U.S. PAT. AND TM. OFF. AND FOREIGN COUNTRIES
—MARCA REGISTRADA
HECHO EN U.S.A.

PRINTED IN THE U.S.A.

*To the memory of my mother, Joyce Ritche,
who never failed to support me.*

There it was, a city on a low, gentle hill, walls shining in the sunlight, houses clustered up against the outer and inner walls like chicks snuggling up to a gray hen. And underneath Mags, the solid, steady warmth of his Companion, jogging steadily toward those walls, taking him back to the only place he could even think of as home. By all rights, Mags should have been half out of his mind with joy to see the walls of Haven in the distance, but all he could muster was relief.

Partly, that was due to exhaustion. After all, a person doesn't get kidnapped, drugged, escape, trek alone and without any real resources across a foreign wilderness, get caught again, get drugged *again,* and fight his way free without being exhausted by it. He'd gotten some rest on the journey back; his Herald and Healer escorts had been very careful to see that the trip had been taken at a slow pace when Mags showed no evidence that he was in a fret to be home. But exhaustion could be mental as well as physical, and he was suffering from both. His sleep was . . . not good. He woke a dozen times in the night, and his dreams were full of strange images, people he didn't know, a life he had never imagined before all this. He knew what they were from, of course: the "memories" that his captors had forced into his head. And none of these so-called "memories" raised even a little interest in him. If anything, he would have liked to be rid of them. They were disturbing on a multitude of levels.

Dallen, his Companion, had been uncharacteristically quiet for the entire journey back to Haven. He was always a steadying presence, but he just hadn't said much that wasn't necessary. Not that the Companion was withholding himself in any way! On the contrary, it was a great relief to Mags to feel Dallen as a bulwark in the back of his mind when he woke in the night. And it wasn't a disapproving sort of quiet, more the introspective sort.

When Mags had finally asked him what was going on, just this morning, he'd gotten a somewhat surprising answer. At least, it wasn't anything that Mags would have guessed.

:I'm examining those—well, I suppose they are "memories"— that you got.: And that was all Dallen would say. So those memories . . . well, Mags supposed it was just as well *someone* was looking through them. It was the very last thing that *he* wanted to do.

It wasn't the first time that Dallen had gone rummaging through Mags' head, and Mags certainly didn't mind, but it was the first time that the things Dallen had examined weren't exactly events that Mags himself had lived through.

I wonder what he's made of all of that . . . He'd probably shared it with other Companions at this point; it would be foolish not to. The men who had shoved those things into Mags' skull had tried multiple times to destroy the heart of Valdemar—first by killing the King, then by destroying the Companions, then by kidnapping the daughter of the King's Own Herald, Mags' sweetheart, Amily. If anything could be learned by going through all those thoughts, Mags would let a hundred Companions rummage through them.

:So?: he asked, as they rode down into a valley and lost sight of the city for the moment. *:Have you learned anything?:*

Dallen made a sort of muttering noise, and Mags got the definite impression that he was not at all happy. A moment later, the Companion's answer explained why. *:Not very enlightening as to the origin of your pursuers. I suppose I would have to say "your countrymen"—:*

:Not mine!: Mags objected, so strongly that Dallen's head jerked up, and the Companion turned to stare at him with one startled blue eye. *:Mebbe I got the same blood, but I ain't the same sorta person as they are! Valdemar's my home!:* No matter what those fiends had said, if there was one thing he was sure of, it was this—he had nothing whatsoever in common with a clan full of assassins who took whatever contract paid most, regardless of how heinous it was.

: . . . I apologize, Chosen,: Dallen said contritely—and immediately. *:I should never have put it that way. Well. There is a lot you don't really remember of what they poured into you, and I think that's just as well. I can get at it with some work and share it back with you, but, honestly, it doesn't seem to be particularly useful. It's mostly about training, clan life, the clan hierarchy, and the bonding that those awful talismans of theirs creates. There's nothing there that I can look at and say, "Aha! That's where they come from!" I don't recognize the language, even. Rolan doesn't.:*

It wasn't the first time that Dallen had shared things at a great distance with Rolan; Mags' Companion seemed to have an extraordinarily long "reach" when it came to Mindspeaking. And that gave Mags some comfort. Rolan knew . . . a lot. He'd been the Companion to the last three King's Own Heralds, and as a Grove-Born, Mags had every reason to suppose that he had access to a wealth of information no other creature—except maybe a few gray old scholars—had ever seen.

:While I've heard of drugs that repress Mindspeaking, I've never heard of drugs that open you up to memories like that. The talisman they used . . . that seemed to be where those memories came from. Something of that sort is completely new to me and to Rolan as well.:

Dallen settled himself back down, as Mags brooded on what he'd said.

:Was there anythin' at all that was useful?: he finally asked.

:Hints. I wish there had been more of their life outside of their training. Or more of their more—esoteric training. Spy work. There were hints of things that could have been enormously useful to you in the path that Nikolas is mapping out for you. The techniques and tricks of an assassin are useful for a lot more than just killing people.:

It was too bad that Dallen had not managed to glean anything more useful, and yet Mags was just as glad he wasn't going to have to re-experience those memories for the sake of learning . . . spycraft. Surely Nikolas could teach him everything he would ever possibly need to know. Mags would just as soon not think too hard about what had been stuffed into his head. The best of it was unpleasant, and the worst made his skin crawl. He was just glad that it was all—secondhand, as it were. Something that didn't *feel* as if he had done it.

And he was just as glad that his parents had escaped that poisonous environment. He didn't like to think what he would be like if he'd been raised that way, with every waking moment in earnest competition with other killers. Being a mine-slave had been bad enough; he still was not sure why it hadn't turned him hard and cruel. But the training that his blood kin went through . . . that was worse. It was *meant* to turn someone hard and cruel. It was meant to turn someone into a ruthless killer who would not hesitate to murder a babe in its mother's arms.

They rode up the slope, and now, again, above the farm fields and meadows that surrounded it, was Haven, close enough to make out people on the road leading in, the low Hill on which the Palace and the Collegia stood rising slightly above the rest of the city, secure behind their stone walls. And farther out, the city walls built of the same mellow stone. Not that the city needed walls anymore; evidence of that lay in the sprawl of city streets that spread out untidily outside them. The walls themselves were not even manned these days, except as a place for the City Guard to use as an easy path for patrolling, and a vantage point for looking down over the streets below. No enemy had come far enough into Valdemar to put the capital under siege in twenty generations or more. Only on the Borders did cities need to huddle inside their walls—and really, not even on all the Borders. Mostly the one with Karse, although there were places in the north and west where small, organized troops of bandits were enough of a threat that no one wanted to build outside a defensive wall.

Spreading out over what was ordinarily a quiet stretch of common land between the city and the river was a second city of tents and canvas booths, and ever since the city had come into view, traffic on the road had been growing thicker. This was a reminder, not that Mags needed one, of how long he'd been gone from Haven. He had been stolen away in early autumn. It was now almost winter. This was the Haven Harvest Fair, the last Harvest Fair in Valdemar for the year. Those merchants and peddlers disinclined to travel in the winter descended on the capital for one last spate of commerce before settling back into their shops and workshops for the winter months. Farmers brought their stock and their produce for merchants to store and sell all winter long. There was a Hiring Fair in one corner, a Horse Market in another. And, of course, where there was a Fair there were always entertainers. With all the other Harvest Fairs over, every traveling player and musician, every roving acrobat and tumbler, every single person who made his living on the road supplying amusement, all converged on Haven for the biggest Fair of the season.

It wasn't the only fair, of course; there were four huge ones, one for each season, plus various other specialty fairs. But this was the biggest of them all. There would be another enormous Fair at Midwinter, but it would be only half the size of this one, if that; it would depend entirely on the weather. There would be no Hiring Fair at Midwinter as all seasonal hiring was done at the Spring and Harvest Fairs, and any entertainer who had any sort of venue for regular income would be sticking to it and not venturing to cross the country in the hard months of bitter cold.

Mags thought of the Midwinter Fair with much more fondness than the Harvest Fair—even though the Harvest Fair was generally the favorite of all the other Trainees. It had been at Mags' first Midwinter Fair, ever, that he had met Master Soren, whose friendship had led to so much—including meeting Amily.

At the thought of Amily, he felt his throat closing; not even exhaustion could keep him from longing for her the way a starving man longs for meat. All of his doubts about whether or not he was in love with her had somehow vanished in those weeks he had been in captivity. If he had anything to say about it, he was never going to be separated from her again.

:I'd be jealous if she weren't worth every bit of your regard,: Dallen said lightly, and teasingly. *:And if I weren't certain she feels the same about you.:*

:Quiet, horse,: he managed, with real humor. *:Do I get jealous of all the mares you chase?:*

:And catch!: Dallen replied archly, and he curved his neck and flagged his tail to prove how handsome he was. *:Even Rolan can't keep up with me. I am a legend among the mares, I will have you know.:* Mags chuckled and felt his spirits start to rise, albeit sluggishly.

It could not possibly have been a more perfect day for a

homecoming. The air was just cold enough to still be pleasant as long as you were under a good wool cloak, the sky sported only a handful of fluffy white clouds. The air was rich with the scent of woodsmoke, fallen leaves, and the last hay crop drying in the fields. Virtually everyone on the road was in a high state of cheer. And how not? From everything that Mags knew, it had been a good and fruitful year, the harvests especially bountiful. Even if the winter was terrible, there was more than enough to sustain the entire Kingdom through it.

The crowds gave way to the easily identifiable three Heralds in their white uniforms who rode at the front of the little group, the remains of the troop of Guardsmen and Heralds that had met Mags and Dallen at the Karsite Border. There were the three Heralds, a Healer, and Mags now, which was a much more manageable number than the original rescue party. They'd been able to spend the nights in comfortable inns rather than tents.

It wasn't surprising that people parted to let them pass. Mags might be in the Grays of a Trainee rather than the Whites of a Herald, but his Companion marked him as one of the Chosen. And a Healer's Greens always got respect, no matter what he was riding on.

Mags must have seemed to be emerging from deep thought, for the Healer perked up and gave him a look of inquiry, which Mags answered with a nod. "I'm looking forward to finally meeting your friend Bear," the Healer said cheerfully, urging his mule up beside Dallen. "He's quite the genius with herbs, and I can learn a lot from him."

That made one of the Heralds turn around in his saddle to stare a little. "But Raynard, you have a Gift!" Herald Farnten exclaimed. "Why on earth would you need *herbs?*"

"Because if I can get the same result using herbs as I can using my Gift, I am going to use herbs," the Healer said patiently, as if he had been forced to make this same explanation far too many times in the past. "That way I save my energy for someone I *can't* dose with herbs. You have Fetching Gift. Do you use it to get an apple from a bowl across the room?"

The Herald chewed his lip a moment. "You have a good point," Herald Farnten replied, nodding. "I never thought of it that way. I just think of Healers as . . ." Then he shrugged. "Obviously, I'm an idiot."

"Not so much an idiot as the first part . . . you *didn't think*," Raynard chided. "But don't feel bad; that's all too common, alas. I wish it weren't. People like Bear would get a lot more respect."

It cheered Mags immensely to hear his friend spoken of with such respect by a Healer who knew him only by reputation. Certainly poor Bear got none of that from his own family, who felt that a Healer without a Gift was no kind of Healer at all.

This engendered a lively discussion between Raynard and Farnten, which Mags stayed out of. They generally agreed with each other, but they seemed to enjoy these debates that were not quite arguments. He'd learned that much on the journey back up from the South. He supposed just some people just enjoyed arguing for the sake of it and somehow managed to not turn an argument into an excuse for an actual fight.

:Yes, well, civility is an art form not practiced nearly enough,: Dallen observed. *:By the way, are you going to be civil enough to buy me a pocket pie on the way through the Fair?:*

:I swear I would, but you know I haven't so much as a bent pin in my pockets,: he apologized. *:I promise I'll beg the cooks for some for you when we get up to the Collegium. You deserve a thousand pocket pies for rescuing me.:*

:I'm pleased to see you properly value my courage.: There was a chuckle under Dallen's mind-voice. *:Not to mention my astonishing good looks and sparkling personality.:*

Mags found himself grinning and felt his spirits lightening some. *:You're almost as handsome as Raynard's mule. And a hundred times better as company.:*

He got a snort for an answer.

The road had entered the Harvest Fair, and it appeared that on the right was the quarter devoted to food and entertainment, and on the left was that devoted to livestock. Clashing bits of music competed with one another, showmen shouted out their attractions, and the aromas of a hundred different things to eat on the one side conflicted with the bawling of cattle, the whinnies of horses, the noise of flocks of chickens, geese, and ducks, the shouts of auctioneers, and the smells of animal sweat and dung on the other. Nearest to the road were the cattle pens, and it made Mags a little dizzy to think how much hay was going to feed the herds—and how much cleaning up it was taking to keep the pens healthy. Although, someone was surely profiting by that; healthy cow dung was valuable stuff, especially for those who had no cattle of their own and fields that would need a good manuring before winter set in.

It might seem a mistake to put the two quarters cheek by jowl, but men who had just concluded a bargain always wanted to drink over it, and the animal market had to go *somewhere.* At least the road divided them—and the rules of the Fair were quite strict about sanitation. Every pen had two boys whose only job was to make sure that the pens were clean enough you wouldn't hesitate for a moment to walk across them without watching where you were stepping.

It did make for a very noisy passage, however, and a crowded one, as drovers competed with travelers for road space. It was almost enough to give him a headache at this point, and it made him weary all over again to be battered by so much noise and crowding. Much as he had always enjoyed a Fair, Mags was glad to get out of this one and onto the quieter city streets.

Unusually quiet, which was all due to the presence of the Fair. Even merchants who could be found at their shops from dawn to dusk had closed up and opened little booths if their stock-in-trade lent itself to impulse purchases. And often enough, even if the merchant didn't close his regular shop, he'd send a 'prentice or two down to the Fair with a booth and some stock.

Mags breathed a sigh of relief as they found themselves on streets that held very little traffic. They were actually able to spread out a little, and the Companions, eager to be back in their comfortable stable and no longer kept to a slow walk by the press of the crowds, picked up their pace.

Mags knew Haven intimately at this point; probably no one knew these streets better than he did except the City Constables who patrolled them. But the familiarity was not giving him a great deal of comfort, and the closer he got to the Collegium, the less easy he felt.

And the more torn.

Because being home didn't really mean being *safe.* Not now that he knew what he was up against.

On the one hand, he was almost desperately glad to be back with Amily, with his friends. But on the other hand—he'd been kidnapped practically right under their noses. All right, he *had* been taken from within Haven, not the inside the Palace walls, but . . . the assassins had penetrated the Palace grounds before. They could again. Now Mags truly knew what he was up against in their skills, and he was not going to underestimate them.

Was he just bringing danger back with him?

:At least you know after that dust-up with the Karsites, the assassins are not *going to be tendering their services there anymore,:* Dallen said, in an effort to comfort him. It was a good effort . . . and what Dallen had said was true. The Karsite priests who had hired the men who had taken him had no idea just what it was they had contracted with. When their goals turned mutually exclusive, well, it was not the Karsites who had triumphed, at least not as far as Mags had been able to tell.

:I don' think they were lyin' when they burned up the contract,: he replied, as the street took another turn upward, and the neighborhood became more genteel, with fewer shops and larger homes. That had been why he'd allowed himself to be infected with those dreadful memories. It had been a bit of a devil's bargain, but the only one he could see his way clear to making at the time.

I won't fight you if you pledge to leave Valdemar in peace and never attack the Royal Family and the Heralds again.

At the time, there was no prospect of rescue. The contract with the Karsites was still to be fulfilled, and he had known that his kidnappers would fulfill it unless he gave them a reason not to.

At the time, all he could think of was that his duty as a Herald was to sacrifice himself to protect the Kingdom. So he had made his offer, hoping that *not fighting* was enough of an incentive to them that they would agree to it.

They had. He still was not entirely certain why, except that maybe their faith in their talisman wasn't all that strong. The fact that he hadn't resisted, and had still managed to remain himself, might very well be the proof that their form of coercive Mind-magic couldn't hold against someone who had training in the Heralds' form.

:An' I kept the letter of the bargain.: He had only pledged not to fight. He'd never pledged not to escape if he got the chance.

Plus . . . well . . . the Karsites had managed to thoroughly and completely muck things up for themselves by first aggressively confronting, then actually attacking the kidnappers. Mags had the notion that even if he'd escaped, his captors would be in no hurry to make another bargain with anyone as duplicitous as the Karsites.

So at least there was that much. *He* might still be in danger, but at least the Kingdom and its leaders were no longer in jeopardy from *that* source.

:I don't think they could lie about that,: Dallen opined. *:I don't think it would ever occur to them to outright lie. The thing I picked out of those memories is that they are absolutely bound by their contracts and pledges unless the person they've contracted with violates the agreement first. Which the Karsites did. Who knows? Maybe they'd already seen that the Karsites were not to be trusted and counted on the priests violating the agreement before it became an issue. I suppose that is only logical. Who would trust a clan of assassins to keep their bargains and not get bought out if they didn't have a stellar reputation? If you can call a reputation for that sort of thing "stellar.":*

Mags considered that. *:Yes, but . . . they made me that promise before the Karsite priests attacked them.:*

Dallen was silent. *:That's true . . . but I still don't think they are going to renege on what they promised you. Valdemar turned out to be a lot nastier to deal with than any of them expected. And we know now that they want* you, *specifically. Taking contracts from the Karsites was just a means to finance their deeper scheme, and they've discovered that the Karsites will break their word without a second thought.:*

Mags was not so sure about that . . . but then again, it was Dallen who had been sifting through his memories. Right now, the only things he could remember clearly were ones that would actually be useful to him. Then there were things that were muddy—like the attitudes these people had. And Dallen had just said there were things he had shoved away so hard he couldn't consciously remember them at all.

Dallen might be in a better position to judge than he was.

He certainly hoped so.

By this time, they were out of the district of merely prosperous houses and into the one of extremely wealthy mansions—passing right by Master Soren's home, in fact. The place was shuttered up, and no surprise, really, with the Harvest Fair going on. Master Soren must be up to his eyebrows in business right now; he was involved in every aspect of the cloth trade since he was on the King's Council, and he would deem it his duty to personally oversee trade at this Harvest Fair. He certainly couldn't wait around his own doorstep on the off chance that Mags would be coming by. And Mags was quite certain that as soon as his business allowed, Soren would personally come to see that his young friend was all right.

Still, he felt a faint disappointment, which he quickly scolded himself out of.

It ain't as if you're all that important, either, my lad! he reminded himself. And since all the Companions and their Chosen up on the Hill had certainly known to the quarter-candlemark when he would be arriving back at the Collegium, he knew he could be certain of a warm welcome from his friends.

:You very nearly got a warm welcome on the road,: Dallen put in, as they passed from the homes of those who were merely wealthy to those who were wealthy *and* highborn. *:It was only being reminded that those who skipped classes would get demerits that prevented a general stampede through the Harvest Fair.:*

Mags smothered a laugh. *:That could have been awkward.:*

:A bit more than awkward. Having us galloping through the Fair would be likely to set all the animals in an absolute uproar, and not all the Animal Mindspeakers on the Hill would have been able to keep them quiet.: Dallen shook his head vigorously. *:No, you'll just have to put up with an avalanche at the—oh, look, here it comes now.:*

"Here it came" indeed. Ahead of them, the main gates to the walls around the Palace and Collegia sprang open, and a flood of Companions—some with Gray-clad Trainees, a few with Heralds in full Whites, and many carrying double with people in Healer Trainee Green, Bard Trainee Rust, and Guard Blue—came pouring out. There were even a few ordinary horses amid the crush, which poured down the road and surrounded the five riders in a shouting, laughing mob.

And then the shouting, laughing mob, having engulfed their prey, turned around and carried the five back up through the gates in a relentless tide of exuberance.

It took all afternoon before people stopped mobbing Mags, pounding his back, and welcoming him home in the heartiest possible manner. He was actually starting to feel a bit bruised by the time he sat down to supper with his closest friends.

Not that the dining hall wasn't full to bursting with everyone who could cram in there, but at least he was finally able to not have to answer a hundred questions at once. In fact, he didn't have to answer any questions at all; his friends kept his plate and cup full, didn't ask him *anything,* and let him have some peace. It was good to be surrounded by his friends. Next to him was the Healer Trainee, Bear, with his round, affable face and his air of peace. On the other side of Bear was Bear's wife (though it was hard to think of her as his *wife,* even now), the Bardic Trainee Lena, tiny, dark-haired, and with the most melting brown eyes he'd ever seen that didn't belong to a baby rabbit. They were literally his oldest friends at the Collegium.

And on his other side was Amily. Amily, who, to him, was the most lovely girl there. Amily, whose intelligence and bravery shone from her eyes, whose beauty was so quiet that most people overlooked it. Not as dark or as small as Lena, they might have been sisters, otherwise. But where Lena was finally acquiring the ability to catch and hold peoples' attention, as a Bard must, most people's eyes slid right over Amily. Which suited her just fine.

Between Amily and Bear, he felt bulwarked on either side by peace.

So he ate, and when he wasn't eating, he held Amily's hand. And sometimes when he *was* eating, he held Amily's hand. Princess Lydia, unmistakable with her mane of red curls and her brilliant green eyes, even managed to sneak out of the Palace in a purloined set of Grays to join them at the table, although, of course, absolutely no one was fooled by her "disguise." She couldn't stay long, of course; only the fact that the Court ate later than the Collegia allowed her to slip briefly away. But she got a chance to give him a welcoming hug, whisper that she was glad he was safe, and add a demand that he allow Lena to make at least *one* song about his misadventure.

"But not immediately," she added hastily, perhaps stricken with conscience at the hint of panic in his eyes.

Once she was gone, he was hit with a moment of something that was a little like despair at the idea that he was going to be answering questions from people over and over—for how long? Weeks? Moons? Probably not years; sooner or later something more sensational would happen, and people would lose interest.

He hoped.

But even as he thought that, he realized that something odd was happening. All over the dining hall, the Herald Trainees were getting that look on their faces he associated with *your Companion is having a word with you.* And as they came out of their little trances, they were grabbing friends from Healers' and Bardic, or the odd Blues, and whispering urgently in their ears. The expressions on most of the faces were a mixed bag of disappointment, understanding, and a bit of stricken conscience.

As this phenomenon spread through the dining hall, people began gathering up plates, making farewells, and leaving, until there was no one left but Mags' closest circle of friends.

"Don't tell me," he guessed aloud. "Dallen had a bit of a say, and the other Companions told people to give me some peace?"

The dark blonde girl across from him, who wore her hair tied up in a tail on the top of her head, laughed. "I told you he'd figure it out," Gennie said, and shoved over a plate of honey cakes. "Just one more thing—Dallen promised he'd give all the Companions the best bits, and they could tell us, and he'd leave nothing out, so *you* won't have to go over it until you're sick of it."

That was a relief, because he was already sick of it. He'd been questioned and cross-questioned to death on an official basis once everyone was sure that the Karsites weren't coming over the Border. Everything he could remember, things that Dallen had pulled out of his mind . . . "I just wish I could fergit it all m'self, at least for a little," he said plaintively, lapsing somewhat into the crude accents of the mine.

"Plagued by nightmares?" Bear asked, pushing his lenses back up on his nose from where they had slid down, as they always did.

"No, and I dunno why not. Ye'd think I would be." He shook his head. "Mebbe it's still all too fresh."

"Well, I've got some good potions if you need them," his friend assured him, patting his hand a little, his brown eyes peering at him anxiously from beneath an unruly shock of dark curls.

"That'll do, granny," teased Jeffers, one of the few at the table who was not in a uniform. He combed his nearly black hair back out of his eyes and grinned. There was a healing bruise on one cheek, which was hardly surprising. He was a member of Mags' Kirball team, of which Gennie was the captain. And Mags was stricken with a sudden sense of loss—because certainly the season was well underway, and certainly they had chosen someone to replace him. He would *never* want to spoil someone else's pleasure by taking back the position—but Kirball might have been one of the few things he could do that would take his mind off everything that had happened to him.

So amid everything else, his kidnappers had stolen his chiefest pleasure from him.

He didn't say anything, though he felt Dallen trying to comfort him. It would be better not to mention it at all, or wait for someone else to say something and then be gracious about it.

But it hurt, and hurt with an unexpectedly deep pain, to know that for the first time since the game had been introduced—he wouldn't be playing it. At least, not officially, and not on one of the four Collegium teams.

While he wrestled with his emotions, the conversation had gone on. No one said anything about the game, although people were doing their best to catch him up on other things that had happened since his kidnapping. This, at least, was soothing. It was all commonplace, comforting stuff. Who was seeing whom, who had gotten Whites and gone out on their first Circuits in the Field with their new mentors. Which Companions had foaled. How Sedric was faring as Prince ("No one worries about Lydia. Lydia is perfect, of course, everyone says so"). Who had gotten full Scarlets and Greens, and had gone— Mags really didn't know any of the people who had, although, thanks to Nikolas's training, he could actually put faces and a bit of a personality to every name mentioned. Court gossip that had percolated down to the Collegia. The fact that it was all so very commonplace—and was stuff that wasn't even remotely important or earth-shaking—was reassuring. It told him he hadn't been gone all that long, because no one mentioned was a stranger except for a handful of new Trainees.

He suddenly realized he was starting to nod over his drink and blinked at Bear suspiciously. "You didn't go dosin' me, did ye?" he asked.

"Not I!" Bear protested. "But when you're finally home from a stressful time, it's common to—" Whatever he was going to say was quelled by Lena reaching around and clapping her hand over his mouth.

"He's not your patient at the moment, and he probably

doesn't need to be," Lena chided him, getting away with the indignity as only a new spouse can. She let Bear go before he could start to squirm and leaned around her spouse to talk directly to Mags. "If I were you, I would be absolutely knackered and looking for my bed. Don't worry. They've made sure your room is ready."

"And I'm ready for it," he admitted, yawning. "Sorry I'm not a bit entertainin'," he apologized.

"Why, you mean you didn't get abducted and dragged across country purely to make us a story for us to chew over endlessly?" asked Pip, tossing his shock of tow-colored hair indignantly. "The *nerve!*"

That was enough to get a laugh out of him, and the entire crew surrounded him to walk him down to the Companions' Stables, where his room still was. They left him at the door so he could get back inside the four walls he knew best, sighing a little as he felt tension slip out of him. It was all the same. No one had moved anything, not even when they cleaned it and put fresh linens on the bed.

He was home at last. And it felt, oh, so very, very good to be here.

By sheerest coincidence, the timing on Mags' return could not have been better, although he didn't know it until he got to the dining hall the next morning after a night of completely exhausted sleep.

It had been deeply restful, quite as if he had spent the entire night curled up in a pair of giant, comforting hands. He felt as if this were the first solid night of sleep he'd gotten since he'd returned, and, for once, his dreams weren't troubled by those memory fragments.

He woke early—probably since he'd gotten to sleep *very* early—and lay quietly for a good long time, listening to the birds singing out in Companion's Field behind the stable and to the sounds of the Companions themselves dozing in the rest of the building. He could, quite literally, feel muscles that had been tense all this time finally relax.

But he couldn't lie here all day, and he really didn't particularly want to anyway. Judging the hour by the quality of the sunlight, he decided that it must be just barely dawn, and he decided to take advantage of the fact that almost no one ever had a bath in the morning to go up to the Collegium and have himself a good hot soak.

He got up and checked the chest where he usually kept his clothing. Someone had made certain there were plenty of changes of freshly cleaned Grays that fit him. He felt a wave of gratitude for his unknown benefactor; it would have been perfectly easy to just leave the Grays that were in there alone, rather than clean the chest out and put in fresh ones, with sprigs of rosemary between each layer.

The bathing room was empty and silent, and he ran hot water from the boiler into his favorite tub, the one in the corner. He felt as if he were soaking out more than just dirt, as if he were soaking out some of the lingering nastiness from his captors' drugs and memories. At last he came down to breakfast with damp hair and feeling entirely presentable for the first time in weeks, to discover the dining room was full again—but it wasn't to gawk at him. The moment he caught bits of errant thoughts from unshielded minds, he knew why, too—all three Collegia had the day off so Trainees could visit the Harvest Fair. It was a real day off, too; none of the teachers had assigned any after-class work or exercises, and everyone would be able to just enjoy their holiday without fretting over the work. In theory, anyway. There would always be Trainees like Lena who never stopped fretting over the work, and would probably still be fretting over the work when she got her full Bardic Scarlets.

This probably wouldn't be the first day most of them had gone down to the Fair. You were allowed to go to any of the Fairs anyway, if you didn't have classes and had leave to go, but this was one day you could be sure of being able to go down with all of your friends.

And fortunately, the same kind soul who had made sure he was going to be properly clothed had also made sure there

were a few coins to spend in his purse—as he had discovered
when he had put everything on.

*:Of course she did. I want pocket pies, and she hopes you'll
get her a little something,:* Dallen snickered.

That answered the question of *who* had made sure everything in his room was put to rights and waiting. He grinned.
Trust Amily!

*:She wanted to be sure you wouldn't feel that people had
forgotten about you.:*

Well, he was fairly sure that someone would have seen to it
that his room was ready and he'd had something to wear, even
if all they had done was see to it that the uniforms already here
had been laundered, and the bed freshly made up. But no one
would have made sure the job was done as thoroughly as
Amily. It made him feel very good.

The dining hall had been one of the first places that had
meant anything to him, and he stood in the doorway, feeling
more of his tension ease away. As a completely starved mine-
slavey, who rarely saw anything more nourishing than thin
soup made with cabbage and bones, the good food so freely
available to the Trainees had loomed very large in his life. The
guard posts on the way here and the Collegium dining hall had
been the first places, ever, where he had been allowed to eat
what he pleased and as much as he pleased. And despite a few
bad moments here, when people had doubted him and he had
picked up on their thoughts, most of his memories of this
place were good ones.

It was a simple room, entirely of wood, with wooden pillars
down the center. Banners bearing the crest of Valdemar along
the walls and hanging from the rafters baffled some of the
noise that so many young people eating together were bound
to produce. There were counters at one end that served as
tables for the serving dishes, and the rest of the room was
filled with long tables with backless benches. Each table had

a stack of plates and cups and cutlery at one end, which were replenished by the servers as they ran low.

He scanned the dining hall to see if his friends were already at one of the tables and quickly spotted Bear, Lena, and Amily clearly holding a spot for him. The dining hall had two sorts of service, depending on whether it was a general holiday or something large and important was being held on the Palace grounds. Most days, like today, you took a seat at one of the long tables, got passed a cup and plates, bowls and cutlery from the end of the table, and then got passed serving dishes of whatever was going at that meal (or waited for one of the Trainees on serving duty to bring more dishes around if your table had run out). On days when everyone was busy—or when there was a holiday and there just weren't that many Trainees here because they were visiting with their families— you helped yourself from the buffet counter at the end nearest the kitchen.

It was a hotcake day, which made his mouth water as the aroma hit his nose. And when he discovered that today the cooks had fried apple slices into the hotcakes, he could not have been happier. The cakes had already been buttered before being served; he had only to lift them onto his plate and drizzle them with honey.

"I love hotcake days," Bear said, around a mouthful. Mags nodded happily. Before he had come here, he had never tasted hotcakes, not even burned ones meant for the pigs. He thought that whoever had invented them must have been a genius. They'd been one of the first things he had begged Nikolas to show him how to cook. Nikolas's version had involved frying bacon first, then frying the cakes in the bacon fat. This was because there obviously would be no butter if you were cooking in a Waystation, and there probably wouldn't be any honey, either. But that didn't matter because everything tasted good when cooked in bacon fat.

"I love the fact that you know how to cook them, because I don't," said Lena, nudging Bear with her elbow.

"I'll teach you," Bear promised.

"Or I will," said Mags. "Everybody should know how to cook." Now that he was not so tired, he was being careful of his speech again. "That's one of the things Nikolas was teaching me." He didn't mention that Nikolas was teaching him how to cook over the tiny fireplace in the little pawn shop the two of them ran in a rough part of Haven—a shop that bought information as often as it bought dubious goods. He didn't have to. Bear and Lena were privy to the fact that King's Own Herald Nikolas wasn't primarily teaching him how to cook— he was teaching Mags how to be a spy.

Ordinarily, some other senior Herald would have been teaching Mags that particular task when they were out in the Field, riding the Herald's Circuit, but the two of them had to eat while they were between customers, and Nikolas never let an opportunity for some kind of lesson go to waste. And after all, no pawnbroker in their part of town would ever lock up to go to a cookshop for food and take the risk of missing a customer. Being able to fry or stew something up for himself merely added to the verisimilitude of the character he was supposed to be.

"What?" asked Halleck, throwing his long legs over the bench and sliding in next to Mags. "Why would Herald *Nikolas* be teaching you to—" For a moment, Mags thought he had made a terrible blunder. Nikolas was the King's Own Herald, and a very important personage; there was no good reason why he should be doing a lowly task like teaching Mags to cook. But then suddenly Halleck colored with embarrassment. "I'm sorry, Mags, I'm an idiot."

Well, that was an unexpected response. Mags gave his friend and fellow Kirball player a sideways look. It appeared that Halleck had given him a reason for something that was unreasonable—he just had to find it out without directly asking. "I know you're an idiot, but why are you admitting it just now?"

Normally Halleck would have mock-punched his shoulder for that, but he only flushed deeper. "Because you and Amily— and up until Bear fixed her leg—" He passed a hand over his face. "It's not like it would've been safe for her to cook if you two were alone somewhere—but, I mean, I shouldn't've just come out and said that."

Finally it dawned on Mags where Halleck was coming from, and he had to work to keep from grinning. Halleck was right, of course—if for some reason he and Amily had been somewhere together where they couldn't just *get* food (like the Collegium) or *buy* food (like an inn or a cookshop or a baker), one of the two of them would have had to do the cooking if they were going to eat. And Amily had been pretty heavily handicapped for kitchen work with the way her leg had been all twisted up. She'd never have two hands to cook with, since one would always be involved in helping her balance. She couldn't handle anything heavy. And she'd have been unable to get out of the way of danger if she'd had an accident. And, yes, Halleck was a little bit of a boor for saying so. But he'd given Mags the perfect explanation of his own slip-up.

"Well, now we both have to learn," Mags pointed out. " 'Specially if she decides she's coming with me on Circuit, which she might well. She's stubborn that way." It wasn't unheard of for the mates of childless Heralds, or those whose children were grown, to accompany them on Circuit. And after seeing Amily's determination to make herself a partner, not a burden, to Mags, he had the notion this was exactly what Amily had in mind.

A few moons ago, he would have had some serious doubts about the wisdom of this idea. Now—well, as long as she could hold her own, defensively, he knew there was no question. Who knew how long he'd be at risk from his parents' clan? And if he was at risk, so was she. He would much rather have her with him than be fretting away half his nights, worrying about her.

"I reckon I'll f'give you for being a ham-handed idiot, but better not let her ever know what you were thinking," he said, and passed Halleck the porridge. "Are we all goin' down to Harvest Fair in a bunch, or what?"

"Amily'd kill us if we hared off without you two," said Bear, knowingly. "Last night she was dropping all kinds of hints about how we should do things 'the way we used to,' and all."

Mags had to chuckle. "You *are* married," he pointed out. "That makes it hard to do things the way we used to." He rather doubted, for instance, that the pair of them would welcome him and Amily staying well into the night in Bear's cozy lodgings. It was rather too bad, though, because Bear's rooms shared the special heating system with the greenhouse that kept all his herbs flourishing in the winter, and that made it a fine place to sit and study, play games, read quietly, or just talk.

"She has a point, though," Lena said, and passed him the bacon. "Just because we're married, we don't have to live in each others' pockets. I wouldn't at all mind spending all day with you."

Mags passed the bacon to Halleck, wondering if he ought to invite his friend to be one of the party. "Well, I'm spoke for," the saturnine Trainee said with a grin. "The Kirball Riders are each getting a new mount thanks to Princess Lydia. The team wants me to cast my eye over prospective candidates."

Mags managed not to lose his smile at this reminder that the team had, in essence, gone on without him. Halleck's obliviousness had made itself known again. And since Halleck wasn't talking about Amily, he was never going to figure out how insensitive he was being. "Better you than me," Mags said, swallowing his own feelings, along with a lump in his throat. "All I know about horses is what other people tell me.

Gods only know what kind of spavined crow bait I'd recommend because I felt sorry for it."

"Funny you should mention that," Halleck replied, and began an involved story of how he had managed to find what *he* considered the bargain of the century, because the horse in question *wasn't* acting all nervous—and, in fact, was dozing away in the paddock!—in the strange environs of the Horse Fair. "People were thinking he was deaf, or old, even though one look at his teeth would have *shown* them he was four, at most. Or sick, or just a slug. He isn't any of those things! He's just too smart to let himself get bothered by other horses getting bothered. He was actually bored by the Fair after being there for a few days, and he's perfect for us! Jeffers nearly went mad after trying his paces!"

Mags gritted his teeth and looked interested and appreciative and was effusive in his praise of Halleck's (and Halleck's Companion's) ability to judge a beast. Not that he wanted in the least to spoil Halleck's pleasure—after the other teams had seen the mounts he'd scored, they wanted his help, and he was justifiably proud of that. It seemed to take an age, but Halleck finally got off the subject and on to other things, and then the Captain of the Greens came to collect him so they could go down to the Fair together.

When Halleck was finally gone, Mags finished his breakfast fighting off gloom. He felt Bear's eyes on him, but he refused to meet them until he managed to get himself into a better frame of mind. After all, what did *he* have to feel sorry about? He was home—a home he had never thought to see again. He was himself, and not some stranger taken over by foreign memories, something that had seemed out of the question not that long ago. He was safe, everyone had missed him and welcomed him back, and absolutely *no one* was giving even a hint that they thought he didn't belong here, among the Heraldic Trainees. Just because his team had—understandably!—replaced him in a *game* was no call for sulks.

He must have been getting better at this sort of thing, because when he had finished the last bite, he had managed to persuade himself out of the gloom and into nothing more than a mild melancholy. "Right, then," he said, meeting Bear's concerned gaze again. "What's the plan? I know you got one, you never do nothin' without a plan."

Bear's expression lightened. "We promised we'd collect Amily about now. She's having breakfast with Lydia; Lydia wants some stuff particularly from the Fair if we can find it, but the Princess can't actually be seen wandering about like you or me."

"So Amily's gonna get it for her." Mags nodded. "I don' mind that, 'specially if you an' me can find things t'look at in the same places." He had no doubt that they would; didn't they both have ladies to buy nice things for?

Bear made a face. "Shopping," he said in tones of resignation. Lena elbowed him.

"I could say the same thing when you get into the herbs," she teased.

Mags was just happy to see them so settled and yet still like themselves. Somewhere in the back of his mind had been the fear that being married would change them. Instead, they were still themselves. Closer to each other than anyone else, but still themselves.

He didn't want to lose himself; he'd come far too close to that already. If Lena and Bear hadn't, then why should he and Amily?

"Plan," he reminded Bear. "I'm the only one with a Companion."

"There're wagons going down to the Fair and coming back, regular," Bear told him. "So, the plan is to get Amily, get a ride on the wagon, and do the shopping first. Then we reckon a bite of lunch, then we go see the entertainers that aren't like what we got up here. Like jugglers, rope dancers—"

Mags nodded. *:Sounds like you're bein' left behind today, horse,:* he teased Dallen.

:Fine. Leave me behind. See if I care,: Dallen teased back. *:Actually I'd be dreadfully awkward down there in all that crush. A couple of the others said it got pretty hot and uncomfortable at times. I have a plan to eat to the bottom of a bucket of windfall apples, then have a long nap, then another bucket of apples, then, well, give me some privacy.:*

Mags chuckled. *:I can do that,:* he promised. "There might be contests," he said out loud. "We might want to watch some of those." If there was a Master Archery contest, for instance, that would be very exciting. He would like to see wrestling, but he didn't think the girls would. Horse races—everyone would like those . . . foot races too. Spear throwing. He could think of a lot of things that would be fun to watch.

"I forgot about the contests, but Amily is all sorts of organized. She says she'll have a list of everything and where it is," Lena said, tucking her hand into the crook of Bear's arm.

"Well, then, let's collect her and see what's what." Knowing that his friends were perfectly capable of sitting there and discussing what they might want to do for another candlemark, rather than actually doing it, Mags got himself out from the table and bench, picked up all their dishes, and took them to the hatch into the kitchen. By the time he turned around, Lena and Bear were waiting for him at the door.

Herald's Collegium was actually stuck at the end of the Herald's Wing of the Palace, so they didn't even have to go outside. Amily was ready and waiting at the door to the Heralds' Wing, where every Herald that hadn't made some other arrangement had quarters. Amily shared a suite there with her father—which made him wonder, would she be willing to live in his stable room with him? There was just about the same amount of space as she had to herself in the suite, but the level of creature comforts probably wasn't as high . . .

He hadn't quite made up his mind whether or not to kiss her, but she took care of the situation by throwing her arms around his neck and kissing *him.* He was not in the least unwilling to kiss her back and was just a little bit disappointed when she broke it off.

"Here's the list of what's going on and a map of the Fair," she said, handing two pieces of reused paper to Lena. "I made two copies." Mags got just a glimpse of what was on the other side; it looked like some sort of very dull document. That was the norm up here at the Palace; there were a lot of things that stopped having relevance after a while, and the backs of them got used for writing-practice, after-lessons work, and anything else that didn't need pristine paper. He'd once written an entire series of assignments on the backs of harvest reports from decades gone by.

The wagon left from one of the small gates in the wall around the Palace-Collegium complex, the one that usually admitted the supply wagons. In fact, this actually *was* a supply wagon, with high, slat sides; low on comfort but very capacious. The four of them squeezed themselves into spots along one side on the plain wooden wagon bed. No one had thought about how they'd rattle and jounce all the way down to the Fair, but, then, most of them were too excited to care. There was just enough room that Bear and Lena, and Mags and Amily, could put their heads together over their lists and the map and make some rough plans.

"Lydia is even more organized than me," Amily said, pointing out the merchants in the list that she had underlined and the rough area of the Fair each would be in. "Then again, she's the Princess—she probably sent someone down to hunt things out for her. She wants a perfume from here, some tinctures from here, some specially good pens and ink from this man."

Mags started to ask why Lydia hadn't just had that same footman pick the things up for her—then he realized why. First, a Royal Footman wouldn't bargain. Second, a Royal Footman would be cheated, probably by being sold inferior goods for an inflated price. And third, a Royal Footman would not have the knowledge that Lydia's friends did. Bear could make sure the perfume was pure and not adulterated and vouch for the quality of the tinctures, while Lena, as a Bardic Trainee, was something of an expert in pens and inks, and might just try out as many as a dozen of the former before she picked out the ones that Lydia would want.

They had to be some sort of special pen, though, to be superior to the ones supplied to the Palace. He wondered just what on earth that was all about.

As he glanced over the list of contests, he didn't see much he was terribly interested in. For one thing, at least so far as he was concerned, he had to actually know at least some of the contestants to have any interest in the outcome. For another, things like "grain-sack hurling" and "pig catching" didn't exactly sound . . . exciting.

"I think the contests today are a wash," Bear said, craning his neck around.

"The good contests are all on the last three days, Lydia says," put in Amily. "And we'll all be back at lessons."

"Look, if I wanta see archery that'll make m' eyes bulge, I'll just ask Weaponsmaster for a demonstration," Mags pointed out. "Now, look here, there's a whole *tent* full of jugglers and tumblers and rope dancers, and the like! What's that about?"

"You pay your penny, go in, and stay as long as you like," Amily told him. "They have seats, and they change performers and acts. Kind of like if the performers at the wedding had come to us instead of us going 'round to them. This sort of thing only happens at the really big Fairs."

"I like that idea," Mags declared. "What about the rest of you?"

"I'm game," Bear nodded. And the girls agreed.

There was a music tent too, but no one suggested going to it. After all, when you lived at the Collegia, you had the music from Bardic all around you all the time. It would be very difficult to find any sort of music that was a novelty.

The wagon dropped them all off at the edge of the Fair, very near the first of the booths marked on Amily's map. This was where the commons started, at the edge of the city itself— mostly "waste" ground that people used to graze beasts they could keep in their tiny back yards, like goats or geese, or their donkeys if they had them. People were free to harvest the grass here to feed rabbits as well. Otherwise, anyone could use it for almost any reason as it was land held in common for anyone living in the city. Sometimes travelers or trading cara- vans camped here, and always the Fairs and Markets were held here. It looked as if a second city of tents had sprung up outside the first one.

Merchants generally lived in these tents as well as sold their wares or displayed their skills in them. Some were scarcely large enough to have room for a collapsible counter and a bedroll. Some were enormous, big enough to contain a hundred or more people at a time. All were laid out in a grid- work pattern, like houses with small spaces behind them. This had been the custom for hundreds of years, and was the busi- ness of a man called the Master of the Fairs, whose entire job was to make sure that each Fair and Market was put together in a sensible fashion, with proper care taken for sanitation and cleanliness.

Here, the tents were all small; a few were quite sumptuous, with canvas painted and even ornamented with touches of gold or silver. Some were small and plain. There was a faint hint of sweet and spice on the breeze, as if the very canvas of the tents had over the years soaked in the redolent aromas of the owners' wares. Since this was the area designated for herbalists, perfumers, chymists, and the like, it was highly likely that this was exactly what had happened. A well-made tent could serve several generations of merchant, after all.

Well, both Bear and Lydia wanted things here. This was as good a place as any to start.

Bear went with Amily to find Lydia's tinctures and Bear's herbs, leaving Lena with Mags to seek out the perfumer.

The tents had been placed in no particular order. Some quite plain ones selling dried herbs were right next to tents beautifully painted with flowers or geometric designs that sold expensive scents. The herbalists' wares were mostly packed away in sealed jars or airtight boxes, although they advertised by having bunches of fragrant things like rosemary and lavender hanging from their front "doors." The most expensive perfumers only needed their exquisite, tiny glass bottles, each one cut, and sparkling, like a gem.

The lesser lights of this profession sold their fragrances in bottles of stone or tiny pots; they didn't confine their fragrances to perfume, though, but also dispensed oils, creams, soaps, and pomades. There were even a few chandlers, which surprised Mags, until he saw that their candles were of scented wax that was molded or carved and colored like works of art. He couldn't imagine how anyone could bear to burn something like that, though he supposed that was the point. If you were wealthy enough to want to be ostentatious, this was the epitome of "burning money."

The perfumer they sought was one of the middling ones. His glass bottles were all plain dark amber in color and all the same shape. He dispensed not only perfume but other scented products as well. He was a tall, thin man, very pale, with hair so pale a color it was almost white.

His clothing was very different from anything that Mags had seen before. He wore a red linen shirt with huge sleeves ending in tight embroidered cuffs and a high neck, also embroidered, with an embroidered placket, not centered on his chest, but off to one side. He wore a broad leather belt and very full black trews tucked into high boots.

He smiled at them as they entered his tent. "Ah, young Herald and his friend, yes? How may I being to serve you?"

"Lydia of the House of Soren asked us to—" Mags began, as Lydia's note had coached him to say. The man clapped his hands together once, with an even broader smile.

"Lydia, of flaming hair, yes? She is being my customer since she is so high—" he measured a height barely up to the bottom of his rib cage with one hand. "I am already to be having package made up, knowing she will either come or send." He bent down behind his counter and came back up again with a basket that was almost as much a work of art as those expensive candles were. It had been made, as near as Mags could tell, of fine coils of pine needles sewn together. They still held a faint scent of pine.

And if Lydia was an old customer of this merchant, there was very little chance he would try to cheat her by passing off an inferior product. Mags relaxed.

"You are being have list, yes?" the man continued, unpacking the basket. "You will to be telling me if I am to be leaving anything out, yes?"

Mags fumbled out his list. "She says here, the scent is Forest." He'd always wondered how it was that sometimes Lydia would smell . . . well, like a forest. It seemed he had found the answer.

"Yes, yes. I am to be the only Scentmaster to be making this scent," the man said proudly. "I am to being Efan Sevanol, Scentmaster. Which, you are to being know already, as you saw sign. Now, of Forest scent. Four bars soap. Two jars cream for hands. Two pots cream perfume. One bottle essential oil. One bottle perfume. Is right, yes?" He beamed at them. Mags just had to smile back, the man's good humor was that infectious.

" 'Xactly right, Scentmaster," he said, and was rewarded with a rich chuckle.

"Good, good. I am to being hear she is to being married yes?" the Scentmaster continued, as he packed the basket up again, carefully cushioning the glass bottles of oil and perfume in tiny, form-fitting pine-needle sheaths of their own before repacking them. "As wedding present, I am to being add this, yes?" He held up a third bottle. "Is to being scent I am to be thinking she will like and will please husband. Is to being Ambar. Men are to being—" He waggled his eyebrows at them, and Lena giggled and blushed. "Yes, yes, young lady understands!" He crooked a finger at Lena, who came closer, and he opened a bottle fastened to the counter with wax so it wouldn't tip over and spill. The cork had something like a glass needle with a blunt point sticking in it. "Please to be giving me wrist, yes?"

Lena obliged; he gently ran the point of the needle over her wrist; it left a glistening trail of perfume behind.

"Now to be rubbing wrists together," the man—suggested, rather than ordered. Lena did, and Mags felt his eyes widen as the rich, dark, subtle scent reached his nose. It reminded him of . . . incense maybe. And honey. And woodsmoke. And . . . well, he understood exactly what the Scentmaster was hinting at, now.

"Oh—my!" Lena exclaimed, her nostrils flaring. "Oh, this is . . . very . . . intoxicating. . . ." She blushed again.

"Yes, yes," the man chuckled. "For married ladies, yes? They will be to having exciting time if wearing, yes?"

Lena laughed, still blushing. "It's a good thing I'm married, then!" As the Scentmaster tilted his head inquiringly, she added quickly, "Not to Mags, he's just a friend. To a Healer."

"And he is off hunting herbs and things not so interesting as scent." The man laughed again. "So, it is my dismal duty, as I am to be having many expenses, to be asking for payment, please?"

Lydia had named a price and given Lena the purse. Although Mags had expected Lena to bargain at least a little, after the addition of that very generous gift, Lena simply handed over the purse without a quibble. The Scentmaster opened the purse casually, counted it out without seeming to do so—Mags had learned that trick from Nikolas—and bowed, pushing the basket toward her. She took it, and hesitated.

"Something is wrong?" the Scentmaster asked quickly.

"I probably can't afford it," she said, a little sadly, "But . . . how much is the *Ambar?*"

"I am devastated to say it is a silver piece for a bottle," the Scentmaster replied, losing his smile. "The resin is difficult to find, the perfume is hard to make."

Mags could see Lena struggling with herself. And a silver piece was a great deal of money for someone like her or Mags, after all, for something as frivolous as a scent.

"But . . . if the lady does not mind a fainter scent," the Scentmaster continued, "I am to be having this—"

He held out another bottle.

"What is it?" Lena asked.

"I am to be diluting perfume with distilled spirits, am to be using much less of scent. Is to be four coppers for bottle." He smiled as Lena's eyes lit up. They exchanged coppers and bottle, the bottle once again being cradled in a little woven pine-needle sheath. "To being very careful. Distilled spirits are to being escape into air, easy. To being sure bottle is well sealed with wax when closed. But . . ." he chuckled. "I am telling grandmama how to pluck chicken, am thinking. You are wife of Healer, you will to being know these things. Thank you, my young friends! Tell others of Efan Scentmaster! I have many fine things for all tastes!"

Mags counted up his pennies in his mind, and asked, without hesitation, "You wouldn't have 'nother of those, would you?" Amily wasn't one for ribbons and the like . . . but he rather thought this would please her. It wasn't quite her usual style; she favored scents like lavender and rosemary, but this wasn't the sort of too-sweet, flowery perfume of the kind she *didn't* care for.

And—of course the Scentmaster had another.

Beaming, Lena thanked him again and tucked her precious purchase into the bottom of a separate belt pouch she was wearing besides the one holding her money, one she had probably put on specifically to stow small purchases. Mags put his in his pocket—after all, he didn't expect to have it long. She and Mags moved on to catch up with Amily and Bear.

They spotted the pair of them in the final stages of bargaining in an herbalist's stall; from the look of things, both of them had found what they were looking for. Mags caught their eyes, then he and Lena waited patiently off to the side until the bargaining was concluded to the satisfaction of all parties.

Bear's nostrils flared as Lena's scent reached him. "What's that you're wearing?" he blurted, getting a little red. "It's . . . it's very. . . ."

"Yes, it is, isn't it?" Lena laughed, and hugged his arm. "I'm glad you like it."

"I like it too," Amily said, wistfully. "Very much."

"Then you'll be glad I got you some," Mags said promptly, grinning as he fished out the little bottle, and watched her expression brighten.

Then they moved on just a little farther. The area for pens, inks, pencils, paints, and fine papers was very small, and it didn't take them at all long to find the stall Lydia wanted. That was when Mags found out just why the pens were so special.

The nibs were made of metal. They'd last ever so much longer than a goose quill. Lena bargained cheerfully with the merchant and got Lydia the three pens and the special ink at what Mags considered to be a good price. So much of what went on in the business of running a Kingdom seemed to be commerce; Mags had been getting a lot of exposure to commerce from the perspective of the little man behind the counter of a pawnshop and the movers and shakers among the various mercantile Guilds. It was not something he would ever have thought he would find interesting, and yet, it was.

If only because a great deal of it was about greed, and greed was something he understood all too well.

When they were all together again, Mags brought out the list of performers and merchants and the map. They all tucked themselves into a gap between two tent stalls, out of the way of the foot traffic, and consulted both, heads huddled together over the papers. "I was kind of partial to trying one of those tents where they got a bunch of different folks rotating in," he said. "I 'spect that'd bring us up to about lunch time."

Bear nodded, Amily shrugged, and Lena looked interested. "Anything we go to see will be something we haven't got up on the hill," Amily pointed out, "So I'm ready to look at whatever you like. I can't think of any particular performers from last year that I'm dying to catch again. They were all pretty good."

As they got to the area of the entertainers, however, despite the large tent with banners depicting the ten different acts going on inside, Mags found himself oddly distracted by something on the very end of the row.

There was a much smaller tent, dyed blue, with white swirls painted on it that looked like representations of wind and cloud. There was no loud fellow outside bellowing out the virtues of the performers within. Instead, there was a quiet-looking . . . person . . . outside, dressed in androgynous robes and a head wrap, all in the same blue and white; a dark blue throat wrap that matched the head wrap, a white underrobe, and a lighter blue overrobe belted at the waist with a dark blue scarf from which an embroidered belt pouch hung. Mags really could not tell if this person was male or female, and the melodious voice gave him no clues. It could have been a low alto or a high tenor. He couldn't see the hair, and the robes were baggy enough to have hidden either a flat chest or a pair of modest breasts.

The person chanted, in a sort of singsong, while a ferret scampered up and down his (?) arms at his direction. "Come, come and see, see what love will earn, see what kindness brings, see how even the lowliest creatures reward a loving heart. You will never see such feats from any other beast show here, never see how eagerly the beasts will answer the call of love. Come in, come in, there are seats still left."

Nothing like as aggressive as the other barkers, but there were plenty of people responding to it—generally people with small children. It sounded like a very good choice for young children, actually—nothing to frighten them, and nothing their parents would feel uncomfortable trying to explain. Right now—well, after being a "captive beast" of a sort himself, Mags was in the mood to see something that sounded so gentle. "Let's see this," Mags urged, and the others seemed just as interested.

"I generally hate animal shows, because the animals are treated so cruelly," said Amily. "But this—sounds nice."

The person must have overheard her, because he turned to the four of them and smiled. "It is nice, young mistress. You will see; my beasts and I are the greatest of friends, and they will do for me at my request what no amount of punishment or harsh training could demand. A penny each, if you please."

Before Mags or the others could respond, Amily had paid for all four of them. The person guided them in, then fastened a rope across the tent entrance, and dropped the cloth door behind them.

The found themselves in a curious little round tent, with two rows of bleacher-style seats around the circumference, and a ring delineated by a low wooden barrier, painted white, with a gap in it in the center. Thanks to the blue coloring of the canvas, the place was shrouded in a pleasant twilight, with the empty center of the ring illuminated by the sun coming down through a hole in the top of the tent. The seats were, indeed, full, and the four of them took the last ones available.

The person in charge went to a stand on which there was a curious instrument, rather like a harp, but lying down. He took a pair of thin rods in his hands and began to tap them on the strings.

"Oh!" said Lena in surprise, her eyes going round with delight. Mags could understand why. He'd heard a lot of instruments up at Bardic Collegium, but never one like this.

Nor had he ever seen an animal act like this. It began with a pack of little mongrel dogs, who did everything he had ever seen a trick dog perform and more besides, without ever seeming to get any direction from the player, except, perhaps, musical cues. They jumped over each other, danced on their hind paws, then balanced on their forepaws, they performed tumbling tricks, jumping and rolling as human tumblers did. The smallest jumped onto the backs of the largest and rode them like horses. They dragged hoops onto stands, leaped through them, and dragged the hoops off again. They ran and jumped off ramps. It was amazing to behold.

They ran off, and three birds with long tails flew down out of the roof of the tent, where they had perched unseen, and flew in acrobatic formations along with the music. They retreated into perches up in the roof, and the dogs returned, arranging themselves around the circular area and then holding perfectly still. A moment later, a quartet of ferrets bounced in and began a race around and around the ring, jumping over and scooting under the patient dogs. That ended with them each jumping onto a dog's back and balancing there, first on their hind legs, then on their forelegs, and then the entire pack of dogs, ferret riders and all, trotted out of the ring again.

Last came a sextet of the smallest horses Mags had ever seen, much smaller than the mine ponies. Without any direction, they began the same sort of pacing "dance" that the Companions had done for the wedding of the Prince and Princess. Bells on their bridles and harnesses chimed in time with their dancing. They wove in and out around each other, making patterns, breaking them, and making new patterns. And just when that was barely starting to lose its novelty, they began executing the fighting-moves that Companions and warhorses were trained in: rearing on their hind legs and pawing the air in front of them, leaping into the air and kicking out, rearing up and hopping forward. Then they went back into their dance, this time joined by the birds.

Then they were joined by the dogs and, finally, by the ferrets, with the horses forming an outer circle, the dogs dancing in a circle rotating counter to theirs inside that, and the ferrets one going the same direction as the horses inside that, and the birds swooping and diving over their heads. Then, as the player created a final series of chords, they all stopped, pivoted outward to face their audience, and bowed.

As one, the entire small audience leaped to their feet with applause.

The animals filed out, with only the birds going back to their perches. The—trainer? keeper?—opened the door of the tent and stood there, bowing slightly, and waving his audience out. Mags felt dazzled with enchantment and admiration.

"Please!" Lena said, as they reached the door. "What sort of instrument is that? I've never heard anything like it! And you play it like a Master!"

"Mistress," the person corrected her gently, with a smile, thus at least solving one question for Mags. "It is called a hammered dulcimer, young Bard, and I thank you for your high praise. My people seldom venture out of our home, but I was overtaken by wanderlust once I attained . . . my proficiency. Originally I had only my horses and my birds, but the others came to join me over time. Now I cannot imagine life without them all."

"Animal Mindspeech?" Mags ventured. The smile broadened. He noticed that the Beastmistress had curiously pale eyes, like a wintery overcast sky.

"Even so. It is our hope that we can show people what love and good will can accomplish and make them lose their taste for beast shows that are created with fear and punishment." The Show Mistress bowed slightly.

"I hope it works," Mags replied sincerely. It had certainly worked on him. Having watched this, he couldn't imagine taking pleasure in any other sort of beast show. And the dancing bears he had seen, so cruelly shackled and goaded, made him shudder with revulsion.

Once outside the tent, they realized they had been in there longer than they had thought; Bear's stomach actually growled, and they all laughed as Bear blushed.

"Well, that says what we'll be doing next," Amily declared.

3

The quartet caught a wagon back up the Hill that left well after sunset, but also well before the Fair closed for the night. It had been a wonderful day; they had eaten odd and tasty things, seen a trained-horse exhibition put on by genuine Shin'a'in horse traders, enjoyed one of the multiact shows with acrobats, rope dancers, and people who had climbed and disported themselves on poles held up by handlers, and one who had done amazing things on silk scarves hung from the top of the tent. They were pleasantly tired, but before too long, Mags knew, they would start to feel unpleasantly weary and begin to be quarrelsome. There would be a huge rush for the last wagons, and almost certainly some people were going to wind up walking back. He put that to the others, and they all agreed that they might as well make their way back to the Collegia.

It was a good decision; the wagon was almost empty, and they were tired enough by the time they reached the pickup point that their purchases were beginning to feel very heavy.

Someone had finally taken pity on the Trainees and put a layer of fresh hay in the bottom of this wagon, so the ride back up was much more comfortable than the ride down.

Mags had been able to lose himself in all the activities of the day, but now that it was all over, he found his mind going over and over the conundrum of his origin—and the worries over what it meant. Now that he knew part of it . . . it was almost more frustrating—and worrying—than when he had known nothing.

And yet, he could not help thinking that until he knew completely who he had been, he would never be sure what was driving his decisions. And if he didn't know what was driving them, how could he be sure they were good decisions?

The other three chattered away for almost half the journey before they finally noticed he hadn't said anything. "You're very quiet," said Amily, and squeezed his arm affectionately. "It's all right. If we're bothering you, just say so."

"Not bothering me," he replied, and after a moment he decided to say more. "But . . . I'm kind of in a quandary, here. It's like I'm on a map, but I only generally know where I've been, so I'm not sure where to go next. I've got no direction. You all, you know exactly who you are and what you come from. Now, I kind of know, but it's all fragments. It's not helping much."

"Well, you know what they say," Lena said, after a long silence. "I mean, it's even in a song. 'Lost and Found,' I know you've heard me sing it before."

He nodded.

"Nothing's ever really lost; it can always be found again if you look hard enough. You can find all about your whole past if you decide you want to. Look what you've already found out! And I think you already know the worst at this point, and it's not so bad, really. So what? You come from some sort of clan of assassins, which doesn't make you an assassin, or a traitor, but when you think about it, all the things that make a good assassin are the same things that will make you *really* useful to the King and Nikolas. Right?" She patted his knee. "The rest of what's lost is just details. Details you really ought to find out but still, details. And you actually do have a direction. You know exactly what my father is training you for."

Well, that was true, and it wasn't as if he didn't agree with it. It would be interesting work, and certainly needful work. But by the same token, this made him profoundly uneasy. Perhaps an assassin's skills would make him a good spy. But they would also make him a good assassin. What if things started to blur? What if he found himself murdering someone and justifying it to himself and others?

:Nonsense. You have me,: Dallen said firmly, before he could get himself wrought up. *:Whatever gave you the idea that I'd let you do something like that?:*

He felt rather stupid for a moment. Dallen was his moral compass, just as every Companion was every Herald's moral compass. As long as he had Dallen, he would be all right—and if for some reason he no longer had Dallen, there would be a *lot* more wrongfulness going on than he really even wanted to consider.

:We learned our lesson with Tylendel,: Dallen said soberly. *:If I have to knock you down and sit on you to prevent you from doing something stupid, I will. Not that I expect to ever have to. If anything, you overthink things. 'Lendel was many things, but thinking wasn't his strong suit.:*

It was extremely odd to hear someone talking about an historical, tragic figure as if he were a—

:Emotional, overwrought, impulsive manchild who made a habit of blundering about regardless of consequences and paid the price, and I would rather not go into it any further.:

Mags blinked a little at Dallen's vehemence. It *almost* sounded as if Dallen had been . . . present at the time of the tragedy! Could that even be possible?

But Dallen had made it quite clear that he was not interested in discussing the situation, and Mags knew better than to press. In fact, Dallen had sounded as if the situation had caused him pain as well as the irritation he was voicing.

Maybe someday he'd find out, but clearly, that day would not be today.

Still . . . there were more to his concerns than that, of course.

One of the large ones was personal, insofar as anything that affected a Trainee or a Herald could be personal. He had *not* extracted a promise from those people to leave him alone— only to drop the contract with Karse. He was pretty sure that they were going to keep coming for him until they got him, one way or another. For some reason, he was important to them, and he needed to find out why. He needed to find out who it was they kept mistaking him for.

It had to be someone important in their circle. That was the only explanation for why they wanted him so badly. If he looked so very like this person, it would probably be extremely useful to them. He could be used as a decoy. This person could appear to be in two places at once, which would certainly impress people.

He needed to figure out how to get them off his trail.

:You know, if it is only your appearance that has them so set on having you, that can be altered. Although scarring yourself that badly would make you more recognizable in Nikolas's service, since if the scars were easy to hide, they would think of that, too.:

Mags shuddered to think of what it would take to get *that* scarred up. *:You are not making me feel any better, horse,:* he replied crossly.

This was . . . a puzzle. So far, he hadn't found the way to crack it.

There was no doubt whatsoever that the answer was somewhere in his personal past, not in the generalized "clan memories" that had been fed to him. If he resembled someone that closely, he had to be closely related to that person. A brother he didn't know about? That seemed unlikely, since both his mother and father were dead—unless, perhaps, they had been forced to leave a child behind when they left their home?

:I agree we need to discover all this. It might be extremely useful, too. We might be able to turn it around to use on your pursuers.:

He wondered if there was a Gift for that—finding things out in the past. If somewhere there were people who could look into your past, the way the Farseers could look into the distance and Foreseers could see the future.

Again, his thoughts returned to that stone in the table in the lower level of the Palace. Could *it* do that? Given the clues he had now? Or could *it* recognize those memories and give him something more to go on? *It* was like the Archives: extremely useful, full of unexpected knowledge, but you had to know where to look.

Amily put her head on his shoulder and drove all of his thoughts into the distance. "I was sure you would be back, but I was horribly afraid when Dallen couldn't sense you," she said softly. "I guess, what I mean, is that I had faith you'd come home again. But faith didn't stop the fear. I never want to be separated from you again."

There it was, another thing that had been in the back of his mind. He knew now that he didn't want to be separated from her, either. "Do you think you could—" he began. She interrupted him.

"Weaponsmaster is giving me special lessons." She chuckled. "He calls them *How Not To Get Killed* lessons. It will take a while before I am as good as any of you Trainees, and since you are *really* good at fighting, I probably will never catch up with you. But I don't have to. I only have to keep myself out of trouble, stay alive, and maybe help you a little if I can. I have to be sneaky, mostly. I have to learn how to spot trouble ahead of time. I have to learn how to find ways to escape or get to spots where I can't be reached. I have to think a lot about that.

But I can do that, I know I can. More important, Weaponsmaster says I can. And that means if you go somewhere, I can go
with you. You won't have to worry about me, because I'm
learning to take care of myself. If someone is after you, the way
they are now, I won't be a hostage or a victim again." Then her
voice faltered a little. "I thought—"

"You thought right," he said warmly, so proud of her he
could scarcely stand it. "You thought absolutely right. And
aye. I want you with me, too." He'd worry a lot less, a whole
lot less, if they were together. And if she got good enough to
actually help guard his back, that would be best of all. Even if
she didn't, two sets of eyes watching for trouble were four
times as good as one.

"Let's count on that," he said, as those thoughts ran
through his head. "Your Pa probably won't like it much, but
he'd like it even less if we was separated and both of us were
frettin' about t'other, and maybe not bein' quite as careful as
we could be, 'cause of it."

"I knew you'd have a good argument," she said happily,
and snuggled down into the arm he put around her, then
craned her face up for a kiss, which he was more than willing
to give her. After all, Bear and Lena were not paying the least
little bit of attention to *them.*

And despite all his worries, a little warm glow bloomed
inside him. The rest of the trip back up went by far too quickly.

———————

No matter how disoriented he had gotten during his abduc-
tion, so long as he wasn't drugged completely insensible, he
had always awakened at the crack of dawn, and that hadn't
changed. He'd parted reluctantly from Amily, thinking again
with envy of Lena and Bear. One thing that they hadn't been
forced to deal with during their courtship was other people . . .
"keeping an eye on them." He and Amily must have a hun-

dred "eyes" on them at all times. Amily, after all, was the daughter of the King's Own. Practically every Companion on the Hill was "keeping an eye on her." Literally nothing they did was really private, and if he and Amily got beyond a little kissing and cuddling, it was absolutely guaranteed that within a candlemark her father would know about it.

Mags wasn't entirely sure what Nikolas's reaction to that would be. He had shown himself to be a reasonable man. His objections to Bear and Lena getting married on the sly had all been rational ones that had everything to do with political situations. Everyone knew that Mags and Amily were a couple. No one objected to that. There would be no political repercussions. . . .

But the difference was that Nikolas was not dealing with a couple of younglings in the abstract, he was dealing with his "apprentice" and his daughter.

From what Mags could tell, based on what his friends here said, things he'd read, and things Dallen had dropped, a man could be perfectly rational about a pair of younglings coupling, even give tacit approval (at least to the young man) right up until that coupling involved his daughter. Then rational thought went flying right out the window.

So . . . for now, kissing and cuddling was all he was going to get.

And, oh, how he envied Bear.

It was, truly, a distinct advantage to get the entire bathing room to yourself of a morning—especially when certain parts of you were not at all pleased about the situation with your girl.

Mind, of all of the many, many things that he loved about being a Trainee, the ability to have a hot bath whenever he chose was very high on the list. For a simple, uncomplicated pleasure, a hot bath was very difficult to beat.

He was far too early for Bear and Lena to join him for breakfast. Unlike him, they were anything but early risers, and they had preferred staying up as late as possible even before they had gone from friendship to love. They both had bought treasures at the Fair they would have to show each other, and then . . . well, he knew the sorts of things that he and Amily would have been doing if there hadn't been a hundred busybodies watching them while trying not to look as if they were dong so, and not all of those things involved being undressed and in bed together. Last night Bear and Lena had probably done some similar things and stayed up later than usual.

Bear in particular. He probably would have had stories to tell Lena about some of the rare and imported herbs he'd gotten. He always talked to vendors, every chance he got, because one of the things he was always telling Mags was "No knowledge is ever wasted." Lena might well have garnered some inspiration from those stories. If she did, well, he knew her; she would be up half the night writing down the bones of a new song. And even if she wasn't inspired right that moment, Bear was constitutionally incapable of telling a brief story.

Even without the Fair yesterday, it was only even odds that Bear and Lena would be up at the same time he was. Mags was almost always one of the first people in the dining hall in the morning. And when he wasn't, it was generally because he had kitchen duty that morning, and ate there with the rest of the helpers.

In his opinion, sleeping late was overrated. He much preferred being the proverbial early bird, because in this case, it wasn't a nasty worm he got but the first of the breakfast dishes straight out of the kitchen, so fresh that you couldn't eat bites without blowing on them. It was lovely getting biscuits or bread still hot from the ovens so that the butter melted in them and soaked into them, and the first round of whatever was on the menu was always better than the later ones.

It was also going to be a good thing for him to be done

early. Like him, Dean Caelen was an early riser, and Mags was going to have to find out what classes he was in and how he was going to catch up with them.

He wasn't looking forward to that part. The Dean couldn't have anything but bad news for him.

Because he was fortnights behind everyone else, thanks to being dragged across two countries drugged and semiconscious. There was going to be a hellish amount of catching up, and there wasn't going to be a choice.

He finished his meal, helped himself to some biscuits and bacon and made little tasty sandwiches of them, wrapped them all in a napkin, and took them with him as an incentive to the Dean to be easy with him.

As he had expected, the Dean was already in his office, which was on the third floor of the Collegium, right next to the library. As he had not expected, the office was . . . clean. There were no stacks of books, no piles of papers. The desk was a little untidy, but there was room to work on it, and there were several places for visitors to sit. He stood in the doorway and stared, open-mouthed, until the Dean looked up and saw him there.

Dean Caelen, a plain brown-haired, brown-eyed, mild-mannered man, smiled self-consciously. "I was told by Princess Lydia that I was getting an assistant and I was not going to be allowed to say no," he said wryly. "I resented it at first, but now I don't know what I would do without the lad. Come in, Mags, I've been expecting you."

Mags put his wrapped biscuits on a bare spot on the desk and waited.

The Dean didn't reach for them, as he normally would have. "I know this is going to sound very odd to you, but . . . I don't have classes for you yet."

"What?" Mags said, startled. "Why not?"

"The general feeling is that we want you to stay out of classes for now, while we assess you, assess what you have discovered, and decide what to do with you."

Before Mags could react to that startling statement, the Dean was continuing. "Nikolas and some of the other senior Heralds basically want you to themselves for a while, several days at least. They are adept at extracting information people didn't even know they had, and you are, at the moment, a veritable treasure trove of information, not only about the people that took you but also the Karsites. In short, a very valuable source of intelligence. So I wouldn't be able to put you into classes anyway, not right away."

What could he say but "Yes, sir, of course"? Although he normally would not have minded having a day or two when he wasn't frantically trying to catch up with everyone else, at this point he was so far behind that his first real reaction was resentment. It seemed horribly unfair—here he was, behind everyone in classes, through no fault of his own, and being forced to lag even farther.

"Mags, I know what you must be thinking," the Dean said placatingly. "But think a little further. Younglings come in all the time as newly Chosen, and at every possible level of education, and yet we manage to fit them in. You won't be in the same classes you'd been taking with the same group of Trainees, it is true, but what of it? You might end up in classes with others of your friends. Remember, not all of you are progressing like—like Blues. We don't have set class-years that begin and end everything together. And meanwhile, you are getting something like a holiday, one that, if you ask me, is overdue. You have been burning both ends of your candle for far too long."

"But what'm I supposed to do with m'self when I ain't bein' questioned?" he asked, plaintively, his hands clasped between his knees.

"What do you *want* to do?" the Dean replied.

It had been so long since anyone asked him that question that for a moment his mind was blank. "I—dunno—" he managed.

"Something will come to you, I am sure," the Dean said dryly. "You might consider reading for the pure pleasure of it, for instance. I can think of few things I enjoy more than sitting next to a fire reading a book. In the meantime, you might ask your friends if any of them need any help. If you are going to insist on being useful, I am certain someone will be grateful, even at this unholy hour of the morning."

That was a dismissal if Mags had ever heard one, so he said goodbye to the Dean and wandered out into the crisp autumn morning. It occurred to him then that he did know someone who could use some help—Bear. After that successful work on Amily's leg, Bear was only technically a Trainee and only at his own insistence. But this was fall, and fall meant that Bear had a great many medicinal herbs to transplant and bring into the greenhouse for the winter—not to mention a great many herbs to harvest and preserve.

So he wandered over to Healers' Collegium to see if he could lend a hand.

Bear greeted him with relief, a sort of breakfast sandwich in one hand and a small sickle in the other. Lena was gone already, probably to her first morning class, having brought Bear back something to eat. "I'll say you can help me," was the grateful response. "There aren't many I know I could trust to do what I tell them, and they're all either busy with patients or classes. Take this—" he thrust the sickle at Mags, handle first. "—and come with me."

Mags followed him out to the herb garden. "You already know wormwood, eyebright, and comfrey on sight," Bear said, and Mags nodded. "I want you to carefully cut each plant off just a little above the ground and harvest it. Make sure to keep your cut clean, and don't crush or bruise the stems. Keep them separate, obviously."

"I can do that," Mags said confidently. "Bring the baskets back when I'm done?"

"Yes, I'll show you how to hang them for drying and

where." Bear hurried off, and Mags knelt in the soft earth between the rows of plants and began his harvest.

Maybe someone else would have found the work backbreaking, but Mags had spent most of his life laboring on his knees in a gemstone mine, and this was infinitely superior to even the best of moments in the mine. He was in the sun, the air was clean and cool, and the work was delicate enough to be interesting. He got into a slow rhythm and was a little disappointed when he realized he had run out of plants to cut.

He brought the three baskets to Bear, who showed him how to bind them with thread at the cut ends, three plants together at a time, and hang them upside down in the drying room. He had only just finished that task when Dallen nudged him in his mind.

:Nikolas and his lot want to see you now.:

Well, at least now he was in a better frame of mind for it. *:Tell 'em I'm on my way,:* he replied, and told Bear.

"Bah. Well, when they turn you loose, if you are still of a mind to help me, come on back," Bear said good-naturedly. "This time of year there's no such thing as too much help."

Following Dallen's directions, Mags found himself at last in a small, comfortable room in the Palace, facing four people: three Heralds including Nikolas, one of whom had set up as a sort of secretary, and someone who looked like a scholar.

"Relax, Mags, take a seat over there on that couch, and make yourself comfortable," Nikolas ordered, as he looked around and waited for them to tell him what they wanted him to do. "The more relaxed you are, the easier this will be on everyone." Mags did as he was told, as Nikolas indicated one of the Heralds with a wave of his hand. "Herald Cende usually assists the Chief Magistrate of Haven when witnesses need to be questioned. Her particular Mindspeech—"

"Oh! I know Herald Cende by reputation!" Mags exclaimed, and smiled a little. This was going to be easier than he had thought. He'd expected he was going to have to pummel his memory until he got a headache from it. "You kind of—nudge things out of being forgotten."

Cende, a vivacious brunette who looked to be in her late twenties, laughed. "That's as good a description as any. No one quite knows what to call my Gift. This is going to get quite tedious, I expect; we'll be asking you to go over the same part of a story several times, and I'm sorry for that, but it's the only way I can get you to keep remembering things."

Mags nodded. "That makes sense. If you're just kinda nudging things, it's gonna take a few times through every story before we fish out all the bits."

"For a while, this is going to make the memories very vivid, and you might even dream about them," Cende warned, tucking her hair behind her ears as Mags made himself more comfortable on the couch. "They'll fade, though, I promise."

:I'll make sure they do,: Dallen put in, which was exactly what Mags hoped to hear. He didn't want to have those recollections right up in the front of his mind any longer than he had to.

"For right now, we are going to concentrate on all of your encounters with the Karsites," said Nikolas. "Not just the ones when you were captive, but also the ones with the young priest who became your friend. We feel we can learn a great deal about their priestly magic from that—things he would probably be reluctant to tell us directly himself."

Mags nodded, as that made perfect sense. Strategically, they needed to get every detail about the Karsites that they could right now. So he settled down, with a pitcher of water at his side, to a session of perfect tedium.

And that was exactly what it was. He would tell the same story over and over, remembering a new phrase or a new detail, for the first several times. That was Cende's Gift at work, of course. Only when he simply could not bring out anything new did they move on to another bit of narrative.

They didn't even break for luncheon; food was brought to

them, though Mags was not minded to complain when it was clear this was stuff straight from the King's table. The ripe grapes were particularly welcome after all that talking.

They finally let him go a candlemark or so before supper, and only because it was clear that they intended to discuss what they had gleaned from him. That was fine with him. He returned to Bear and harvested another herb, and he and Bear and Lena went off to supper together.

Amily was waiting for them, saving them seats. After all that talking, he was much more in the mood to listen to the others than to say anything himself. He had been afraid that going through all those unpleasant memories would put him out of sorts, but in fact, as he listened to the others chatter about nothing, he realized he had nothing to fear. He'd done well, especially for someone with absolutely no resources but the clothing on his back and a single blanket, and by concentrating on that, and allowing himself to feel a bit of pride in what he had accomplished, things didn't seem quite so horrible after all.

The next several days passed in the same way, although the topic of the questioning changed to his captors rather than the Karsites.

Then, after four days, there was someone new with the trio of Heralds, taking the place of the scholar. This was a fellow in the robes of some religious order or other, though nothing that Mags recognized.

"This is Father Seneson," Nikolas said, after Mags had taken a seat. "He's an expert on languages. We're going to try to get a sense of where your captors came from."

Mags brightened at that. He'd been getting a bit tired of being the one giving all the information without getting anything in return. If this Father Seneson could come up with some answers, that would be a welcome change!

"First, Mags, do you still remember your kidnappers' tongue?" the newcomer asked.

"I've been dreamin' in it," he replied truthfully. "It ain't likely to leave me any time soon."

The priest nodded. "Excellent, the answer I hoped to hear. All right, then. I'm going to give you a word, and I would like you to tell me the same thing in their language."

Mags almost snorted. That was child's play, really. Or so he had thought . . .

"There ain't a word for that," he said, when Sorensen asked him for what seemed extremely odd to him, the word for *games.*

"Are you saying they don't have a word they use for that concept, or that they don't have a word in their own language?" Seneson asked, looking up from his notes.

"Don't have one in their own tongue," Mags replied. "They don't do games." They didn't, of course. Everything was serious with those people, and as far as he could tell, nothing was ever done for sheer pleasure.

"Tell me the word they use, then," the priest replied, and noted down what Mags said, asking him to pronounce it carefully several times to make sure he got it right.

And that was when things got . . . interesting. Mags had *thought* that these people had an entire language, and for some things they actually did. But there were entire concepts missing, mostly having to do with, well, *living.* They didn't have words for too many kinds of food, for instance. Or anything that someone might do in his leisure time. They had to borrow words for these things from some other language, and it didn't take long before Sorensen put down his pen with an expression of satisfaction.

"I'm done with you, Mags, at least for now, although if you ever want to help me compile a full dictionary I would be very pleased to monopolize your time for as long as Herald's Collegium will let me," he said, and turned to the others. "Heralds, I have your answer. As I suspected, when you described this culture to me, they are not nearly so far away from us as we had thought. And rather than being a *culture,* they are more of a—sect, of sorts. A very secretive clanlike group that lives almost unknown within a greater Kingdom. And that Kingdom is Thurbrigard. I suspect they are hidden in the mountains, and not one person in five hundred thousand knows they exist."

"Well, that explains why Karse got involved," Nikolas said thoughtfully. "And why they had some tokens from the Shin'a'in with them, if they went straight west at first, looking for the boy, then doubled back and went north."

"Even so," the priest agreed. "And being in the midst of Thurbrigard, they have their own language only for those things that are important to them. For anything that is foreign to the clan culture, they must use the words of the people around them."

"Having their own language would allow them to speak in front of others without giving themselves away," Nikolas observed. "Well! Now we are *much* farther ahead than we had been. Possibly there are some in Menmellith or Rethwellan who have diplomatic or trade ties there—"

Mags had no idea what on earth good that would do *him,* but at least now he had a location for "his" people.

"All right, Mags, consider yourself released," said Herald Nikolas, with *that look* in his eyes that told Mags that he really wanted the Trainee to be elsewhere so he could discuss things with the others. Mags was adept at taking Nikolas's hints, and made himself scarce.

Besides, he wanted to go to the library, the Heraldic Archives, and the Guard Archives. Whatever there was to learn about Thurbrigard—he was going to find it.

Mags leaned up against the fence and watched the Reds and the Greens skirmishing against each other in Kirball practice. He'd had to get outside for a while; the dust in the Archives was beginning to make him sneeze, and his eyes were getting tired from perusing all the closely written pages of ancient reports. The sun was warm on his back and the air so clean out here that it made him wonder why he was bothering to spend so much time inside when this weather was so fleeting.

Well, he knew why. The Archivists wouldn't let him take the boxes of reports outside to read.

So far he hadn't found terribly much. Mostly, anything useful had been buried in the interviews that the Guard did with traders and entertainers before they were allowed to pass the Border. Thurbrigard was so *very* far away that no one had taken much thought to gathering intelligence on it. There were a very few mentions of it, and only then as places that traders said they carried goods from. Carved semiprecious gems for

58

the most part: high value, small size. That made it worth carting them all that distance.

He could see why no one considered Thurbrigard any sort of a threat worth investigating. First, it didn't seem to be a very prosperous Kingdom, so it was logical to assume it didn't mount much in the way of armed forces. In the case of the gemstones, they were *semi*-precious. It was really the intricate carving that made them valuable, not the intrinsic value of the stones. If that was their best export, they weren't a wealthy land. Second, before Thurbrigard could be a threat to Valdemar, its army (if it even had one) would have to wade across two or three other countries, one of which was the ever armed and ever hostile Karse. There would be plenty of warning long before it got as far as Menmellith if the rulers decided to get up to no good.

For that matter, the sudden abandonment of our Border by Karse would be a good clue that there was something up, he thought, watching as Gennie and Jeffers passed the ball back and forth between them.

And third—why would they ever bother to come this far north? What could Valdemar offer that was worth trying to invade it across three other countries? Nothing that they couldn't get by going to war much closer.

No one could ever have anticipated that some remote assassin clan would decide to come calling.

He felt someone coming up behind him and recognized her by the "sense" of her as Amily long before she actually reached the fence. "You could ask for your place back," she said, putting her arms up on the top rung and leaning her chin on it as he was doing. "On the team I mean."

"They already offered it," he replied, ruthlessly pushing down a feeling of melancholy. "But it don't feel right, takin' it from Wolf. He's good."

"Not as good as you!" Amily protested—truthfully, actually. Wolf and his Companion weren't as fast or as agile as

Mags and Dallen. Wolf couldn't Mindspeak to every other Companion and human on the team, either.

Still, they could *learn* to be as fast and agile, and Wolf's Gift of Farsight could prove just as useful as Mags' Mindspeech.

"But he ain't gonna get better 'less he's pushed to it, an' if I take my place back, he ain't gonna get pushed." Mags suppressed a sigh. He didn't say aloud what he was thinking—that after having all those memories shoved forcefully into his head, he just couldn't look at Kirball the same way anymore. He'd been indoctrinated into the mindset of people who literally did not have a word for *game.* Sure, in the back of his mind he had always known that Kirball was training for warfare—and he and his fellow players had even used those moves to help rescue Amily and capture—briefly—two of the assassin clan. But he hadn't felt it, not deep inside. But now, he did. Now whenever someone made a move, his mind overlaid it with how that would play out in combat. He could still play, and play well . . . but the game would never be free of that for him, ever again.

He'd never again be able to lose himself in the game, which was half the fun of playing it in the first place.

Maybe this was why the experienced Guardsmen—the ones who had combat experience—hadn't volunteered for the team.

"Nah, it wouldn't be fair," was all he said. "You busy?"

"Well, there are always things I can do . . ." She hesitated. "I was going to see if I could get a lesson with the Weaponsmaster." She brightened. "I really love Weapons work! He's been really kind about fitting me into every class I turn up for."

Well, that would be something both of them could do. "Good idea." He smiled at her. "Reckon we can both use as many of those as we can get."

The Weaponsmaster, of course, was already putting a class through training. And as usual, it was a mixed class of mixed ages and levels of expertise. That hardly mattered; the Weaponsmaster was so skilled a teacher that this was merely a slight challenge to his abilities. Weapons classes were the one place where Trainees of varying levels of advancement actually *could* be taught together, so long as the teacher was a good one.

In fact, he welcomed them with a half smile and a nod and directed them to pair up with other Trainees for some sword work. Mags expected he'd be set up with one of the young Guardsmen who would have qualified as "advanced," and indeed he was, but he was pleasantly surprised to see that Amily was put up against one of the Herald Trainees who was certainly "intermediate" if not a bit higher.

The helmet obscured the face of the young man he was paired up against, but the way the fellow moved let Mags know this was someone he had never fought with before. The young Guardsman's introduction confirmed that. "Helden," said the Guardsman, giving him a salute. "You're Mags, right?"

"Aye, that'd be me." Mags made sure that the straps holding all of his padding were snugged down tight, then tamped his helmet on. "Would you be a bodyguard in training?"

"Aye." Helden shifted his posture into the ready position. "Queen's men. Want to lead off as attacker? I've been hacking at Grell for the past three days, it feels like. I need some defense."

"Trust me, it only seems that long," Mags replied with a laugh, and went into the attack.

He spotted Helden's weakness immediately as he scored a shoulder hit that would have taken his left arm off if it had been a metal blade and would have probably broken the joint if Mags hadn't been pulling his blows. "Hold up a bit," he said, "I want to see something. Hold out your left arm and fight what I'm doing."

Helden obliged. Mags pressed up on it from below, and got heavy resistance. But when he pressed *down* from above, he felt the arm trembling and giving way. "There's yer problem," he said. "Ye need t'be exercising both sets of arm muscles."

"But that's my off arm," Helden objected. "I won't be holding a shield when—"

Then he stopped. He realized that if the Weaponsmaster had put Mags in charge of him, then Mags knew what he was talking about. So he properly shut up and let Mags explain.

"Ye'll have armor on that arm that's almost as heavy as a shield, and meant to serve as one," Mags explained patiently. "Except that it don't work exactly like a shield does. Ye gotta be careful with that kinda heavy arm armor. Ye don't *block* with it, ye gotta learn to move and deflect. And ye can't just tuck yer arm behind ye like ye been doin'. Started on Court fencing?"

Looking puzzled, Helden nodded.

"Thought so. Court fencing's good training, but not for this. It's all rules and lines. Bodyguardin' is no rules at all, and figure the one comin' at ye is gonna play dirty." Absently he noticed that his speech had lapsed again, but Helden didn't seem to notice or care, so he continued on. "That's why ye'll get armor on yer off arm, and yer to use it sorta a shield, only not the kind yer used to. Get off the line of attack if ye *can,* but ye may be pinned in—look, I'll show ye. Come at me."

Helden did, using the same pattern that Mags had—a stab at the gut, which was parried and turned into a cut down to the shoulder. Only Mags had brought his arm up in such a way that the wooden blade glanced along it and down, and while Helden was gawking, Mags closed with a hammerlike blow of his hilt to the gut, and as Helden staggered back, a cut to the neck that he stopped short of connecting.

"See?" Mags said. Helden nodded.

"It's a whole different way of thinking," the young Guardsman said, rubbing his neck.

"Right, so, instead of thinkin' of it as unlearnin', think of it as learnin' something new. Like ye did when ye learned sword and shield work for in the line." Mags scratched his head. "Got an ideer."

He went to the equipment room and procured a tiny shield, not even the size of a dinner plate, to strap onto Helden's left wrist.

"This'll remind ye t'keep that arm out, not tucked behind," he said with satisfaction. "Weaponsmaster'll have some weights for the wrist, I reckon. Or heavier padding for yer off arm. But this'll do for now."

Out of the corner of his eye, he had been watching Amily with astonishment and pleasure. She had changed into a pair of trews that she bound at the ankle and up her calves, and she was giving her partner as good as she got. She was favoring her bad leg a good bit, but compensating for it, and her partner wasn't good enough to take advantage of the weakness. This was making Mags extremely happy. She hadn't been exaggerating when she had said she could take care of herself.

He went back to turning the young Guardsman into a proper royal bodyguard. He suspected this fellow was destined to be part of Princess Lydia's entourage rather than going to the Queen, since the Queen already had a contingent of men she knew and trusted, and he was in for a rude shock when he discovered that Lydia was probably as good as he was. Still, Lydia would often be hampered by robes of state and other impediments, not to mention being surrounded by half a dozen potential hostages in the form of her ladies-in-waiting. She'd need all the help she could get from her bodyguards in the event of an emergency.

When both Mags and Helden were soaked with sweat, the Weaponsmaster called a halt to the class. He'd come by a few times to suggest something but otherwise had been content to let Mags do the teaching, which had tickled Mags no end.

"Are you and Amily scheduled for anything?" he asked Mags, as the rest of the class went off to clean up.

Mags shook his head. "Caelen ain't put me in any classes," he replied. "And I guess Nikolas ain't got any more questioning for me." He glanced over at Amily, who was just coming over, pulling a helmet off her sweat-damp hair. "You got anything?"

"Anything to do this morning? Not really. Nor the afternoon, either," she replied, with a curious look at both of them.

"Good." The Weaponsmaster smiled thinly. "I've got just the thing for you." His gaze unfocused for a moment as he spoke to his Companion, and when his attention returned to them, he smiled again. "It's all arranged. Until Nikolas and Caelen decide what is to be done with you two, you are my new assistants."

Mags gaped at him. "All day, sir?" he stammered, although it was not out of dread for the work. If anything, it was with a certain measure of relief. He wasn't going to be able to think of *anything* while he was schooling others in weapons work.

"I see no reason why not," the Weaponsmaster said, then shrugged. "Well, perhaps not Amily for the whole day. Not because she is a female, but we do not wish to place too much stress on her leg while she is still technically healing. But you? Yes."

Mags felt himself smiling. "That sounds good to me, sir!" he said with real enthusiasm. Then he looked over at Amily. "Sound good to you?"

She rubbed the lobe of her ear thoughtfully. "I've never done . . . physical things . . . for days at a time before. It doesn't sound like a bad idea at all to me." She considered a moment more, then smiled. "Actually, sir, I wouldn't mind more practice parrying while sitting. That would make me a perfectly adequate set of pells for the youngsters. More than adequate, since I can correct them as well as deflect them."

"Good. There's a pump and a sink in the changing room. Clean yourselves up a little. The next class will be archery and other distance weapons." Now the Weaponsmaster's smile turned sly. "Amily is going to give you some unexpected competition, Mags."

It ain't unexpected if I was expecting it, he thought, but he didn't say anything, just followed Amily to the changing room.

After all, if the Weaponsmaster wanted him to be surprised, well he could simulate that. Who was he to deprive the Herald of a little pleasure?

He blinked as he realized *he didn't actually know the Weaponsmaster's name.* No one ever referred to the man except by his title. *Well, that's embarrassing. . . .*

He sensed a chuckle from Dallen. *:Not as embarrassing as the Weaponsmaster's real name. Marion.:*

He was in the act of plunging himself head and shoulders into the filled sink of cold water and came up spluttering and coughing. *:Marion? Are you joking?:*

:Can you blame him for preferring his title?: Dallen replied.

:Not the tiniest.: No wonder the Weaponsmaster was as good as he was. With a name like that, the poor kiddie must have had to fight practically from the cradle. *:What kind of sadist gives a boy a name like Marion?:*

:Never asked. Don't intend to. Suggest you don't, either.:

Amily was giving him a peculiar look. "Water's colder than I thought," he said, and began toweling off. There were piles of old uniforms just one step up from the rag-bag in here, and he rinsed his tunic out in the sink when Amily had finished washing and hung it up to dry, taking another that was approximately his size and was either a gray so faded as to be almost white, or a white so dingy it was almost gray. It wouldn't matter what color it was when he was done with the next class, because it would probably be soaked through with sweat again.

"I should do what you did," he said, nodding to her. She had changed out of her regular gown and into a set of tunic and trews that were a red so faded they were pink. "Nobody'd take me serious in pink." She snickered.

"I'd love to see you in pink," she said.

"I might take that challenge," he replied, and they both went back out as the sound of the next class arriving filled the *salle.*

Of course, the class only remained there long enough to get bows, arrows, and other distance weapons, like sets of throwing knives. This time the Weaponsmaster put Mags in charge of an intermediate group and Amily with the advanced students. There were as many Healer and Bardic Trainees in this class as there were Heralds. Guards did their own drilling in distance weaponry. But Healers and Bards were often enough out in the wilderness alone and would need to defend themselves or hunt for food, so this training was mandated for them. Mags' group was a mixed set of Healers and Bards, four of them. He set them at targets at twenty paces and kept increasing the distance until their arrows were falling short. Then he set to work with them, now that he knew what their base distance was. Of course, there was only so much distance you could get out of a bow with a given pull in the hands of an expert, but this lot was by no means expert yet.

Amily's bunch, however . . .

Amily herself was setting the bar for each flight of arrows. She would shoot first, then the rest were to place their arrows as close to hers as possible. They were all Herald Trainees, and they were using man-shaped targets with multiple hit spots marked out on them. Amily was consistently placing her arrows in the lethal zone.

He felt himself grinning at her with pride, his smile fully wide enough to make the corners of his mouth hurt a little. The Weaponsmaster turned at that moment and caught his expression, and nodded with evident satisfaction.

He had to turn his attention back to his own pupils, though; they sorely needed it. Evidently the Weaponsmaster had not yet had the time or opportunity to press them past their current state of achievement, and being, like most younglings, a

little lazy, they hadn't pressed themselves. Well, he could understand that. The Weaponsmaster was only one man, and
there were a *lot* more Herald Trainees now than there had
been in the past. They were certainly adequate for fieldwork,
and even battle conditions. Mags just wanted them to be excellent rather than adequate.

He kept his group on the archery targets, but Amily's group
moved on to throwing knives, then axes, then javelins. She
was superb with everything but the ax, which didn't seem to
be much of an issue to him. The ax was a weapon for someone
with a strong arm; it took an entirely different sort of skill to
throw it than to throw a knife. Heralds didn't carry axes for
anything but cutting wood, and the likelihood that Amily
would be in a position where that was the only weapon she
had to hand was pretty slim.

And if it was the only weapon she had to hand, it would be
pretty foolish of her to throw it away anyway. He remembered
the Weaponsmaster's admonition to all of them the first time
they began using throwing weapons. *The person who throws
his only weapon at the enemy is an idiot. A few moments after
that, he will be a dead idiot.* Facing someone with a bow, her
best bet would be to drop and roll and knock the assailant's
legs out from under him if she could, and at least make herself
a harder target to hit if she couldn't. Against someone with a
sword or a knife and no option to run, her best bet would be
to wait for him to attack, take his measure, and use the ax as
a hand-to-hand weapon.

He sent his group away to try out some more bows, ad-
monishing them to look for ones that had a harder draw than
the ones they were using now. He reckoned it was about time
for them to try more powerful bows. While he waited for them
to come back, the Weaponsmaster left his group for a moment
to come talk to him.

"Amazing, is it not?" the Herald said with what—in anyone else—Mags might have called "glee." "Who would have

guessed? It is as if a natural warrior, not unlike you, was simply sleeping inside her, waiting for her leg to be repaired before leaping out fully formed."

"She's a natural, that's for certain sure," Mags agreed, watching as she set her pupils another challenge. "There's nothin' magic about it, though," he continued. "She's been playin' darts t'pass the time since she was about old enough to fling 'em. And her pa made her a little grapple on a cord she could use to fetch things to her so she didn't have to struggle to get 'em. Clever bit of kit, that. Wonder who thought of it?"

The Weaponsmaster gave him a long look, as if to make certain that Mags was not trying to pull some sort of joke on him. "Darts, you say?" He repeated, sounding a bit incredulous. "And a grapple?"

"Well, think about it. When you gotta drag a near-useless leg around, so yer pa set you up a target you can pull to you, and pull back into place, you got a lot of incentive to learn to hit it, so you don't haveta go chasing scattered darts," he pointed out reasonably. "And if you got a way to hook a basket, or a book, or an apple and bring it to you, well, you get good hooking things real fast."

The Weaponsmaster nodded thoughtfully. "The skill of hand and eye would translate somewhat to the sword as well," he mused. "But not, say, the staff. Which explains why she is not much better than I would expect in staff."

"I dunno about that, but I'd have her at my back with a bow any time," Mags said with open admiration. And then his pupils returned with their new bows, so he moved them closer to the target to begin all over again.

The next class was swordsmanship again, and Amily tired quickly after teaching two classes in a row. The Weaponsmaster put her to correcting the youngest and least experienced in the class, something she could do without having to partner them, while Mags took another group of mixed Heralds and Guards. And then it was time for luncheon—or, rather, it was just time to get themselves clean before going to luncheon. They all set off for the bathing rooms and filled the place. No Trainees ever wanted to present themselves at the dining hall stinking of sweat.

The afternoon was much the same as the morning, except one of the classes was in staff rather than sword, and Mags saw for himself that Amily was barely adequate. In a way, that was a little bit of a relief—it would have been just a bit depressing to discover she could outfight him in every aspect of weapons work!

At least he could be sure she would never be able to scramble across rooftops the way he could. She didn't have much of a head for heights, and with her leg still strengthening, she would likely never be able to climb and leap the way he could.

Just as well. Her pa'd murder me if I took her roof-walkin'.

:He would murder you and find a way to bring you back so he could murder you again, Chosen,: Dallen chuckled.

Amily arrived at the dining hall at almost the same time as he, both of them with wet hair from a good dousing, and Mags had the feeling they even looked much alike: tired, but satisfied. Lena and Bear gave them startled looks as they sat down at the table, took plates, and began helping themselves.

"Dare I ask what you two have been up to?" Bear ventured.

"We're the Weaponsmaster's new chew toys," Amily said dryly.

Bear looked confused, and Mags chuckled. "She means we're his new assistants. All day, every day. Tell you what, we're getting more'n our share of exercise."

"I can believe it!" Bear explained. "But . . . why?"

"Dean Caelen wants t'hold me outa classes for a while. Dunno why," Mags said, making it public knowledge for the first time. "Weaponsmaster reckoned he can use the help, and I ain't arguing with *him.*"

"Don't blame you, but that doesn't explain Amily," Bear retorted. Amily shrugged. "What else have I got to do?" she asked reasonably. "And you wanted me to exercise more to strengthen the leg before the snow came. This is certainly exercise."

"It's all of that," Bear replied, though he sounded a little dubious. "Just don't overdo it—"

Mags and Amily looked at each other and burst into simultaneous laughter. "Don't tell *us,* Bear," Mags choked out. "If yer really serious 'bout us not overdoing, you need to tell Weaponsmaster!"

Bear looked away for a moment. "Not sure I'd dare," he confessed.

Amily patted his hand fondly. "That's all right, Bear," she said. "Not sure I would either."

Whatever else the new regimen was doing for him—and Mags was pretty certain he was getting very damned good at weapons work, and his stamina was increasing—it also wore him completely out. Despite being with Amily all day, he was untroubled by fantasies about her at night because the moment his head touched the pillow, he was asleep. Sometimes he wondered if it hadn't been Herald Nikolas's idea to put them both to work like this, because it left them neither the time nor the energy for "getting up to mischief" as some people delicately put it.

But Amily swore that when she'd gone back to the rooms she shared with her father that first night, it had all been news to him. So maybe it had been a completely legitimate need of the Weaponsmaster, after all.

Mags was discovering, however, that there were some very physical memories that he had picked up among all the others that the assassins had tried to shove into his head. He discovered it when, two fortnights after they had begun as his assistants, the Weaponsmaster had brought out a new sort of knife to throw, small, heavy, and looking a bit like a dart without a feathered end. Mags had picked up several, and with a sideways flick of his wrist that he had *never* been taught, he sent them in rapid succession—one, two, three—into the center of the target. The three had been placed so closely together that their tips touched.

Weaponsmaster had given him a *look,* but had said nothing, except to order him to teach the others the same throw. Mags was pretty certain there was a lot being said between the Herald and his Companion, and from there onward—probably being relayed on up to Nikolas. He expected a new interrogation after dinner, but all that happened was that Dallen nudged him a little as he was parting from Amily.

:Nikolas says if you come up with anything else useful, be sure to let him know.:

He agreed wordlessly. Nikolas seemed satisfied.

That night, he dreamed briefly in the assassin's tongue again. He seemed to be witnessing two powerful men arguing. It didn't last long enough for him to determine what it was they were arguing about; his dream began about the time they were both disparaging each other's character. And "witness" was all he could do, for he couldn't move or speak, and they didn't appear to notice his presence.

When he woke he still didn't have a clear sense of what had been going on. It had been rather like coming into the middle of a disagreement, so that all he got was the knowledge that the two men were never going to come to terms with each other.

It'd be nice if I were Farseeing, he thought wistfully, *And those men are the leaders. It'd be awfully useful if that lot were fightin' among themselves.*

He fell back asleep again, to find himself dreaming of training among the assassins, making his way back and forth across a sort of obstacle course, except that it was about a story above the ground. The dream-him was extremely good at this, and he took mental notes of some roof-walking techniques that he had never seen nor thought of. Acrobatics, actually. It seemed that by incorporating tumbling moves rather than simple jumping, you could get more distance.

He was better than the other young men in his dream, and their instructor bestowed sparse praise on him that left him glowing and the others glowering. It appeared that such praise was not often forthcoming, and marked him as something special. It felt good in the dream, but when he woke up, the good feeling faded and was replaced with consternation. That was the first time he'd dreamed something about these people that had attracted him to them and their way of life. Were those memories starting to take root?

He could only repeat to himself that Dallen knew his mind better than he knew it himself, and if something was wrong, Dallen would certainly raise an alarm about it.

:Yes I would,: Dallen said patiently and sleepily at about the fifth repetition of this. *:Mags, you are still you. There is nothing about you that has changed, just . . . grown. Do you understand what I'm saying?:*

:That I've had t'grow up?: he replied, feeling just a trifle irritated.

:That is exactly what I am saying,: came the reply. *:Trust me, no one likes being forced to grow up. It's damned unpleasant. You learn you're never safe. You learn that people you depend on to protect you might not be able to. Not even me. You learn all sorts of things you would really rather not have known. I hated it. You hate it. Everyone hates it.:*

Yes, but that didn't make these things less true. And he hated that, too. Well, maybe hate was too strong a word, but he certainly didn't like it, not one bit.

He realized at that moment just what it was that was peculiarly attractive about the assassins.

No one ever has to figure out anything. They get told what to do, an' they do it.

After everything he had gone through, all the uncertainty, there was comfort in that. Heralds were supposed to make decisions all the time. Heralds had to make decisions not only for themselves, but for other people. Big, important, life-changing decisions. Becoming a Herald like Nikolas— effectively a spy for the King—meant he would be making all *kinds* of decisions that would affect people for the rest of their lives. Or shorten those lives. *Could* he do that? Would he ever feel ready to do that?

He'd come here in the first place from the mines, where everyone knew his place and what he was expected to do— and, almost as important, was expected to *keep* to that place and never step out of it. The assassins had a similar life. They didn't make the decisions and were not responsible for the decisions, only for carrying them out.

A Herald's entire life was spent finding his own way.

Right now . . . knowing your place seemed a lot more attractive than finding your way.

:Oh come now, you're too intelligent for that, Mags. Even if conditions at the mine had been good, you'd have been bitterly unhappy being confined like that. And if you were to go join your "cousins," or whatever they are, even if everything was wonderful, you were never assigned to murder anyone who wasn't a hideous villain, and you had friends there, you'd be bitterly unhappy at being confined and not trusted to make your own decisions about your own life there.:

"I suppose . . ." he said aloud, into the dark.

:My impression is that—just as an example—if these people decide that someone should be fathering children, they fling a selected woman at you and expect you to breed like a prize bull. I rather doubt you'd care for that.:

Well . . . that was true enough,

:And seriously, can you lie there and tell me that you wouldn't be questioning every single time you were told to go and murder someone?:

Mags sensed Dallen—laughing?

:Of course I'm laughing. The idea is utterly absurd. Admit it.:

Well . . . it was absurd.

:All right then. Get some sleep, the gods know you will need it. Who knows, something new might be turning up tomorrow.:

5

And in the morning . . . something did turn up.

:Up, you,: he heard in his mind as he first swam up into wakefulness. *:The Dean wants to see you. I told you someone would have something for you soon, and I was right.:*

That woke him up in a hurry.

By now mornings were unpleasant. Not in the sense of having to get up, but in the sense that it was always dark and perishing cold outside when he did. There were brick ovens built into the outside of the stable, one at his end, one at the opposite end. When he'd first returned, it was still warm enough that no one bothered to fire them up except at night. Now they were kept burning all night long, imparting heat to his room and the rest of the stable.

:Do you know what it is?: he asked, scrambling out of bed and hunting for a fresh uniform. It was too blessed cold to wash up at the stable pump, but he did have a basin and a reservoir of tepid water here; when he first moved into this room, someone had kindly arranged for a tank of rainwater to

be stored right up against the chimney brick, and as long as there was a fire there, the water was bearable. He dipped out enough to wash in, since it seemed there was going to be no time for a proper bath.

:I haven't been taken into their confidence,: Dallen replied, sounding a little miffed. *:All I know is that the plan also includes Amily, Bear, and Lena.:*

All right, that was more than a bit of a puzzle! How could a plan include Bear and Lena that had to do with *him?*

He made great haste to finish his washing, got himself into that clean uniform, and hurried to breakfast. There was no point in going to the Dean's office on an empty stomach.

:Do Amily, Lena, and Bear know about this already?: he asked as he loped up the path. There was heavy frost everywhere, and the leaves were all in their autumn colors and already starting to fall. His breath puffed out in clouds, and he was glad of his cloak. Winter would not be long in coming.

:I doubt it. I think this is something Nikolas and Caelen cooked up between them.:

That was even more interesting. He hurriedly got himself his food and bolted it without tasting it. At this point, he was beginning to feel that almost *anything* would be better than spending his time in somewhat disorganized research and being interrogated until his head hurt.

The Dean was right in his office, as usual, and Mags wondered for a moment if the man ever *left.* But Dean Caelen was clearly waiting and watching for him, for as soon as Mags came into view, the Dean waved him in, then closed the door.

"Mags, I'm sure you are aware that your situation is making some people nervous about your continued presence here at the Collegium." The Dean took a seat behind his desk and clasped his hands on the top of it, peering at Mags earnestly. "Let me make one thing perfectly clear: No one is at all concerned about your loyalty or stability, but they are concerned about what your presence might bring here."

"Can't say that I blame 'em, sir," Mags replied honestly. "I'm more'n a bit nervous m'self. I dunno how much of those memories they dumped into me are really for true. For that matter, I dunno what else they got into that could bring other trouble here. I mean, *I'm* sure they broke that contract with Karse, and *I'm* sure they ain't gonna go and write up a new one, but—"

The office was curiously quiet; with all the Trainees slowly fumbling their way toward breakfast there was none of the usual background noise penetrating the Dean's sanctuary. The Dean held up his hand. "You can rest your mind easy on that score," he said, with a slight, encouraging smile. "We do have agents inside Karse. The Karsites are not at all pleased with those fellows. In fact, there are orders out to kill them on sight, and we've good reason to believe that the Karsites have set their demons to hunt for them as well. So—no reconciliation likely there."

Mags nodded slowly. "That's one less worry, then. But they're still after *me.* And everything I know says they'll come here to get me. And . . ." he let his voice trail off, because anything else he would say would just be obvious. That the assassin clan had already gotten onto the grounds of the Palace and Collegia not once, but multiple times. That *maybe* that strange stone embedded in the table in the lowest level of the Palace could tell where they were, but not very accurately, and there were not very many people who could talk to the stone in the first place. That—

He could go on forever, really, with good reasons why people would, and *should,* be nervous about his presence. And he was only one fairly common Trainee, no matter how much Nikolas liked him or thought he had potential. It wasn't as if Nikolas couldn't train, say, Corwin to replace him. Or Barrett. It wasn't as if he was the Heir. There was no good reason to muster resources to protect him. It had been bad enough when quite a number of resources had been gathered to rescue him. He just was not that important.

"Mags, are you listening to me?" the Dean's voice rose, breaking Mags out of his preoccupation.

"Oh, no, sorry, Dean Caelen," he said, shamefacedly.

"I thought you looked as if you were miles away." Rather than sounding annoyed, the Dean sounded sympathetic. "Mags, we've put our heads together, and we are going to try something to shake them off your trail. Oddly enough, it was a helpful suggestion from some of those who were not happy about Heralds going to a Collegium system in the first place. They pointed out that in other years, you'd have just gone off with a mentor, just like every other Trainee. You'd be hard to follow in the Field. And the mentor in this case would eventually send back word of your tragic death at the hands of bandits or something of the sort. Your pursuers would not know that the Death Bell *always* rings when a Herald dies, but your friends, of course, would, and would not be fooled." Dean Caelen shrugged. "Then, once your training in the Field was complete, you'd return with a new name and identity, get your Whites, and be sent off to some other remote Circuit."

"But—" Mags faltered, unable to see how that applied to him. There were so very many things he still needed classes for!

"But you're thinking you still need classes," the Dean responded. "Actually, we looked into that. We're not sure that you do. Perhaps some other Trainee might—but you are not destined to be sent into the Field, Mags. You don't really need to know how to run a survey, you don't really need a class in adjudication, you'll never be asked to do a score of things that Heralds riding Circuits need to know how to do. What you *will* need to know are things Nikolas is already teaching you— things you've proven yourself proficient in. You're a natural with weapons. And you'll need to know how to properly survive in the wilderness, without any sort of help at all, because it is entirely possible in your line of work that you will find yourself forced to do just that. You need to learn how to read people, how to know what they mean, rather than what they say. How to know when they are hiding something. How to get it out of them. To get to the point, Mags, you don't need classes to get the rest of what you'll need to know, you can get it all from being tutored, directly, with a senior Herald. So for the remainder of your time as a Trainee, we are going to revert to the old ways. You're going out in the Field with a senior Herald."

"Yes but—" He could already see a huge hole in this. The assassins knew all about his closest friends, about Amily, and they wouldn't hesitate to take *them* and use them against him.

"Mags, we've been discussing this for days, Nikolas and I," Caelen told him, interrupting the frantic flow of his thoughts. "I am fairly certain you are worried about your friends. That's why they'll be going with you."

Mags felt his jaw dropping. "What?"

Caelen shook his head wryly. "It's so mad an idea it practically has to work. Lena is ready for Scarlets and needs to go on her Journeyman's ride to gather the material for a Master piece. Healers don't have an equivalent, but Bear is more than ready for his full Greens. He is going to be granted them so that he can go with her to continue teaching the use of his healing kit to an even wider audience. The Healers will approve when Dean Lita suggests it; they've already been discussing sending him out anyway, and only the fact that his wife was still a Trainee was stopping them."

It occurred to Mags that for Lena, having a husband like Bear was the ideal situation. He wasn't a Gifted Healer, so no one would object that he was being "taken away" and leaving a hole in the Healers' ranks. Sending him out with Lena, however, was going to allow him to disperse his vital information even faster than he had before—and away from Temples and Houses of Healing, some of which had senior Healers who, like his own father, objected to anyone who wasn't Gifted practicing any form of medicine.

Best of all, with the Collegium supporting Bear monetarily, they didn't have to rely on the whims of Lena's audiences for their income.

Eventually—Mags suspected it would be sooner rather than later—she would find a permanent patron and settle. And Bear would settle with her, probably as the family Healer, or in addition to the family Healer.

That gave Mags a sudden pang of sadness. Because that *was* going to happen. They were all going to part ways, eventually. They'd write . . . he might be able to visit them . . . but they would never again be as close a group as they were now.

But Dean Caelen was continuing. "Amily will supposedly be sent off to visit relatives. You won't leave together; it will look as though each of you is heading off in a different direction, and then you'll catch up with each other at some point outside of Haven."

Mags felt a little dazed at this plan. Caelen was right, it was an absolutely mad notion. Except it was incredibly sane. Amily was a brilliant fighter, obviously whichever Herald was to serve as Mags' mentor would also be a good armsman. Mags reckoned himself the equal of most now—

:Two Companions are not to be sneezed at, either,: Dallen pointed out.

They could easily defend themselves *and* Lena and Bear if it came to it. But with luck, it wouldn't. With luck, all would go according to plan, Mags would be reported dead, and the trail would stop. They'd all return in a year, or maybe two, and . . .

Well, that was when they would all part ways. But they would have had a final, wonderful year together.

"The initial plan is this. We'll send Bear and Lena out first, with a caravan big enough to sleep all of you," the Dean continued. "That way no one will be able to track your passage by looking for you at inns. You'll actually be rather comfortable,

I would think, since I expect you'll be camping at Waystations."

"And . . . where will we be goin', sir?" Mags asked, unable to think of anything else to ask.

The Dean rubbed his hands together, looking satisfied. "Well, now, this is the beauty of it. The Circuit we're sending you to cover is out in the hills not desperately far from that mine you came from. Once you get to the hard winter part of it, you'll actually be able to make a sort of headquarters in a part of the hills known as The Bastion. From there, it is an easy ride to each of the villages you are to visit."

There was something here Mags was missing. "So . . . there's somethin' special about The Bastion?"

"There certainly is." The Dean smiled knowingly. "It's the place where the bandit horde that captured your parents was laired up. If there is anything left that can tell you anything about them, you'll have plenty of time to look for it over the winter."

Mags left the Dean's office with feelings so mixed he was having trouble sorting them out. His room at the stable seemed a good, quiet place to try to get a grasp on everything that was about to happen to him, so that was where he went, sitting quietly on his bed, back to the wall, staring blankly at the opposite wall.

He couldn't exactly argue with this plan. It was a good one. He could, quite literally, vanish. No one would be looking for him when he was declared dead, and yet not one of his real friends was going to suffer a moment of grief. Even those who weren't Heralds or Trainees would be quietly put in the know by those who were.

He'd be *with* his friends and be able to *protect* his friends.

Everyone who was truly at risk would all be in the same place, and they could watch each others' backs.

He'd be with Amily—and finally away from all those all-too-watchful eyes that seemed to think they needed to keep him and Amily under supervision. Not that they'd be unsupervised, obviously, but at least there wouldn't be the feeling that every single person—and Companion!—on the Hill was reporting back to Nikolas on everything they did.

This was not going to be easy, though. He had no real experience of wilderness living in the hard conditions of winter. Not to mention everything else that was going to be expected of him.

And just *which* Herald was going to be his mentor? Not Nikolas, of course; the King's Own couldn't be spared. Mags dreaded going off for months with a stranger; what if whoever it was didn't much like him?

But . . . they were going to be spending time, and a lot of time, in the last place his parents had been alive. What chance was there he'd find some clue as to who they had been? Now that he had the benefit of those memories dumped into his head, he knew he could infer quite a bit from very little, if he could find some belongings of theirs. Even fragments would help!

He couldn't help but also feel some panic at the idea that suddenly, with very little warning, he was going to be thrown out on Circuit. No matter what Dean Caelen said about him "not needing" to learn how to stand in judgment on people, that was exactly what Heralds on Circuit were often required to do! What if he made mistakes? What if those mistakes hurt people? Heralds were often the only recourse people in these remote villages had to an impartial judge—what if he made the wrong decisions?

What if he—

:*That's why you go out with a senior Herald, dunce,*: Dallen chuckled, making those concerns, at least, evaporate.

:What, you think the idea is to throw you into these situations and make you flounder? You do nothing but watch and learn for a while. Then the senior will ask your opinion before he makes a decision, then he will let you make a decision, but has the option to override you if he thinks it's a bad one. And that is just assuming that your senior even bothers to go through the motions of the usual Circuit with you. Most likely, what you will be doing is to make his job easier—spying. Using and honing the skills you already have. Finding out the stories behind the story they are giving him.:

Oh. Well. Now he certainly felt foolish. *:Good thing I didn't go blurtin' all that out, then, I guess. And the wilderness survival? I guess that'll be part and parcel of being out in the dead of winter.:*

:Personally, I think you did very well at that. You'll just be picking up a few more tricks and skills, I expect. You should have been taking that class this fall. The Judgment class, as well.:

Well, yes. A little kidnapping had put paid to that . . .

But Dallen was continuing. *:It's no matter. Now that I know what the plan is, I can simply* show *you everything you would have learned in the Judgment class so at least you have an idea of what your senior is doing, so you can anticipate what he might want from you. Want me to?:*

It had been a while since Dallen had done something like that. Mostly, it had been during his first year here, when he'd had to go from an uncivilized half-feral thing that had never seen a bath and didn't know how to behave like a human. If it hadn't been for Dallen, he would probably still be a half-feral thing that didn't know how to behave like a human.

Well, maybe that was an exaggeration, but it wasn't too much of one.

Since then, Dallen had been careful never to "give" him anything that might have constituted cheating. It would have been easy for Dallen to merely bestow on him things he was supposed to be learning in class, but Mags had never asked for that.

Until now, that is. But then, this one time, it wouldn't be cheating, would it?

:Please,: he said.

Having Dallen share information like that was *nothing* like the way the assassin's talisman had flooded his mind and tried to drown him in memories. In fact, there really was no "experience" at all. He simply said *please,* and everything he needed to know on the subject was just there, in his mind, exactly as it would have been if he had learned it the hard way. There weren't even specific memories attached to the knowledge, which was much better than having it the other way around.

As he sat there contemplating the new information, it occurred to him that the assassins were idiots.

Because if they had really, truly, *wanted* him to join them of his own free will, they wouldn't have tried to turn him into someone else with that talisman. Instead, they would have done what Dallen had just done. They'd have given him everything they wanted him to know gently, painlessly, unobtrusively. And he would just *know* facts about them. He'd have had no reason to doubt what he knew, no reason to question what was there.

With Dallen blocked out of his mind because of their drugs, it would have been much harder to fight against them, if all they had done was give him plain facts and information. Even if everything they had given him was purely biased in their own favor—as long as it was facts,

But instead, they'd tried to force it all on him. They'd tried to flood him with memories that weren't his. All his instincts had been to fight back.

And a good thing, too.

He was just thinking that, when there was a tap on his door, and he knew from the *feel* of the presences on the other side it was Bear, Lena, and Amily.

"Come!" he said aloud, and the three of them practically tumbled into the room, all talking at once.

He got up and opened his shutters, which he had left half closed. Light flooded in, making up for the fact that some cold got in, too. The glazing on the windows didn't keep all of the cold out.

It took a little time before they managed to settle down enough to talk sensibly, and it was very clear from the beginning that they were wildly excited about this plan. Bear and Lena shared a seat on the top of his clothing chest, which doubled as a bench. Amily cuddled up with him on the bed.

Bear was the quietest of the three, but Mags got a sense of quiet vindication from him, and who could blame him? He was going to get his full Greens before they all went out, so he and Mags' mentor would technically be the most senior people in the group. It wasn't unusual for quiet young Healers to get full Greens, but most of them were very powerfully Gifted. Bear might be the youngest Healer who relied entirely on means other than a Gift to accomplish his Healing to ever get his Green robes.

It was a huge vindication for Bear, and was going to be an enormous slap in the face to his father. Deservedly so.

Lena was wildly excited. She'd never been away from home until she came to Bardic Collegium, and she'd never been away from Bardic except for visits home, since. She had already been to see the caravan they were going to use and was full of descriptions of every nook and corner of it—

He couldn't imagine why she was so taken with the thing, but then again, it might just have been the novelty. A room that moved . . . that was pretty different. He suspected that she hadn't yet contemplated the fact that there would be an awful lot of them squeezed into a place that was, maybe, the size of his room here at the stables.

Mags might have been more interested, except he already had memories of what caravan life was like from Dallen. A novelty, but living in nice tight rooms in winter was much preferable, at least in Dallen's estimation, and Mags didn't see any reason to argue with him. He could see where tempers could get out of hand with four to six people crammed into the same tiny space, barely the size of two of the stalls that the Companions shared.

But then, if they were going to The Bastion, presumably there would be some sort of shelter there . . . wait, Caelen had said something about caves, hadn't he?

He closed his eyes a moment and thought back to those old Guard reports. Yes! Caves! That was it! There were caves—the reports had definitely said several of them. That wouldn't be so bad. Mags knew from his mining days that caves stayed about the same temperature all year round, once you got away from the entrance some. He knew a lot about mines and caves—if there was a place that had a crack or fissure that went all the way to the surface, often enough you could make yourself a decent sort of fireplace there. And they wouldn't have to hunt for such places themselves, because the remains of the bandits' old fires would show them where such places were. Provided they got themselves in place before the snow fell, they could make things quite comfortable, more comfortable than in a Waystation, probably as, or more, comfortable than in the caravan itself.

"What are you thinking about so hard?" Amily asked. "You haven't said a word."

"Thinking about the best way for all of us to set things up so we don't want to tear each others' faces off before winter gets too deep," he said dryly.

"I suppose of the lot of us, you're the closest to guessing

what this is going to be like," she replied, and made a little face. "And that's without having to evade your hunters."

"Living together that close is gonna be a strain, no matter what. We just need to be careful about things from the very beginning," he assured her, and squeezed her hand. "We've been friends a long time. We'll just have to keep reminding each other why. We just have to be . . . easy with everybody else's bad habits—or what we think are bad habits. Get my meaning?"

He looked over at Bear and Lena, who were giving him thoughtful looks of their own. "It's hard living so close like we'll be doing," he told them. "Sometimes, the least little things'll make you mad. Habits, little ticks, that kinda thing. There won't be much privacy, 'less we can arrange some when we get to The Bastion. You lot ain't never lived without some privacy. It'll take getting used to."

They all considered that for a good long moment, long enough to make him satisfied that they had actually taken in what he said and hadn't dismissed it with an airy, "But we're all friends, we could *never* get angry with each other!"

On the other hand, they'd all had experience with getting angry with each other. Granted, it had been because their emotions had all been manipulated in a sense. The talismans that the assassins had carried had had some unexpected side effects—there was something about the protections here on Valdemar that made the things act like irritants to everyone within close range. So, perhaps that made his friends more inclined to take Mags' cautions seriously.

"Pish," Bear finally said. "If we all start acting too tetchy, I can brew up a tea to mellow us all right down."

Mags had to smile at that. "Just so that we aren't *so* mellow we don't take danger seriously," he cautioned.

"So do we know who your mentor is?" Bear wanted to know.

At that moment, a tall shadow filled the doorway, making them all turn to stare.

"That would be me," said Herald Jakyr, stepping into the room. "Hello Mags."

Jakyr had been the first Herald Mags had ever seen. In fact, before he met Jakyr, he hadn't even known there were such things as Heralds. Jakyr had come in response to a desperate plea from Dallen, who had been unable to get anywhere near his Chosen, thanks to the efforts of Cole Pieters and his sons. At that time, Mags had no more idea that things like Heralds and Companions existed than if he'd been brought up on the moon. Cole Pieters had done a stellar job of making sure every one of his slaves was as ignorant as he could get away with. The less they knew, the better he could intimidate and rule them with fear.

In fact, when Dallen turned up at the mine where he was little more than a slave, he'd thought, from the way Master Cole and his sons acted, that the Companion was a demon or monster skulking around the compound.

Then when Jakyr, his Companion, and Dallen fought their way into the compound itself—well—that was when his life absolutely turned upside down.

They heard the commotion before they emerged from the mine, but it didn't sound like monsters were invading Master Cole's property. It sounded more like the day some fool from the local highborn had come nosing about, or at least trying to. He'd brought an armsman with him, but it didn't do him any good. There was two of them, and a half dozen of Cole Pieters' sons, and if they didn't know how to use swords, they didn't need

to, *as anyone around would know they were damned good
with their crossbows. Master Cole had run the man off then,
and no mistaking it. He hadn't come back either.*

*Cole had been hollering about his rights then, and he was
doing so now. His voice echoed harshly down the mine shaft.*
"I know my rights! Ye can't just swan in here and make off
with whoever ye choose! These are my workers, homeless
criminals every one, signed for and turned over to me to use
as I need until their time runs out!"

*Criminals? Now Mags knew that was a lie, and a big fat
one too. None of them were criminals, not even he. No one had
been signed over by gaolers. Everyone here was here through
no fault of their own . . .*

"Evidently," *drawled a new voice, sounding lazy, but with
a hard edge of anger beneath the words that Mags doubted
Master Cole was hearing.* "Evidently you don't know your
rights as well as you think you do, Cole Pieters. I do have the
right to 'swan in here' and take whomever I please. You are
the one violating the law, denying a Companion access to his
Chosen, and preventing a Herald from exercising his duty."

*Mags relaxed. He didn't really know what a Herald or a
Companion were, though the latter sounded dirty, and he really didn't care. As long as it wasn't monsters come to tear
him to pieces, or devils to torment him, he didn't care.*

*He emerged, blinking as usual, into the bright light of
noon. And there was something of a standoff going on in the
yard between the mine and the house and its outbuildings.*

*There was a man all in white, with two white horses,
standing right at a barricade hastily thrown up across the
lane leading to the yard. Behind the barricade were Cole Pieters and all of his sons, just like the time when that other fellow had come snooping. Only this time the crossbows weren't
trained on the stranger, much to Cole Pieters' obvious fury, as
he kept looking back at his sons.*

"Pa," *said Endal Pieters, his voice flooded with uncertainty, crossbow pointed at the ground and not even cocked. "Pa, that's a Herald. That's a Herald, Pa!"*

"I can see that!" Pieters snapped. "And the man's daft, and so's his horse! There's nothing here for them to take! I ain't letting go of any of you, no more your sisters, and there's nothin' in that trash—" he waved at the emerging mine crew "—that any of them should come calling for! This is just an excuse to come snooping where they ain't wanted, and they can turn around and—"

"Pa, it's a Herald—"

"I don' care if it's the King hisself! I know my rights!" Pieters' face was getting very red indeed. Mags wondered if he was finally going to have that apoplectic fit he'd been threatening to for years now.

Well, Pieters might or might not know his rights, but the kiddies knew when to stay out of the way. The mining crew going in scuttled across the yard and down the shaft as quick as may be, while the outgoing crew scuttled toward the eating shed as fast as they could. It didn't do to fall under Master Cole's eye when he was like this because if he saw you, then you would be the next thing he took out his anger on when things settled down. It was especially true if he saw you looking at him.

So they all kept their heads down and got across the yard as quick as they could, heading for the colorless daughter waiting in the shed for them, and the equally colorless cook ladling out bowls of soup nervously. And it was a sign of how bad things were that there was no one to take the little sacks from them, the sacks that held their sparklies.

Mags caught Davey looking sly then, and he knew that Davey was thinking up some deviltry to be sure. And right enough, Davey was just about to snatch Burd's little sack from him, when up comes Jarrik and takes it from him, then takes Davey's with a dirty look. Mags was quick to hand his over before Jarrik could even put his hand out for it. He

couldn't be rid of it soon enough. Then he headed off across
the yard as Jarrik headed for his brothers and the standoff at
the gate.

But at that moment, everything changed again.

"That's the one!" the man shouted imperiously, every trace
of lazy drawl gone. "Him! You there! Boy!"

Startled, Mags looked to see who the man was shouting at
and, to his bewilderment, saw the finger pointing straight at
him. And one of the horses began rearing and prancing and
carrying on like it had a burr under its saddle, tossing its
mane and flagging its tail.

Bewilderment turned to panic as all the rest turned to stare
at him. Mags looked from side to side for a place to get into
hiding, but there wasn't anything. He was caught like a
mouse in the middle of a kitchen floor, with hungry cats on
every side of him.

"I didn' do nothin'!" he squeaked. "I bin workin'! I bin
workin', I tell ya! It ain't me!"

Truly, he had never seen this man or anyone like him in all
his life, so how could the fellow be so sure it was him he
wanted?

"I will be damned if ye take my best worker!" Pieters
roared. "Ye kin take yer damned horses and be off with ye, or
so help me—"

But the man had an even louder voice than Pieters, and the
boys were all looking very alarmed now. "You will turn over
that boy to me, or I'll bring the Guard here and turn over
every stone in the place and find every last lie and every last
penny you've cheated the Crown out of and every last mis-
treatment of your servants you've done since you were in
swaddling clothes!" he shouted, as Endal plucked at his father's sleeve and begged, "The Guard, Pa! He's gonna call the
Guard on us! We cain't hold off the Guard! Be reasonable!"

And that was when things got very strange indeed.

Jarrik pulled Endal away from their father, and shoved him

toward Mags. "Get him! Bring him here!" Jarrik growled, and then motioned to two of his brothers, who surrounded their father and bodily shoved him off to the side, arguing with him in harsh whispers.

Meanwhile Endal had crossed the yard, seized Mags by the ear, and was dragging him toward the man, with Mags hissing in pain the entire way.

Endal only let go of his ear when they were within touching distance of the man and the horses, if the barricade hadn't been in the way. Mags had never been this close to a horse before. Not a real horse. The mining carts and machinery were all pulled by donkeys, and he had never been allowed near the stables, nor the Pieters boys when they were mounted.

These horses were big. Very big, They smelled sweetly of cut grass and clover, with overtones of leather. Truth to tell, now that he was this close to them, they scared him. Something that big could mash his foot flat with a silver hoof and never notice, knock him down and trample him and move along without even noticing.

He stared down at the ground, unable to move, while the men shouted over his head. What could this fellow, this Herald, want anyway? He hadn't done anything! He never left the mine!

This . . . couldn't be about his parents, could it? But what did he have to do with what they'd done? He'd only been a baby. . . .

"This boy is coming with me." The man was not shouting now, but he didn't have to, the anger in his voice was like a bludgeon. "You try to stop me, and so help me, I will do exactly what I said I would. The Guard will be here. They will tear this place apart. If you have done one thing wrong, we will find it. And then you will be for it, Master Cole."

There was some urgent whispering as Mags stared and stared at his own two feet, until he had memorized every dirt-encrusted line, could have measured out his clawlike toenails in his sleep, knew he would be seeing them perfectly even if he closed his eyes. He couldn't make out what the whispering was about, but it sounded as if the boys were getting their way with the old man. Finally Cole growled, "Then you'll be paying me for him."

The man barked a not-laugh. "Pay you for him? Slavery is illegal in Valdemar, Cole Pieters. You can be thrown in gaol for owning slaves, or selling them."

"I've spent a fortune feeding and clothing this boy!" Cole sputtered. "Eating his head off, taking my charity, giving back naught—"

"A fortune is it?" The angry drawl was back. "What kind of a fool do you take me for? I'm neither blind nor ignorant. I can see from here what kind of slop you feed these children. A good farmer wouldn't give it to a pig. And if there is a rag on their backs that isn't threadbare and decades old, I will eat it. As for shelter, where are you having them sleep? I don't see a house big enough for them. Are you keeping them in the barn? In a cellar?" His tone got very dangerous, and Mags shivered to hear it. "Exactly what have you been spending all the money given to you for the keep of orphans on?"

What money? Mags thought, dazedly. But Cole was right on top of that one.

"What money?" he sneered. "Nobbut one person wanted these brats. No fambly wanted 'em, no priest wanted 'em. And their villages couldn 'ford another mouth to feed. Charity! It was my own charity that took 'em in, useless, feckless things that they be! My charity that feeds 'em, and me own kids going short—"

"Oh, that's a bit much even for you, Cole Pieters." There was a growl under the drawl. "If you are going to claim all that, then I think perhaps a visit from the Guard and Lord Astley's Clerk of Office would be a very, very good thing."

There was a great deal more of that sort of thing, most of it so far over Mags' head that it might as well have been in a foreign tongue. But the man was winning.

Mags only wished he could tell if that was a good thing, or a bad one. Usually he would immediately have said that anything Cole Pieters was against was going to be good for him, but now, he wasn't so sure.

Finally, Pieters literally picked Mags up by the scruff of the neck, hauled him off the ground like a scrawny puppy, and shoved him over the barrier at the man, shouting "Take him, then! Take him and be damned to you!"

Without a word, the man mounted one of the two horses, reached down and grabbed Mags' arm and picked him up like so much dirty laundry, and dumped him on top of the other horse.

Mags froze stiff with fear, his hands going instinctively around the knobby part of the thing he was sitting on, his legs clamping as hard as they could to the horse's sides. But—but—but—

"I dunno howta ride . . ." he tried to gasp out, but it didn't come out any louder than a whisper, and anyway it was already too late. The man was off, the other horse right behind him, and Mags squeezed his eyes and hands shut, and his legs hard, and clamped down his teeth on the chattering they were doing.

I'm gonna fall off. I'm gonna fall off and die.

———

As the memory flashed through Mags' mind some of it must have shown on his face, for Jakyr grinned. "If I were to stand you and that scrawny, filthy little mine-slave side by side, I'd never know the two of you were the same person. The years have improved you out of all expectation, Mags."

"They'd kinda have had to," Mags pointed out. "There

wasn't all that much of me to begin with. Anything would'a been an improvement."

Jakyr laughed. "This will be a first for both of us. I've never mentored anyone before."

"Well," Mags said, and grinned back, "I *been* mentored, so when you mess up, I'll be sure'n let ye know."

"Insolent brat!" Jakyr aimed a blow at Mags, but of course, he never connected. Or, rather, he turned the blow into a rough tousle of Mags' hair. "Introduce me to the rest of your fellow sufferers, then."

"Everyone, this is Herald Jakyr," he said obediently. "I 'spect you know Amily, Jakyr."

"By reputation, your father's stories, and from afar, and I'm very pleased to see you looking fit and healed, milady," Jakyr replied, and sketched a bit of a bow. "Also pleased to hear of your martial progress from our Weaponsmaster. I am completely confident in your ability to hold your own."

Amily flushed with pleasure and bowed a little herself.

"This is Bear and Lena. They're giving Bear his Greens afore they leave, and Lena's gonna be on her Journeyman's travels. They're married," he added hastily.

Jakyr eyed the two of them with interest. "So you two are the cause of that near-incident last year. I'm surprised you haven't made a comic song of *that,* Trainee."

"Call me Lena, and what makes you think I haven't?" Lena asked, tilting her head to one side. Jakyr broke out into laughter.

"Well done. Just picking your time to debut it?" he asked.

"Some things are like wine and cheese: They need to age properly before you bring them out in public," Lena replied archly.

"Well said. Now, if you don't mind my joining you?" Jakyr waved a hand at the bed, which at the moment was the only place to sit.

As an answer, Mags and Amily moved over on the bed, making room for him. Jakyr took a seat.

"Here's the rough plan. Mags and I, Amily's escort, and you and Nikolas will be the only people knowing your route. You will be avoiding inns, buying supplies as you need them, and overnighting in the caravan at Waystations. Bear, you and Lena will take the caravan. You were probably told that, but I have made a change, and Nikolas approved it. You'll have a third party hidden in the caravan the entire time. Amily and her escort will leave once you're gone and will catch up with you at a Waystation; the only people who will know *which* Waystation it is will be the person with you and Amily's escort. At that point, the person with you will take Amily's place, and Amily will go into hiding in the caravan. Meanwhile, Mags and I will leave going in another direction, double back, and pick you up on the road somewhere between here and the start of our Circuit. We'll know your route, so it will be trivial to find you. And at that point, we'll all become a team. This district has a reputation for being a particularly thorny one. The bandits that holed up in The Bastion were only the most obvious of the problems. This is no sinecure; it will be a real job, even a difficult job. We'll have our work cut out for us." He looked at each of them in turn. "Bear, I am counting on you to win people over with your skills and willingness to share them. Lena, these folk don't see Bards all that often; they are more likely to talk to you than to me and Mags. You'll be very valuable to us."

"What about me?" Amily asked, sounding just a touch forlorn.

"*You,* my dear, will be your father's daughter, possibly the most valuable of all," Jakyr said with conviction. "I've been told of how you have mastered the art of seeming invisible, quietly observing and listening. Healers often have assistants. I know you've helped Bear out in the past, so you will be Bear's assistant. You will be the one that goes to the locals and the markets for supplies, which will allow you to talk to them without anyone official-looking about. The more you can act like a common servant, the better. People will take you for being at their social rank, as opposed to the rest of us, and they'll put down anything elevated in your speech as simply a matter of coming from the capitol. What Lena doesn't uncover by coaxing it out, you likely will by gossip and eavesdropping."

Amily nodded happily. "I've watched Bear and Mags bargain enough, I think I can do it too."

"Don't bargain too sharply," Jakyr chuckled. "We want them to think they've been more clever than the city girl. That will put them off their guard with you. We can certainly afford to be a little bit cheated in return for getting a lot of information."

This was a side of Jakyr that Mags had never seen, one of the network of Nikolas's intelligence agents as well as a Herald. Clearly, he knew his job and how to do it well.

"All right then, I'll leave the four of you to plan. I don't think I need to emphasize that we keep this just among us, right?"

"Everyone else gets told Lena and I are going out on her Journeyman's round, and I'm going with her to teach," Bear agreed. "And we got lucky to get offered the caravan, so I can carry a lot of supplies with me."

"And I'm going to visit unspecified relatives," Amily added. "I'm going to be quite unhappy at being separated from Mags for at least a year and maybe more, but, then, I would be just as separated from him if I were here, which is something I'll tearfully tell people over and over so they can comfort me."

"Excellent," Jakyr said. "I'll leave you to it then."

He let himself out, and the four of them put their heads together.

6

"**I** think we should go look at this caravan," Bear said. "We need to figure out how much room there is for each of us."

:The caravan is stored in the wagon shed. It should be obvious. It's the white one with faint flowers and vines bleeding through the paint.: Dallen sounded highly amused for some reason. *:Six coats of paint, and the designs are still bleeding through. If we could ever figure out who made that paint in the first place, we'd never need to paint anything with more than one coat again. Oh, and there are people around there who can tell you exactly how much space there is for personal gear and supplies for Bear and Lena. So multiply that by three for the supplies you think you will need for two of you, and divide the remaining storage by three for the personal gear and you'll be able to figure out what you'll get.:*

That sounded promising. Mags relayed that to the others, and they went to look for the promised caravan.

There was only one building on the grounds where vehicles were kept. Most of them were homely, working wagons and vans. There was one Royal Carriage, which held eight, but it had been decades since any Royal Family of Valdemar went on a Royal Progress, so all of the fancier wagons that would have carried their luggage and baggage had long been pressed into more practical service.

The caravan wasn't difficult to spot. It was actually taller than most of the other vehicles here, taller even than the Royal Carriage. It had exceedingly high wheels; the ones in the front were smaller than the ones in the rear, but the ones in the rear came almost to Mags' collarbone. It was very far off the ground. From where Mags stood, it looked like an entire cottage on wheels!

He measured the rear wheels against himself, wonderingly, as he gazed at the contraption in the light coming in through the open doors.

"That's so she can ford rivers," said someone behind them. They all turned.

It was an older man, quite gray-haired, and tough and wiry looking, with formidable muscles, in a rougher version of the blue-and-silver Royal livery, clearly made for a hard working-man who expected to be outdoors a great deal.

"That's why she's so tall," the man continued. "She's meant for the road, and rough road at that. Tall, so she can ford rivers. You want to hope there are always bridges, but sometimes there ain't. So, I reckon these two are the ones that'll be taking her out, and you've come to see her?" At Bear and Lena's mutual nods, he grinned. "She's built for six, so you two will have heaps of room. I'll show you about."

Mags noticed at once that the wheels were outside the body, but that the wagon itself had been built outward over the open wheels, which would add some to the interior of what was undoubtedly going to be very cramped living space. There were racks along the side where you could store boxes; the boxes themselves were stacked up to either side, out of the way. There were railings along the top as well; presumably you could store more things up there. Mags approved.

"This here's the front," said the fellow. "Oh, I'm Ard Ardson. I'm the Wagonmaster, as was my father, and his father before him, and his father before *him*. If it goes on wheels and belongs to the Palace or the Collegia, it's my job to keep it in trim."

"Then I'm right glad you were here, Master Ardson," Bear said earnestly—and looking daunted. "I've—ah—never handled a wagon before . . ."

"And you won't be handling one now," Ard told him. "One of your teachers, I misremember who, found out about this scheme and reckoned she was due for a trip. I guess teaching you lot's harder than driving and tending to a wagon and pair!" He laughed at his own joke. "She and I had a short run with this beauty. I've already checked her out, we had some hands-on, and I am here to tell you I'd let her drive any rig in this building, including this one, so no fear there. Two-hitch, four-hitch, wheel-changing, there's nothing I wouldn't trust her with."

This was the first any of them had heard of it, but Mags was extremely relieved to hear it. *He* certainly didn't know anything about wagons and horses, and he rather doubted Jakyr was an expert—although you never knew. But at least Bear and Lena would have an expert with them from the beginning.

"So as I said, this is the front." Ard gestured to what looked like a little porch with a door in the middle. There was a fold-down seat currently locked in the "up" position for the driver and fold-out steps that were in the "down" position between the shafts. "As you can see, driver is all cozy, or as cozy as you can be driving in bad weather, which I would advise against. Horses won't like it, and you're better off losing a day. The storage boxes on the outside are for supplies, so you can keep clothes and the like on the inside, out of the weather. The boxes are all waterproof, I just checked 'em myself, which is why they ain't loaded up now. Canvas bags for fodder and wood on the top, or anything else that's light and easy to haul up or throw down."

The more Ard spoke, the more admiration Mags had for him. He definitely took his job extremely seriously.

"The boxes on the top are going to be lashed into place. Don't take 'em down unless you have to. They will have canvas, stakes, and rope. Two bow tents, a skirt for around the bottom of the wagon and a floorcloth for under the wagon, if there's more than six to sleep, and they'd rather sleep under the wagon." He raised an eyebrow. "As I said, she sleeps six, but it's a tight six, and if the weather ain't bad, the last lot to take her out preferred to have two sleeping below. With four, it oughta be fine. Yer teacher and the assistant can use the benches. I reckon, women don't seem to toss as much as men. Oh, there's a cupboard-box that bolts in under the rear; that's for your pots and pans you use over the fire. They'll get black and nasty and stay black and nasty, and you won't want 'em in the wagon 'cause they'll get smuts all over everything. Now, go on up into her."

He gestured that they should go up the stairs and into the wagon itself.

It was bigger than Mags had expected. Inside it was all handsome varnished wood, which should be easy to keep clean. The middle part of the roof was both raised and bowed, with thin sheets of horn inset along the sides of the raised part, bringing in a lot of light and giving far more headroom than he would have expected. Not even Jakyr was going to have to stoop in here.

"Two of your beds are there at the rear," Ard went on from the door. Mags craned his head around to look. Sure enough, two beds had been built into the rear, one above the other, with the bottom one on the floor and a small cupboard built above the upper one. Both had little windows looking rearward, also with horn panels. "Those windows open for air, but if it's snowing, you won't want em open, obviously. Shutters on the outside to close up against bad weather. Shutters on all the windows except the mollicroft up here." He tapped the narrow windows up in the roof. "Mollicroft windows open, see?" He demonstrated by unlatching one and opening it on a hinge at the bottom. "Two more of your beds are built on this side." He slapped the right side, where Mags had already seen two very narrow bench-type beds, with cupboards over and under them. There were a series of horn windows here, too. "Plenty of room for four."

There was literally not a bit of space that wasn't in use. Cupboards, some hardly big enough to hold a few knives or spoons, or maybe a mending kit, had been fitted in anyplace there was some useable space.

"This side, as you can see, nearest the door, there's a nice metal hearth and chimbley." He slapped what looked like a tiny metal fireplace with a cast-iron pot in it, standing on three legs. "What you do is, you fill that there pot with coals, and she heats the wagon at night. Come morning, you make sure to dump that pot, I'm sure I don't need to tell you. Also, more storage for your things." The rest of that side was, indeed, cupboards. "And that's your wagon. She can be fixed when she breaks by just about any blacksmith or wheelwright. But treat her right, and she shouldn't break unless you have mortal bad luck."

Ard backed down the steps and off the wagon; the rest of them followed. This wasn't going to be impossible, not by any means, but. . . .

:But we had all better work on our temper-keeping skills,: Dallen chuckled. *:And I suspect that unless it is bloody freezing cold, those tents are going to be getting some use.:*

———————

Amily looked up from her calculations. "Well," she said, finally, "as far as I can tell, we'll each have room for four standard packs worth of . . . stuff. Which is not a lot, but it's two packs more than a solo Herald on Circuit has." She raised her pen at Bear before he could say anything. "I allotted extra room for your herbs, Bear. Lena—I don't know what to tell you—"

"All I need is my small gittern," she said firmly. "Maybe a flute. I'll manage. A Bard on Journeyman's round isn't able to carry any more than a solo Herald."

"That's more'n I'll need, Amily, if you want one'a my packs'-worth for yourself," Mags said generously.

"I'd rather you took it and carried armor," she replied seriously. "Just in case." She sighed a little. "I'd hoped to bring some books, but . . . they're heavy and bulky and I can't think of any that would actually be *useful* under these circumstances."

"Well, if you do, we'll find a way to get it in," Mags promised. For his part, he hoped that they would be able to reach The Bastion before any serious weather came in. They were going to need a *lot* of fodder, with two horses and two Companions to feed all winter. There was no way that wagon could take even a fraction of it. They'd be hard pressed to carry enough to supplement grazing on the trip itself. They'd probably have to stop several times to buy more.

:Rest easy,: Dallen replied to the thought. *:The Bastion is being supplied for you by the Guard even as we speak. As you know, there are caves, plenty of good, dry places to store supplies for you and those of us that eat hay.:* There was a suggestion of a heavy sigh. *:But, alas, there is no good way to store pocket pies.:*

Mags laughed silently. *:Guess you'll have to suffer with plain old apples.:*

:The horror,: Dallen mourned.

———————

There was a slight change of plans before it was all said and done.

There seemed to be no reason why Mags and Jakyr should not leave first. They were going to have to circle back once they thought they had left a sufficiently confusing trail, and that was going to take time. Jakyr, as always, was eager to leave the Collegia as soon as possible, and Mags didn't see any reason why he shouldn't indulge his mentor.

There was a good reason for this haste, of course, at least as far as the Herald was concerned. Jakyr was avoiding someone.

In fact, for as long as Mags had known Herald Jakyr, he had been avoiding that same someone.

Strangely enough, it was not another Herald.

"That will be the new Healers' Collegium," Jakyr said, pointing toward one of the unfinished structures, "And that will be the new Bardic. I hope to blazes they're done by this time next year. Meanwhile, we have all of you younglings crammed into the one building. Damn and blast Healers and Bards to perdition anyway!" He ran his hand through his hair in the first demonstration of irritability that Mags had seen from him. "Couldn't they just have waited—" He broke off, and looked over at Mags with a rueful expression. "Never mind me, lad. I go off on a rant about this—"

"Aye, you do, Jak, and on any excuse whatsoever." They both turned their heads at the sound of the voice, which had been pitched to carry. There was a woman approaching, sauntering slowly toward them with her arms crossed over her chest. She looked about the same age as Herald Jakyr but was dressed all in red, with a hooded coat rather than a cloak. "And I'm certain-sure he'll hear it all enough times to be sick of it. Is this the new lad that Dallen called for help in fetching?" She nodded at Mags, and a graying blond curl escaped from her hood at her temple.

Jakyr's expression went very stony. "Aye, Lita, it is. Now if you don't mind I've—"

"You've got to take him off to Caelen, and then you have urgent business to be off on," she interrupted him, with just a touch of waspishness. "Which was precisely what you always have. Lots of urgent business taking you elsewhere, and none of it keeping you here. Which is why you are in that saddle, and your bed is narrow and cold. Nah, be off you with on your urgent business!" she continued, as Jakyr's expression went from stony to stunned. "I'll take the boy to Caelen. You fair can't wait to shake the last of Haven dust from your feet, so be about it. It'd be a sad day when a Bard can't extend a bit of courtesy to a new Trainee."

As Jakyr sat there, looking very much as if he could not make up his mind between going or staying, she added, "You think I'll eat him? You think the leader of the Bardic Circle can't be trusted to take one Trainee from here to Caelen's office?"

That made up Jakyr's mind for him. "Thanks, Lita," he managed, as if he were strangling on the words. "I really do have—"

"Urgent business, aye, I know," the woman sighed. "Go, and wind at your back. I'll not wish you ill, no matter what our differences."

There was no other word to describe Jakyr's abrupt departure but "fled." And when he was out of sight—which happened so quickly that Mags suspected he had deliberately chosen the route that would put buildings and trees between them the soonest—the woman looked at Dallen. "Well met, Dallen," she said, reaching out and giving the Companion a friendly pat on the neck. "So you finally got you a Chosen?"

Dallen nodded. She smiled, then looked up at Mags. "And what would your name be, then, lad?"

"Mags." He stared down at her, feeling rather dumb-

founded. Whatever had just happened here left him entirely in the dark.

"Don't mind Jak. He and I have some history betwixt us." *She sighed. "Not always good history, especially toward the parting end of it. And now I can't help myself; whenever I see him, I goad him." She shook her head. "Come along, we'll turn Dallen over to his minders and get you into the hands of yours." She turned and headed up a stone-bordered, well swept path, without looking back to see if he was going to come along.*

———————

Lita wasn't just any Bard. Lita was the Dean of Bardic Collegium and the head of the Bardic Circle. And the "history" wasn't just a bit of a quarrel.

Mags knew now that Lita and Jakyr had been a couple at one point. He also knew that Jakyr had all but fled the relationship. Lita clearly did not understand why, and since Jakyr made it a point to *never* get past mere friendship with anyone, not even fellow Heralds, it appeared no one else knew, either. Maybe Nikolas knew, since he knew just about everything else that had to do with life up on the Hill, but if so, he had never told anyone.

Mags certainly couldn't figure it out, although he'd been more than a little hurt when Jakyr, the first person to ever be kind to him since he was a toddler, had done his level best to deflect any attempt Mags had made to make a connection with him.

Only when Mags had demonstrated over the years that he really had no intention of trying to put Jakyr in the position of being a surrogate father did the Herald finally relax.

Mags had to wonder, though, if this wasn't the real reason why Jakyr hadn't mentored anyone before. The Herald didn't want ties to anyone except his Companion, yet there was no question that you could not avoid such things developing when you lived so closely with someone over the course of a year or more.

At least he didn't seem reluctant now. Maybe he figured that with Amily along, Mags would not be making any emotional attachments to *him.*

No fear there.

It took only a couple of days to get everything ready. Jakyr had advised them every step of the way. Traditionally, Mags had been told, Heralds and their charges left in the gray light of early dawn.

Jakyr, clearly, was not the sort to hold with tradition.

"We'll leave when we leave," he told Mags the night before. "Get a good night's sleep and a good bath and breakfast in the morning. I'll inspect your packs, and when I figure we are ready, we'll go." He had made a face. "I don't like leaving or arriving when people expect me to. The only people who *need* to know my comings and goings are Nikolas and . . . well, Nikolas."

So Mags did exactly as he had been advised. He and Amily spent all evening together, as if they were not going to see each other for a very long while, and whenever someone commiserated with them about the coming absence, he pulled a long face, and Amily looked as if she was about to burst into tears.

In reality, she was fighting to keep from giggling.

But they trailed about tragically, exactly as anyone would expect for a couple about to be separated against their will. They picked at their food in public—and had a celebratory picnic in his room with goodies Lydia had sent down from the Palace kitchens in the hopes of tempting his appetite and comforting him. It was very kind of Lydia, who had absolutely no idea that this was not exactly what it appeared to be, and they enjoyed the unexpected feast greatly.

There was no one about to be impressed with how doleful he

was in the morning, so he enjoyed his usual hearty breakfast after a good bath—because no telling when he would next get one, breakfast *or* bath—got his packs, and went into the stable proper to await Jakyr. It was just chilly enough that he preferred to wait in the stable itself, over by Dallen's stall. The stable-hands had already begun firing up the ovens that stood at either end of the stable, ovens that warmed the huge masses of brick of which they were made, and thus kept the entire stable warm without the danger of fire.

Mags loved the stable; he'd always loved living here instead of up at the Collegium. His fellow Trainees were a noisy lot; here it was always calm, with nothing more than the occasional stamp of a hoof or a whicker or mutter as the Companions conversed wordlessly among themselves. The air always smelled of clean horse and straw, scents that meant comfort to him. In winter, it was warm, and in summer, when all the windows were open to a prevailing breeze, it was almost never too hot. But most of all, it was peaceful.

As the Herald approached, Mags had plenty of time to watch him, because he wasn't hurrying his steps. Jakyr had aged a bit in the last several years, but not so much that he'd lost any of his somewhat rough-hewn good looks. The few times that Mags had seen him around others—ladies in particular—women didn't seem to find him ugly, but he never responded to overtures with anything but cool politeness.

And it wasn't because he preferred men to women, either.

Dallen had once remarked that Jakyr preferred "company that he paid for." Mags hadn't understood that at the time, but he did now, after seeing Jakyr going nonchalantly into one of the better and more ethical brothels down in Haven, one where the ladies plied a trade and paid their taxes just like any other business. And where they had ample protection from those who might take that as a license for something other than the services advertised.

Mags had no issues with brothels of that sort, and he

doubted anyone else did, either, except priests of sects that held congress without marriage to be a sin.

But it was highly unusual for a Herald to make use of their services, and it probably never ceased to surprise the ladies there. It was the easiest thing in the world for a Herald to find even a casual partner without having to pay for it—Heralds were almost as popular in that regard as Bards.

But seeing Jakyr enter the House of Red Silk, Mags suddenly understood what Dallen had been saying. When the exchange was for money, it ended with money, and that was how Jakyr liked it. No ties. No promises. Nothing implied.

It seemed a sad way to live, at least to Mags. But he had no intention of telling Jakyr that. Logically, Jakyr could have some excellent reasons for his standoffishness; where others looked at the life of a Herald, found it often short and violent, and chose to *make* ties to others, it could be that Jakyr found it needful to break them. Or, at least, never make them in the first place.

So, as the Herald stopped at Dallen's stall, borrowed a bit of thong from the saddlery supplies that Mags always kept there, and tied back his graying brown hair into a tail with it, Mags just kept his mouth shut on his thoughts and said instead, "Ready for inspection, Herald," and sketched a comic salute, as if he were a Guardsman about to be inspected.

Jakyr laughed. "All right. But I'm not about to unpack everything just so you have to pack it back up again, like a drill sergeant would. Tell me what's in this one." He poked the rightmost one with a white-booted toe, then looked up. His eyes gleamed with sardonic humor. "If you've done your job right, you'll know down to the last leather scrap."

Mags had had some inkling that Jakyr would do something like this, since that seemed to be a common thread among the Trainees who had been taking the wilderness survival classes. So he did know, and he proceeded to recite. Jakyr's eyebrow rose approvingly.

"And this one?" he asked, poking the other. Mags obliged.

"And the ones that are going off with the caravan?" he persisted.

"Every spare uniform that isn't in these, 'cept the special ones. Ink and paper, cause I reckon I can get goose quills anywhere. My clothes that ain't uniforms, I got three changes. Armor, light armor, since ye said that heavy armor was gonna be worse'n no armor in the snow. Needles an' thread. Harness-repair stuff. Saddlesoap. Extra blankets for Dallen. Went t' Stablemaster an' got his list of simple stuff for ailin' horses, an' he give me a little book t' go with it an' give t'Bear. You said we'd be stoppin' at Waystations, so I got them smoke things that kill bugs. Extra soap, chilblain salve, that kinda thing. Second heavy cloak, light cloak for when it gets warm again. Extra fire-startin' kit. Fishhooks an' arrowheads. Couple more knives." Oh, how many years of his life would he have paid to have had the kit, a knife, fishhooks, and arrowheads when he'd been trying to make his way back across Karsite territory! "All of Dallen's hair what got combed out an' I saved. That's it."

"Oh, that's right, I remember, you braid things from it. Good idea, we might be stuck somewhere because of weather, and you'll need something to keep your hands busy." Jakyr nodded with approval. "Is there any room in there?"

"Aye, a bit. Not much. Reckon we can get 'em to ship us up more uniforms if we need 'em with Guard supplies and pick 'em up at the Post. In fact, I packed up some books an' asked 'em to be shipped there for us to get later."

"Better to have a bit of room left," Jakyr agreed. "We're having women along, and they always overpack. And yes, excellent thinking, we can almost always have things sent with the supply trains to the Guardpost."

Mags shrugged. "Lena an' Amily're used to havin' everything they want an' need. Might be hard for 'em to pare down."

"Well, then. I think we're ready," Jakyr said with satisfaction. "I left my packs here last night. I'd planned for you to have to repack a little, but since you don't need to after all, we can start right now, wander our way at a leisurely pace into the East, and come on a very nice inn I know in time for luncheon." He made his way over to his Companion's stall and started saddling him. Mags made a note of which set of saddle and harness Jakyr was using and did the same. This was a set he'd never used on Dallen before; it had only two bridle bells, rather than the full set of bells on bridle and barding on his formal gear, but those could be taken off easily and stowed. Jakyr did so now on his Companion, and Mags did the same. Otherwise, the gear was the same blue and white as the formal gear, rather than the utilitarian brown of the set that they used to practice everything from Kirball to the obstacle course.

As they rode out of the stable, there was no one to bid them goodbye. Even the Guards at the gate merely waved them through without a farewell or a greeting.

And Mags had absolutely no doubt in his mind that this was the way Jakyr wanted it.

———————

Perhaps if it had been anyone other than Mags who rode at Jakyr's side this morning, they would have been out of sorts by now. Possibly even angry. Jakyr had done everything possible to prevent friends from making their farewells and waving them off. He'd made sure all the Trainees were in class. He'd prevented Amily from knowing exactly when they were going to leave. Not even the stablehands had been around to say goodbye to Mags, and Mags knew every one of them by name, all about their families, and as much about them as he knew about any friend.

Many entirely reasonable people would have reacted poorly to this sort of treatment.

But Mags had spent most of his life fundamentally friendless. He didn't remember his parents. Farewells were things he just wasn't used to getting, so not having them didn't particularly bother him. The people he most cared about he was going to be seeing again in a few days anyway.

:As you are thinking, that is one reason among many why Jakyr has never been asked to be a mentor,: Dallen said dryly.

:You know, I could do with a bit less mystery, horse,: Mags responded. *:If you know what the devil happened between him and Lita, I'd like to hear it.:*

:It wasn't anything dramatic,: Dallen said. *:No great tragedy, no sudden misfortune that befell a friend and made him rethink things. I think perhaps Lita got a little aggressive about wanting some sort of formal acknowledgement, but I don't know for certain. All I do know is that things cooled off rapidly enough that it was the cause of gossip for some time, and things have been uncomfortable between them ever since.:*

Mags felt a certain amount of sympathy for them both. Who knew? There might not have been any great tragedy, but certainly *every* Herald and Trainee knew that the nickname for those in Whites among the Guard was "moving target." Maybe Jakyr had been having second thoughts about having a romance with *anyone* when he might be killed without warning.

And maybe, after the blowup with Lita, it just became a lot easier for him to prevent any further ties from developing.

:It did happen about the same time that Nikolas recruited him. That might have had something to do with it,: Dallen observed.

Hmm. Perhaps Lita had known and objected. Perhaps Jakyr had just been made aware that his potential to be a target had just increased a *lot* when Nikolas recruited him as an intelligence agent.

Perhaps Lita had known and wanted to be included.

I think I am just going to stop speculating and enjoy this ride. It ain't my business, it's his. I don't like it when other people get all up in my business, and I don't reckon he likes it either.

"We don't get too many chances to enjoy ourselves, young-ling," Jakyr said aloud, in an uncanny echo of Mags' own thoughts. "I don't know how much of this expedition of ours is going to be pleasurable, but right now, it's a treat. Take my advice and drink it in."

They were practically the only people on the road, in fact. The fields to either side were full of farmworkers getting the last of the harvests in. A little while ago, they'd passed work-ers drying hop cones, stirring the cones on their drying sheets. The air had been scented heavily with the pleasant bitterness. At the moment, they were passing through apple orchards with some folks gathering up the windfalls to feed to pigs and cattle, some up on ladders getting down the last of the ripe and green apples. The green were just as good as the ripe ones, if you knew what you were doing, as Mags had found out when he'd helped in the Collegium kitchen. The farmer had a press going in there, just out of sight of the road. The winey scent of freshly pressed cider was enough to intoxicate.

Jakyr inhaled deeply. "There's the thing I think about come autumn! Now, I like cider better when it's had a chance to age," he said, philosophically. "Just hard enough to make a man feel pleasant."

"I like it hot, with spices," Mags said. "Maybe a drop of mead in it. Like Master Soren sets out at his Midwinter par-ties." He sighed. "I am going to miss that. Midwinter, we'll probably be living in caves. Master Soren sets a mighty table at Midwinter."

"Caves with villages near enough that we can buy our-selves the makings of a nice little Midwinter feast," Jakyr re-minded him. "And caves we can make all cozy before then. I've spent many a Midwinter in a Waystation that hadn't been kept up as well as it should have been, and I'd prefer a nice dry, draftless cave any day over a Waystation with holes in the wall you can stick a finger through." He paused a moment in thought. "Now that I consider it, if we offload everything from the caravan into the caves, we can drive that caravan to one of the biggest villages and load it up well—and do it over again at another village. If vermin turn out to be a problem in the caves, we can keep it all safe in the caravan. I think getting a cat would not come amiss. She can live in the caravan and keep out the mice."

"I know you can't cook," Mags said. "I *can,* but not a lot of things." He made a rueful face. "Wish I could say different, but if we depend on me, we'll be eating a lot of porridge, beans, and eggs."

"I can cook very well, actually, although I would really rather people think I can't. My mother and father are both cooks, they run a good inn, known for its food." Jakyr flashed a grin at him. "Don't fear you're going to starve around me. What you *will* do, is learn to cook as well as me."

"I'd like that," Mags said honestly. It seemed not only a generally useful skill, but a skill he could use. He could walk into just about any inn and have a job, if he could cook, and inns were fine sources for information. If he were to be sent someplace where he wasn't supposed to be known as a Herald, he wouldn't have to concoct much of a disguise at all if he could cook.

"I was cooking before I learned to read." Jakyr shrugged. "Ma was either cooking, having a baby, or both, and once you were old enough to be trusted in the kitchen, it was your job to feed yourself. Once you could feed yourself, you had a job, either cleaning or cooking, and I hated cleaning, so I learned to cook well, and that right soon. At least with so many of us, we weren't worked past what was reasonable for a youngling.

"I just let people think I am a terrible cook so no one argues with my choice of eating at inns."

Mags nodded. Though the highborn would have been astonished at such a statement, to him, it seemed normal for

kiddies to begin work as soon as they could walk. The difference between a good home and a bad one, or a good master
and a bad one, was whether they made sure you got your
basic learning, good food, and plenty of rest. And, of course,
if it was your own family, love, and plenty of it. He, obviously,
had none of these things. "Must have been good to be working alongside your kin."

Jakyr snorted. "There were so many of us you almost
couldn't call us 'kin' at all. Half the time Ma and Pa called us
kids by the wrong names. It wasn't that they had so many
because they needed that much help at the inn, either. They'd
have done just fine with only half of us. It was religion. They
belonged to some religious sect that said you had to have as
many younglings for the Glory of God as you could manage."

Mags blinked at that. "Uh. Why?"

Jakyr shrugged again. "I have no idea. They were so busy
having the kiddies, they never bothered to teach us why.
Seems a backward way to go about things, to me. Every sen-
nite there they were, in the Temple, telling everybody how
much they loved God and us. Oh, how they loved God, giving
Him so many children! When I left? According to the brother
I still talk to, they never noticed. He says they *still* haven't
noticed. And as for their God, whenever I see one of their
Temples, I turn around and ride in the other direction."
Abruptly, he changed the subject. "Anyway, since I know good
cooking when I taste it, I make a habit of keeping track of
good inns. The one we're heading for right now is excellent for
plain, farmer food, and they make a specialty of pocket pies."

:Pocket pies?: Dallen's head came right up, and his ears
perked.

Jakyr noticed, and laughed. "You'll get your fill, Dallen.
They love to spoil Companions there."

:Tell him I approve of such attitudes.:

"Dallen can't wait," Mags said.

"My Jermayan is looking forward to it too." Jakyr patted his

Companion's neck. "It's a fabulous place to eat. Terrible rooms, though. Maybe because people rarely stay there. It's situated just close enough to Haven that people coming out get there about luncheon time, and people coming in want to press on and get to Haven proper. I got stuck there in a blizzard once." He shuddered. "Never again. Two tiny rooms, the mattress on the bed was practically flat, the pillows were like boards, and it was like sleeping in a shed, it was so cold. I ended up taking my pack and curling up in my cloak by the hearth."

They left the orchard and entered fields that had been recently reaped. The grain was standing in shocks, waiting to be collected. Off in the distance was the grain wagon, and people tossing the shocked grain up to the man on top of the growing mound. All the colors seemed to glow in the sunlight—the golden grain, the yellow and red of leaves on the trees, the green of the hedgerows between the fields.

"We'll be in inns until we break our trail, so enjoy it while you can. Now, when Heralds are actually on their Circuit, they don't stay in the inns, unless there is no other choice. They stay in the Waystations or occasionally Guardposts. This is to prevent people from trying to bribe them with comforts and luxuries," Jakyr went on. "On the way to and from a Circuit, though, you can stay in inns, Waystations, or Guardposts, it's your choice. Most of us prefer the inns or the Guardposts. It always seems to happen that when you hit the worst weather and choose a Waystation, the one you get is the one that somehow got neglected on the last inspection. Innkeepers get a chit out of it, lets them out of some taxes, so they're happy with the arrangement."

Mags scratched his head. "Seems like a good one to me," he ventured.

"It's terrific if you know the good inns," Jakyr agreed. "Not so good if you don't. That's why we're going out on this road—I know all the good ones here." He paused a moment. "Huh. I wonder if the reason my parents never noticed I was gone and that instead they were getting the Trainee Stipend was because they thought it was part of the chit system. We always had Heralds coming through."

"Trainee Stipend?" Mags asked.

"If you lose a working youngling, the Crown compensates you while he's a Trainee. They figure once a Trainee goes into Whites, he'd have been old enough to strike out on his own, so you couldn't count on having him. Of course, if he's an only child, and you figure he'd have been supporting you in your age, you get a different sort of stipend." Jakyr waved his hand in the air. "I don't know who figured all that out, but it's all to make people happy about their offspring haring off on the back of a white horse. Or, at least, not *unhappy.*"

"You mean—" Mags said, something suddenly occurring to him. "If Cole Pieters had been treating us decent—paying us wages—feeding and clothing us proper—"

"As your guardian, he'd have gotten a stipend, aye." Jakyr snorted. "In fact, that just proves how damned stupid he was. He would never have gotten exposed at all if he'd just been smart about things. When Dallen first showed up, all he needed to do would have been to let Dallen have you, shut up, and present his papers to Haven. He'd have been collecting a nice little packet every year until you got your Whites, and all for doing nothing. If anyone asked about the shape you were in, he could have found a way to explain why you were in such bad condition. Orphaned and running the streets alone or something. The smartest thing would have been if he'd claimed he'd only just gotten you when Dallen showed up for you. *You* wouldn't have told the truth, would you?"

Mags shuddered. Even now, sometimes, he had fleeting nightmares about Cole Pieters. "Never. I'd'a been sure no one would believe me. Not even Dallen could'a got me to tell."

"So, there you are. Dumber than a box of rocks." Jakyr snorted. "And how many younglings of his own did he have?"

"A lot," Mags told him, though he had no idea why Jakyr

had asked that question. "A whole lot. He was under the skirt of every maid in the house, plus the ones from his wife."

"And there you have it!" Jakyr exclaimed, throwing his hands up. "Like my parents. Just because you *can* have a quiverful of youngsters, it doesn't mean you *should.* Or *any.* Right?"

"I guess," Mags replied, completely bewildered now as to where *that* statement had come from. What on earth had prompted it?

:Huh . . . I wonder . . . : Dallen said.

:You wonder what?: Could it be Dallen had gotten some insight about Jakyr that would explain . . . a lot? *:Care to let me in on the secret, horse?:*

For once, Dallen seemed reticent to say anything. *:Right now it's just a . . . speculative insight. I'll let you know if it comes to anything useful.:*

————————

The inn was as good as Jakyr had said it was. To Dallen's intense pleasure, they indeed made pocket pies—but, oh, *such* pocket pies!

These were not just the tasty, but unvarying treats made by the Collegium kitchens, nor the pies of uncertain quality you found at Fairs, whose contents could be dubious.

Oh, no.

There was no doubt at all as to the quality and provenance of the contents of these pies. You could *taste* every ingredient, separately and as a harmonious whole. And the list of what you could get filled two boards on the wall of the inn.

Mags hardly knew what to choose. There were pies full of chopped beef or pork, minced carrots, onions, peas and barley, all seasoned and savory, with just a touch of juice, enough to keep it all from being dry. Pies full of something like stew, only thicker; "gravy pies," those were called. Chicken pies.

Game pies. Egg-and-cheese pies, flavored with bacon. Apple, currant, blackberry, quince, pear, and cherry pies. Mince pies. The crust was amazing, and for any *other* pie that Mags had ever tasted, it would have been the best part, but here it was something that was part of a delectable whole. Mags had a half-and-half—half chopped beef, half chopped pork—and a cherry pie. These astonishing pies were washed down with exactly the sort of cider that Mags like best—spiced, with a touch of honey, and served warm. Evidently the beer was just as good, as Jakyr sipped his as slowly as Mags sipped his cider.

The fruit pies would keep and were just as good cold, so they rode off with some for later. Dallen and Jermayan were stuffed full, and Dallen didn't complain in the least that he hadn't had enough. Mags was just glad that the constitution of a Companion was a *lot* more robust than that of a horse. That many pocket pies would have sent horses straight to the Healer.

They rode past sunset to reach the next inn, but it, too, was worth it. It didn't have the variety of fare that the first inn did. The custom here was that everyone was offered the same thing, and tonight it was roast pig with roast vegetables and very good bread. But the food was cooked perfectly, the beds were good, and there was a bathhouse.

If Jakyr had been conducting a pleasure trip, the next three days could not have passed better. Sometimes they ambled, sometimes they went at the Companions' ground-eating lope. Jakyr said this was to throw off anyone who was attempting to follow them, but Mags secretly suspected their varied pace had more to do with Jakyr's favored inns than the stated reason.

He didn't mind. He was enjoying himself to the top of his capacity. The weather remained fine. He studied the people around him assiduously, keeping in mind he might have to pass as one of them some day. He took pleasure in the good food and the comfortable accommodations. There was something to be said for Jakyr's philosophy of enjoying oneself as one could, in the moment.

After three days, they cut North and spent two nights in Waystations rather than inns. This was to break their trail; Jakyr was, indeed, a very good cook, and he'd made certain to get provisions before they went off the roads. He introduced Mags to a fantastic dish made of white beans and a little sausage that Mags thought he could probably eat five or six days in a row before he grew tired of it.

Then they cut West again, this time back to the pleasant pattern of using inns—but under different names. Jakyr was "Herald Boyce," and Mags was "Trainee Hob." Mags could only assume that either Jakyr was known by that name on their new route—entirely possible, since he was an intelligence agent—or he had made very certain not to be memorable on his last visits to these inns. Whichever reason it was, no one hailed him by his real name, nor did anyone look puzzled when he gave the false names.

They were not going truly West; it was a bit North as well. Mags was very glad that they were staying at inns at this point, as the leaves were starting to drop rapidly from the trees, and the nights were getting bitter. When they stopped it was lovely to walk into a warm common room, full of the smell of cooking food, knowing you wouldn't have to tend the Companions, build a fire, and wait until your dinner was cooked before you could eat it.

"We're close," Jakyr said, one morning as they rode out under a sky that was overcast and leaden instead of cloudless. A wind too cold to be called "brisk" was finding its way down Mags' neck past the upturned hood of his cloak.

"How soon will we catch up with them?" Mags asked.

"Tonight. It'll be after dark, but if we ride good and hard, we'll meet them at the Waystation tonight." Jakyr glanced at

Mags for a reaction. "I imagine you'll be glad to see Amily again."

Hang you and your problems, Mags thought, with a touch of irritation. *Whatever they are, that's no cause for me to pretend I'm indifferent.* "Very," he said, "It can't be soon enough, in fact."

"In that case—" Jakyr didn't do anything, but his Companion surged into a lope that was almost a canter. Dallen snorted and matched the other, pace for pace.

At least Jakyr wasn't scornful of his wish to see Amily soon. In fact, he seemed to be going out of his way to accommodate it. They barely stopped for food, pushing hard; although the weather threatened, nothing came of the threat, and nightfall found them forging along a river road, with the river at least a full story below them, at the bottom of a steep and stony bank. Mags was very grateful when Jakyr led the way off that road and onto a little trail; putting a foot wrong would have sent them tumbling down that nasty little cliff into water that could not be much warmer than ice.

He was even more grateful to see the glow of light through the trees ahead of them almost immediately. By now he was chilled, and the prospect of a warm fire was almost as enticing as the prospect of seeing Amily again.

When they trotted into a clearing, it looked as if their friends must have been there since early afternoon at the latest, and possibly for a couple of days. Things were very much in order.

The caravan was pulled up beside what looked like a substantial little stone cottage; there were two horses in a lean-to stable that would easily accommodate four, Lanterns had been left alight outside the stable, and as they rode up to the cottage itself, the door opened.

A female form was silhouetted against the light from the doorway. "We've been expecting you for the last two days," said a strangely familiar voice. "Were you gorging yourself at inns at the Crown's expense again?"

Jakyr nearly tumbled from his saddle in surprise. *"Lita?"* he gasped.

"It's not the Crown Princess," the (former?) Dean of Bardic Collegium said testily. "Get your friends bedded down and get in here. It's bloody cold and I'm not holding the door open all night."

The Waystation was warm and stoutly built; the stone walls were quite thick, and the windows had bullseye-glass in heavy frames, which didn't seem to be leaking cold air at all. There was a fine fire going on the hearth, and there was space in front of it for two bedrolls. But the atmosphere within the four walls was decidedly frosty.

Bear and Lena sat together, with Amily sitting apart. Mags' happiness at seeing them again was tempered by discovering that Master Bard Lita was going to be the other mentor here. Every time he'd seen Lita and Jakyr together, sharp words had been exchanged. And yet, Lita *had* to have volunteered for this. Why?

The other three looked a bit discomfited. Mags decided he wasn't having any of it. However, he also wasn't going to directly confront Master Bard Lita, who was probably still head of the Bardic Circle and was definitely still a Master Bard, even if she wasn't Dean of Bardic Collegium anymore. "I'll take care of the Companions if you cook, Herald Jakyr," he said, and before Jakyr could reply, he looked over to Amily and asked, "Want to help?"

"When have I ever turned down a chance to get my hands on Dallen?" she asked rhetorically, and got up from the box bed on which she had been sitting. There were two of those box beds, with bedrolls in each, and another pair laid out on the floor, so there was no telling what the sleeping arrangements were going to be. Mags decided he'd let Lita and Jakyr sort it out.

Hopefully they would manage to do so without coming to blows.

The first thing he did as soon as the door closed on the others was to take Amily into his arms and kiss her as thoroughly as ever he could manage. She wrapped her arms around him under his cloak and held him close, warming him with her body. It was bliss, right up until the wind whipped the cloak away from him and blasted them both with ice.

She squeaked, and he swore, then they both laughed. "Let's get this over with, so we can get back in the warm," Mags said.

:I second that. I want two blankets, thank you. And we both want a warm mash. Jermayan just told Jak as much.:

The Companions had already moved into the shelter of the stable, which turned out to be built right at the chimney wall, so some warmth was radiating into the space from the heated stone. Mags got the packs off both Companions and deposited them just inside the door, while Amily took off their bitless bridles, hung both up, and uncinched the saddles. By that time, Mags had gone to the caravan and retrieved the bigger blankets and the rubbing cloths from the storage box on the side that had been helpfully labeled "blankets" in blue paint, and the two of them got the saddles off and into the racks, took off the smaller saddle blankets and draped them over the rails to dry, and rubbed both Companions down before blanketing them cozily. The two horses watched all of this with mild interest.

These horses were not like the draft horses that Mags was used to seeing, whose shoulders were easily as tall as his head. These fellows were compact, giving an impression of enormous strength, and standing about fifteen hands tall—not small by any means, but not as tall as the great draft horses that pulled the working wagons up at the Palace. They didn't have feathered feet, but they did have big blocky heads and heavy, almost furry, black and white coats. They were clearly all ready for winter. One of them finally bumped Mags' shoulder with his nose and whuffled in his hair. He seemed gentle and intelligent. Well, intelligent for a horse.

:*They are intelligent for horses,*: Dallen agreed. :*They won't give you any trouble. Rather like big dogs, really. Good-natured. I don't know who chose them for you, but he or she did a good job.*:

They were tied up to the manger—being tied was necessary for horses, though the Companions could be left loose, of course. They'd already cleaned out their food to the last wisp of hay, though their water buckets were mostly full. And they looked longingly at the fresh hay and measure of grain that Mags was putting in the mangers for the Companions.

:*It's cold, they could use the energy. It'll be safe enough to give them another round of hay.*:

No reason not to trust Dallen's judgment on this. Mags loaded up their mangers again, and the two horses gratefully buried their noses in it.

"Dallen says Jak's Companion asked for a warm mash," he told Amily, as he grabbed a pitchfork to get rid of anything the horses had deposited. The Companions were fastidious about their lodgings and wouldn't care to step in anything nasty any more than a human would. "Can you see if it's done yet?"

She ducked inside and came back out again with two wooden bowls of steaming bran mash. The Companions practically inhaled it, but they'd been putting on a lot of speed today, and they probably needed it. By the time Mags was done cleaning the stabling area, the bowls were licked clean and ready to store. Amily took them and stowed them in one of the outside boxes on the caravan.

Finally they couldn't put going back inside off any longer. They looked at each other, sighed a little, held hands and went inside.

The atmosphere had at least warmed from "frosty" to "formal." That might have had something to do with the fact that Jakyr was bent assiduously over a three-legged pot on the fire, and the lovely aroma told Mags that he was making that white bean dish again. It's hard to be nasty to someone who is cooking you something that smells so good that you want to eat the steam coming off the pot.

The little building was a bit crowded with six people in it, but it wasn't bad. There was no furniture in here as such; just the two box beds built into the wall, some storage chests that could serve as seating, and storage cupboards. Someone had been doing a bit of arranging of the bedding while Mags and Amily had been outside. There were two sets of two bedrolls at the hearth now, one set on either side of where Jakyr was crouched, and Mags recognized his own bedroll as one of the two to Jakyr's right.

So . . . sleeping arrangements sorted. It looked as if Lita and Jak got the bedboxes—which was really only fair, since they were older and probably wouldn't do as easily on the floor as the younger pairs—and the rest of them got the hearth. The beds weren't really wide enough for two, anyway. They'd been filled with what looked like bracken, which would be a lot better than resting on hard planks.

As for those on the floor—there in a pile, as far from the fire as possible, was more bracken. They'd have to be very careful about banking the fire when they went to bed so that random embers didn't jump out and set fire to their bedding, but the hearth had been built to accommodate that.

There wouldn't be any "canoodling" with Amily with everyone practically on top of everyone else, but that was all right. Well, it wasn't all right but . . . it wasn't horrible either.

And Bear and Lena would be in the same situation, so no reason to feel envious.

"Anything else we can do?" he asked, looking at Lita.

"Bear and Lena offered to clean up, and after that I think bed for all of us," Jakyr said, still assiduously tending his pot and not looking up from it. "It's been a long day for everyone."

"Where are we heading tomorrow?" Mags asked.

"It's three days to our Circuit, four to The Bastion, and that's at a wagon's pace," Jakyr replied confidently. "Now that we are officially on our way to our Circuit, we can go back to being ourselves. We can safely stop at inns if you want. I can put us at either inns or Waystations as you prefer."

Lita smirked. "You're always the one that wants to stop at inns."

That sounds like a comment that has a long, running history behind it.

Jakyr finally turned and looked her straight in the eyes. "Hot baths," he said, succinctly.

She flushed and looked away.

"Right, then. Inns it is." He turned back to his beans.

As Mags and Amily combined their sleeping rolls into one much more comfortable whole, Mags was extremely glad of his powerful Mindspeaking Gift. He hadn't used it often with Amily, but as the two of them cuddled up together, he projected his words into her mind as gently as possible.

Is this uncomfortable?

He sensed her tensing, as she tried to form a reply as clearly as possible so he could read it without getting any "leakage" she didn't want.

No. Not used to it, though. It's . . . odd-feeling.

He was actually a little surprised at how clearly her words came through, however. Was it possible she had a latent Gift?

If she did, it would probably only be a matter of time before it stopped being latent if they continued to "talk" like this. Gifts had a way of triggering in that way.

Hope flared in him at the idea that such a thing might happen. He couldn't imagine anything better, or more convenient, than being able to talk to Amily without anyone overhearing them.

Carefully, they "spoke" together. Mostly he wanted her to be reassured, to know how happy he was that she was along on this trip, and that he considered her as brave, clever, and skilled as any of them. He didn't *think* Lita was at all likely to have given her any indication to the contrary, or hinted that she was some kind of burden, but he wanted to be sure. The Dean—former Dean—wasn't always diplomatic when she was under stress; and there was no doubt that traveling with Jakyr was putting her under stress.

Finally even he was feeling the strain of Mindspeech with someone who wasn't a Mindspeaker, so he switched to whispers. "When did Dean Lita turn up—and why?" he asked softly.

"Just before we left—which obviously was after you left. I guess she didn't want Jakyr to get wind of her plan to go along with us and get Father to veto it," Amily breathed back. "It was supposed to be Bard Kendiss, not her, but she got herself substituted and swore the Wagonmaster to secrecy. She said she wanted Bard Purchel to get a trial period as Dean to see if he could handle it—he's the one she's been training as her successor—and it was going to be easier on him if he didn't have her breathing down his neck all the time. She comes from a family of drovers, and really, it's quite true that she was a *much* better choice to handle the horses than Bard Kendiss. Kendiss knows horses, how to handle them and care for them, and she has had experience driving as well as riding, but she's never had the experience with wagons that Lita did."

"Right, I can see that," Mags agreed. "But . . ."

Amily sighed. And a moment later, Mags sensed her thinking hard and opened his mind to her.

And she also said she was not going to sit back and allow Jakyr to ruin one of the most promising Trainees she'd ever had. And I have no idea what she thought Jakyr was going to do to Lena to ruin her. Neither does Lena, or Bear, but that was what she said.

That took him entirely aback.

Oh, was all he could manage.

"Exactly," she whispered.

Well, this was promising to make the next year quite the challenge. Even without all the other complications.

———————

Jakyr was first up in the morning, and making griddle cakes. It was the smell that woke Mags; he'd slept long and hard, as hard as a hibernating bear. Someone had providentially gotten butter to fry them in, and Jakyr had sliced apples into the batter as they fried. Mags was starving, and he thought he had never smelled anything so good. The cakes tasted as good as they smelled.

Someone among the group had passed away the travel time by weaving hay into holders for food—not so much "plates" as grass napkins. That made cleaning up for Mags and Amily a lot easier; just toss the grass squares into the fire, and it was done. There was nothing to wash; since the cooking pots and pans and griddle for over the fire were all of well-seasoned cast iron, cleaning was a matter of wiping them down thoroughly with more hay, then stowing them.

Lita went out first, to get the horses ready. By the time Mags and the rest came out with their bedrolls neatly bundled and the cooking gear and supplies to go back into the wagon, she had both horses harnessed. Amily and Lena scrambled up the steps into the wagon after stowing the pots in their outside box, and Bear handed everything up to them before following and pulling the steps up behind himself. It seemed they had gotten things down to a routine so far as Mags could see.

While he and Jakyr tacked up the Companions, Lita moved the horses into position. By the time he had Dallen saddled and was ready to mount, she had finished the harnessing, working so smoothly and efficiently that it was obvious she had done this so many times it was as second-nature to her as tacking Dallen was to him. What surprised him was something he hadn't noticed when he'd first seen the caravan. There was room for only one horse between the shafts; the other was harnessed alongside the first, on the right, outside the shafts. When the horses were buckled up, Lita got herself into place behind them and took up the reins. He watched in utter fascination as, with a series of remarkably economical maneuvers, she got the wagon completely turned around and pointed in the right direction.

Never did the horses seem confused; never did they seem to put a foot wrong. It was almost like a dance, forward while turning, then back, then forward while turning, until the caravan was completely turned around, all in a space that wasn't much bigger than two of the caravans put end to end. Mags was impressed.

So was Jakyr. Mags could tell it from his face. He didn't say anything, though, just gave a hand-gesture to Mags to follow, and skirted around the wagon and onto the path out as soon as Lita was ready.

Mags had been a little afraid that the horses would just plod along, but their pace was a good, steady, brisk walk. They seemed to enjoy their work and weren't straining at all. Lita didn't use the little seat; she sat on the "floor" of the porch with her feet braced against a beam that separated the shafts, both hands full of reins, her Scarlet hooded coat wrapped and tied tightly around her, with the hood snugged down with a Scarlet wool scarf. It was clear that of all of them, she was probably the best prepared next to Jakyr for the trip. In her Scarlets, she was the brightest bit in the landscape; the color of her uniform and the few spots of blue on the Companions' tack, and the faint pastels of the vines and flowers on the wagon were the only touches of color in all the gray and brown.

:It isn't as if she's never done this before, you know,: Dallen chided him. *:She's more used to living on the road than you are. Before she was a teacher or the Dean, she was a Journeyman, and then a Master Bard, and Bards wander. And before* that, *she was a drover.:*

Jakyr forged on ahead, though he at least had the courtesy to stay within about five lengths of the caravan. Mags asked Dallen to drift back to Lita once they were properly on the road. Fortunately, that river below them was moving along placidly, or the noise of rushing water would have drowned out any attempt at conversation. Even the river was gray, moving along with scarcely a ripple on its surface. There wasn't much sound other than the clop of the horses' hooves, the faint chime of the Companions' feet, and the sounds of the wagon. There was the steady creak of wood, the sound of the metal-rimmed wheels crackling through the layer of dead leaves on the road, and the steady breathing of the horses in time with their pace.

It was peaceful. Just as peaceful as the slow, ambling pace he and Jakyr had taken on the first leg of their journey. If it hadn't been so cold, it would have been perfect.

I better get used to the cold again. There'll be a lot more of it afore there's less.

"Dallen says you was a drover," Mags said, as he caught Lita's eye, and she nodded cordially enough to him. "What's a drover?"

"A drover is anyone who drives animals," she said, "Now, that can just mean someone who herds them for long distances, when you take a herd of sheep or cattle or horses to market, for instance. That's done afoot sometimes, sometimes ahorse. But in my case, it literally meant that I was a *driver.* My whole family worked as wagon, cart, and caravan drivers over great distances. We were the ones who got trading caravans where they were supposed to go. I used to live in a van like this one, only not nearly as new." She chuckled. "Six of us, my pa, ma, and me and my three sibs. Two girls in the cupboard bed below, parents in the bed above, two boys in hammocks slung over the benches. I had reins in my hands at the age most farming younglings are toddling after their folks for their first planting." She raised an eyebrow. "Probably the same age they put you down in that mine."

He nodded. Suddenly he felt as if he had a lot more in common with Lita than he'd had before. They were both working at an age when people like Amily, Bear, and Lena were still allowed to be children.

"Don't get me wrong, I loved every moment of it," Lita continued, and chirruped to the horses, who cocked their ears back at her. "I drove a vanner just like these fellows. They're a breed apart, I can tell you. Smart, steady, calm, and gentle. Willing, oh, you'll not find a horse as willing as a vanner. We used to play among their feet and never a care that we might get stepped on. That's one reason why I stepped in when I got wind of this. I went down to the Horse Market, called on my old friends, and looked over a good many pairs before I picked these two. I knew you'd need the right horses, and I knew you'd need someone who'd done more in the way of driving than take the reins on a pair now and again."

"Well, I'm mortal glad you did," Mags told her sincerely. "I dunno nothin' about horses. I reckon I'd've had to ask Dallen."

"Given that your lads can actually *talk* to horses, you might've been all right," Lita replied, but she sounded dubious. "Still, things can go wrong in the time it takes to blink, and plenty of trouble can happen between a horse spooking and Dallen or Jermayan noticing. Still, I wouldn't trust anything between the shafts of a caravan but a vanner. I won't say that vanners won't spook, but they trust their drover more than most horses, and if the drover stays calm, they settle pretty quickly."

"Do you—would you teach me to drive?" Mags asked hesitantly. If Lita would—well, it seemed like a valuable skill to have. Did they make smaller caravans? They must; single traders wouldn't need this much room, and a trader would make a good disguise. Too bad that Companions wouldn't take dye . . .

:Don't you dare even try.:

"I intend to," Lita assured him. "I intend to teach all of you to drive. Even the All-Alone-Herald up there, if he can climb down out of his self-imposed isolation long enough."

She said it with an ironic twist of her lips, but Mags caught the underlying bitterness. He deemed it prudent to pretend he hadn't noticed.

"Vanners are all-arounds, and these two have been trained for riding as well," she continued. "We'll probably not be able to move the caravan until the snow melts once it sets in, so the Three Inseparables in there will have to ride out to the villages. That's not a problem, you saw the muscles on these lads. They could carry two riders and four packs and not strain themselves." She chuckled. "I'll bet Bear and Lena and Amily are walking stiff and sore for a while, though, once they start riding. Striding a vanner is like trying to get your legs around a small house."

Mags laughed, because he had noticed how broad a barrel these horses had. He didn't envy his three friends one bit. Even *he,* who rode constantly, would have a little trouble adjusting to a horse that large.

"It feels good to get the reins in my hands again," Lita mused. "You know, Mags, I think I was getting stale and bad-tempered, cooped up in the Collegium, spending all day solving everybody's damned problems. I never got to teach anymore. I didn't get to write or perform nearly as much as I wanted. If Purchell does well in my absence, I think I may just step down and go out on the road again for a while, at least while I'm still fit enough to do it. Or I will if I get to steal this caravan to do it."

Mags had to laugh at that, because as cramped for six as the caravan was, it would be quite luxurious for a single person. "Not asking much, are you?"

Lita straightened up and struck a pose. "I'm a Master Bard, head of Bardic Circle, and Dean of the Collegium. If I don't deserve it, who does?"

Mags had to admit, she had him there.

"And think how jolly this rig would look painted all in Bardic Scarlet! Pick out those vines and flowers in black and gold . . . she'd be a treat. I think, regardless, I'm going to see about keeping these boys for myself." She grinned. "I just might commission myself a new caravan if I can't have this one."

He wondered what the other three were doing inside that rolling cottage. He was pretty sure he knew what Bear and Lena would have *liked* to get up to, but Amily's presence would put a damper on that.

Amily was probably reading. Lena was probably practicing— the notes of a softly plucked gittern couldn't be heard outside those stout walls. Bear? Either making notes, or maybe sorting out herbs into his kits. He had one full cupboard devoted to just the herbs for his kits in there, but he had explained that it was better, so far as taking up space was concerned, for him to store them in bulk and make up the kits as he went along.

Last night, the wind had blown most of the leaves down off the trees, and the sky had gone overcast. The wind had died down, but it was almost as cold as it had been last night, with the leaf scent gone bitter, and the air feeling even colder with the damp in it. There was the least little hint of fog, less fog and more a chilly haze in the distance and blurring the tops of the trees. The entire world was painted in shades of brown and gray now; autumn was nearly over, and winter right at hand.

Mags was glad that Lita had given in to staying at the inns Jakyr planned to choose. *I've gotten soft since I got to the Collegium,* he thought wryly. *Beds, regular hot meals . . . hard to do without 'em when you got used to having 'em.*

He wondered just how well the Guard had stocked The Bastion—and just what the purported caves looked like. If they were just shallow indentations, enough to shelter supplies but not much more, it was going to be a very cramped and crowded winter, unless they could come up with some auxiliary shelter.

He and Dallen mulled that over as they trotted alongside the caravan. Lita seemed perfectly content just to drive, humming to herself under her breath. Jakyr dropped back a little, riding just in front of the horses, but he didn't seem inclined to conversation. That left Mags and his Companion free to consider options.

:It might just be best to make a second bedroom under the caravan. We could wall it all around, give it a floor. Use the canvas to cut the wind, back it with firewood or pack straw in between canvas and, say, some laths. Then Bear and Lena would have some privacy and you'd have privacy from them.:

Mags thought that over. *:Might could do the same sorta thing with a wall for one of them indentation caves. If we did that, could put a fire in there, wouldn't be so cold.:*

Neither option seemed particularly comfortable however. He went over what he remembered from the reports. Surely the brief descriptions had suggested *real* caves. . . .

:That's how I remember it,: Dallen agreed.

With real caves they could have real comfort. Real beds,

even; easy enough to make a fine bed with a little wood, a lot of hay, and some canvas. Why, if the cave entrance was big enough, they could move the caravan inside, and whoever was lucky could sleep in it!

:*What'm I thinking? Bear and Lena'll get it, sure as sure.*:

As the morning turned to noon, the terrain on either side of the river turned hillier. Mags didn't envy the farmers who had to plow their fields here. Though most of the land seemed to be given up to orchards and grazing, there were still fields that had been cultivated, the plowing following the contours of the hills, giving them a slightly terraced look. He spotted more than one farmer out covering the fields with old straw or beanstalks or even leaves.

:*That's to hold the soil on the side of the hill over the winter,*: Dallen told him. It seemed a sensible precaution. :*In the spring, all that will be plowed under. You won't find anyone burning leaves or straw out here; no one wastes anything.*:

Lots of sheep here, which moved slowly away from the strangers on the road in an uneasy, woolen cloud, as their guardian dogs kept a wary eye out.

By contrast, the cattle paid no attention to them at all, and the few horses—ponies, really—that were out in the fields came up to the fences to stare. Some whickered at the vanners, who replied but didn't stop moving.

:*This is where some of your Kirball ponies are from,*: Dallen told him. Well, he could see how they would have to be sure-footed on this terrain.

Around noon or a little after, Mags spotted a thin stream of smoke rising from somewhere near the road ahead. Since Dallen had made a point of saying that no one burned leaves or brush here, or fired their fields before winter to burn off the stubble, he guessed it must be an inn.

And so it was.

They didn't stop for long—just long enough for all of them to go into the kitchen for a quick washup in hot water, drink down some excellent soup and mulled ale, and take away some packets of roasted vegetables in crust. Not quite a pocket pie, but not unlike one either. When they got back on the road, Lita had Bear sit beside her for a driving lesson. From the way he was handling the reins, with confidence instead of hesitation, Mags guessed it wasn't his first.

The afternoon was much the same; gradually the hills got steeper, but they never left the river road. When they saw people in the fields or at farmsteads in the distance, no one seemed at all curious about the strangers. Not even children came down to the road to see who it was.

Mags was beginning to get a sense of why this district was considered a challenge. Only at infrequent public houses and small inns did anyone show any curiosity about them, and even then, it was just to stare at them. None of the waving and calling out of greetings he had seen coming back from the Karsite border or on the first leg of their trip.

The sun was just setting when another plume of smoke heralded another inn, and this was, indeed, the one at which Jakyr intended to stop.

Mags couldn't tell any difference in this one from any of the others they had passed; it was built of rough-hewn timbers, a single low, broad building all on one level, with a stable around the back. But there was a very great difference once they had pulled into the stable yard. A stable boy appeared immediately to help Lita position the caravan and unharness the vanners, and he pointed out two open, capacious loose boxes to Mags and Jakyr.

"Help yourselves, Heralds. I'll be along with water and fodder shortly." He grinned, showing a gap between his front teeth. "There's only me, but I'll get to it."

Well! At least that was friendlier than the folk they had seen so far on this road!

Amily, Bear, and Lena came down out of the caravan as soon as the steps were down, each carrying two packs. Lita took one from Lena and led the way into the inn itself while Mags and Jakyr tended to Dallen and Jermayan.

By the time that they got inside, Lita had everything sorted out. "Steam bath that way," she said, pointing to the right. "Rooms, follow me. This is mostly the local pub, and the rooms are usually used more in spring and summer, for traveling traders and entertainers. There's not a lot of call for them this late in the year, so since no one else is likely to turn up, we got all three. Dinner's when we're done with the bath, locals will be turning up after, Lena and I are singing."

Since there seemed nothing else to say, they followed Lita. Inside, the building was built to stand for a good long time, it seemed. The floors were the same rough-hewn wood as the walls but worn smooth by the passage of many feet. The ceilings were low, and the roof had scarcely any slant at all; in that, it was much like Cole Pieters' house, where a servant was sent up to shovel snow off the roof as soon as it fell, to prevent it building up and causing leaks. Mags hadn't noticed, but he guessed that the roof itself was slate or wooden shingles. The walls had been plastered white, but time and smoke had turned them a deep cream. There was a very pleasant smoky scent in the air as well.

Lita took them to a plank door in the side of the common room with an iron latch and iron hinges. The rooms were all in a row, with doors leading from one to the next, rather than being on a corridor.

That made sense; if you were at all uneasy about your guests leaving without paying their due, this was the best way to keep them from doing so.

The rooms were all alike, the white-plastered walls a lighter shade of cream than the common room, barely big enough to hold a bed that could sleep as many as six and a small table with a rushlight on it. And each bed probably did sleep that many when the inn was crowded; few people coming along this road could afford a room to themselves. Whole families shared a bed, and even strangers would bed down together to share the expense.

Bear and Lena took the end room, Lita decreed that she and Amily would have the middle, and Mags and Jakyr the one that let out on the common room. Jakyr gave Mags a commiserating pat on the back but said nothing. Mags sighed, but he didn't object, in no small part because he could not imagine Jakyr and Lita actually sharing a bed without being able to somehow erect a wall between them. And even then . . . no.

"You'll like the steam bath," was all Jakyr said, and he led the way to it.

There were two steam baths actually. Jakyr took the first. The steam bath was exactly what it sounded like: a room filled with hot steam, with an unheated entrance room with a barrel in it and a drain in the floor. You stripped down and went and sat on wooden seats in the main room until you couldn't stand the heat anymore. Then you left and washed down with cold water from a barrel, then you went back in again for another round. You did this as many times as you liked—Mags only managed twice, Bear called a halt at one, but Jakyr stayed for three—then you washed off a final time, got dressed, and went back out to the common room, feeling rather like a pleasant puddle of yourself. Lita and the girls presumably took the second room, since there was no sign of them until Mags went out to the common room again.

When they were all sitting at a table in the common room, the innkeeper brought them supper: bread, a smoky barley and vegetable soup, baked leeks, and smoked meat of some sort. Mags couldn't tell what animal it came from, only that it was so tender it fell apart, and the smoky flavor was delicious. Now he knew where the scent in the air came from; it appeared almost everything that was cooked here got at least a taste of the woodsmoke, and it was delicious. He had to wonder what their bacon was like.

There was hot cider to drink—no spices, but there was a roasted crabapple floating in each mug that had been cooked in honey.

As they were finishing their dinner, the locals started to arrive. It appeared that everyone who ordered food got the same thing that their group did, though there weren't many of them. Mags immediately grasped the significance of the menu—smoked meat kept a good long time, and soup—well, you just kept adding to it, because as long as you kept it hot, it stayed wholesome. Nothing would be wasted, even if you got fewer customers than you had expected.

Most of the locals ordered beer or cider and roasted nuts. They settled down in groups and talked among themselves, only surreptitiously glancing at the strangers in their midst. Lita and Jakyr similarly paid them no heed, so Mags followed their example.

:It isn't always like this. In fact, it isn't mostly like this,: Dallen told him. :Usually people come up, want to know the latest news, share what's going on locally. Even if you aren't there on Circuit, Heralds are looked to as people who can solve problems. Evidently Jakyr was briefed on this, even though we weren't. I can see how this sort of attitude would give a Herald some difficulty in doing his job.:

Mags considered the people around him. :Well, these folks keep to themselves right close, I reckon. Seems like they make a virtue out of it, which 'splains why Cole Pieters could get away with what he did. Nobody was gonna get in his business unless he invited them to, and damn sure he wasn't gonna invite 'em.:

:That makes sense,: Dallen agreed, and then Lita caught Lena's eye, and nodded to her. The two of them went to the rooms and came back with a small assortment of instruments: two gitterns, a flute, a hand drum, a small harp, and a fiddle. The two of them moved to stools on the hearth. Lita picked up the fiddle, Lena the drum, and they began.

The locals might have been insular, but they weren't deaf. Conversation ceased. Table tapping began.

Here Lita showed the skill and the Gift that made her a Master Bard. Within moments, the locals had accepted her as if she was one of their own. It was without a doubt that she was the best musician they had ever heard in their lives, and Mags was certain they would be talking of this evening for years.

She chose well. Even if people didn't know these exact melodies, they knew something *like* them.

A few lively tunes on the fiddle came first, then she and Lena switched to double gitterns, singing and playing in two-part harmony that had people listening with their mouths dropping open.

Lita played the crowd like she played her instruments. At her direction they laughed and wept, listened intently or sang along, clapped and stomped their feet or held their collective breaths. It was in every sense a masterful performance, and they knew it—instinctively if not consciously.

Mags mostly watched Lena, who in turn was so riveted by her mentor that he suspected nothing else in the room registered with her. This was, he thought, entirely as it should be. This was not just a lesson, but an object lesson. Lita was demonstrating every possible thing that Lena must conquer in order to be called a Master Bard, and Lena knew it.

Mags halfway expected Jakyr to return to their rooms long before the performance was over—after all, he had surely seen or heard performances like this many times before, and he was not on what you would call *good* terms with Bard Lita at the best of times. But he stayed, listening and watching just as intently as any of the locals, but with a completely unreadable expression on his face. Mags wondered what he was thinking, but knew he would never dare to ask.

Finally there came a pause in the music. "This will be the last song, and we thank you for your kindly listening," said

Lita, and began at once before there could be any objections voiced.

> *"Of all the money that e'er I had,*
> *I spent it in good company.*
> *And all the harm that e'er I've done,*
> *Alas, it was to none but me*
> *And all I've done for want of wit*
> *To mem'ry now I can't recall*
> *So fill to me the parting glass*
> *Good night and joy be with you all."*

Half melancholy, half celebration, Lita and Lena slowly played and sang this song that Mags had heard before, at one of Master Soren's Midwinter celebrations. It appeared to be new to the locals, but Mags knew it was very old indeed; he'd been told it might go all the way back to the founding of the Kingdom. And as Mags happened to glance over at Jakyr, he could have sworn he saw a tear in the Herald's eye.

But if he had, by the time the applause died down, it had been surreptitiously wiped away.

Lita and Lena strolled back to the table with their arms full of instruments, pausing frequently to say something to each of the people who stopped them to thank them for their performances. "Not bad for a greenie and a rusty old bag," Lita said with some satisfaction when they finally got back to the others. "Not bad at all."

"If you can repeat that at will, I'll have no problem getting cooperation," Jakyr said dryly. "I expect you are going to be quite useful." Mags couldn't tell if he was being sincere, or trying for irony—or just hoping to spark annoyance in the Bard.

Lita only raised one eyebrow at the backhanded compliment, then yawned ostentatiously. "That's harder than driving," she said. "I'm for bed."

"Us too," Bear said, as Lena and Amily nodded.

Lita headed for the rooms before Jakyr could say anything more, with the others following. Mags got up, then paused, and glanced inquiringly at Jakyr.

"I'll just have a beer, then be along," the Herald said, his face unreadable again.

Mags nodded. He took the side of the bed farthest from the door and left a rushlight burning.

But he was hard asleep in moments and never heard nor felt Jakyr join him.

The remaining three days were identical to the last. The sky remained threatening, the air damply cold, and yet (thank the gods) there was no inclement weather. Lita and Jakyr did verbally snipe at one another, but they confined their acerbic comments to a couple of barbs in the morning, when they all rode out, and the evening, before everyone retired. Their stays at inns were also nearly identical to the first: decent, wholesome food and drink, standoffish silence from the locals until Lita and Lena played. Then there was a kind of reticent welcome. Once they shared a room with three beds in it. Once they all had cots in a room with a dozen lined up like a common barracks.

The local folk, with the exception of the innkeepers and staff, seemed to regard them with guarded wariness, as if at any point they might all do something unsociable. It wasn't strong enough to be called "dislike" and it certainly wasn't overt hostility, but it was as if the locals mistrusted them. Except for Lita and Lena. Mags would have thought that this was because the two Bards were females, but they regarded Amily with the same wariness.

"At least," Jakyr commented, when Mags ventured something about it, "thanks to the Bards, we aren't likely to be murdered in our beds."

"Does that happen often?" Mags asked with alarm.

Jakyr shrugged. "I have never heard of it happening to Heralds or Bards, and I picked these inns on the best recommendations, but, yes, it does happen to travelers who might not be missed. Usually traders alone, with enough goods to make them worth murdering."

That didn't make for an easy rest that night.

Finally, on the third day, Jakyr brought them not to an inn but to a Guardpost. Like all such Posts it was a walled compound right off the road for easy travel. Very conspicuous even at a distance, since the trees had been cleared around it to prevent possible hostiles from using trees to get in over the walls, there were three plumes of smoke arising from three substantial chimneys, one at each end of the big building and one in the middle.

Mags was very glad to see it, as the unmistakable timber walls loomed up in the distance. Finally there would be some faces that were friendly from the moment they rode up! It would be a blessed relief from the closed-in wariness of the locals. Even the scent of the chimney smoke on the air was a harbinger of comfort, part woodsmoke, part cooking food.

And so it proved. From the moment they first came within view of the walls and the sentries got sight of the Companions, the distant figures waved a welcome. The Guardsmen on duty hailed them from the top of the walls as soon as they came within shouting distance, and by the time they entered the gates around the walled compound, there were several dozen welcomers waiting for them. There were plenty of eager hands waiting to take their packs, take the caravan around to the stabling area, and see to the Companions. Here, Mags had

no fears about letting someone else tend to Dallen. Guardsmen knew very well what Companions were and spoiled them
like favored children. Dallen winked at his Chosen as he followed three of the uniformed Guard around back to the stables.

:Don't eat yourself sick!: Mags cautioned, knowing that
the Guardsmen were going to press sweet things on both of
the Companions, probably more than they should ever eat at
one time.

:Me? Never!: Dallen said in mock indignation, flagging his
tail as he pranced out of sight.

The rest of the party was escorted to the main entrance.
The building within the walls was two stories tall. All the windows could be shuttered and barred from within, and Mags
knew that the shutters themselves were reinforced with metal
plates, while the drop-down bars were solid steel. The exterior
walls were stone, unusual in this area where most buildings
were made of timber. Even the roof was of slates. Anyone who
actually got into the compound would be unable to set fire to
this building from the outside.

Yet there was nothing foreboding about the structure; on
the contrary, it looked very much like a comfortable manor.

The main door, like the shutters, was sheathed in metal.
Good luck taking it down with a battering ram.

"You lot go find some beds. I'll be with you, Mags, shortly,"
Jakyr said, as they passed through the door, and went off on
his own. Mags followed the Guard who had appointed himself
as their guide to the guest quarters. The rest followed him.

The guest quarters were upstairs, where the barrack rooms
were, all by themselves in the center of the building and surrounded by the officers' quarters. They comprised a block of
rooms about the size of a highborn's closet, ascetic but comfortable enough, on either side of a corridor that also served
as an armory. But once he had picked one of the tiny rooms
for himself, he left his pack on the bed and went looking for

Jakyr; he ran into him in the hall. Jakyr was already looking for him.

"Ah, good. We're going to go meet with the Quartermaster and then with the fellow who'll guide us to The Bastion, who also happens to be the one who oversaw storing supplies out there. Come along." Jakyr headed off down the hall at a fast walk without bothering to look back to see if Mags was following; Mags made haste to keep up with him.

All Guardposts were laid out on the same plan, so it was no problem to find the Quartermaster's office. It was directly downstairs and in the same general position that the guest quarters were, which was (not at all coincidentally) near the central chimney. When a job requires that one have fingers that are not stiff with cold, it makes sense to put him near the chimney. On the other side of the chimney wall was the kitchen hearth and the ovens . . . which might make things uncomfortable in summer, except that in summer most of the long cooking moved out of doors to big ovens in the yard.

This particular Quartermaster clearly had a passion for neatness. Every accounting book was lined up in military fashion in bookcases; every paper was squared up on the desk. The office was no bigger than one of the guest rooms upstairs, but it managed to seem uncrowded because of that very neatness.

That worthy had been expecting them, knew what they needed before they even asked for it, and wordlessly handed over a small sheaf of papers before introducing them to a Guard Sergeant, who was likewise waiting patiently in the tiny office.

"This is Sergeant Milles," the Quartermaster said, with the air of a man who didn't like wasted words any more than he liked wasted money. "He'll tell you everything you need to know." The unspoken look of veiled impatience said what the Quartermaster did not say aloud for politeness: *And now get out of my office, if you please.*

The Sergeant crooked a finger at them and took them to the Post library, where he already had maps spread out for their perusal. Guardsmen were generally not known for being great readers, so the Library was in a room that was barely big enough for the bookcases that lined the walls and the table in the middle. "This one is yours," he said, handing a map that he rolled up to Jakyr. "I'll guide you tomorrow, of course, but you should have your own map of the route in and out. There're a lot of trails going in and out of that spot; there are always treasure hunters hoping to find a secret hoard somewhere in there. As a consequence, it's easy to get lost until you know your way. This map is more detailed than the one you've been given, I expect."

Jakyr unrolled it and cast an eye over it with approval. Mags craned his neck to look over Jakyr's shoulder. The map, insofar as he could judge, was the equal of any of those made by men whose business it was to draw them. It wasn't as fancy as the one the Royal Cartographers did, but it was well made. "It is. In fact, this is excellent work. Yours?"

The Sergeant shrugged, but he smiled. "A hobby of mine. Now, let's sit down and I'll show you the map of The Bastion itself."

The three of them pulled stools out from under the table and sat down on them. The Sergeant took weights and put them on the four corners of the map of The Bastion he had obviously made himself. The valley was roughly oval, and the Sergeant had detailed caves in the hills with blue paths.

The moment Mags saw the map he could have cheered. The hills around the valley of The Bastion were, indeed, laced with a system of caves. Real caves. The Sergeant had made an effort to map as many of them as he could, but of course, he hadn't been able to penetrate too deeply into most of them. "We had a lot to do and not a great deal of time to do it in, so I hope you'll forgive me for not exploring more. My main concern was getting the supplies stowed for you, not mapping out things. And I'm not a surveyor, Heralds. I haven't got the knowledge or the tools. I measured as best I could, but things could be off, and maybe by quite a lot."

"Anything is better than nothing," Jakyr replied. He bent over the map and put his finger near one branching area. "So, I think I have your system worked out properly. These are the hay caves?"

"Yes, here, here, and here." Sergeant Milles tapped three marked with yellow spots of paint. "We laid in more than we think you will need, because some might spoil. We did our best to find the driest spots, but since none of us know caves all that well, it's mostly guess and a lack of watermarks. We also laid in extra because hay is useful for more than feeding the horses. This is the straw cave, and this part here—" he pointed to a bulge to one side "—has a good base of sand. If you want to bring the horses down into the cave for an extended period of time, this will be good bedding for them and easier to keep clean than straw."

Jakyr nodded with approval. The Sergeant pointed out all the other storage areas and detailed how the stores had been put up, as Jakyr went over the Quartermaster's list.

"Now, here is what you'll probably want to use as your living quarters, at least those of you that don't use the caravan," the Sergeant continued, tapping a section of the caves marked with a green dot. "What you can't see on here is that with care, you can probably bring the caravan down as far as here and get it back up again. As you can see, you can easily reach all the provisions from this spot without going outside. There's a water source in there, an actual 'well' of sorts right here. My personal feeling is that it is actually an opening leading to a deeper water cave. I wasn't able to explore that, but I did test the water, and it's sweet and good. Also, there's a chimney crack here; the bandits built a firepit under it. I tested it, and it draws, so there's no danger of waking up choking to death. Keep the fire going, and the heat should keep the opening up top free of snow."

"At the risk of having it drip right down into the fire, but I think we can put up with that," Jakyr said with a slight smile. "Sergeant Milles, we are already indebted to you. You've done brilliantly by us."

The Sergeant, who was a lanky, dark-haired fellow with a baby face and was probably much older than he looked, nodded appreciatively. "It's good to get a Herald up here; maybe with your entourage we can put a dent in the local pattern of being closed-mouthed and actually get something accomplished. That nest of bandits that holed up in The Bastion? They'd been there for decades. I'm fairly certain half or more of them were related to villagers around here, so of course, the villagers wouldn't say a word about them. We only started getting somewhere when someone started a blood feud with someone *else* who was related to the chief. And even then, mostly we got half-literate messages and sketchy maps left stuck to the door with thorns or in the top of the feed bins."

Jakyr just nodded. "I've run up against that very situation before," he said. "I'll see what I can do, but you're coming up against custom that dates back centuries, and that's mighty hard to dislodge."

Mags nodded to himself. Now the situation with Cole Pieters was even clearer. The mine-kiddies hadn't been related to anyone around the mine, so no one really cared a toss about them. Cole Pieters, meanwhile, had a lot of money, a lot of influence, and a lot of offspring he could arm up to cause trouble if anyone caused it for *him*. There were two powerful reasons why no one had ever done anything about the conditions at the mine. Anyone he hadn't bought off—like the visiting priests, who were supposed to ensure that conditions were good for the orphans—he could easily have intimidated.

"You recollect that situation over on Lord Astley's lands

with the mine full of slavey-kids?" he asked, wondering if the story had gotten this far—and if there was anything like the same situation.

The Sergeant shook his head. "Too far away; there're at least two Lords with holdings between us, two whole districts and Astley has his own Guardpost, he doesn't use ours. The only time we ever hear of anything from that far off is when someone transfers here."

He recalled how Dean Caelen had said that this district was "not that far" from the mine where he had grown up. *Too far away, hmm? I guess "not that far" is pretty relative when you're sitting in Haven . . .* Ah well, it wasn't as if he needed his own story known in order to be effective here.

The Sergeant rolled up the rest of the maps and handed them to Jakyr. "These are all for you, Herald. I've made maps that show your Circuit as being a series of spokes coming off of The Bastion, rather than the usual spiral you Heralds do. I think that will help you a fair bit. We'll be off first thing in the morning; it'll take us a good day to get to The Bastion. We'll camp with you there overnight and leave you. After that, you know your own business better than me, I'm sure."

"I'd better after all these years." Jakyr chuckled, and the sergeant joined him.

"Beer?" Milles suggested.

"Don't mind if I do." Jakyr glanced over at Mags. "Go off and find that girl of yours, give her a tour of the Post or something. You know the drill around here. Meet me up for supper."

Mags laughed. "Yessir, I do," he said, since at least a fortnight—or more—of his first days as a Chosen had been spent in a Post exactly like this one, recovering from the abuse and neglect he'd suffered at the hands of his master. Without that considerable rest period he would never have been able to make the trek to Haven; he wouldn't have been able to sit Companion-back for more than a candlemark or two, and he never would have been able to endure the blizzard that shut them into another Guardpost. He still wasn't sure how much time he'd spent there; much of it had been eating and sleeping in the first few days—the first time in his entire life he'd had a full belly and a warm, soft bed, the first time he had ever been completely clean, the first time he had ever owned clothing that wasn't rags. The first time since he was a baby that people had been kind to him. "I'll do that."

He went back up to the guest rooms—tiny little boxes all in a row on either side of the hallway, with comfortable but narrow beds that barely fit inside. Well, all but two, which were at the end, slightly larger and with larger beds that *did* fill the room. He found Amily in one of the little ones, staring at her pack in the gathering gloom as if she was trying to work something out.

"Yer gonna go blind if ye don't get a light," he said, making her jump and squeak. He reached inside the door, and plucked the candle from its holder over the bed. There really was just barely enough room to move around the bed, not even enough for a table beside it. "You'd best close the shutters or it'll get damned cold, even with a brick in your bed. I'll get a light for you."

He went down the hall in time to meet the Guardsman who'd been sent to light all the main lamps and got a flame from him, then brought the candle back to Amily. She had closed the shutters as he suggested but was still contemplating her pack. "What're ye doing, staring at the pack like that?" he asked. He couldn't imagine what was in it that would make her look at it as if it held a snake.

"Do you change for dinner here?" she asked, worriedly. "I didn't bring anything nice."

He didn't laugh at her; after all, she *had* been brought up in the Palace, where everyone turned up at dinner in fancier dress than they wore during the day. "No, it's just like eatin' at the Collegium. All ye do is make sure ye don't come to table all over filth. Guards usually wash up good afore dinner, so I reckon we leave 'em the hot water an' get a wash after. Water'll have hotted up again by then."

"Oh, good! I already washed my face and hands in the caravan. I'm glad you know how things go," she said, and held up her face for a kiss. "Can you show me around?"

"Nothin' I'd like better," he lied—because there was definitely something he would like better, but—well—no privacy.

———

The dinner summons came when he had just about finished showing her the last of the Post. "We'll prolly sit with the Captain and the officers," he told her. "I didn't the last time I was at a Post, but I was just a little'un. We're all, like, honored guests and all. You want it known who your Pa is?"

She shook her head. "Not really. Just saying I am Bear's assistant should be reasonable. I don't want to be fussed over."

He squeezed her hand as they went down the hall. "Well, then, just let Lita and Lena get all the attention, which they will. The rest of us might as well be invisible when there's a Bard in the room."

The mess hall wasn't that far from where they had been poking about—looking over the armory—so it didn't take them long to get there, and as Mags had expected, the Captain's servant intercepted them at the door and took them to the officer's table. Jakyr and Bear were already there; Lita and Lena arrived shortly, and once they were seated, the meal was served.

Which was to say, the men got up and got their food from the mess line, and the Captain's servant brought them each plates that he filled for them. Mags didn't mind; the food was good, with a couple of things he'd never tried before, and he wasn't in the habit even now of leaving good food on a plate because it wasn't exactly what he was hankering for.

Mostly, he remained quiet and listened, and ate, as the Captain and Jakyr and (to his surprise) Lita exchanged stories. Or rather, it seemed a little as if Jakyr and Lita were in a kind of competition to come up with the most outrageous and amusing story for the entertainment of the table. They didn't *quite* descend to the level of telling tales on each other, but he had the distinct feeling that in other company, or with more beer, it could have devolved to that.

It might still have, except that Lita had already arranged to have a semiformal concert for the entire garrison once the dishes were cleared away, and that is what she did. Once again, Mags had the intriguing experience of watching a Master tune her art to please *exactly* the audience she faced. Not only the audience, but the mood they were in—winter was coming, always a hard time. Shorter days meant less light, depressing to the spirit. And this garrison was full of men who were far from home, far from their loved ones, and far from women, serving people who were, if not overtly hostile, certainly nothing like friendly. It was hard on them, far from home with Midwinter coming, and Lita's concert was purposed to raise their spirits.

It was a shorter set than the ones she'd done at the inns that they had stopped at, but, then, she wasn't playing for an audience she had to win over—they were hers from the beginning. She began with purely comic songs, just to test the crowd, but before long, she was working into material like drinking songs that everyone knew, so everyone could sing the chorus.

Mags held Amily's hand as soon as the concert started, but as the audience got completely caught up in a lively ballad that relied heavily on double-entendres and allusions rather than coming out and *saying* what was going on, he felt her squeeze it tightly. Glancing over at her, he saw her nod ever so slightly toward the door. He let go of her hand, and she slipped away under the cover of the chorus. Giving her a bit of time—not that he thought they were fooling anyone, but for the sake of pretending to propriety—he followed.

With the rest of the concert as a muted background, they spent a very satisfactory, if also somewhat frustrating, candle-mark cuddled up together in her bed, kissing and holding each other, but not much more. There was no telling when someone would come along, and he understood without her saying anything that she would be painfully mortified if anyone caught them getting farther than that. They broke apart, reluctantly, and only when they heard the first lines of "The Parting Glass" floating in from the mess hall.

He had the distinct feeling that Lita had chosen that song deliberately to warn them that the concert was over. Finally someone was on *their* side!

When a Guardsman says that "they are leaving at first light," he is being literal. Mags already knew that, but Lena, Bear, and Amily were still scrubbing the sleep from their eyes as they mounted the steps to the caravan and Lita took up the reins.

At least they can go back to sleep, Mags thought, a little glumly. He wasn't used to sleeping in a place as busy as the Guardpost was at night. There had been men coming and going down the corridor as the watches changed, and each time they had, it had woken him up. As if she had heard the thought, Lita looked up at him from the driver's position. *She* looked like she'd slept like a baby—but then, she was used to sleeping in Bardic Collegium, where it was never quiet.

"You know, there is no reason why you have to ride for the first part of this journey," she pointed out, then looked over at

Jakyr, who looked very much as if he had stayed up too late last night. Evidently he'd found a convivial comrade in Sergeant Milles. "Nor you either. Although . . . if you were—" She mimed drinking "—you probably would be better off riding than being in the caravan, the way it's going to be swaying over those rough roads."

Somehow she made it sound as if Jakyr made a habit of getting drunk. And Mags could not imagine how she'd done it. Jakyr predictably bristled, and Mags didn't blame him. Lita hadn't made any effort to keep her voice down. Deliberately, he was sure.

"As it happens, I was ironing out some last-minute details with Sergeant Milles," he snapped, "I was seeing to some extra supplies that he had not thought of, and those were mostly for the comfort of you ladies. So thank you, yes, I will take to the caravan for a candlemark or two." He looped Jermayan's reins over the saddle horn and reached for the side of the porch. As Lita hastily scooted out of the way, he swung himself over onto it, pulled open the door, and ducked inside, brushing the Bard with a foot near enough that, although he didn't actually kick her, it was clear he *could* have if he had chosen to be a cad, and sloughed it off as an accident.

Mags decided that a closed mouth was the better part of valor, and just said, politely, "May I?"

"Be my guest," Lita replied, staying where she was. He eased Dallen up to the side of the caravan, and copied Jakyr's moves—without the near kick—and climbed into the wagon. Lita shut the door behind him, and a moment later the caravan lurched on its way.

This was the first time Mags had been in the vehicle while it was moving, and it did sway, quite a bit. He clung to an overhead rail, while Jakyr rolled himself in a cocoon in blankets on one of the narrow beds, pulled a corner over his head, and turned to put his back to the rest of the caravan.

The little doors leading into the two cupboard beds were

closed. Amily must be in the lower one alone, and probably asleep already again. She'd had a lot of practice by now in sleeping in a moving van. Despite the fact that he would dearly love to have cuddled up with her, Mags decided not to disturb the occupants, and instead took the other narrow bed. It was surprisingly comfortable. There was a featherbed in the box, and it was thicker than it looked. He nestled down into it and closed his eyes, and decided that he liked the swaying of the wagon. Of course, he had never been a baby that had had a cradle—at least, he didn't think so—but he imagined that was very much what it felt like. As soon as he got cozy-warm, he fell right back asleep.

When he woke again, he turned over to see that the other bed was empty, and he heard someone softly practicing scales. He realized he must have been hearing that for some time, and he sat up.

"Want to help me make food for everyone?" Amily asked from somewhere about the level of his feet. "It's about luncheon time, and there are no inns on this road, but the Cook loaded us with enough food to give everyone something to eat. I thought I'd just put packets together; we can pass them out the windows here at the back."

"Always happy to give you a hand," he said, turning to see her peeking out of the bottom cupboard bed. She came out and sat next to him, and together they put up something people could eat in the saddle. Rolls split and buttered, with a thick slice of cheese, a couple of small leeks, and a bit of bacon in the middle. Then they opened the rear windows and stuck their heads out.

"I've got food!" Amily called, and handed the packets out as the half-dozen Guardsmen rode up and reached over their horses' heads to take them. There was enough in the supplies for everyone to have two, which seemed to satisfy all of them.

He helped Amily clean things up and tidy everything away, shaking the basket the rolls had been in out the window. It was clear that in a space this small, you had to tidy up every-thing as soon as you were finished with it, or you'd soon have no room to move.

:Need me out there?: he asked Dallen.

:Not in the least. Jakyr is sulking, and he and Milles are exchanging stories about insufferably rude women, and how it's impossible to understand females in the first place. I think you would only get in the way of their fun.:

Having, in the course of his duties to Nikolas down in Haven or at the Palace, been forced to listen to far too many such conversations, Mags was inclined to agree. If there was one tune that got harped on over and over, it was how unrea-sonable women were (among men) and how unreasonable men were (among women). He was inclined to think that everybody just got burrs under their saddles from time to time and got unreasonable in general.

"All I can say," Mags said to Amily, "is that it is a very good thing that Jakyr and I are going to be out of The Bastion as much as in. I just hope we don't get snowed in together too much."

"If we do, we have several options," Amily said thoughtfully. "We could move to another cave. We could tell *them* to move to another cave. Or we could tie them together and make them work out whatever it is that they've been quarreling about."

Mags shuddered. "With the third?" he said. "I think there'd be blood afore it was over. Lita, I know she's got a tongue like a sword, and Jakyr ain't far behind. They'd flay each other alive with words afore any making up happened."

Amily grimaced. "Then we make them move to other caves. Maybe they'll go into hibernation like grumpy bears and spare us all."

————

Jakyr seemed to have worked off his irritation in a couple of candlemarks . . . no doubt by making sure Lita was within earshot of stories she couldn't respond to and had to pretend not to hear. That was when Mags swung himself out of the caravan and managed to get Amily up behind him, all without anyone stopping or slowing down. The road—if you could call it that—was little more than a track among the trees at this point. Mags had the feeling that if the supply wagons hadn't worn it down some, they'd have had a hard time tracing it.

There was a great deal of wildlife out there among the trees. More than once, they heard something crashing through the underbrush, running away from their convoy. *:Deer,:* Dallen informed him. Once, a fox just stood there and watched them pass, bold as you please. Rabbits fled, as did tree-hares, and squirrels by the dozen raced up trunks and scolded them from imagined safety. Since several of the Guardsmen amused themselves by taking out tree-hares and rabbits for their dinner tonight, the squirrels wouldn't have been nearly as safe as they thought they were.

Overhead, birds flitted among the branches like leaves, watching them without any sign of fear. Evidently, few people came here, and fewer still hunted. Mags wondered why.

"You can see why the bandits picked this part of the country," Milles said, as another deer went blundering away. "Plenty of game. It's been so long now that the wildlife has gotten fearless again. Impossible for anyone to get through here without alerting the wildlife, so if you paid attention and were quiet, you could easily tell when someone was coming up on The Bastion. You only need to put out a few sentries to guard quite a big area." He shook his head. "We must have scouted through here dozens of times. I was just a first-year Guardsman at the time, so I was part of that. All they had to do was to pull back into their caves and make sure we never found the entrance to the pocket valley. We probably went past them a hundred times before we finally got someone to guide us in."

"And then?" Jakyr asked.

"We sent one scout to verify that The Bastion was where the informant said it was. He was truly a genius at what he did and was undetected. We gave them no indication we knew they were there. We waited until we had a double garrison ready to go, and if you've ever seen the report, you know how that went." Milles let the sentence trail off, inviting Jakyr to say he had or had not. Mags eavesdropped shamelessly.

"I only found out about the gang because of The Bastion being central to my Circuit," Jakyr lied smoothly. "When I did my research. It looked like a natural place to set up a headquarters, rather than relying on the Waystations. So?"

"So, we'd planned all this in as close to absolute secret as we could. No one outside the Post knew about it. We even managed to hide the doubled manpower. On the day, we sent men in over the top of the hills before dawn, and killed their scouts as they took up their posts, then filled the hills with archers. We blocked off the entrance, then one full garrison went in, on foot, wearing full plate. Hard to move in, but it made it almost impossible for them to do us much damage. We moved in squares of four, so nobody could get hit from behind. Anybody who tried to escape up the cliffs and over the hills met the archers. The entrance is barely wide enough for a supply wagon, so men in armor could just bull right through until we got ourselves a foothold; then we just kept feeding them in. The bandits tried a rain of arrows, but they never got anything going thanks to our archers above."

"Good gods," Jakyr said, sounding stunned.

"Aye. It was a slaughter. A sheer butchery. Mind you, they got quick deaths, which was more than they deserved. Remember, we caught them by surprise, so they got very little chance to get into armor themselves. It wasn't so much a fight as—well, we were like some sort of reaping machine that took men instead of wheat." Milles ran his hand through his hair. "Not the sort of battle you boast about. When we got a look at what they'd been up to in that camp that we *didn't* know about, I have to say I'm glad they're gone, but it was the sort of fight that sickens a man of fighting."

Some of Milles' memories were strong enough that he actually projected them, and Mags felt nauseated by them too, before he shut them out. He hoped he would never find himself in a position like the one Milles had been in. The bandits had been all but defenseless against the Guardsmen—highly trained, heavily armored, heavily armed. Most of them hadn't so much as a shield; they'd just picked up whatever weapon was closest to hand, tried to fight their way out of the valley, and been met by arrows everywhere. The ones that survived that had been insanely desperate, or they would never have tried to fight their way past the Guard.

Then there had been the fights with the ones trying to hide in the caves. That hadn't lasted past the Guard tossing in balls of pitch and tar that were on fire and put out huge clouds of choking smoke. Again, there was no choice: choke to death on the smoke or face the Guard. And for whatever reason, few of them seemed to consider a third option—surrender.

Maybe because they knew they'd probably be hung anyway if they did. According to the reports that Mags had seen, they'd been responsible for hundreds of deaths that the Guard knew of. Which meant there were probably two times more that they didn't.

"Give me a nice clean battlefield any day," Milles was saying fervently. "I never want to do that again."

"There's a lot to be said for that," Jakyr agreed. "Although sometimes a battlefield is no cleaner. I'd rather have been in your shoes than face Karsite demons."

Since that was a conversation Mags *really* didn't want to listen in on—having *far* too vivid memories of the Karsite demons still—he had Dallen drop back to the caravan again. Lita had slowed the vanners; the caravan was pitching a little on the uneven track.

"Problems?" Mags asked.

She shook her head. "As long as it gets no worse than this."

"It don't, milady Bard," offered one of the Guardsmen. "In fact, this's the worst of it."

Sure enough the track smoothed out again, and it wasn't more than a candlemark later that they found themselves threading an entrance between two sheer stone faces. It looked as if a giant had cleft the hill with an ax, making a passage between two halves of an exceedingly tall hill. A small mountain, *he* would have said.

It was a good thing that he was used to the mines, because that passage would have been claustrophobic. As it was, a couple of the Guard looked very uneasy until they came out on the other side.

And the other side was a pretty, if unremarkable, tiny pocket valley, ringed completely by hills with very steep—in fact, he would have said, sheer—cliffs on the valley side. It was as if that same giant had taken his fist and punched a cup into the hills.

"Now . . . this is odd," Jakyr said, looking around himself. "Very odd . . ."

"How odd?" asked Milles.

"Well . . . I've been to a lot of strange places, so I've seen a bit more than your average Herald," Jakyr replied. "And if I had just come on this place . . . I'd say it was a Hawkbrother Vale. . . ."

A Hawkbrother Vale?

:You know, he's right,: Dallen said. *:It has the look of a Vale, a long abandoned one, but a Vale nevertheless.:*

"Huh." Milles looked surprised. "I thought they were a myth."

"Not even close." Jakyr dismounted. "I've met 'em. I've been to two Vales. The only thing missing here is the giant trees, but those won't flourish once the Hawkbrothers leave, and they'd have fallen a long, long time ago. Or got cut down.

Those big trees, they're mighty tempting to a woodsman. You could build your entire Guardpost from the wood from *one,* and who knows? Maybe someone did. One way to know for sure. Go on, Jermayan. You're better at this than me."

The Companion shook his head briskly, then closed his eyes and raised his nose as if he were sniffing the breeze. Then he trotted straight over to a little grassy depression, like a bowl about the size of a four-room cottage, and pawed at the center of it.

"That tears it," Jakyr said with some satisfaction. "He says that's where the Heartstone was. It *was* a Hawkbrother Vale, but it's been abandoned for a long, long time. Probably long before Valdemar took this piece into its borders."

"Couple hundred years, then?" Milles replied speculatively.

Jermayan trotted back to his Chosen. "Oh, at least," said Jakyr. "I'd reckon more than that. There's no hint that there's anything uncanny in all the Guard reports hereabouts. If you had the weirdling beasties you generally find around a Hawk-brother Vale, trust me, you'd *know* about it."

He looked over at Lita, who had been watching all this with her mouth open in astonishment. "Did you hear all that?"

"I heard it, but I can scarcely believe it," she said. "If I didn't know you better, I'd suspect you of tale spinning."

"It's no tale, Jermayan agrees," the Herald told her smugly. "Well, you always wanted to see a Vale. Now you can."

:Guess I won't be the only one digging through this place,: Mags told Dallen.

:By the look on her face, she's likely to be digging more than you,: the Companion replied.

The caravan fit very nicely into the side of the entrance to what they were already coming to think of as the "living quarters." It would definitely be out of the way of wind and snow;

that kettleful of coals would heat it up nicely for sleeping, and Lena and Bear were already acting as if it were their own little cottage. Not that he blamed them; it was the one place here where they could be guaranteed absolute privacy without leaving the comfort of the group cave.

So far as Mags was concerned, they could have it. A heap of straw, one of the canvas bow tents atop that, and the feath-erbed from the lower cupboard bed atop that, plus his and Amily's bedrolls made a place just as cozy. There were a lot of little side caves, like private rooms, with hollows in them that were just bed-size. They were all off the main cave, tucked into the wall in such a way as to give a great deal of privacy. He reckoned if there was a way to fit a curtain across the en-trance, he'd have almost as good a situation as a room with a door. If this had been a natural cave, he would have regarded this configuration as wildly unlikely, and would have assumed that something was drastically amiss—most likely, that this place got flooded on a regular basis and the hollows were water-worn. But if this had been a Hawkbrother Vale, any number of things became a possibility.

Really, the fact that it had been a Hawkbrother Vale ex-plained everything that had seemed far too convenient. The chimney area . . . the well . . . the storage caves that were so bone-dry it was safe to store fodder in them . . . it all made perfect sense. Someone had been living here for a very long time, and the Hawkbrothers had shaped the place to suit them.

As they all settled in—the Guardsmen temporarily, the rest of them more-or-less permanently—he asked Lita who those "someones" would have been.

". . . because I thought Hawkbrothers lived in trees," he concluded, helping her move all of her instruments and per-sonal things to areas cut into the side of her chosen side cave that were so flat and even they could only have been shelves or open cupboards for the previous occupant.

"You thought correctly," the Bard said. "What would have been living here were the *hertasi*. Gentle, manlike lizards, about so tall." She measured the height of her breastbone. "They were—are—the servants to the Hawkbrothers, and they prefer to live in caves or tunnels underground. All this—" she waved her hand at the cave around them, now brilliantly lit by lanterns placed in niches that clearly had been made explicitly to hold lanterns "—is just what they would have had when everyone first moved in here. Before they left, they'd have made themselves all manner of structures and comforts. It would have been every bit as nice as the Collegia down here. I'm serious. The *hertasi* like their little comforts."

"It's not bad now," he observed. She laughed.

"It's a blessed sight better than what I thought we'd find. Jak promised me once he'd take me to a Vale." She made a face. "Well, this is as close as I'm like to get, so I'll enjoy what I have."

With the Guards' help, Jakyr had already set up a kitchen, and there was a good dinner cooking away. He was making flatbreads, grilled on a griddle, while a good rabbit stew bubbled in a pot. The vanners had been tethered outside while it was light, but just to be safe, Mags had moved them in and tied them to the caravan when it got dark. The Guards had brought their mounts in as well. Now the little herd stood, hipshot, dozing, with the remains of their hay and grain within easy reach.

The Companions had inspected every hollow and settled on one each. Mags had filled the chosen spots with straw, and they had settled in, too. It had been a long day for all of the hoofed ones, and they hadn't gotten the benefit of naps in the caravan the way the humans had.

"Well, now I envy you," Milles said, as he came up to Mags, watching Jakyr for the sign that the food was ready.

"Because of what this place was?" Mags hazarded.

The Sergeant nodded. "I'd give a hand to be able to explore

it properly." He sighed. "Who knows what you're likely to find!"

Mags smiled. "Know what'd suit me best right at this moment?" he asked, then answered the rhetorical question. "Supper!"

The sergeant laughed. And a moment later, Mags' wish was answered.

The Guardsmen left first thing in the morning; Mags, as usual, was awake even before he heard them moving about. They were quite quiet; moving carefully so as not to make much noise, drawing water, building up the fire, preparing to make use of the cold rations they had brought with them.

Well, it was going to be a very long, chilly trip, and Mags couldn't see sending them off on little more than a couple of bars of trail rations. Not that the things weren't edible; they were, and really not bad, either, so long as you didn't mind gnawing on them like a beaver on a branch. Still.

Mags used one of his cooking lessons to make them a basic sort of breakfast; he took the trail rations and some cut oats and made a very good porridge with it, which was even better when he loaded it with dried berries and added a little honey. They were more than happy to wait for him to cook it when he offered, and they were equally happy to clean up the dishes after they finished. When everyone had a belly full of hot food and the mess had been disposed of, Mags saw them off—

everyone else was *still* asleep—and got a lantern. He had a good idea how he wanted to spend his time until Jakyr woke, at the very least.

Knowing that this cave had served the former occupants as a living space, there was one thing that should be here that no one had yet located (or at least had yet identified) that was pretty vital to comfort. He had a pretty good idea where he would put such a "room" if he were the one laying out the cave, so he went looking for it. Knowing that the cave complex had been created by Hawkbrothers made his task a bit easier. If this were all a natural cave, the former occupants would have had to make do with how they found things. But this was, in part at least, not so much a cave as an excavation. So positioning should follow rules of logic.

He was looking for a small room. It would be off the main cave, accessed by a narrow, but smooth-floored, descending tunnel . . . and hopefully with ventilation coming into it and going up through another chimney crack.

As soon as he found such a tunnel, he followed it, and . . .

Well, well, well. Logic had not failed him. The tunnel ended in a small roomlike area. At the back was a large niche, big enough for three people to fit in with room to spare. The niche was about knee height, with a flat bottom, a sort of floor to it. The sort of thing that, if you were in, say, a Palace, would have a statue standing in it. But here, there were three equally spaced, carefully smoothed depressions, and in the depressions were large holes.

This was the privy. And this was, by the standards of what they had planned on creating, a very nice privy.

Even if the bandits had used this, it had been so long ago that whatever mess they had created here was long since cleaned away by time, insects, and the atmosphere of the cave itself. He peered down one of the holes, holding his lantern over his head and deflecting the light downward; it was too deep to see the bottom.

That was a good sign. The deeper it was, the farther away the deposits would be.

He dropped a pebble down one; he heard a far-off "tick" when it landed, not a splash of water, which was what he was hoping for. The last thing they needed was to have their water supply contaminated. So the well they were getting their water from was either a true well, or the water source had no direct connection to this cave.

Of course, if *he* were building such a thing . . . beneath the well opening above would be a good deep pool, preferably rain fed or fed by a slow spring. Something with high walls around it. Overflow would only be periodic, and it would flush what was deposited here down deeper into the caves and away from the drinking source.

Maybe some day someone will come here and get into these lower caves and see if they did make it that way. Meanwhile, judging by everything I've read about the Hawkbrothers, we can trust them to have made good work of this.

There was more, because this had been Hawkbrother-made. On the left side of the little room was another niche that ended at about waist height, with another, deeper depression. This depression had a much smaller hole in it.

In short: this was a basin for washing the hands and face. It had probably once boasted a plug for the bottom.

This could not have been better unless it had the same sort of flushing-water setup the Palace and Collegia had. With a slight smile he left the little room and went hunting for supplies.

Amily woke up first. It had been very nice sleeping cuddled together (at last!) even if they hadn't done anything but kiss and fondle. They'd certainly kept each other warmer than they would have been sleeping separately. He rather thought that no one had noticed that they had gone off together last night, since Bear and Lena had retired right after supper to the caravan, Lita had gone to bed not that long after, making up for the fact that she had not had the luxury of a nap on the way, and Jakyr had stayed up with Milles, talking. It wouldn't be too long before someone noticed, however . . .

Well, cross that river when they came to it. Amily wasn't a Bard, so Lita probably wouldn't say anything. Bear and Lena certainly wouldn't. That left Jakyr, and if Jakyr took against it, Lita would almost certainly come out on their side. The ensuing argument would probably cause both the Herald and the Bard to forget what they were arguing about.

When Amily emerged from their cavelet, still sleepy eyed, he took her by the hand and conveyed her wordlessly to his little discovery in all its newly decorated glory. Beside the latrines, a big bag of soft hay. In the other niche was a wax plug that fit in the hole of the "sink", and on the stone shelf of the "sink," a lit lantern, a box of soft soap and a bucket of water with a dipper.

Amily stared. "Was all this—I mean the stone—here already?"

He nodded. "I tried it out. The latrines are made for something with a wider behind than a human, but it still isn't a bad fit. I have to warn you, though, it's startling cold to sit on, and it's going to get worse the colder the winter gets."

"And here I thought we'd have to be digging our own! It would have been even colder out there in the valley, sitting in a canvas-sided box on a couple of boards or something." She kissed him, then shooed him out. He left, chuckling. He knew very well how to deal with a deep-pit latrine like this one; collect the ashes from the fires, and toss them down as often as you collected them. Even if there wasn't a bit of runoff to clean things up periodically, it would all compost nicely, and probably provide for cave insects.

He was organizing the kitchen area a little better when Amily came out, all smiles. "I even had a good wash. Now, if you find some sort of *hertasi* bathtub, I will be in sheer heaven."

"For all I know, they made something of the sort. I'll see what I can find," he began, when Lita appeared from her own cavelet.

Unlike Amily and Lena, she was wearing breeches. The other two had opted for divided skirts, like very wide trews, on this journey. Mags had a notion he wasn't going to see any of them in skirts or gowns or even Bardic robes at all, which didn't bother him in the least. One less thing for them to worry about; he just hoped that the locals were not going to get their knickers in a knot over it.

"Found the *hertasi* jakes, did you?" Lita said cheerfully. "One less thing that I have to look for then. Point me in the direction?"

Amily did, then helped Mags set up for a more substantial breakfast than he'd made for the Guard before they left.

A lot of things had been left when the bandits had been cleared out that weren't worth the looting. Mags had found three slabs of stone that set up to make a very passable sort of oven when set against the rock wall. He raked all of the coals back there while he built up the fire again, and he got out all the three-legged pots and pans that you used over an open fire when you didn't have a way to suspend them, arranging them on and in their cupboard. He didn't remember if there was a tripod to hang pots from in the supplies, but there certainly hadn't been one in the pot box that was slung under the caravan. He started a pot of water heating and got the frying pan on the fire. They still had bread, they had eggs, and they had plenty of bacon. That would suffice for toad-in-the-hole, which to his mind, was about the best breakfast there was. The smell of bacon brought out Lena and Bear, and eventually Jakyr, who took over after he'd visited Mags' discovery.

"Mags," Lita said, around a bite of hot egg and bread, "do you want to go hunting for the *hertasi* bathing room, or shall I? There will be one; the *hertasi* are as fussy about cleanliness as their masters are. I can tell you what to look for, and you're probably handier at crawling around caves than I am."

"What am I looking for?" Mags asked, not at all averse to trying.

"Mostly, a small spring. If there is one around here in these caves, they'll have built the bathing area around it. There'll be a bigger basin cut into the rock, bigger than the bathtubs that we're used to, but at the moment, the spring will just run through it." It was Jakyr who answered, not Lita. Mags looked at him curiously, and he shrugged. "Remember, I've been to a working Vale, as opposed to reading about them."

Evidently Lita was in good enough humor not to rise to his baiting. She just shrugged and had another bite of yolk-soaked bread.

Jakyr looked faintly disappointed at her indifference but continued. "It'll be a variation on how they make their big hot-spring soaking pools for the Hawkbrothers. There would be several of these bathing-basins, but I doubt we'll find more than one still working, and the bandits probably used it—if they used it at all—for watering their horses and livestock. They probably had no idea it was for taking a bath. Though I could be wrong; for all I know, they were hedonists who lolled about in baths all day." A quirk of his mouth and a lifted eyebrow invited Mags to chuckle, which he did. "So. Spring, which will be running into a big basin, which will be filled and overflowing into some sort of escape drain into a lower cave."

"Think I'll find it here?" Mags asked.

Jakyr shook his head. "If there were a good place to put it here, we'd have heard the spring the minute we got inside the caves. It probably won't be near this one, because the well for drinking water is here. They are fastidious about keeping dirty water away from clean, and they won't have taken the chance of contaminating the well."

Mags nodded.

"Anyway, the basin just overflows straight into a drain, but if you look at the inlet end, you'll see a diversion channel for the spring," Jakyr continued. "They'd probably use dams of clay, and we can too. You divert the water away from the basin, have your bath, let the clean water in to flush out the dirty, and there you go." He sighed. "If there were Hawkbrothers here, they'd have some way of heating the water, and it would be flowing in hot. But I expect we can use hot stones to get it bearable anyway."

Mags sighed as well. That would have been nice. Still, it was far better than no way to get a bath.

"Or we can use the canvas tub we already have with us," Lita pointed out, and nodded to what looked like a thick door or thin cabinet propped against the wall.

"Oh, well, be logical, then!" Jakyr retorted. "Personally, I'd rather tote around *one* kettle of hot stones than twenty of hot water, not to mention emptying it after!"

"Suit yourself." Lita finished her meal and scrubbed the plate and fork clean with sand from the bucket Mags had provided for that purpose. She got up, and stretched. "I'll see to the vanners. Are we here for the day?"

"It will take us at least that long to properly set up," Jakyr replied. "I don't want us scrambling to get things done and end up with everything only half done. The Guard left us a lot of supplies and other things that need to be stored right the first time."

"Sir, yes, sir," Lita said laconically. Mags was afraid she was going to salute, which might very well have been enough to set Jakyr off, but she didn't. "Suit you if I set up the stables?"

"Suits me fine," Jakyr replied, brusquely. "Mags, you and I went over the inventory and where it's all stored, so you and I will be doing most of the moving."

"I'll help," offered Lena. "Amily and Bear can set things up here if you tell them where you want things."

The actual moving of things out of storage and into the

main cave took most of the morning. There were a lot of heavy objects, at least when it came to the kitchen area— Mags had seen the inventory, but he hadn't quite believed what he'd read. Yet, there all those things were . . . they were going to have a kitchen that many housewives in cottages would envy.

Jakyr made them all lunch, then they *all* worked on set-up. By the time night fell . . . well, you would not have been able to tell the main cave area from the interior of a very comfortable cottage.

Mags discovered that his construction of the stone oven was entirely unnecessary. There was an iron stove that somehow had come packed in pieces that fitted together with sturdy metal pins, and a load of firebricks to stack around it and act as a heat-mass the way the chimneys in the stable did. The kitchen was moved to one side, though still situated where the chimney crack would take the smoke from the stove, and the firepit they had used to cook in was turned into a communal fireplace with heavy rugs and cushions stuffed with hay around it. Everyone now had more blankets, more pillows, waxed canvas to put on the ground under the hay in their beds, and feather comforters. There were cleaning supplies tucked away in their own area, a canvas sink for actually washing dishes in, and the aforementioned canvas bathtub waiting to be set up next to the fire when someone wanted it.

At the entrance of each of the sleeping caves, Amily had found sockets carved into the rock to hold poles. Bear went out with the measurements for each of the cavelets in use, and cut poles to fit from the piles of wood that the Guard had left for them. Now there were canvas curtains hung up across the opening of their sleeping caves, for privacy.

The Guard hadn't just left fodder for the horses and the Companions. In the piles of supplies there were storage chests that could be sealed against vermin thanks to gaskets of tarred rope around the lids, and each of these chests was already laden with foodstuffs like dried fruits and vegetables and dried meat.

There were chests of candles and lamp oil, chests of lanterns, the chests they had already robbed of their blankets and ground canvas, an entire chest of soap. . . . In short, everything you could possibly want to turn a cave into a home was here.

"Why would a Guardpost have all this stuff?" Mags wondered aloud, as they put the finishing touches on the central space.

"Because the highborn have been known to want to come on a campaign," Jakyr grunted, "And the comfort of the highborn must be seen to. All of the extra stuff—the rugs, the folding furniture, that sort of thing—is kept in storage in a Guardpost in case it's needed. Milles tells me that, packed away, it doesn't take up much room, so no one really objects to keeping it around."

"Can't object much when we're gettin' to use it," Mags pointed out.

With a reluctant smile, Jakyr agreed.

At that moment Amily discovered, with a cry of joy, that there was a little chest of books among the candles, and Mags found himself grinning.

A proper stew had been simmering all afternoon once they got the stove set up, and the aroma was enough to drive a person half mad. Jakyr was still puttering with his kitchen, Amily had settled with a book, Lena and Lita with their instruments, and Bear with his herbs. Mags decided to go look for that bathing area before the stew scent drove him to eat something he shouldn't—like the last of the bread. He took a lantern and went out into the valley.

The Companions and the horses were cropping contentedly enough at the tall, withered grasses, which were roughly knee high in most places. The sun was somewhere on the other side of the hills and sinking fast. Not much time to look.

But then, he realized he didn't have to *look*.

:Dallen. Have we got a running spring in one of them caves?:

Dallen's head came up. *:I'll ask Jermayan to help me search. Shouldn't take long.:*

The two Companions split up and checked the entrance to each cave in turn, using their superior senses of hearing and smell. They would hear the spring or smell the water long before Mags could.

Mags took the opportunity to explore the little valley while they hunted.

He thought he could see signs of where the enormous trees that the Hawkbrothers were said to live in had once stood, but there was no trace of them now. There didn't seem to have been too many of them, either, and that made him wonder if they had also lived in the caves, as their *hertasi* did. The valley had definitely been cleared of anything like a tree at or around the time the bandits took it over, but it had been long enough for trees to have reseeded themselves in several places, making compact little groves here and there.

He was sure he found the place where the legendary bathing pools had once been. On the one part of the valley wall that wasn't sheer rock, there was a sloping hill, with six basins built into it. He could see where water would have started at the top, cascaded down to the next two, and then into the last four. But if there had been a spring that fed these basins, it had dried up a long time ago. The basins themselves were more like depressions, partly filled in with soil, and covered with turf and weeds.

This would be a nice place in summer though, and was not bad now.

He also inspected the huge pile of wood that had been left for them by the Guard. The bigger logs had been chopped up and split and piled in several pyramids off to the right of the entrance of the cave they were using. Branches had mostly been cut into fire-sized pieces, but there was a pile of uncut ones as well; this was what Bear had used for their curtain poles, and Mags expected there would be other uses for them. It looked like an impossible amount of wood, but he knew from experience that keeping fires stoked used a lot of fuel. His best guess, though, was that there would be enough here to keep them through spring. It looked as if the Guard had dragged every dead tree within easy reach of the entrance inside, and chopped it all up here. There was a substantial pile of wood chips that would make good kindling.

It didn't take long at all for the Companions to find the *hertasi* bathing room. The cave in question was along the same wall as their living cave but deeper into the valley, located behind one of those little groves of trees, but Jermayan found it quite quickly. Mags went in to inspect it as the shadows deepened and the light began to fade from the sky.

He was glad he had the lantern; it was dark, and although you could hear the spring faintly from the entrance, it was around several draft-killing twists and turns in the tunnel. It was a tunnel and not a natural cave this time; he spotted the telltale signs that someone had been working the rock.

When he emerged into a small room, he knew immediately that the place was going to take some work before it was usable.

There had been some rockfall along the wall, which made the footing a little treacherous there and diverted part of the water. But more importantly, the basin—which was rather like a huge bulge in the middle of a small stream—had a thick layer of fine mud on the bottom. Certainly no one had cleared it since the bandits called this place home. And the water was just one step above ice. He hurried back to report to the others.

"I think maybe they was using it for a lotta things," he said, after describing what he'd found. "I think washing clothes and maybe watering horses. Diggin' the mud out ain't gonna be nice, cold as that water is." He sat down on one of the wool rugs with his back to a hay-stuffed cushion the size of a horse's torso. The hay smelled nice; he suspected Bear had packed some herbs in there as well. The cushion rustled a little as he settled himself.

Jakyr dished him up a bowl of stew, stuck a chunk of bread in it, and handed it to him. "Maybe that portable tub is a better answer then."

Mags took a bite of gravy-soaked bread. "Well," he said, "I can tell ye, as some'un who's had his arms in cold water in winter, that it won't be but a couple of moments afore your hands start to hurt like fury. And then you start to get cold all *over,* once yer arms get cold. We didn't have a choice back then but to do it, but I don't think none of us now could work for longer'n a verse in a drinkin' song afore we'd have t'quit." He shivered, feeling chilled just thinking about it. "That mud'll be packed in there good. It'd take candlemarks t' get it all out. I'm thinkin' that's a job for warmer times."

Lita gave him an *I told you so* look. She didn't say it. She didn't have to. It was Bear who quickly defused things before they started snapping at each other again.

"We got a *lot* of these sleeping caves," he said. "Any reason why we couldn't heat up rocks an' use one of em for a steambath? I liked the one we used back at that inn."

"Huh. We'd want one far enough away from where we're actually sleeping that the damp doesn't get into our bedding, but . . ."

"I hope this doesn't immediately make you against the idea," Lita said dryly. "But I like it, I like the idea a lot. I favor steam baths in winter. We could set up the canvas tub in there to use for water for the rocks and to wash in. Plus, steam is good for winter ailments."

"If we get sick, steam's good for carrying medicine into the lungs," Bear pointed out.

"In that case, I appoint you in charge of seeing it done," Jakyr said, handing Bear his dinner. "Try to find one where the damp will be carried farther into the caves rather than toward the living space."

"I can do that," Bear nodded.

Amily looked around, and sucked in her breath. "I never would have thought we could do anything like this," she said. "I thought—well, I thought things would be harder than this."

"More primitive, you mean?" Jakyr laughed. "They still will be. When we go out to the villages, Mags and I will still be using the Waystations, and you and Bear and Lena and Lita will be living in the caravan. We just have this very comfortable place to retreat to, and if the weather looks like it's going to close in, we'll leave the village to sort itself out for a time and get ourselves back here."

Amily chuckled a little. "I wouldn't call the caravan primitive."

"You won't have to cook for yourselves if you don't want to, either," Jakyr pointed out. "Mags and I will."

"If you youngsters get on my nerves, I can trade a room at the inn, if there is one, for singing," Lita pointed out. "That's pretty standard for Bards. Well, so is trading music for a space on the hearth, but I think I am going to hold out for rather more than that. I'm not exactly the average traveling musician."

"You have a far better command of music and speech than that. One sharp, scolding sentence from you will have them offering you the inn to go away," Jakyr replied.

"I'd take that as a compliment," Lena put in before Lita could respond. "That sort of command would take a Gift."

"Oh, she has a Gift, all right," Jakyr said. "The Gift of flaying someone's hide from his back with a few words."

Lita was opening her mouth to respond when she was interrupted by the sharp stamping of hooves on stone and two explosive equine snorts. She snapped her mouth shut, as Jakyr's head jerked up.

:*Chosen,*: said an unfamiliar Mindvoice, :*You can stop*

being an ass, or you can walk to the village in the morning. It's up to you.:

Mags hid a smile. He'd bet that Jakyr had forgotten that Mags could Mindhear any Herald or Companion. He'd also bet that Jermayan bloody well remembered.

"Why're we leaving now?" Mags asked Jakyr, as they rode out through the entrance into The Bastion in the thin light of early morning. "I thought we were gonna let the Bards an' Bear go in first."

"I don't think we'll need them," Jakyr scoffed. "They can be just as useful finishing up making our headquarters fully functional. More."

:Someone has his knickers in a knot,: Dallen sniggered.

Mags couldn't disagree. But he also didn't mind seeing what happened if they approached this as if it were just any ordinary Circuit, and not one where the locals considered them intruding strangers. He wanted to see how Jakyr handled that, because that was the hallmark of a good Field Herald.

Mind, Mags was unlikely to be called on to fulfill the duties of a Field Herald . . .

But unlikely things had happened to him in the past.

It took them all morning to get to the Waystation just outside of town. Jakyr had told Mags that the condition of the Waystation, which the locals were required to keep supplied and tended, told you a great deal about the attitude of the locals toward Heralds.

So the condition of the Waystation they approached didn't bode particularly well for their reception.

It was shuttered up tight, and while it wasn't dilapidated, it was not by any means in particularly good shape. The pile of firewood beside it was meager. There was barely enough hay for a few days, and it looked and smelled like last year's.

When they opened the Waystation and checked the supplies, it was clear that no one had restocked this one since the last Herald had come through, about six months ago. There were no human supplies there, only grain for the Companions. Last year's, just like the hay.

"We anticipated this," Jakyr reminded Mags, as indeed they had. There was still enough green browse to satisfy the Companions without resorting to the dubious hay. They had brought their sleeping rolls and plenty of food for several days. They left the Waystation and proceeded to the village.

Shepherd's Crossing was two streets crossing the main road, with a village square. A little girl out herding geese spotted them first, in the distance, and they could see her shooing her birds on ahead of her as she ran to report their arrival.

"I want you to keep your mind open for what you can pick up," Jakyr said, a little grimly, as they watched the little girl disappear into a cottage. "I don't need to tell you what and what not to do, just Mindspeak me if they're hiding something."

Mags nodded. The bells they had hung on their Companions' bridles when they left the Waystation chimed cheerfully; they were the only thing cheerful hereabouts. The sky was overcast, and the village itself was anything but welcoming as they rode into it.

They were met at the village square by an authoritative man and four others. There was no sign of anyone else, not even peeking out windows or doors.

"Gi'ye afternoon, Herald," the man said, his closed face revealing nothing.

"Afternoon, Headman Blakee," Jakyr replied with casual cordiality. "When and where will your people hear the reading?"

"Here and now," the headman said. Jakyr *tsk*ed.

"You know better than that, and I know you know," he said immediately. "The law is the law. All your people above the age of ten years are to hear the reading of the King and Council's Will in the new season. So, when are you gathering them, and where?"

There was some discontented muttering among the men; Jakyr waited while they talked, patient and stolid as an ox, without the least sign of impatience on his face. Mags brought all his shields down and allowed a few thoughts to brush against his, but it was all sullen resentment that every six months some white-clad busybody would show up, interrupt everyone's working day, and waste their time reading out new laws that almost never applied to them.

"Inn, one candlemark," the headman said, finally. "Get this over with."

The inn was obvious by the wheat sheaf tied up over the door. Jakyr nodded acknowledgement, and the Companions moved the few paces over to it.

No one came to take them; Jakyr dismounted and began to lead Jermayan around to the back. Mags followed his example. There was a small lean-to stable and no visible stablehands. Jakyr left Jermayan under saddle but heaped both mangers with hay and a measure of grain—only fair considering the state of things back at that Waystation. Mags brought buckets of fresh water, and the two of them went around front and entered the common room.

The innkeeper took his time in coming over to them, considering there were no other customers at the moment. Jakyr ordered beer for both of them and paid for it on the spot before payment could be demanded.

Technically they were entitled to be served for nothing, and the chit Jakyr would leave would more than cover whatever they got. Obviously, though, the innkeeper would have been unpleasant about the chit. Jakyr anticipated the trouble and cut it off before it arose.

Gradually the room filled. Mags was pleased to see that both men and women were coming. At least the Headman was going to abide by the letter of the law.

At last the Headman reappeared. "This's all my people," he said gruffly to Jakyr, his eyes resentful. "Let's get this over with."

Jakyr stood up and read out the new laws, slowly and carefully, into the silence. Mags sensed some amusement over things that didn't apply to these people—regulations regarding the number of goats that could be pastured on common land, for instance, since a village this far out didn't have or need a commons—and some irritation over things that did, even when the law was a good one, like the yearly marking of borders by a surveyor from the Guard. But he didn't pick up anything that seemed to require Jakyr's attention.

As soon as Jakyr finished and sat down, people began deserting the room so quickly that you would have thought he had an infectious disease. Jakyr kept his face expressionless, but Mags sensed his irritation.

"Is that all, Herald?" the Headman asked, starting to move toward the door himself.

"I would be a poor Herald if it were," Jakyr replied, with the unspoken *and you know that very well,* implied by the silence at the end of his sentence. He let that silence hang for a moment, waiting for the Headman to volunteer, and sighed when he did not. "I'll be needing the records of your judgments for the last six months, if you please. We'll be going over them together."

Well, I don't *please!* the man's thoughts shouted, but with a great sigh, he pulled a large book out of a satchel at his side, and sat down across from Jakyr and Mags.

One by one, with his finger tracing under the words, the Headman read out the date of his judgment and what it was.

"Dannel Brewer beat his wife. Fined four coppers."

"Why four?" Jakyr interrupted. "The law says eight."

"Foreby the bitch threw a stewpot at his head," the Headman growled. "With the stew still in it."

"And why did she throw a stewpot at his head?" Jakyr persisted.

"Foreby he came in drunk from reapin'." The Headman said, exasperated.

"Ah." Jakyr nodded. "I'd have thrown a stewpot at his head, myself. A man can lose a foot, reaping drunk."

The Headman's attitude lightened, an almost imperceptible bit. "Which is why I didno fine her. 'Twas a waste of good stew, but he got no dinner, and she refused to cook after he beat her, so I recked fourpence was enough on top of a empty belly."

"Have they learned better?" Jakyr asked.

The Headman shrugged. "There's no gettin' drunk in that house afore dinner time and no more beatings."

Jakyr nodded. "Next?"

They waded through judgment after judgment, until people began to file back into the inn, obviously wanting their beer and whatever they were accustomed to get with it. Jakyr stood up.

"We'll begin again tomorrow morning, Headman," he said formally. "Thank you for your time."

With that, he headed for the door, with Mags following. It was already dark, and the innkeeper had lit the torch at the front door. They went around back, mounted up, and headed back to the Waystation.

"Anything?" Jakyr asked, as soon as they were clear of the village.

"Nothin' important," Mags replied. "We're city folk with no call to be tellin' them what t'do. They don't like that the Guard's gonna make sure they keep their boundaries straight. Headman thinks you got pride the size of a house, but you just might have a lick or two of sense."

"I'm flattered," Jakyr said dryly. "At least they don't want to poison our beer."

"It's mostly they don't like people outside of their own Lord tellin' 'em what t'do, and they ain't too fond of their own Lord doin' it, neither," Mags reported. "Guard was right. This's gonna be a sticky Circuit."

"I don't mind, so long as it gets no worse." They rode in

silence the rest of the way to the Waystation, with Mags pondering that in his mind.

In the morning, their session with the Headman over small beer and buttered bread was interrupted by a commotion from outside. Jakyr paid no attention to it, and the scattered bits of thought that Mags picked up told him that the commotion was due to the arrival of the others. He expected all four to come into the inn, but it was only Lita and Lena.

The innkeeper greeted them with a *lot* more enthusiasm than he had Mags and Jakyr, and he and Lena engaged in a spirited bargaining session that nevertheless managed to be quiet enough that it didn't interrupt Jakyr and the Headman. When they had struck a bargain to Lita's liking, she and Lena left and came back again with an assortment of instruments. These, they set by the hearth, and the innkeeper fed them.

The Headman's heart was obviously no longer in defending his judgments like a badger defending his sett. He kept eying Lita and Lena as if trying to figure how good they were just from how they were eating their luncheon (which was much better than the one the innkeeper had offered Mags and Jakyr). And instead of making Jakyr pry out every little detail, he was offering it all in one go, almost blurting it out. Mags caught the corner of Jakyr's mouth quirking a little. Whether she meant to or not, Lita was making their job much easier.

The Headman heaved a great sigh of relief as they got to the end of his judgment book, shortly before supper. "I've nothing to complain about, Headman," Jakyr said, as the man closed his book and stowed it away in his satchel. "I'll not be needing to see anyone you called judgment on, unless *they* wish to bring something up before *me.* So I'll be back in the morning to give them the opportunity. Meanwhile, the Crown thanks you for your cooperation."

At any other time, the Headman might have muttered something uncomplimentary about the Crown, but there was a Bard and her Journeyman sitting not four lengths away from him, and it was clear there was going to be some excellent entertainment in less than a candlemark. So he just mumbled something marginally gracious back, and hurried out, the image clear in his mind that he was going to return his judgment book, tell his wife that the children could be given their dinner by the cook, and he was treating her to the inn tonight, and hurry her back here.

Jakyr raised an eyebrow. Mags shook his head slightly. Jakyr relaxed, and before the inn got too crowded, he ordered a meal for both of them. The innkeeper at this point was so beside himself with happiness that his inn was going to be crammed full tonight that he didn't even bother to charge them real money. He accepted the chit absently and hurried back down to his cellar to bring up another barrel of beer. There would be a lot of drinking tonight; throats got dry when people were encouraged to sing along, and when people were choked up with emotion, they tended to drink as well, and a Bard who wanted the good will of the innkeeper would see to it those moments came often.

The food wasn't as good as Jakyr's cooking, but it wasn't anything you had to choke down. The inn slowly filled, and Mags and Jakyr moved to the farthest corner of the room to make way for people for whom this was going to be a rare treat.

:Should we leave?: he Mindsent to Jakyr.

He sensed the effort it took his mentor to reply. :No. Would look odd. Understand?:

After a moment of thought, he did understand. Why would the Heralds leave—presumably for an ill-tended Waystation, isolated outside of town—right when the inn was full of people, warm, they were getting a good meal, and not just one, but *two* Bards were about to perform? People would ask why, and there was no good explanation for leaving like that.

And anything they tried to do to *make* it believable would

only make the whole situation look odder. Shoulder their way out, muttering loudly how much they hated music? Very bad idea. No one would ever believe it. Pretend a sudden headache or illness? Ridiculous. And there was no way, in their Whites and Grays, that they could get out inconspicuously.

The best thing they could do was what they were doing; it was courteous of them to get to the back of the room and allow others a better view. That would reflect well on them. But they should be listening as if they had never heard Lita and Lena play before, and show their appreciation. Not that this would be difficult, after all.

And this would be an excellent way to see if there was anything amiss among the people of this village. Most of them would be here tonight, and if anyone was harboring guilty secrets, given the usual content of the songs that Lita performed, sooner or later something would leak out where he could "see" it. So as they listened to Lita and Lena tune up, he let stray thoughts brush against his mind, looking for ones that were out of the ordinary.

He really didn't find anything. When they weren't being surly and resentful, these were just normal farming folk. There were no dark secrets here. People did stupid, sometimes unkind things. People did things that were a little bad, things that they were ashamed of. People cheated a little on their taxes, got a little greedy, sometimes they pilfered something that wasn't properly theirs, they quarreled, they abused each other (but never to the point that it would call for a Herald's intervention) and were basically just . . . people. A little good, a little bad, mostly just getting by. Not even *close* to the level of evil that Cole Pieters and his sons maintained.

And when they hurt someone, in general, they made it up later, were kind, generous, thoughtful, contrite.

Ordinary folks, a muddle in the middle, just trying to get by with the least amount of pain and the greatest amount of joy. He could not argue with that.

He caught one thought that was directed at him just as the ladies finished tuning and were about to start.

Mags. I know you can hear this. Bear and I did well. We're up at the front. We'll talk back at the caves.

That was Amily. He thought about Mindsending to her to ask if she and Bear had run into anything he and Jakyr should know about, then he realized that if she *had,* she would have found a way to get a message to him. Everyone in the village knew where they were all day, after all.

So he relaxed and stayed alert, but he prepared to enjoy himself.

Might as well enjoy himself. There was a cold ride back to a cold Waystation waiting them at the end of the evening.

At the end of four days, he and Jakyr packed up their things and headed back to The Bastion. He was not sorry to leave that Waystation; it was drafty, and they had to heat stones in the fireplace to warm their beds enough that they could get to sleep at night. The only reason they had eaten well was because Jakyr had been warned to carry a sizable purse with him to buy the things that they should have been offered. So, that was one village. If the rest of them were going to be just as "welcoming," well . . . that cave was going to look very good.

Actually, it was appealing right now. There had been ice on the water in the buckets *inside* this morning. Despite stoking the fire, they'd only gotten the temperature in the Station to the point where the ice melted before they left. He was looking forward to a steam bath as soon as possible. Maybe the next village would be better.

"Are we going back to the cave or on to the next village?" he asked, as they rode away from the little Waystation on the morning of the fourth day. The third day had proceeded without any drama at all. The people of the village had still been standoffish, and the Headman had marginally thawed but still was not what one could call "friendly." But prowling around with his shields down still yielded nothing they needed to concern themselves with. Jakyr summoned everyone together again, announcing that anyone who wanted to appeal a judgment or bring a grievance up could come to him, and still there were no flares of anger, or guilt, or . . . anything, really. Mostly a wish that the Herald would stop interrupting work.

"Back to the cave," Jakyr said with resignation, as the Companions loped their way down the trail to The Bastion. "I see now why the Guard supplied us so well, why I was told to carry money, and why everyone suggested we use The Bastion as the hub of a wheel instead of riding the usual pattern. If all the Waystations are neglected like the last one, we'll have to bring three days' worth of supplies with us to each of them. I wish now we had a pack animal, but I suppose we can carry enough grain and some hay that the Companions will be all right."

:We'll be fine. We have a knack for taking care of ourselves when we need to.:

"Dallen says not to worry about him and Jermayan," he reported.

Jakyr smiled faintly. "Jer said much the same thing. It's true that somehow they seem to be able to find food where not even a goat would be able to browse."

"I'm glad we have Lena and Lita and Bear with us. It will make getting real information out of these people much easier," Mags noted, ducking under a branch. "The people in this district seem to be just as suspicious of authority as the people down around Nikolas's pawn shop."

"Not suspicious of authority," Jakyr corrected, holding aside another branch on the overgrown trail. A moment later, Mags did the same on his side. There was room for them to ride side by side; in fact, there was room for the caravan, and there were faint traces of its wheels on the ground, where the fallen leaves had been crushed into the damp earth. Mags had to wonder, though, how many times they would be able to use it . . . how many of these "roads" would stay passable and for how long. "They are perfectly content with their own people who are in authority, like the Headman. It's outside authority they have a quarrel with. They think that they can do just fine without us. All they see is what we demand of them and conveniently forget what they get from us."

Mags pondered this, then tucked it into the back of his mind. He needed to think about that. It might come in handy if he had some answers to toss back at anyone who objected openly, and he knew enough now about governance to put together quite a little list.

Hazard—or benefit—of having to stand through all those Council meetings disguised as a page.

Jakyr looked over at him and smiled a little more. "You did very well there, Mags. Kept your head. Gave me exactly what I needed when I needed it. If I didn't know better, I'd think you'd done this before." He paused. "That last was a joke."

Mags grinned a little and ducked his head. "Just doing what Nikolas taught me to do; I figured that was mostly what you needed from me. Stay in the background an' just . . . listen. Amily says she has some stuff to tell us, but it ain't bad. An' Lena and Bard Lita did a hell of a job distractin' people."

Jakyr frowned a little but nodded. "Much as I am loath to admit it, the ladies are doing us very good service on this assignment. We *could* do it without them, but it would be harder."

"Well . . . what can they do to help more?" Mags asked. There was a long silence punctuated by the calls of crows, rooks, and starlings. "Because they'll do it, 'specially if I ask Lena and Lena asks Bard Lita."

"I'll think about it," Jakyr said, then changed the subject to what sorts of supplies they would need to pack out from now on and how much the Companions could carry.

The Bastion seemed very quiet without the other four there, but Mags was sure that between them he and Jakyr could probably make enough noise that it wouldn't seem completely empty. Just getting the steam bath going would make plenty of noise, for instance, and he was looking forward to getting a good long one. While Jakyr stoked up the fire, got luncheon ready, and put things to rights, Mags took care of unsaddling the Companions and turning them loose.

He headed into the cave with every intention of first starting rocks to heat in the fire for the steam bath, then getting a book and settling down to read until the others returned. But he never got that chance.

"Mags, go sit down a moment," Jakyr ordered, as soon as he had cleared the entrance and gotten down into the living area. The Herald's voice made it an order, and Mags heart dropped. What had he done wrong? Or was—was it something that he hadn't done? Omission was as bad, or worse, as commission . . .

He sank down on one of the rugs, and pulled his knees up to his chest, quaking inside with dread. Because surely something terrible had happened, or he himself had *done* something terrible. Or—not done something critical. Or overlooked something important.

Jakyr had already started a fire in the firepit, and it was slowly warming the area. Now he dropped carelessly down on the cushion next to the one Mags was using and wrapped his cloak around himself. "Well, now. This should have been your father's little lecture to give. Or Nikolas, but that would make things altogether impossibly awkward, wouldn't it?" Jakyr's square face twisted in an ironic smile. "It hasn't escaped anyone that you and Amily have put your sleeping gear together and you're using the same cave. So, how far has it gotten? I'm not accusing you, not even close, I just want to know what stage you two are at."

This was not how he had expected that question to come up. Or the direction he had expected it to go in.

"It hasn't!" Mags blurted, all the things he had been planning to say flying right out of his head now that the moment was here. "It hasn't gotten anywhere! I mean, we been kissin' and gettin' ourselves all up and bothered, but—we ain't done anything yet!"

Jakyr looked taken entirely aback by the confession. "Uh . . . why? I mean, why not? You love each other, you're both certainly old enough to know what you're getting into. I would have expected you to be—well—" For the first time, ever, Mags saw Jakyr flush with something other than anger.

" 'Cause I dunno what t' do, an' I don' want to hurt her," Mags choked out. There was the crux of it, really. He loved Amily, he knew that the first time always hurt, and—how could he love someone and still want to do something that hurt her? Besides, the only sort of sex he'd seen with the mine kids had been . . . mindless. Like a couple of dogs just pounding away because they could, with no thought in it. "I mean, the mine kids was always up in each other when they got old enough an' they wasn't completely dead tired or starvin', but I don' want it t'be like that!"

"Huh. Well, well. As the saying goes, 'Two virgins in a bed is one virgin too many,' I suppose. This is certainly nothing I expected to hear from you." Jakyr got even redder. "I'm at a loss—there goes *my* planned speech about the proper precautions and all of that."

"Lena tol' Amily all them things and give her th' herbs. She's been takin' 'em all along," said Mags, now blushing painfully himself. From feeling as if he were a little'un who'd been caught doing something wrong, he had gone to feeling like someone who *should* have been doing something but didn't know how. Which, of course, was the point. All the other Trainees who were . . . keeping company with girls never seemed to have any difficulty keeping everybody pleased. "Bear wanted her t' do it anyway, on account of I guess it was gonna help her heal faster. I jest . . . I dunno how t' make things good for a girl . . ."

He just could not go on. He just sat there, feeling hot and hideously embarrassed. Why couldn't they have lessons in these things? Why couldn't Dallen at least have helped? It's not as if he would dare to make himself look stupid in front of the rest of the fellows for not knowing something so basic!

"It's not the sort of thing you could talk about to your friends, is it?" Jakyr said sympathetically, echoing his thoughts. He crossed his legs and leaned back against the hay-stuffed cushion. "Or Dean Caelen. He's not supposed to know that you Trainees have that sort of interest in each other. It keeps things simpler."

"Or *anybody* at the Collegium," Mags pointed out. "I mean, Amily's Nikolas's daughter, and people were already watchin' us like . . . I dunno, it's just that everybody was always watchin' us, and anybody I mighta been able to talk to was one of the ones watchin'!" He stared at Jakyr in something like despair. "No matter who I talked to, it was gonna get back to Nikolas, an' then what?"

"Bear?" Jakyr ventured. "Bear is not just your friend, he's a Healer, and he's a married fellow. Couldn't he help?"

Mags shuddered. "Even worse. Either he'd go over all Healer, and that'd not be a lotta help because he'd just talk about how this part fits inta that part and not give me any good idea about how to make her happy, or he'd get more embarrassed than me. And that'd take a lot, t'get more embarrassed than me, but he'd do it."

As if he couldn't help himself, Jakyr started chuckling. "Oh, poor Mags. I don't know how your situation could be made more difficult. I really don't. On the whole, coming out here like this is probably the best thing that could have happened for you two. You are at least out from under the eyes of all but three of those would-be guardians of Amily's virtue. Unless

Dallen is also on your side, which would make it two would-be guardians."

"An' now you're gonna—" Mags began, feeling sure now that Jakyr was going to tell him that he and Amily had to separate their sleeping arrangements and start behaving in a chaste manner.

But Jakyr interrupted him. "No, in fact, I am not, and I just told Jermayan to shut his hay-hole about it." His chuckle deepened. "He was very offended for as long as it took him to read me a lecture on responsibility. So the last two dragons of virtue have been vanquished."

"Uh—so—" Mags began.

"The upshot is that despite the fact that I have been trying to squirm out of acting like a parent to you, I am going to have to act—hmm. Come to think of it, this probably isn't going to be acting like a parent to you." Jakyr's face turned thoughtful, as the fire crackled and hissed cheerily, and a gentle warmth crept over Mags, making him relax a little. "Only a very careless father would be inclined to tell you what I am going to tell you. I suppose I am about to act like the disreputable uncle who everyone fears to leave the boys with because he encourages them to drink distilled spirits, stay up late, and do more than merely kiss girls."

"Uh . . . what?" Mags replied, utterly bewildered now.

"I am going," Jakyr said, leaning toward Mags, his eyes dancing with laughter, "to tell you how to please a woman."

Mags thought for a moment his face had caught fire, because surely it couldn't burn like that without some outside help.

When Mags got over the worst attack of embarrassment he had ever suffered in his life and somehow managed to get his head wrapped around the idea of treating Jakyr's help just like any other lesson, he listened closely, did *not* exclaim several times—as he was tempted to—"you're joking, right?!"—and when he was in the least confused, asked questions until he wasn't confused anymore.

Jakyr, for his part, kept strictly on the subject and did not, as he often did under other circumstances, wander off into reminiscence.

It was . . . highly instructive.

And Mags was very, very glad for it all. He'd known the first time was going to hurt Amily; it always had with the mine kiddies. He hadn't wanted to hurt her, or at least, he'd wanted something good to happen beforehand so she wouldn't be revolted and not want to do it anymore when it did hurt her. As it happened, Jakyr had several ideas on that score.

They talked—or, rather, Jakyr talked and Mags listened—for so long that both of them were starving. Last night they had put in an order with the village baker for bread, they had gotten it first thing before they rode out, and Mags had taken the bulging saddlebags to the kitchen area. Jakyr made the simplest and quickest possible meal for them out of bread and cheese and some apples, and he kept talking. Finally, it seemed that he'd managed to exhaust even *his* considerable knowledge of women and how to please them. Physically, at least. Mags was grateful that Jakyr made no attempt to tell him how to please a woman in any other way than physically, since current observation would suggest that Jakyr was not a very good source for that information. They finally finished eating in—at least in Mags' case—slightly embarrassed silence.

"Now, if I were you," Jakyr said, when they had both finished and were sipping lukewarm tea. "What I would do is check how sound carries from where your sleeping spot is set up. If you haven't already, that is. I can promise you that there is nothing more uncomfortable for someone than to hear the sounds of someone *else* enjoying him- or herself carnally."

Then he added dryly, "Except, perhaps, discovering that your own adventures were keeping other people awake."

Mags shook his head. "Never thought on it," he said, blushing all over again. "I was thinking more *where's warm* than *where is it we won't—*"

"Well, do. Make sure sound won't carry or echo to the rest of us. If it does . . . well, might try deeper into this cavern. Lena and Bear have the walls of the caravan to keep sound from traveling, but we have stone walls, and as a miner, you know how those echo." Jakyr shrugged. "You might even think about going to another cave entirely. It's not as if you are going to be cold for very long with what you two intend to get up to. There's still plenty of bedding . . . the only drawback I can see is that it's going to start snowing soon, and when that happens, a trek through the snow to come and go is going to get unpleasant."

"If you don' mind, I'll get a lantern and see what I can find now," he said, getting very tired of blushing.

"Please do. Remember that young love gets tedious in a great hurry when it wakes up the poor fellow sleeping solitary—or keeps him from going to sleep in the first place." Jakyr got up. "I'll see about a proper dinner. I don't think we can expect the others until tomorrow at this point, so it will just be you and me."

Mags nodded, scrambled to his feet, and got a lantern.

There was one thing true about sound in a cave or a mine: If you could hear it from where you were, someone *out there* could hear your noise from where he was. So he knew he wasn't going to have to further embarrass himself by calling out to Jakyr, "Can you hear me?" All he had to do was to listen for Jakyr's rather noisy cooking. Jakyr liked to sing while he cooked, especially if there was no one immediately around, and most especially if Lita was far, far away. Probably because Lita would have made fun of him. That was going to be useful tonight.

Venturing down what looked like a promising passage, he discovered that it must have served as a kind of dormitory, for the sleeping nooks were spaced along the walls on both sides, more or less evenly. The tunnel itself had a low ceiling, which kept sound from bouncing around too much, and it had a layer of thick sand on the floor, which also muffled noise. Someone had taken thought for sound carrying to the main room as well—or, possibly, *from* it—because the tunnel kept turning, like a snake. He wondered if this passage hadn't been where the occupants bedded down their youngsters, once they were old enough to sleep away from their parents safely. It would make a lot of sense in a communal space to put all the little ones together with a supervisor or two.

The passage made a hairpin turn, then another, and he realized he could hear absolutely nothing from the main room. With glee, he examined each of the nooks in this new section until he found the best one. It actually had a ledge all around the sleeping hollow where they could put things and a hole in the wall that surely had been intended for a hook or support for a lantern. That seemed to indicate his guess had been right, and this was the sleeping place of one of the older supervising—beings? No way of telling if these nooks had been for lizards or humans.

He spent the rest of the time moving everything from the existing nook to this new one, adding more hay and another feather comforter, then went out to the smaller woodpile inside the cave and rummaged until he found a forked stick of about the right diameter to hammer into that hole in the wall.

"Listen for me whacking on somethin' would you?" he asked Jakyr as he passed. Jakyr nodded absently, intent on something he was simmering. "I'm gonna pound a lantern hook inta the wall, and if you cain't hear it, you won't hear nothin' from there."

It wasn't easy to drive the branch home without ruining it, but after a couple of false starts, Mags got it hammered in securely enough it would actually take his weight as he tried to pull himself up off the floor with it. The lantern hung perfectly on it; it would certainly take an earthquake or worse to dislodge it. Pleased with the results, he went back out to the main cave. Jakyr looked up at him as he entered.

"Just in time, the soup is ready. When are you going to do your hammering?" the Herald asked.

"Done," Mags smirked, and took the bowl and the bread that Jakyr was holding out to him. "If you didn't hear *that,* 'specially the swearin' I did when I hit my hand, you ain't gonna hear nothin'."

"Congratulations," Jakyr said, with no more than faint irony. "And now you will also be spared Lita's snoring. Perhaps I should go looking for a similar nook."

Since Lita had not snored once to Mags' knowledge, he just held his peace and ate his soup. Jakyr made the most excellent soup. Somehow no two batches ever ended up tasting the same.

"What's the plan for the next town?" he asked instead. "Let Bards and Healers go first, instead of us, and feel the place out for us?"

Jakyr paused in his eating, as if that hadn't occurred to him. "That's not a bad thought," he said. "Provided we can get her Bardic Majesty to agree with it, I like the plan."

Mags smiled to himself. If there was one thing he was certain of, it was that he knew exactly how to get Lita to agree.

Even if it meant he was going to get one less night with Amily than he really wanted . . .

"Lemme say somethin' about it, then you come up with all kinds of ideas why that won't work," he suggested. "Lita's bound t'object, you fight a bit with her, then let 'er get 'er way."

Jakyr eyed him favorably. "Mags, you are a manipulative young man. You have unplumbed depths to you. I like it."

It had been a long ride, and Mags was tired. He was also keen to try the new sleeping nook and make sure it was going to be comfortable and warm enough for Amily. He volunteered to wash the dishes and did so; Jakyr retired to his own nook before he had finished, so he was left to bank the fire and make sure all was safe until morning. The Companions had come in by themselves, of course, so after making sure they were warmly blanketed and had water and fodder, he took a lantern and went to his new bed.

It must have been fine after he'd warmed it with his body, because he didn't remember anything past starting to relax in the silence and the dark.

He went out hunting while they waited for the others to arrive, and a plump young buck with only two points to his antlers made too tempting of a target to turn down. A clean shot through the eye took him straight to the ground, and Dallen turned up wearing a spare horse-collar so that Mags could lash together a rough drag of branches to bring the carcass home with little effort. Alerted by Jermayan, Jakyr, clad in a set of old, faded clothing that was *other* than Whites, was ready at a spot in the valley where there was a tree big enough to take the deer's weight. With Dallen's help, they hauled the buck into the tree, head-down, bled him out, and butchered him. Dallen and Jermayan, meanwhile, went to stand watch at and outside the entrance, to guard against trouble and watch for the caravan's return.

It was Mags' first time at butchering anything bigger than a bird, and he found it far more fascinating than repulsive. He and the other mine-kiddies had eaten what they could get or catch either entirely raw, half-burned and half-raw, or entirely burned; it had depended entirely on whether they could sneak their catches into a fire or not and for how long. Several of them had tried to tan rabbit hides into something they could use for shoes, but the results had been less than successful.

Watching Jakyr however, and working under his direction, Mags developed great respect for the butcher's work.

Jakyr thriftily saved the blood in a couple of the biggest pots they had, then made a smallish cut in the belly of the deer, removing the entrails carefully. "I'd just as soon not use the stomach or intestines," he explained, as he set them aside, absolutely intact. "We haven't got a good way to make sure they're clean enough to eat safely."

Mags nodded; perhaps the others might have been revolted by the mere idea, but back at the mine, those rejected organs would have fed six or seven kiddies, and some of them might not even have bothered to try to clean out the contents first. Jakyr told him where to bury them; he followed the directions and returned to the butchering.

Once the rest of the organs were out, Jakyr carried them and the pots of blood back to the cave. He came back just long enough to show Mags how to start skinning, then returned to the cave. "I'll be back as soon as I get the stew started," he called over his shoulder.

I expect I better not tell 'em where the meat in the stew came from, Mags thought, as he painstakingly started the task of separating the hide from the hind legs with tiny, careful cuts of the extremely sharp knife that Jakyr had left with him.

He had the hide stripped off both legs and was starting on the torso when Jakyr returned, looking quite pleased— probably with the progress of his stew. Mags was very much looking forward to it. "Not bad," the Herald said, examining the work. "You'll get better, but not bad."

As the two of them worked together, Jakyr corrected Mags until Mags was working almost as smoothly as he was. "Fortunately, we have oak trees right here," the Herald said with satisfaction. "And plenty of salt for the first step of curing. I was always taught to waste nothing of an animal you take down."

At just that moment, Mags felt something cold on his

cheek. He looked up, to see tiny snowflakes coming down out of the sky. Jakyr followed his gaze and grinned.

"Could not have come at a better time. We won't have to worry about any of this going bad, nor about smoking or salting it—although I probably will be smoking it piecemeal over time."

"When did you learn all this?" Mags asked, curious now. He hadn't taken Jakyr for much of a hunter. Just showed how much he didn't know!

"What, did you think I was brought up in the city?" Jakyr mocked. "Our inn was in a little village just like the one we left. Father would never pay for anything he could do himself, so he butchered his own animals, and we used *everything*. Nothing went to waste. He'd have had a right fit over me burying the guts, let me tell you. The intestines would have gone for sausages and the stomach for tripe and onions. I just don't have a good place to properly clean and wash them." He sighed. "Too bad, because I make a very, very good tripe and onions."

They worked together in silence except for Jakyr directing Mags' knife. With two of them working together, they got the hide off and salted, the meat stripped from the carcass and packed away where it would get and stay good and cold and out of reach of vermin, and some of the smaller bones stewing, crammed into a stockpot to make broth by the time they were hungry. Jakyr added the tongue and handfuls of the diced scraps to the stewpot; they both cleaned up and changed. Jakyr insisted that they carry the bloodstained clothing to the cave where the bathing basin was, soak it in the cold water, and leave it there, weighted down with rocks. "Give it a day or two and the blood should be gone," he said, "And if it's not, we'll scrub with some salt and that will be that."

"Huh." Mags scratched his head. "Useful—"

"Usually in every couple of villages there's someone running a laundry who knows how to clean Whites—but they get very upset when you bring them Whites with dried blood on them," Jakyr said with a laugh. "I learned how to take the blood out first to keep my head from being threatened."

:*Caravan is nearby,*: Dallen said at that moment in Mags' head. Judging by the way Jakyr's head had come up at about the same time, Jermayan had warned his Chosen as well.

The caravan clattered in through the entrance in a swirl of tiny flurries, the vanners looking very happy to see a place they associated with food, shelter, warmth, and peace. Lita was driving, as usual, and brought the whole rig right into the cave, backing the caravan into place with a skill that made Mags feel great envy. Mags ran up to them, with Jakyr strolling at a much more leisurely pace behind him.

Lita tossed Mags the reins, and jumped down off the driver's seat, her eyes widening as she caught a whiff of the savory stew. "Blessed gods, what is that heavenly smell?" she exclaimed, as Bear, followed by Lena and Amily, popped out of the door. They didn't wait for Mags to unharness the vanners and lower the stairs, they jumped right down after Lita.

"We got a deer," Mags said, and then was occupied with welcoming Amily, leaving the rest of the explanation to Jakyr. Bear knew better than to lift the lid on the stewpot, having had his knuckles rapped hard by Jakyr the last time he'd tried, but he did poke at the pot where the bones were simmering away, looking interested.

"Huh. Broth," he said. "I wonder if it's gonna be as good as beef broth."

"Probably," said Jakyr. "It should actually be richer than beef broth. Venison makes good broth. Why do you ask?"

Mags and Amily got to work unharnessing the vanners, wiping them down, blanketing them, and giving them fodder.

"It'd be damned useful if we could preserve some, somehow," Bear pointed out. "In case someone gets sick."

Jakyr considered that idea, then shook his head. "I'll try, but we haven't got a lot of jars I can seal easily, and I can't think of any way of keeping vermin out," he said with regret. "Don't worry, though; if someone starts to get sick, we can pot a rabbit or a bird and make broth out of the whole thing."

"What's in that stew?" Lita demanded, and then, when she saw a look of faintly malicious mischief cross over Jakyr's face, she waved her hands frantically. "No, no! I changed my mind! I don't want to know! I want to enjoy my food in ignorant bliss!"

For a moment it looked as if Jakyr might tell her anyway, but he glanced at Lena and Amily and shrugged. "It should be ready, anyway. Good thing you made it in before nightfall; running that trail in the dark could have been a hazard."

They queued up for bowls of the thick, dark stew, and chunks of bread to go with it. It had a rich, wild taste to it, and the bits of organ were tasty, oddly familiar, oddly unfamiliar in his mouth. Whatever odd, metallic flavor that the blood might have given to it, Jakyr had neatly disguised with seasoning.

"So I was thinking," Mags said, after he'd had a couple of mouthfuls, "I was wondering if maybe you lot ought to go out ahead of us this time. That way you could sorta scout the village and let us know what's what once we get there."

Jakyr frowned. "I don't think that's all that good a notion, Mags," he said—and Lita predictably cut him off.

"Of course you wouldn't. You don't trust us to be able to suss out the situation," she said with scorn. "I've been gauging audiences since before you were in Whites, Jak. I think it's a splendid idea."

She paused to inhale a few more bites of stew, and Jakyr winked at Mags while her attention was still on her bowl. Then he launched into his counterargument, an argument that was as frail as a cobweb and just as easily destroyed. He put up a brave mock fight, though. They went through two bowls of stew each before he put down his bowl, threw up his hands, and said, "Have it your way! You will anyway! It's all about you winning!"

"As if it wasn't as much about *you* winning, you hypo-crite!" she snarled back, and they were off, this time with some real vitriol.

The others hastily gathered up the dishes, worked together to get them quickly washed and put up, took lanterns and retreated—Lena and Bear to the caravan and Mags and Amily to their sleeping nook.

"Where are we going?" Amily asked in puzzlement, as Mags led her by the hand past the now-empty spot they had used, and deeper into the cave.

"It's a surprise," Mags said, and chuckled. "Or maybe not, since you saw we ain't got the same place."

"Ooh," was all she said, and let him lead her down the twisting passage. The arguing voices faded away as they made the first turn, and after the second, they could not be heard at all.

He hung up the lantern on the hook and was pleased with her reaction to the new bed. Now . . . to follow Jakyr's instructions.

Although there was one thing they were certainly not going to do. Jakyr had suggested that he start undressing her slowly, caressing her and kissing her as he did, but she was already stripping away her clothing and huddled under the feather comforters in next to no time, and he didn't blame her. It was cold enough to make his teeth chatter, and he was glad to follow her example, blow out the lantern, and join her under the covers.

This was the first time they had ever been undressed to-gether. He felt excited, and awkward, and hot and cold all at the same time. But he kept his head and did as Jakyr had suggested, starting with the same sort of kissing and cuddling they'd done all along. Then he started doing the other things that Jakyr suggested. Some things had made sense and some hadn't—but all of them seemed to work just fine, and her little sounds started making him hot and things almost got out of hand—until he let down his barriers and concentrated on picking up little bits of thought from her.

He was pretty sure that if he had been an Empath and was feeling what she was feeling, that wouldn't have gotten the results he wanted. But having to concentrate on listening with his mind, that was work, and it calmed that unruly part of him right down and let him work on getting her to that big happy place Jakyr had told him about.

Then her thoughts went all incoherent, and she began to gasp, and all of her shuddered and arched under his ministrations, and with great satisfaction he knew that he had done it.

He held her and cuddled her while she panted and slowly relaxed, then started it all again. Except that this time, now that she'd been taken care of, it was going to end in his turn.

Just when he was about to make his move, she wiggled and got herself under him. That made him pause. He couldn't see her in the thick cave dark, but he whispered to her, "Are you sure?"

"Yes," she whispered, and *yes* said her body under his and *yes, yes,* her hands and her lips, and so he did what he'd been dreaming about for months and months.

And he hurt her; he heard her gasp, and it wasn't a gasp of pleasure, but at this point that part of him that was not to be reasoned with had the bit in its teeth and it was going to gallop away to what it wanted regardless. He couldn't have stopped it and, really, didn't want to. He'd pleasured himself, of course; what fellow didn't once that part became aware of what it was for and how good some things felt—but, oh, this was better, better, so much *better!*

And then it was his turn to gasp and groan and shudder and then collapse over to the side, shaking.

But when he could think again, he remembered what Jakyr had told him. *"After you've hurt her, make her feel good again."* So even though he would have liked to fall right asleep, he kissed her and cuddled and caressed her, and finally the plaintive little breaths and the pain-thoughts turned into pleasure again, and he made her happy.

And then they slept.

With a wink at Mags, over a breakfast of oatmeal cooked in the deer broth—which was surprisingly good—Jakyr suggested mildly to Lita that they might want to start right away for the next village. But this time Lita didn't exactly rise to the bait. Maybe she had figured out she'd been manipulated last night; after all, she was anything but a stupid woman.

"Tomorrow is soon enough," she said. "We won't be taking the caravan anymore; we'll be riding double on the vanners. With snow in the air, we can't take the chance the caravan will get stuck somewhere."

"For once, I agree with you," Jakyr said, and that was that. Mags and Amily had a second night together, which went even better than the previous one, and in the morning, with Lena up behind Amily and Bear up behind Lita, the four of them headed off at a brisk trot for the next village on the Circuit. He hoped she wasn't still sore so that riding the wide-barreled vanner was going to hurt her, but she seemed cheerful enough as they trotted off.

Mags and Jakyr gave them a half-day head start, which would become a full day after they overnighted at the next Waystation. Jakyr spent the morning bottling up as much of the broth as he could, which was not nearly as much as he wanted, and cleaned the kettle, while Mags secured the site for another five or six days of absence. Then, after a good lunch, they were off.

But as they approached the Waystation, they immediately knew that something was . . . not right.

There was a smell of woodsmoke in the air, and there shouldn't have been anyone around to build a fire. *Maybe* the scent had traveled from the village, but the wind was in the wrong direction, and that seemed unlikely.

They approached the Waystation cautiously. Unlike the previous station, this one was not only in good repair, it was in *suspiciously* good repair. The roof was newly thatched, every stone in place, and all the woodwork repaired and stained. And, yes, there was a very thin curl of smoke coming up from the chimney.

They looked at each other. "Someone's moved in and is helping themselves," Jakyr said, with a hint of a growl in his voice.

"I thought that was against the law," Mags replied.

"It is. And we're going to put a stop to this. But whoever is using it might be armed, so we'll treat this as if an enemy had taken it." At Jakyr's nod, they both dismounted and turned the Companions loose. The Companions ghosted through the trees, somehow becoming practically invisible, and scouted the area around the Station.

:Nothing out here. And we don't scent anyone in the Station itself,: Dallen said. Mags and Jakyr glanced at each other, and Jakyr nodded, but they both kept their swords in their hands as they eased up to the door.

Someone had modified it so that it had a real latch and a lock instead of the string latch that Waystations were supposed to have. Jakyr made a face, but Mags waved a hand at him.

"I got this," he said, and sheathed his sword, taking a slim dagger from his belt instead. Of course, if he had known that he was going to have to pick a lock, he would have brought the set of lockpicks with him. But who could have predicted that someone would have helped themselves to a Waystation?

Mags had been taught by an expert, a member of the City Watch who'd once been a thief. He himself was by no means an expert, but this was a very crude lock, and that was being generous; it yielded to his efforts long before Jakyr got impatient.

When they opened the door, it was to find that the unknown someone had not only helped himself to the Station, he had moved in, lock, stock, and barrel.

One of the bed boxes had become a curtained bed. The other had been turned into a storage chest, complete with a lid. The storage cupboard had been joined by a second as well as a wardrobe. There was a table with a basin and a pitcher, a little table with a chair, a rug on the floor, a chamber pot in the corner, and very little room left in which to move.

There was also a pot simmering over the fire in the fireplace, which suggested that the occupant could be expected to return at any—

:He's coming up the path,: Dallen warned. Mags and Jakyr positioned themselves on either side of the door, weapons ready. They waited, scarcely breathing. The door swung open.

Before the man could react to the fact that "his" door was now unlocked and unlatched, the two were on him, Jakyr's sword at his throat, as Mags snatched away the ax in his hand.

Now, any reasonable person, at least in Mags' estimation, who found himself confronted by an angry Herald in full Whites—scarcely someone whom you could mistake for anything *but* a Herald—would acknowledge the fact that he'd been caught red-handed doing something he shouldn't and surrender.

This fellow was evidently not a reasonable person.

He tried to knock the sword aside and went for Jakyr. Jakyr was handicapped by the fact that he really didn't want to hurt the fellow, and the fight that ensued, though short, turned into something rather brutal. By the time it was over, the chair and table were good for nothing but kindling, the pottery in one of the cupboards and the basin and pitcher were shards, Jakyr had a black eye and bruises on his throat, and the only reason that the fight had ended at all was because Mags had managed to get behind the man and brain him with the flat of his own ax.

After they'd bound him and shoved him into a corner, swept out the broken pottery and thrown the ruined furniture— and the lid on the bed box—into the woodpile, Jakyr woke the interloper up with a rude pail of ice-cold water from the little well to the face.

The man spluttered into consciousness, tried to rise, discovered he was bound, and glowered at them.

"I'm trying to be charitable here," Jakyr said carefully, "but it's damned difficult. *What* are you doing in a Herald's Waystation?"

"What are you doing in my house?" the man roared back.

"It's not your damned house!" shouted Jakyr.

"Wait!" Mags interrupted, holding up a hand. "This ain't gonna get us nowhere. Lemme Truth-Spell 'im."

Jakyr paused and blinked at Mags. "You're right. We don't have to get consent for the Truth Spell when we catch someone breaking the law." He waved at their captive. "Do it, Mags."

It was Dallen, not one of the teachers at the Collegium, who had taught Mags the Truth Spell. Dallen had taught Mags practically everything he knew about his Gift, and since Mags had an exceptionally powerful Gift of Mind-magic, Mags could lay the strongest possible variation of the Truth Spell on a miscreant—or someone who simply wished his story to be believed. This version could compel the truth out of the person it was placed on, and more. It would compel them to tell the *whole* truth, blurt it out in fact, without needing specific questioning.

This would be the first time Mags had ever put the Truth Spell on someone who wasn't a fellow student, and it felt very odd to be doing so. Even odder was the part of the spell where you concentrated on a pair of . . . eyes. He actually *saw* the eyes hovering over the miscreant's head for a moment, and from Jakyr's start, so did the Herald.

Then they blinked out, and the blue aura of the Spell enveloped the man.

Mags could not help thinking, though, as Jakyr moved in and took his place to question the man, about the eyes. Because the assassin's magician who had gone mad had babbled about eyes watching him. Were these . . . the same eyes?

He didn't get a chance to think about it for long, however, as Jakyr barked, "What are you doing here?"

"This is my home!" the man snarled back. "My father gave it to me! What the hell do you *think* I'm doing here?"

"Now what do we do?" Mags asked aloud. The man had finished ranting, he had dismissed the Truth Spell, and they had gagged him because he still kept ranting about "his house" and "his rights." He was sitting on the edge of the empty bed box, and stared up at Jakyr, hoping that the senior Herald had an answer.

"I confess I am at a loss," said Jakyr, staring down at the man, who glared back at him and issued muffled and incoherent sounds from behind his gag. "We clearly have a problem here. This should not have happened. At all. Someone at that village—what is it?"

"Therian," Mags said, consulting the map. He wasn't surprised that the name had flown out of Jakyr's mind; it had gone from his as well. What should have been a routine, if somewhat irritating, Circuit was turning into something unexpected and ugly.

"Someone at Therian thinks he has the right to give away Crown property, and I will be unsurprised to discover it is the

212

Headman, given the general attitude out here." Jakyr paced back and forth—even though there wasn't a lot of room to pace in. The man continued to glare. Jakyr continued to ignore him. "He couldn't do that unless one of two conditions obtains. Either the rest of his village doesn't know, or the rest of his village is convinced they don't have to obey the law. If it's the first, we can probably come down like the Wrath of the Gods Themselves and frighten them all into appropriate behavior—probably even get the Headman dismissed. If it's the second, we have a real problem on our hands. Right now we don't know which condition is the one we are about to face." He paced some more. "I'm minded to turn right back around and get the Guard. Except that might make things worse."

Mags thought about this very hard. He could see how getting the Guard would make things worse. The whole idea was that villages were to enforce the laws on themselves. But if they brought the Guard into it—there would be even more resentment, if not outright rebellion, and there would be no way to enforce the laws without *keeping* a detachment of the Guard there. "How about if I sneak down there, get hold of Amily, and find out what they've learned?"

Jakyr stopped pacing. "That seems to be our best option. Meanwhile, I am going to help myself to dinner here, since our thief has provided it." It was Jakyr's turn to glare down at the man, who was uncowed. "Perhaps a lecture delivered while I eat might bang some sense into his head."

Mags nodded and went outside. Jakyr would probably need his Companion soon, but Jermayan couldn't be left to stand in the cold, unprotected. He threw a blanket over Jermayan, but did not unsaddle him, and mounted Dallen. A brisk gallop through bleak forest got them to the edge of cultivated land and within sight of the village just about sunset. There was a glare of light on the western horizon, and the sky was a deep and sullen crimson.

There he dismounted near a hedgerow and used it as cover

to get into the village itself without being seen, slipping along the bushes bent over, so as not to show above the top. When the hedgerow ended, he crouched and peeked around the bottom of it, assessing the two or three dozen buildings of the village. He found the inn quickly enough by the wheat sheaf carved into a board above the door and by the fact that it was roughly twice the size of any of the other buildings in the town. Making sure there was no one about to spot him, he ran to the shelter of the nearest house, put his back to the wall and edged toward what passed for a street, ran across to the inn, and slipped in behind it. Still keeping his back to the wall, and moving as quietly as possible, he slid over to the attached stable—an actual stable, this time, a not merely a lean-to shelter. As he expected, the stable held the vanners, who regarded him with benign indifference as he hid himself between them. There were no other horses here, but the fact that this inn actually had a real stable told him that it got a respectable amount of traffic, probably in the warmer part of the year.

Then he crouched down in the straw between the horses, closed his eyes and sought the familiar sense of Amily's mind. As he searched for her, he tried to make note of the contents of stray thoughts, and at least he didn't sense any overt hostility. Although when the villagers discovered how they had treated that interloper, that could change in a heartbeat.

He found her; the connection seemed a lot stronger between them now, and once again he wondered if she had a Gift that was somehow late in coming, and whether it was slowly awakening now that he was "talking" to her. *:Amily. We got problems. I'm in the stable,:* he sent to her. He caught her startled assent and the general sense that she was coming to him.

He waited, crouched in the straw, relatively comfortable in the warmth being radiated from the two vanners. It was hard to tell in the darkness whether the stable was kept up well or not—but it certainly didn't smell poorly kept. Even an empty stable that hasn't been mucked out regularly had a stink of ammonia and old droppings to it. From where he crouched, he could see the door and the yard outside it clearly. After what was probably a quarter-candlemark, he spotted someone hurrying to the stable in the thin moonlight. As soon as the girl—he could tell it was a girl by the shape—got close, he heard Amily call, softly, in the direction of the stable.

"Mags?"

"Over here, 'tween the vanners," he called back softly. She waved once and joined him, dropping down into the box stall with him so that no one coming in would see her.

"What did you mean by problems?" she asked breathlessly. "I hurried as fast as I could. I was helping Bear with the local farrier and a patient. A human patient. The farrier is the closest thing they have to a healer here. Except for the inn, there isn't much. It's all herders and farmers. From what I gathered, Lord Hallathon doesn't even claim them, they're too far outside his holding."

"When we got to the Waystation, some fella had took it over," Mags explained. "We caught 'im, and he acted like we was the ones at fault. Said his pa had given it to him."

The straw rustled as Amily startled. "Wait—what?" Amily replied. "But that's illegal!"

"Well, aye. We know that, but it seems like the fella we caught either don't know it or don't care. So we kinda need to know just how far this village has gone afore we come ridin' in with him all trussed up like a hen fer the pot." Mags rubbed his temple unhappily. " 'Cause if most of this village reckons that Crown laws don't hold, we could have ourselves a bigger piece of trouble than we thought. Reckon the people to find out are Lena and Lita. Lita mostly. If she ain't found out already."

"I'll go find out," Amily said immediately, and stood up and ran off before he could say anything else. Not that there was anything much more to say, really. That left Mags still crouching in the straw, unhappy, and not getting any happier as the time passed. He was cold, he was uncomfortable, he was hungry, and he was acutely aware that he was surrounded by a village full of people who might very well consider *him* some sort of criminal.

Not the most pleasant situation to be in at best. It was certainly not one he had envisioned himself to be in before they started this trip.

Course, I could be trussed up in a wagon bein' kidnapped again, 'bout to be drugged, and turned into some sort of . . . I dunno . . . shell for a ghost?

There certainly was that. Given the options, this current situation was better. It wasn't as if, even if the worst happened, he and Jakyr couldn't mount up on their Companions and be out of there before anyone could blink. A handful of villagers, however angry, were not going to be able to prevail against a Companion in full fighting mode. Since the Bards, Bear, and Amily weren't obviously connected with Heralds and had already been welcomed, they would be safe enough. The villagers were hardly likely to pursue as far as The Bastion, and they could continue on down to the Guardpost at need, bringing back retribution.

But he didn't want to do that. Jakyr didn't want to do that either. That would, in many ways, just make things a whole lot worse. He wanted some way to work this out so that the fools who had done this realized how much they had transgressed and how much was at stake when they lost. Which they would. Bringing an armed Guard troop down on a bunch of poorly armed villagers—or even a bunch of *well*-armed villagers—would earn no credit for the Crown. Valdemar governed by cooperation, not by repression. Mags wanted this lot of empty heads and grabby hands to figure out they were the ones in the wrong.

He wanted them, in short, to figure out on their own that they'd been idiots.

Wish I could con 'em like Jakyr conned Lita; go to give 'em what they think they want, an' they quick find out they don't want it—

Amily returned about a candlemark later. "Lita's trying to find out what she can. She hasn't seen any overt rebellion; these people are pretty much like the last village. She thinks that if there is a problem, it's just the Headman getting above himself. Maybe since they don't answer to Lord Hallathon, the Headman thinks they're independent and don't have to answer to anybody."

That sounded better. He and Jakyr might be able to work with that. "Lemme tell Jakyr. I'll Mindspeak him. No point in my ridin' all the way back just to turn around again."

"Do that, and I got you something to eat," she said, pressing some bread and cheese into his hand. "I can't warm you up here, but at least I can make sure you don't faint from starvation."

"You're a star," he said gratefully. He couldn't imagine how she had guessed how hungry he was. He'd been thinking about chewing on a handful of the horses' oats at one point.

"I just heard your belly rumbling," she giggled, and kissed him, then sat back on her heels and let him work.

He closed his eyes, reached out into the wilderness where the only minds were birds and animals, found Jakyr's mind, and relayed what Amily had told him.

:Stay there, we're coming,: the Herald replied. *:I'll meet you at the edge of the village fields. One way or another, this is going to have to be dealt with, contained, or quarantined, and right now. You tell Amily when we're there, so she can tell Lita. At least under circumstances like this I can count on Lita to have some good ideas about what to do.:*

Hmm . . . that sounded interesting. He suspected that Jakyr had been having the same thoughts he'd been. Well, of course, he must have been; he was a Senior Herald. He must have seen exactly this sort of situation at least once in his life. Even if he had seemed as blindsided by it as Mags had been. But you could be blindsided by something and still have plenty of ideas about how to fix it. Jakyr was one of the smartest people he knew, and among Heralds, that was saying something. *Concentrate on solutions.*

"I'm goin' to meet Jakyr," he told Amily. "I'll tell you when we're 'bout to get into the village, you tell Lita, an' follow her lead. We'll figger out what's goin' on, and we'll figger a way to fix it afore it all gets outa hand."

Amily squeezed his hand, kissed him again, and ran off, stopping long enough at the stable door to make sure no one saw her leave. He took the time while he was waiting for Jakyr to arrive to devour every crumb of the food she had brought him, then slipped back out the way he had come. People were starting to head for the inn, which made getting across the street a little dodgy, but they also weren't looking for someone skulking about, so he was able to flit from shadow to shadow and get to the hedgerow without being spotted. Handy thing, Mindspeech; he had an infallible means of knowing whether or not someone had seen him; the jolt of the unfamiliar and possibly dangerous would jar a thought out where he would pick it up.

He got down to the trees without incident. Dallen was waiting impatiently for him in the shadows, and after some interminable time later, they heard Jermayan's hoofbeats approaching, thudding softly into the leaf-covered track rather than chiming as they would on a hard surface. Jakyr had removed the bridle bells from Jermayan's bridle, as Mags had removed Dallen's when he headed for the village.

The miscreant had been slung and tied face down over Jermayan's rump. It was not a comfortable position. Mags and Dallen joined Jakyr and Jermayan, and the four of them made their way into the village.

Someone going to the inn spotted them before they were halfway across the fields. Mags suspected Lita's hand in that. Whoever it was shouted for the rest, and by the time they reached the inn, half the village was out there waiting for them.

The villagers couldn't see the captive until Jermayan turned. Jakyr cut the ropes holding the man on, and between them they unceremoniously dumped the miscreant onto the road in front of the villagers. Jermayan pivoted on his heels, and Jakyr stared at them all with a face of stone.

"Does anyone know this criminal?" he thundered, as the villagers recognized one of their own with gasps and mutters.

Several reached for the man, pulled off the gag, and untied him. He, of course, at once began to shout that these *outsiders* had broken into his home, thrashed him, and—well, the tale built from there. Jakyr remained stone-faced, and he and Jermayan could have been a statue. No matter what the man said, no matter how he cursed them, no matter that he looked about himself as if for a weapon, they remained unmoved.

Most of the villagers, at least, seemed uncertain about all of this; the man they had captured was the only one making a great deal of noise. Many began frantic talking among themselves. One old lady cackled, "I told you so, Loran! I told you so! Now you and yer pa are for it!"

But others clearly backed the man; about a dozen surrounded him, and with clenched fists and threatening looks, they pulled him back among themselves. They were the only ones with torches, which didn't make Mags any easier. Of course, you couldn't spook Dallen and Jermayan by waving a torch at them they way you could a horse, but he didn't fancy having them, or himself, burned either.

Finally the Headman appeared, shoving his way through the crowd in front of the inn door. He was a burly fellow, clad in leather and furs, with a bald head, broad shoulders, and almost no neck, and his face was red with anger. "What the hell is going on here?" he bellowed, seizing his son's shoulder, and stepping in front of the young man in a threatening manner. "What have you done to my boy!"

"Pa! They—" the interloper began.

"Silence!" roared Jakyr, and at the same time Dallen and Jermayan reared and screamed, and flailed the air with their hooves. It was a very effective way to get attention.

The entire mob backed up a pace, leaving this "Loran" and the Headman standing alone. The torches wavered in a slight wind. No one so much as whispered. The only sound came from the uneasy shuffling of feet.

"We, Heralds of Valdemar and agents of the Crown, found this man occupying our Waystation, in complete and utter disregard for the law," Jakyr said into the silence in tones of ice. Mags had never seen him look so implacable. The wind cut down the back of Mags' cloak, making him shiver. "This is theft of the second degree, and the law says that the miscreant will be punished by no less than a fine of twenty silver pieces and not more than a year in gaol. You, I presume, are the Headman of this village. What do you intend to do about this clear violation of the law?"

Some of the villagers looked askance at this. Others looked to the Headman. But some looked as if they found this amusing. The Headman folded his arms over his chest and sneered. "Nothing," he said, flatly.

"Nothing?" Jakyr repeated. "Really? A clear violation of Crown Law and you propose to do nothing?" He pretended to crane his neck to look over the crowd, his eyes falling on Lita. "Milady Bard, will you witness this?"

"I do so witness," drawled Lita, ambling to the front of the crowd with her gittern slung over her back, her Scarlets making her stand out among the drably clad villagers. "As a Master Bard, I do so witness. As does my Journeyman."

"And I," Bear said loudly. He stepped to the front as well and planted his hands on his hips. As with Lita his green Healer's robes were vivid against the browns and grays of the clothing around him. "I witness. I'll swear as much to any official."

"So what?" The Headman continued to sneer. "What are you gonna do about it, Master Fancy White Pants? There's dozens of us and only two of you. We can run you right out of town, and you won't be able to stop us. The most you can do is run away." Emboldened by Jakyr's silence, he continued. "What are you gonna do about it? We don't need you, and we don't need Haven to come sticking its nose into our business! That *Waystation* of yours was a perfectly good cottage that stood empty most of the year, and I took it for my son, and I intend to keep it!"

"Really. And how do you intend to house Heralds on Circuit, pray?" Jakyr asked, in a deceptively mild tone of voice.

The Headman howled with angry laughter. "You can buy a room at the inn, just like any other man, Fancyboy." His face could never have been called handsome, but it was particularly ugly with his face contorted into a superior sneer. "You can pay for it, with all the coin you get paid for doing nothing."

Jakyr's right eyebrow rose, slowly. "Buy? Oh, really? That's truly your answer to the theft of Crown property?"

"And then you can take your *laws* and your *justice* and you can pack them up and ride off with them on the mule that brought you!" Mags rather wished that he were watching this as a play rather than being in the middle of it. At this point, the audience would have been roundly booing. It was a very uncomfortable situation, standing here, being uncertain as to which way the villagers were going to jump. They *could* win this, if the entire village managed to see where the Headman was trying to take them all. But how to get them to realize that? "We don't need you! We don't need Haven. And we damn sure don't need some King who never got his white boots dirty!"

Huh . . . little do you know . . .

"So, Fancyboy," the Headman was in his element now. He had a passive audience, and if that audience wasn't exactly with him, it also wasn't against him. He had his pulpit for preaching his particular brand of grievance. And he thought he was facing opponents helpless against his arguments. "What do you intend to do about it?"

With every word, he got more aggressive. It was clear how the Headman had gotten that position. He had bullied his way into it, and no one had yet stood up to him. By now he was used to bullying to get his way, and so far he hadn't done anything so egregious that people had completely turned against him.

But from the muttering, and the fact that about half of the villagers were sidling away, this might be the thing that did it. They weren't entirely sure what was making them so uneasy about what the Headman was saying, but—there was something about the way he was insisting that the village could stand alone that was making them think otherwise.

And that was when everything clicked for Mags. Because, of course, the last thing this village could do would be to stand alone. And once they made that plain—

"I'll tell you what we're gonna do," Mags said, as Dallen moved up to stand shoulder to shoulder with Jermayan. "If that's what you *really* want, then bein' left *completely alone* from now on is what you're gonna get." He raised his hand casually, as if none of this mattered in the least to him, and looked critically at his fingernails. "Be a shame when this town gets burned down by bandits, but, hey, that's what you wanted! Hope you are all good at rebuildin' fast, on account of you're gonna be doin' a lot of it after word gets out."

"The Guard will be overjoyed to discover they won't have to ride out this far just because someone lost a sheep or a cow," said Jakyr, picking up Mags' cue. "And they'll be thrilled to scratch this place off the list of towns they need to safeguard the next time a really big raider band sets up around here. And I can tell you from experience that once word gets around that you no longer have Guard protection, as my young Trainee pointed out, you will be a target, over and over and over."

:Well done, boy!: Jakyr Mindsent, *:I'll take it from here.:*

Now the villagers who had been pulling away from the Headman moved *right* away from him, with murmurs of real alarm. Everyone here still remembered what life was like when bandits held The Bastion, and no one wanted those dark days to return.

"They'll also be thrilled that they won't have to clear the road, once the snow starts, or mend it in the spring," Jakyr continued, with a malicious grin. "But of course, you are all independent! You can do that for yourselves! You don't need the *Crown's* help! I'm sure you all cannot wait for the snow to start so you can get out with your sledges and pack those roads down! It will be just like a winter festival every day! And when the roads and the bridges need mending? Well, I'm sure you can all take the time away from your fields and herds and run out immediately to mend them!"

At this, a couple of the Headman's supporters started to move away.

Jakyr's smile had become positively poisonous. His voice held entire volumes of malicious pleasure. "It's true, you'll save on taxes, because you won't be paying them to the Crown anymore, but do you know what it will cost you to hire mercenaries to guard you? Bard, would you happen to know that?"

"The last time I was pricing a mercenary to act as my bodyguard, it was ten silver pieces a month *and* food *and* lodging," Lita replied, standing hipshot, with her arms crossed over her chest. "So that'll be fifty silver a month for a company of five, and either you'll be building 'em a place to live, paying for 'em to be put up in the inn, or five of you will have a new houseguest who might take a liking to your wife or daughter. Ever tried to get between a merc and a girl he fancied?" She chuckled dryly. "Of course, you might get lucky. The lad might not be the sort that fancies women. Then you'll only need to be able to keep him off your own back."

A few more of the Headman's supporters peeled away. Now he was standing in front of no more than half a dozen, but he didn't yet seem to notice.

"We don't need to hire mercenaries! We can defend ourselves!" he shouted. "What do you take us for?"

"Farmers. Herders. Hunters. Woodsmen. Mothers. Servants," said Jakyr. "You all have things you need to do every day to make a living. When will you have time to do that *and* learn to handle weapons? Hmm? Swinging a sword isn't like cutting firewood. Bandits and raiders do nothing all day *except* practice to kill people—except, of course, when they're actually killing people. Do you really think the lot of you would be a match for an equal number of bandits?" His face darkened. "I've seen what happens when that's tried. It's called a massacre."

"And even if you was," Mags put in, "You'd have to get there afore they stole your sheep or your silver or your daughter. Bandits want a profit, an' they ain't gonna profit if they have to make a fight of it. You think they're gonna tell you when they're gonna come? They hit you when you ain't expectin' it. Their way is get in, get out, get gone. By the time you all come from your work and run to the rescue, they're gone and you're robbed. And maybe someone's dead, too."

"But while we are on the subject of bandits and robbers, let's just talk about the road again," Jakyr went on. "Let's just say that you're lucky, and no big bandit group decides to set up around here and prey on you. Let's say you actually *can* manage to fend off most of the scum that would come attack your town. The Guard not only keeps the road clear and mended, and keeps your bridges from falling to pieces, the Guard *guards the road.* You've got a fine inn there, a fine, big inn. How many travelers do you think it will see when robbers discover there is no one guarding the road, and they can swoop down on anyone any time they like? How many peddlers and traders will take that chance, do you think? It doesn't take a whole horde of robbers to shut down a road, you know. All it takes is one."

"And no Bards or other entertainers will take the chance, I can tell you that, for certain sure," Lita put in. "That's one of the things the Bardic Circle makes sure that *all* entertainers are kept apprised of, what roads are safe and what aren't. In fact, I'll make a point of sending a message back to Bardic Collegium as soon as I can get to a Guardpost, warning them that Therian is no longer safe to travel to, nor is the road that Therian is on safe to use. From there, it will travel to every corner of the Kingdom, and in six months there won't be an entertainer out there who will take the chance on coming here."

"Nor Healers," said Bear, causing just about everyone to gasp. He shrugged, not looking at all regretful. "Sorry, but that's how it is. Simple fact, we can't Heal anybody if we're risking our own lives. You'll just have to make do with your horse doctor there."

The Headman went red, then white, then red again. Two more of his supporters backed away. "We'll appeal to Lord—"

Jakyr cut him off with a rude gesture. "You're daft if you think he'll listen to you without you being willing to live on a quarter of what you do now. Lord Halloran doesn't think you're worth his time and money," he said cruelly. "He'd lose money protecting you and tending to you. You think the taxes you pay to the Crown are terrible? You should see what you'd have to pay Lord Halloran before he would be willing to send his men out here to keep you safe. Twice the Crown tax, at a minimum, and I'd not be surprised to find it three times as much. Not to mention that he'd expect an additional tithe of every harvest on top of the taxes."

"But you're independent!" Mags said, in a mocking voice. "You'll be free! No one will tell *you* what to do! That's what you wanted! Remember how they say *be careful what you wish for?* You wished. You weren't careful. Enjoy your freedom!" He looked at Jakyr. "Let's head back to the Guardpost and start sendin' our messages."

Jakyr nodded. "I think they might even cheer when they realize how much road clearing they won't be faced with this winter. It certainly will make their jobs ever so much easier." He chuckled, then turned to Lita and Bear. "Lady Bard, Master Healer, would you care to accompany us? I'd like to register your formal witness, and I really don't think this town is safe for you anymore."

"Oh, I agree," said Lita, and turned to Lena. "Child, go get our things. We're leaving."

"Yes, Master Bard," Lena said obediently. She headed for the inn.

"Us too," said Bear. "Amily, get the kit, would you? I'll go saddle up the horse so we don't keep the Heralds waiting. That'd be right rude."

"Wait!" One of the villagers ran to Bear and clutched at his sleeve. "You can't do this! What about your oaths? You take an oath to Heal the sick and the injured, you take an oath!"

"My oaths don't cover stupidly putting myself at risk," said Bear, bluntly. "It's what they call the lifesaver's choice—if I drown trying to save you, what about all the other people I *could* have saved? Sorry. You'll have to make do with your horse doctor."

"They'll have to make do on their own!" called a man in a farrier's apron, halfway into the crowd. "Wait while I get my things! I'm going with you!"

At this point the Headman and his son were standing completely alone. The son looked as if someone had hit him in the head with a brick and stunned him. The Headman was turning red and white in turns and seemed to have completely lost the ability to speak. His mouth kept opening and closing, but nothing came out.

Jakyr started to turn Jermayan to ride away. Lena came out of the inn, burdened with the instruments and their gear.

Amily turned toward the smithy, which must have been where they had been tending a patient. Lita and Bear headed for the stables. Then, as some of the assembled villagers turned to each other in alarm, and a couple of them actually started to wail, Jakyr turned back, as if to add an afterthought.

"Of course," he said, casually, "You all do have another choice. You can elect another Headman and toss these two in the gaol." He shrugged. "It's up to—"

Before he could finish the sentence, the villagers rushed the guilty pair, and engulfed them.

———

Four days later, and a great deal of messy business behind them, Jakyr and Mags rode away from Therian as snow started to fall in good earnest. The former Headman and his son had already been sent off in manacles by cart to the Guardpost. It turned out, when their homes and account books were investigated, that they had been up to a great deal more than mere stupidity about appropriating the Waystation. They'd been skimming off the taxes by overcharging the villagers and keeping the overage for themselves. They'd also pressured villagers to sell them prime goods at bargain rates. They had been extorting the innkeeper; forcing him to let them and their "special friends" eat and drink free. They'd probably been up to even more mischief, but that was what had come out immediately. The "special friends" had been as quick to turn on them as the honest villagers had been.

After that, a great deal of minor harm needed to be undone, and the decisions that the Headman had made that *were* good had to be ratified. He actually had not been bad at governing when he was honest, but it appeared that the moment he had a chance to make a profit off something, he did so.

The other four had gone on ahead; it was likely that Mags and Jakyr would get there at almost the same time, since the

Companions were faster than the vanners even when the vanners weren't hauling the caravan, and both the Companions were eager to get back to The Bastion. They were using a ground-eating canter whenever they could, and Dallen was thinking fondly of the apples in storage and wondering if there was a way Jakyr could bake pocket pies.

"That was a bad business back there," Jakyr observed, glancing over at Mags as the two of them trotted side by side on a track that led through a tunnel of bare birches. "If that bully of a man had managed to get more people on his side, we'd have had to go through with the threat."

"Would we have?" Mags asked. "Done it, that is? Gone to the Guard, told them we were cutting them off?"

"Of course we would," Jakyr said, a little grimly. "It's exactly what Bear quoted—the lifesaver's dilemma. If we forced those people with the Guard, there would have been resentment, ill will, and covert, if not overt, rebellion. It would cost the Kingdom three times as much to take care of them as it does an ordinary village. Much more than they're worth, to be blunt. We can't help people who deserve it if we're spending money and resources on people who claim they don't want us. It wouldn't be the first time we've cut a village off from help, and it probably won't be the last. Generally they come back begging to have us back within a couple of moons. Sometimes people just don't realize what they have until it's gone, and taking it away is the only way to teach them." He laughed ruefully. "Though, of course, once we put the consequences in front of them, even the Headman was about to say he wanted us after all. I don't know how he would have extracted himself from the hole he'd dug himself into, but it would have been amusing to watch."

"I'd'a paid good money to watch 'im squirm for a couple candlemarks," Mags said thoughtfully. " 'Pears to me, now that I think about it, these villages out here, they cost more to protect than they bring in with taxes—"

"*Aha!* Very good! Very perceptive!" Jakyr cheered. "And entirely correct. They do. You'd have been told that in the classes that prepared you for your first Circuit. These border villages, out here where banditry and other problems are a constant hazard, are supported by the taxes that people pay in the cities and towns and far more peaceful villages."

"Huh. So . . . why do it?" Mags wanted to know. "Why keep 'em in the Kingdom at all?"

"Well, for one thing, you can't raise sheep or grow wheat and barley in a town, and we need them to supply us with food and other things you can only get from those who are living in the country," Jakyr chuckled. "But for another, eventually, these places will stop having problems all the time, settle down, come to have only an occasional problem, and become less of a burden." He shrugged. "And for a third, because eventually they will come to deserve being protected. They'll willingly send us their youngsters for the Guard. They'll supply Heralds and Bards and Healers. Their children who went to the Guard will return home and train their neighbors to defend themselves. They'll begin to protect each other, taking some of the burden of doing so off the Crown. It's how these things happen, once they realize that no one can survive alone, that we all depend on the work and willingness of each other."

"And if they don't?" Mags persisted.

Jakyr shrugged. "Then if they still persist in being a problem and claiming they don't want us, we cut them off permanently, the way you cut off a rotten branch. Sometimes you have to prune to save the tree. That takes a Crown edict, but it's been done, though it's rare. I've never seen a case of that in the Archives where the village survived for more than a few years after being cut off."

"Well," Mags said after a bit, "I surely would like to see a sound branch at some point. I'm gettin' truly tired of the bad lots, and that's a fact."

In the next village—much more "town" than "village," in Mags' estimation, he got his wish.

The first indication that all was well came when they rode up to the Waystation, which looked like a charming (and un-tenanted) little cottage. They opened the door on the latch-string and found it to be well-maintained and well-stocked, as good on the inside as on the outside, complete with provisions that looked as if they must have been placed there as soon as the weather turned cold enough that insects would not be a problem and the cold would help keep them sound. Dallen was delirious to find there was a small barrel of apples, as well as oats, sweetfeed, and this year's hay—and a couple of extra blankets. Inside, there was the barrel of apples, a couple of bags of fresh root vegetables that would hold all winter, a smaller barrel of pickles, a string of onions. In a sealed chest was a crock of pickled cabbage, bacon, cheese nicely sealed in wax, smoked meat, smoked fish, dried summer vegetables and dried fruit. They didn't even need the tree-hares that

Mags had shot on the way in, by way of precaution, in case this Waystation proved to be as poorly provisioned as the first. They used them, of course, but in a tasty hare pie, rather than the grilled hare spitted over the fire that Jakyr had planned on making.

When they arrived at the town the next day, children ran out to welcome them at the sound of their bridle bells. As soon as they stopped in the village square, the Mayor was there with a list of all of the things he needed their help on. He took them to the village hall, which doubled as the Guild Hall. There was a stableman each for Dallen and Jermayan to take them to stabling at the biggest inn.

They'd barely settled the Companions and returned to the village hall, and already there was a line to get in to hear the reading of the laws and the news. The hall was packed. Everyone listened in attentive silence.

People smiled to see them. Young girls flocked to the stable to pet and spoil the Companions. The contrast with the last two towns could not have been greater.

It took all day to read the laws and the news, because only so many people could fit in at any one time, and the Mayor was anxious that everyone over the age of twelve got to hear. He confided in Mags that this was considered something of an important date in a child's life, the day that he or she was first taken to hear the Herald read the law. And when the child got home, he was quizzed on what he'd heard to be sure he understood it.

Finally Mags understood why most Heralds enjoyed being on Circuit, if most towns were like this. All the danger, all the discomfort of living in Waystations, all the difficulties were more than made up for when you were treated like this and appreciated for what you did.

Lita and Lena were spoiled as well; there were three inns in this town, and all three vied to have them. Lita finally decided that Lena and Bear should stay at the smallest of the three, and Lena would entertain on her own there, while the Master Bard would divide her time between the other two. That seemed fair to Mags, and evidently it satisfied all three innkeepers.

Bear actually found a small House of Healing here and was overjoyed to discover that the Head Healer was one of the people he'd taught the use of his kit to back in Haven. For his part, the Head Healer was just as pleased to have Bear there to give a more intensive set of lessons to everyone in the House—and on the third day, to the apothecary, the farriers, the barber, and every midwife that could be got to the town before they all left.

For their part, Mags and Jakyr's duties were lengthy, if not exciting. There were quite a number of discontented people who wanted to appeal law-court judgments. There were a couple of quarrels about land and inherited property that the court had not been able to settle. Amusing, though to Mags' mind, absurdly trivial, were the number of parents who hauled disobedient children in their teens in to have the Heralds "talk some sense into them"—though the sense that Jakyr talked was not to the parents' liking, more than once. *"No, preferring your own sex to the opposite is not something you can 'grow out of.' Be happy you have a healthy child who loves you."* Or, *"No matter how hard you try, you'll never get a pig to sing, and you'll never get your child to be a blacksmith. He'll make a very fine clerk and support you handsomely in your old age. Let him and get used to it—and find an apprentice who likes hammering."*

Most often, though, what he said was a variation on a theme. "You want to get out on your own and have your own life," he told more than one sullen youngster. "That's right and proper, how it should be. But you're not going to be allowed to get out on your own if you don't stop playing the fool and doing your best to make your parents miserable so that they'll *throw* you out. And you," he would say, turning to the parents. "I understand that you think your child isn't old enough to know his own mind, but I promise you, he *is*. He may well be wrong, but he does know his own mind, and he's got a perfect right to think that way. And you need to stop letting him prove he's smarter than you are by rising to the bait he throws out to make you angry!"

No one on either side of those disagreements was entirely happy with the answer, which Mags supposed meant it was probably the right one. But Jakyr was the Herald, and that made the answer stick.

It kind of surprised him. He hadn't thought that Jakyr was that . . . clever . . . when it came to quarrels within a family. Especially not when you looked at the way he and Lita sniped and battled with each other.

But then again, maybe when it was happening to someone else, it was a lot easier to see what needed to be done. When it was happening to you, things got blurrier, the way a picture did when you brought it too close to your eyes.

What with all the work, they stayed a full seven days. Jakyr seemed to be getting impatient after a while, but Mags thought that he had never learned quite so much about ordinary folk. He knew all about the very poor and the very rich, but about the sorts of people in the middle, not so much. He picked up a lot of useful trivia about various trades, about how a village was run, and about good ways to handle all sorts of problems.

On the whole, it was a very instructive stop. With Lita off in her own inns, and he and Jakyr able to go and relax in the smaller inn that Lena was playing in before they left for the Waystation, things were quite pleasant in the evenings. Lena seemed to appreciate having them in her audience as well— though, really, with Bear there, giving her adoring and en- couraging looks after every song, she didn't need them to bolster her spirits.

But their luck started to change as soon as they left the town and headed back toward The Bastion.

It was a glorious morning, if cold. There was a heavy hoar-frost coating everything, which was pretty enough but made Mags more than glad for the fur-lined winter cloak that Princess Lydia had insisted he have as a present from her. The sun beamed down from overhead; they'd wanted to give the others a good head start and had decided to stay long enough to have luncheon. People waved them out of town, and Mags' spirits at least were high.

When they were into the forest, Mags happened to glance back at the unusual sound a bird made, and what he saw behind them through the skeletal branches of the trees made a chill go down his spine.

"Jakyr!" he said urgently, as Dallen whipped his head around to see what had alarmed him. "Behind us! Blizzard!"

Jakyr swiveled in his saddle and saw what Mags had seen: charcoal-gray clouds on the horizon, looming closer with every moment.

"Do you carry some sort of blizzard attractor?" Jakyr asked, in mingled irritation and alarm. "I swear, every time you and I go anywhere in winter, there's a blizzard. Never mind, time to move. It's a damn good thing the others started so early this morning!"

As Dallen and Jermayan went from an easy lope into a full-out gallop, Mags had to wonder if Jakyr was right. Blizzards certainly did seem to play a large part in his life—far larger than he liked, to tell the truth.

There had been the early one that had nearly caught them on the way to Haven when Jakyr had first rescued him, for instance. That blizzard, like this one, had caught them on the road. They'd barely made it to the Guardpost they were aiming for and had been snowed in there for two days. Then, later that same year, there had been the blizzard that lasted three whole days, shut down all of Haven for a solid week, and had kept it under snow for a good long time after that. He'd been caught at the stable and had nearly died trying to get from his stable room to the Collegium in the teeth of it. If it hadn't been for having Dallen in his head, he probably would have just given up, laid himself down in the snow, and that would have been the end of it.

On the other hand, that blizzard had been very useful to him. That was when he'd first really used his Mindspeaking Gift and had found out how powerful it was. With people scattered among all the buildings on the Hill, and no way to effectively and quickly communicate with them, there was no way to tell whether everyone had made it into safety. He'd volunteered to "look" for people who might have gotten trapped between buildings up on the Hill, for there was always the possibility that some of them had not realized how powerful and deadly the storm was until it was too late. He'd found five people that way, with Dallen's help. It had been easy, really, easier than raising shields in the first place had been.

And that was when the true scope of his power had been uncovered. He, it seemed, could Mindspeak to anyone and Mindhear anyone. That was, so they kept telling him, incredibly rare.

That was also how he had found Bear when the assassins kidnapped the Healer.

They hadn't come there—in disguise as envoys—for that purpose, of course. No one had any idea there was such a thing as an entire clan of killers, killers who wore some sort of talisman that both guarded them from Mind-magic and would murder them if it thought they had been caught.

All anyone knew was that they came from somewhere no Valdemaran was even remotely familiar with.

He knew now that they had all taken a contract from Karse to disrupt or even cause the overthrow of the Valdemaran monarchy, but no one had known that at the time. All that was certain was that they had come to spy and perhaps make trouble; but more by accident than design, he and some of the other Trainees had managed to uncover the fact that they were frauds and scare them out.

He also knew now why the assassins had taken that contract in the first place—it helped them finance their quest to try to find Mags' parents. Mags' foreign parents, who had been murdered by the same bandit band that had lived for so long in The Bastion. Mags' parents, who, it seemed had been members of the assassin clan and had fled so fast and so far that even the best of their kind hadn't been able to stop them.

The assassins hadn't actually been looking for Mags. They hadn't known Mags existed, and the first lot hadn't recognized him at all. But the one who had been sent to help get them out when they were exposed and who had kidnapped Bear certainly had. . . .

Mags would never forget that moment.

Mags stepped into the light, his hand clutching his sword hilt.

The thin, dark-haired man dressed in strange, dark clothing stared at him.

"Not YOU!" he screamed. "YOU are not supposed to be here!"

He would probably see that moment in nightmares for the rest of his life.

:You might want to concentrate on the nightmare closing in on us.:

Mags looked back over his shoulder. There was definitely more black cloud back there, and that didn't bode well. It seemed cruel that ahead of them was a bright, sunny, nearly cloudless sky.

:Dallen, keep me from fallin' off. I gotta try to warn the others.:

He didn't wait for an answer; he dropped all of his shields, which was safe enough out here, where there was nothing but birds and beasts and—

Wait. Woodcutter. The man was intent on the tree he was

chopping down; wise, since when a woodcutter's mind was on other things, bad accidents often happened. Mags concentrated as hard as he could. *:BLIZZARD!:* he "shouted" into the man's mind, timing his warning for the moment when the ax blade would actually strike the tree. *Let's not make things worse by choppin' his foot off!*

He sensed the fellow jump; the ax lodged in the tree and stuck there. The man looked up and spotted the ominous clouds. The first thing that leaped into the man's mind was relief that his cottage was not far away. The second was to get his ax out so he could run for its safe walls.

Good. Mags left his mind behind.

He found two more people out in the woods, a hunter and a trapper. He managed to alert both of them before moving on. He hoped they would get to shelter, though he probably would never know for certain, since neither of them had a destination in mind when he pulled his thoughts away from them. But they had a better chance now than they had before he'd found them.

At last, he found Amily and the rest. With a surer touch now than he'd had when he'd first tried to talk to her this way, he didn't so much shove his way into her thoughts, the way he'd done with the three strangers, as he slipped into them, a welcome guest instead of an interloper. *:Amily! Blizzard behind you!:* he Sent urgently.

:What?: he Heard—and it was almost exactly like a deliberate Sending. Then *:Oh, gods! Don't worry, we're not that far, and we'll run for it!:*

He could have cheered at the clarity and strength of her thoughts, except he had other things to think about right at that moment.

It was going to be easier, for him at least, to Send to Jakyr than to try to shout over the pounding hoofs of the Companions. He crouched farther down against Dallen's neck and closed his eyes. *:I warned the others,:* he Sent.

:Good,: came the labored response. *:I think we'll make it, but the storm will catch us before we get there. This is going to be a near thing.:*

:Just get us there,: he replied. *:You an' Jermayan know yer way around woods better'n me. We'll follow you. Just don't lose the track when it hits!:*

As they pounded along the track, Mags began to wonder if waiting for that steak-and-kidney pie for luncheon was going to prove to be the mistake that cost them dearly.

Maybe it would have been better to ask for the sausages in rolls and eat in the saddle.

Well, too late now to undo that mistake. And hindsight was always crystal clear.

He kept shooting glances over his shoulder, and the view didn't get any better when he did. The clouds boiled up behind them, still charcoal-gray, still closer every time he looked. The wind picked up behind them, colder and damper, cutting through the cloak and making him wish Lydia had got one lined with sheepskin instead of fur. Ahead of them, the trees swayed, and the wind moaned in the branches.

It seemed they had been running forever, with the menace coming on fast behind them, and the landscape never varying. If he didn't know better, he'd have thought they were running in circles, except that you could still see the clear track passing through the trees ahead of them, with the hoofprints of the vanners clear in the damp earth and moss, huge horseshoe shapes squashing leaves into the mud.

He fell into a kind of trance, concentrating on making himself the least burden to Dallen he could, using every muscle in his body to stay in perfect rhythm with the Companion. Were they closer now? They'd been running flat out for a couple of candlemarks or more, and he knew that Companions could achieve incredible speed for very long periods of time. They'd have been about four to six candlemarks away at a simple lope when he first noticed the storm. How far at a gallop? He actually didn't want to look down, because he knew that the ground would be going past at a rate that would make him dizzy.

Now he could hear the wind and the storm howling behind them, and the branches of the trees ahead of them and around them lashed the sky as the wind strengthened ahead of the blizzard. The clouds were right overhead, like a shelf of rock overhanging them.

How far away from the caves were they now? He didn't recognize anything around them, but then again, there weren't really any landmarks out here.

The storm pounced on them.

Suddenly they were enveloped in streaming curtains of snow, carried on a bitter, bitter wind. He felt Dallen gasp as it hit them, felt him put in extra effort. All he could do was hold on and close his eyes, trying to lend his strength to his Companion and praying with all his might that Dallen wouldn't trip or stumble into a hole. It had been one thing to run at a full gallop when the track had been clear—but now?

And then, suddenly, the wind stopped, and Dallen stumbled a little into a walk.

He opened his eyes.

They were in the cleft in the rocks that led into The Bastion. They were safe!

He almost fell off with relief.

They came through the cleft into the pocket valley, and now into snow falling mostly straight down. And there was a *lot* of it. Already it was hoof deep here.

The hills cut the wind but not the snow; it was coming down so hard that it was like being in a thick fog, and despite the fact that it was barely midafternoon, it was as dark as thick dusk. But there were two lights burning through the white, about where the cave entrance should be, and Mags knew that the others had put lanterns out there to guide them in.

:Feel your way. Walk slow,: he told Dallen sternly. *:Don't*

*need to have run all that way only to break an ankle now! In
fact, I'll get off and help. You just follow me, right on my
heels.:*

He slid off Dallen's back before the Companion could object. Jakyr looked at him oddly through snow coming down so
thickly it almost obscured his face, then did the same. Mags
took the lead, walking slowly, shuffling through the snow to
find any dangerous spots. Dallen walked directly behind him,
in his footsteps, Jakyr in Dallen's, and Jermayan's in Jakyr's,
as the best way to find a safe path. The floor of the valley was
littered with stones, the odd branch, little depressions. Those
were not a problem when the ground was clear, but now—step
on the wrong thing and a sprained ankle or hock could be the
best outcome. Dallen had already suffered one broken leg
thanks to Mags; Mags was not going to let him suffer another.

The cave entrance had never looked so welcoming. When
they reached it, Dallen and Jermayan paused to shake off
snow that had already managed to build up a good two fingers
deep on their saddles, necks and haunches, then trotted down
into the stabling area. Mags and Jakyr each took a lantern
from the front of the cave and headed into air that felt almost
summerlike in comparison with the white hell outside.

Amily came flying out of the darkness and caught Mags by
surprise in a frantic embrace. He managed to keep her from
burning herself on the lantern only by a last-moment maneu-
ver that put it over their heads. She didn't say anything, but
she didn't have to; Mags understood all too well just how
frantic and worried she had been. *He* had been pretty frantic
and worried himself!

When they were done kissing—which in itself was very
warming and welcome—they held hands and followed Jakyr
down to the blessed light and further warmth of the central
area. Lita, Lena, and Bear were already seeing to it that Dallen
and Jermayan were rubbed down, blanketed, watered, and
fed. The vanners were drowsing, blanketed, and content.

Mags caught a glorious aroma and peered into the light around the kitchen. There was a tray of pocket pies warming on the top of the stove, which was a very welcome sight indeed. Mags suddenly realized he was absolutely famished.

From the way Dallen and Jermayan were head down in the grain buckets, they were famished too. Not surprising considering how fast and hard they had run.

He took off his cloak, shook it out vigorously and tossed it over a storage chest to dry, then sank down on the rugs nearest the fire. Jakyr did the same opposite him, and he wondered if he looked as dull-tired as his mentor did. Amily brought him a warmed pie and a mug of hot tea, and he murmured thanks. Lita did the same for Jakyr, and to Mags' shock, all Jakyr said was, "Bless you."

But he couldn't dwell on that when he was ready to eat his own hand. He bit into the pie, and either it was the equal of those godly pies at that inn Jakyr had first taken him to, or else hunger made it seem so. He ate it down to the last crumb, just as Amily brought him another with an understanding grin. Only after he had finished a third did it feel as if the gnawing monster in his belly had been appeased, and he leaned back into the cushion and put an arm around Amily and let the heat from the fire soak into him.

"I think we are going to be here for a while," Lita said into the silence. "There was a weather-witch back at the town who said we were about to get snowed in hard, here in The Bastion, with several storms, one after the other. I wish I'd paid more attention to her."

"Well, why didn't you?" Lena asked. Then proving it was a completely rhetorical question, continued, "You didn't, because the mayor said she never predicted anything but terrible weather for The Bastion."

"I should have asked if, when she predicted terrible weather, the weather actually came," Lita replied with a shrug. "But I suppose if they never came out to The Bastion, they'd never know for sure. If we can't break through at the entrance, we're going to have to slowly dig our way out or wait until we get a thaw."

"This might be the reason why this Circuit is so hard to run," Jakyr observed wearily. "If Heralds get snowed in that often, they aren't going to see the villages as often as they should, and we got what—" he waved a tired hand "—we got. Unruly, surly, and resentful."

"It's as good a theory as any," Lita agreed. "I'm thinking this Circuit should be divided into smaller ones. And I need to get more Bards out here. There's nothing to persuade people that they need Heralds quite like flinging the Vanyel cycle at them until they are sick of hearing it."

Jakyr gave her an odd look. "What?" she asked, defensively. "I don't hate Heralds. I like Mags. I like Caelen. I even like Marion."

Jakyr rolled his eyes a little, but he managed not to make a sharp retort. Instead, he turned to Mags. "This might give you an opportunity to see if there is any sign left at all of your parents," he said. "Our friend Milles marked the two caves that had been the bandit treasury and the area where the captives were kept. They are quite clearly picked out on the map. You probably won't find anything, but you never know."

They had had so many other things to worry about that the possibility of looking for some piece of his past had entirely slipped his mind. But if they were going to be snowed in here for a while, that was as good a task as any. "I think that's a good idea, Mags," Amily agreed, nodding slightly. "That's why Caelen sent you out here in the first place. At least even if you don't find anything, you won't be tormented by wondering if you *might* have if you'd just looked."

He smiled, and hugged her. "Well then, reckon I will," he said. "But not till the storm clears. We don't need nobody lost in it."

"No, we don't," Lita agreed. "It was a near enough thing with you two as it was."

———————

Bear had kindly gone around to everyone's bed and left a hot stone in each to warm them before sleep. Jakyr went to bed first, complaining about old bones and storms. Lita yawned hugely and left shortly after. Lena and Bear cleaned up the little there was to clean from a dinner of pocket pies, and slipped off to the caravan. That left Mags and Amily alone.

"How come," he said aloud, "it was Dallen doin' all the work, but I feel like I was doin' the running?"

She groaned a little. "Because you were, sort of, you just don't think about it anymore. Remember when you first learned to ride, how sore you were? Riding uses an awful lot of muscles, love, and just because you know how to ride and you don't hurt anymore, that doesn't mean you aren't still using them." She made a face. "That's what happens when you play at being a Healer's assistant. After a while you stop playing, and you realize you *are* a Healer's assistant."

"You like it?" he asked.

"Like isn't the right word, really," she said after a long moment of thought. "Some of it is pretty horrid. Wounds and things are nasty. People sicking up in buckets is nasty. But I feel useful. I suppose I would rather be doing something that wasn't so nasty but I like feeling useful."

"You're braver'n I am," he said honestly. "I allus hated helping Bear out. It's strange, but I can kill an animal and butcher it, no problem. I can kill a man if I have to, and it'll make me sick to do it, but I can do it. But when I gotta change a dressing on a wound, or worse, a burn—" he shuddered. "Just makes me go all collywobbles inside. I think Healers are the bravest people ever."

She chuckled. "I don't think Bear would argue about that.

He gets quite cross when some great big man rears back and acts like a coddled highborn confronting a mouse when Bear starts to tell him how he'll have to take care of his own wound or nurse a sick child. And he laughs when they faint at the sight of their own blood."

Mags laughed aloud. "Not to their faces, I hope."

"He's been tempted." She snuggled into his shoulder and sighed. "It's nice here. I don't want to get up. But the longer we stay here, the colder that stone in our bed gets."

Our bed. He loved the sound of that. "Well, then," he said. "Let's go get it out and take its place."

The blizzard lasted three days, just like the one that had snowed Haven in completely, all those years ago. He wondered how bad it was over at the villages they had left. Had they gotten snowed in this hard? The Guard was going to be mighty busy cleaning roads, that was for certain sure. He hoped that the worst of it was falling here, in The Bastion. He wouldn't wish this on small villages. He hoped people had managed to get their herds into shelter before it hit, because three days in the snow without food would probably kill most cattle, sheep, and horses. And when the storm was over, it would be hideously hard work to get out to them, even in shelter, and get food to them.

It snowed them in hard. Because there was very little wind to speak of in the valley, there were no insanely tall drifts, but the snow in the entrance was fully waist deep. There would be no getting out of the cave without a lot of work. Mags had been afraid that Jakyr and Lita would be so restless and irritated by being confined together like this that they would start actual fights by the middle of the first day of the blizzard itself.

But strangely, they didn't. They stayed out of each other's way. Jakyr went into a food frenzy, making trail bread, smoking most of the venison, and making the rest into meat pies that he set near the entrance to freeze. That seemed eminently sensible to Mags; it meant that they'd have pies waiting when they returned from a village, and if they were tired, all they would have to do would be to put one on the top of the stove to thaw and warm. And trail bread kept nearly forever in this weather; it wasn't his preferred meal—it wasn't *anybody's* preferred meal—but it was a good deal better than making porridge out of the Companions' oats if they were forced to use another ill-prepared Waystation.

There was no point in trying to shovel any paths through the stuff or even clear it from the entrance until it finally stopped. It would just pile back up. So mostly, they all rested, and the cave was strangely quiet and peaceful. Oh, he and Bear had a couple of silly snow fights right in the entrance, and coming back into the warmth of the living area was heaven. The steam bath was in near constant use, and Jakyr had even introduced Mags and Bear to a curious custom of using it, then running full-tilt through the cave—in nothing but a breechcloth—to throw oneself into the snow, then running back to it again. He said that people did this up north. Bear was not a fan of the practice at all. Mags found it invigorating, but he wasn't a fan of running mostly naked through the caves while the ladies laughed at them.

As for the ladies, Lita was in the throes of composition, and so was Lena. They washed clothing, hanging it from the caravan, which imparted a nice scent to the air. They all read and slept. Or in Mags and Amily's case—and likely Bear and Lena's—"slept."

And on the fourth day there was sunshine.

Mags was the first one out, because as usual he woke before anyone else, and went to poke at the mound of snow, expecting to discover that it was heavy and wet. Instead, he came back to where the rest were gathering to get breakfast to report some good news. "Sun's out, and snow's deep, but it ain't too hard to clear away," he said. "Stuff's pretty dry and fluffy." He accepted a plate of hotcakes and bacon and tucked in.

Lita sucked on her lower lip and took a sip of tea. "Well, there's the question: Do we want to try to clear a way to the cleft and see how things are beyond it? With that wind, we might end up lucky, with the track drifted to either side but otherwise clear."

"I'd still prefer to wait for something of a thaw," replied Jakyr. "And don't forget what that weather-witch said. Not just *a* storm but several storms. Maybe she'll be right, maybe she won't."

Mags shrugged. "I'm gonna break a path to them two caves, anyway. If we're stuck here, I wanta see what's there. While I'm at it, I'm gonna break a path to the cleft when I'm done. Might as well. Less to clear even if it does snow again."

Jakyr shrugged. "I'll help until my old bones won't let me, once I'm done with feeding you and cleaning up," he offered. "No guarantee how long that will be. You are right, though, Mags. The more we clear to the cleft now, the less we'll have to clear if there is a second storm."

"I'll give you a hand," Lita offered, putting down her gittern and capping her ink. "I was born and raised in the country before I got sent to Bardic. I'm not afraid of a little snow. Not like some people city bred."

Ah, there it is, that's more like I expected. Mags was almost relieved to hear Lita start sniping again. At least now he wasn't waiting for something to erupt.

"Suit yourself," Jakyr retorted. "It's not as if you were doing anything useful in here. Just making us crazy by plunking the same notes over and over with minor variations."

Lita stood up and actually looked as if she might hit him, her eyes flashed with such anger. Mags handed Lita her hooded coat and hurried her out before she could start anything.

While the storm had been raging, Mags and Bear had

looked for anything like a shovel in the stored supplies. At first, they hadn't found anything of the sort, but after staring at some inexplicable "broom handles" and something that looked like oversized shingles, they had suddenly realized that the two were meant to go together to form flat, broad-bladed wooden shovels. Perfect for shoveling snow. And also a lot easier to store in that form than as a single unit. It turned out that there were even holes bored in the right places, and bolts of the right diameter to hold the things together. If the shingle broke, you just unbolted it and bolted a new one in place. It would be easy to find someone to make you more shingles, too, if you broke all of them.

He and Bear had put four of the shovels together, figuring that it was unlikely more than four people would want to shovel at any one time.

Now he hurried Lita up to the entrance and gave her one of the four he and Bear had left there.

"I think we ought to clear the entire entrance, not just a path," Lita said, considering the waist-deep snow that confronted them. "If it does start coming down hard again, we don't want to find ourselves sealed in here."

Mags didn't think that was likely to happen, but he was no expert on snow. So the two of them worked until they were both losing feeling in their feet and getting chilled enough for their teeth to start chattering. By that point they had cleared the entire entrance and a good distance out past it. What was more, they had made bulwarks of the discarded snow to try to hold back drifts from the cleared space.

It was a perfectly gorgeous winter day, if you liked winter. The air was cold enough to keep the snow from melting and turning hard—but it was rather hard to breathe unless you wrapped your face in a scarf as Bear had done. It cut into the lungs like a knife. The sun would have been blinding, except that for most of the morning it was just behind the hills. But Lita had an answer for that; when it did poke over the hills, she went in and brought out straw summer hats, which they tied on their heads over the hoods to shade their eyes.

They came back in around luncheon, cloaks snow-caked, and ready to eat just about anything. Bear took their cloaks and went off with them. He came back with all of them beaten clean of the snow, and he spread them over a cushion to warm. "I beat the snow off in the steam bath," he said with a shrug. "Not like it isn't already wet in there."

Jakyr handed them fresh meat pies and mugs of hot tea and went back to something he was working on without a word. Whatever it was involved harness straps and big, thin squares of wood. Lita didn't ask him about it, but, then, she looked exhausted. She really had been working terribly hard.

When Mags was warmed up, he fetched his cloak and his shovel and went right back out again. He meant to cut a path to the nearer of the two caves that interested him—and maybe to the second one, if he could manage it. He reckoned that by sticking close to the cliff wall, he'd deal with slightly shallower snow. Lita was half asleep on the cushion, and he wasn't about to ask her to come out and help again.

But Bear followed him, bundled up to the nose. "Reckon I can help a bit," he said, his voice muffled by the scarf he had wrapped around his face. "I'm pretty fit, I reckon, and I think I got a few more candlemarks in me of work. Besides. If I don't get some sun, I'm going to start talking to myself anyway."

"You already talk to yourself," Mags teased.

"There! You see!" Bear retorted. "It's happening already!" There was a grin in his voice, and it was infectious. Mags felt himself grinning back.

Since Mags only intended to make a path one shovel wide, the two of them took turns; when one tired, the other took his place.

"I haven't asked, how are things going with your herbal kit?" Mags said over his shoulder when it was his turn to shovel.

"Better than how things have gone with you Heraldic lot," Bear replied. "Nobody's met me as if they figured I was that cousin nobody likes. So far, everybody's been right happy to see me. I got treated real well." He sighed heavily. "If I'd known people were that desperate for something they could use when there isn't a Healer around, I'd have done the kit a long time ago."

"You'd have had to fight your pa over it, and afore you pretty well proved yourself at the Collegium, I dunno that you'd'a got anywhere," Mags pointed out. "You had to fight your pa over it, anyway, but at least you had the Collegium backing when you did. Sometimes ye gotta wait for exactly the right time."

"Like you and Amily did?" Bear teased.

Mags flushed bright red, and suddenly his cloak felt far too warm.

"Hey, I understand," Bear continued as Mags shoveled faster, trying to work off his embarrassment. "It's not like you two woulda been able to do anything with everybody and his dog trying to play guardian."

"Guardian of *virtue,* more like," Mags grumbled. "And every one of 'em self-appointed. I didn't hear Nikolas sendin' out a call for people to tell him every little thing me and Amily done, but they sure figgered they *needed* to. Not just Heralds, either. Everybody on the Hill, it seemed like. I was even startin' to think the cats and dogs was lookin' at us funny."

Bear patted him clumsily on the shoulder. " 'S all right. Me and Lena got lucky. After my father showed up and made a damn fool of himself, *especially* after the second time, people were practically throwing me and Lena together. Only reason there was a fuss when we up and got married was cause we didn't tell anybody but you."

"Makes me almost wish her pa were someone other than Nikolas." He sighed. "Nikolas is . . . I wish he was my pa, an' I'm real happy to have him for—whatchacall?"

"Father-in-law," Bear supplied.

"Aye, that. But I wish he wasn't King's Own. It makes things a lot more complicated." He sighed again. "As if things weren't complicated enough."

And if she wasn't the daughter of the King's Own, she wouldn't have been kidnapped, either, he thought. His stomach still lurched whenever he thought of her, scared and alone, in the hands of those bastards. How in hell could they even *dream* he'd want to join them when they had done that to her?

Resolutely he turned his thoughts away from that grim period of time and quizzed Bear about his view of the goings-on in Therian. Bear had seen an entirely different village than Mags and Jakyr, of course; the village he had seen was one where people still felt secure enough to complain a bit about their Headman, but they were beginning to look over their shoulders while they did it. It seemed that the Heralds had come and stirred things up just in time.

Mags was beginning to feel weary as the afternoon wore on and the sun dropped behind the hills again, but the end was in sight. The entrance to the cave was not more than a few arm lengths away.

"But, you know, about Nikolas not being Amily's father . . . if he wasn't, then she wouldn't be Amily," Bear pointed out, when the conversation circled back around to how things were going between them. "And now you two are really together, and Jakyr and Lita don't care and won't preach, and by the time we get home again, you're gonna get married anyway. Oh, and don't worry about . . . uh . . . needing to think about getting married in a hurry, I got all the stuff we all need, enough to last all the way into summer. And if I can't find more by then, everybody in this part of the Kingdom's gonna be in trouble."

That took a bit of weight off his mind. Amily hadn't been forthcoming about it, only assuring him she was taking great care that there were no unfortunate accidents. Mags knew, from listening to the lecture everyone got on the subject, that the herbs in question were almost foolproof—so much so that some people regarded a child that happened *anyway* as being a child that the gods were determined you would have! He just wasn't sure how big a stock Bear had with him, and now would be a bad time to discover they were running out.

A clatter back at the entrance to their living cave made both of them look up.

The first thing they saw was one of the vanners, in harness, coming out of the cave. The second thing they saw was that the horse was pulling something that looked like a giant plowshare made out of wooden shingles. The horse plunged into the snow, and the "plowshare" dug in and began turning the snow over and to the side, making a giant "furrow" in the snow itself, creating a small path in its wake. The horse seemed to be having a grand time, plunging into the snow like a happy dog. His shaggy coat was soon sparkling with the snow crystals he was throwing up.

He got the plow about two lengths into the virgin snow. Then the horse stopped, evidently at a signal from someone on the other side of him, out of sight.

Jakyr's head and hands, and then the rest of him, appeared as he heaved himself up onto the vanner's back.

He turned and waved at Mags and Bear, gathered up the driving reins in great loops in both hands, and chirped to the vanner, who went back to forging a path through the snow, the plow cutting along in his wake.

Mags heard something from his friend that sounded like choking. When he looked to see what was wrong with Bear, he found the young Healer convulsing with laughter, doubled over, laughing so hard that he could hardly breathe.

"What?" he asked.

"He gulled her!" Bear choked. "Lita! He gulled her into clearing out the entrance the hard way, so he could put that plow together, get the vanner out, and cut the actual path the easy way! Oh, glory! He gulled her! You know how Bards are always so sure they can't be gulled, 'cause they know how to use words so well! Oh, she has got her comeuppance!"

Well, now, he didn't know that. But Bear lived with one, so Mags was going to take his word for it. Lita especially was likely to have that kind of pride, he considered, given that she was not just a Master Bard, but the head of the Bardic Circle. He wondered just what Lita's reaction was going to be.

"Tell you what," he said. "Let's get this finished up quick. We might need a place way outa earshot when she finds out."

Amily had persuaded him to do one thing before he began his explorations: move wood, food, bedding and some basic supplies into each of the caves he was going to look through, enough to hold him for a week, at need. He didn't see any problem with that. The Guard had cut them enough wood to last for two winters at the rate they were burning it, and that was assuming that they ended up spending the entire cold season here instead of in Waystations. He wondered if they had a weather-witch of their own. It would make sense if they did. They needed to be as prepared for a hard season as everyone else put together.

In the treasury cave, he had filled all of one side of the first big room—the one that supposedly had held all the loot—with wood stacked as high as he could reach. He'd brought in plenty of the frozen meatpies, and, since Jakyr was using actual kitchen stuff to cook in, not pots you put on a fire, he and Bear had lugged over the box of pots that was usually slung under the caravan. Several armloads of hay and some of the extra blankets that the Guard had left completed the preparations. When he was done here, he would move it all to the cave where the prisoners had been held. He didn't actually expect to find anything there. The bandits would have stripped everything from them that even looked as if it might have some value.

But still, he wanted to go through the cave anyway. If nothing else, it was where his parents were buried. It didn't seem right to be here and not put some kind of marker there. Pay his respects. He didn't remember them . . . but that didn't change the fact that they had probably died to save him.

Anyway, Amily was right. It was better to be prepared. What was the worst that could happen? He'd have a fire to keep him warm, food right at hand, and—well, a place to retreat to if Lita and Jakyr escalated their quarrel.

"If that weather-witch is right, and we do get more storms, I want to know you aren't going to be in any trouble, or *get* in any trouble trying to get back to us," Amily had said, earnestly. It had been a sensible precaution, and one that cost him only a little effort with Dallen's help, so he'd given in.

The nearer cave was the one where the bandits had kept their loot, fortunately. Obviously everything of real value had long since been taken away, but as he sifted through the dirt and trash on the floor, he was finding little bits of things, brass and glass and semiprecious stone. Which was promising; it suggested that he might find some bits of things that had belonged to his parents, things that had escaped because they were worthless. It looked as if small animals, mice or rats or something, had been in here. But there were better, less open places for them to go, and they hadn't found anything to eat or bed down in, so they had mostly left the area alone. What was here was mostly the remains of the few leaves that had been blown in over the years and the churned-over dirt from people digging, trying to find one last bit of treasure that had somehow missed being discovered.

The work was tedious, but he didn't mind it. In a way, it was soothing. He had a fire going behind him for heat as well as light and a lantern above him so he could catch the gleam of metal or polished stone as he patiently sieved through the sandy soil. It was like the better parts of sluicing through the gravel looking for sparklie chips, back at the mine—with no one hectoring him or threatening to thrash him, no one growling at him to work faster. He could rest when he wanted, warm himself when he wanted, and there was peace in doing something so repetitive and simple.

Already, he had an interesting collection of bits. Lita might want them; she was a bit like a magpie herself, for collecting odd and shiny things. If nothing else, perhaps they could give the collection to some child along the way.

He was getting the strangest feeling of being . . . watched . . . as he worked, though. He couldn't shake it. He began to wonder if maybe the place was haunted. A lot of people had died here, after all.

Finally his back and shoulders got weary, and he took his collection up in the scrap of cloth he was using to hold things, put out the fire, and headed back toward the living cave.

He handed over the pile to Lita, who was glowering over her work, hoping it would put her in a better mood. It did at least distract her, which was positive. Anything to prevent her from starting another argument.

She and Jakyr had finally come to open quarreling. Last night they'd actually started shouting at each other. Lita had taken exception to Jakyr harnessing up the vanner and cutting the path to the cleft with him. Lita seemed to think that only *she* had enough experience with the vanners to do such a thing, even though Jakyr had clearly known exactly what he was doing, and the vanner had returned to the stabling frisky and in fine fettle.

It seemed that Lita was angrier than ever. He must have missed something while he'd been sifting dirt.

"What's going on?" Mags whispered to Amily, who was assiduously working on mending some of Dallen's barding where the stitches had broken. He settled down next to her, enjoying the feel of the fire on his front instead of his back.

"This time Jakyr is in the wrong, and he won't admit it," Amily whispered back. "The vanner is a little lame this morning. It isn't bad, and Bear thinks he'll be fine in a couple of days, with poultices, but it turns out the plow is supposed to be pulled by two horses, not one. The vanner probably didn't notice he'd pulled his hock muscles until they stiffened up overnight, he was so glad to get out into the sunshine. Now Jakyr won't admit that he was wrong for using only one horse, wrong for not checking him periodically as they plowed, and wrong for just rubbing him down and blanketing him instead of checking all four legs for pulled muscles before he left the horse alone. If the leg had been properly wrapped and poulticed, the horse wouldn't be lame today."

"And Lita is gonna glare at him until he apologizes." Mags nodded. "Well, I didn't find much, but it was pretty spooky back in that cave. I kept feelin' like someone was watchin' me."

Amily's eyes widened a little. "I was exploring those sleeping tunnels, and I felt the same!" she exclaimed, this time loudly enough that Lita looked up. "I even thought I *saw* something out of the corner of my eye! I—I usually don't get feelings like that. Is there something about these caves, do you think?"

"Well, lots of people died here," Mags said, repeating his own earlier thought. "Lots of 'em were people the bandits were holdin' prisoner. I dunno, you'd'a thought if anyplace'd be haunted, the mines I worked would'a been, and I never actually felt or saw anything there but . . ."

"But ghosts are supposed to be the spirits of people who have unfinished business, things unresolved," Amily put in, her brows creasing. "If I had died working in that mine, I wouldn't be able to get away from it fast enough, but the people the bandits killed—maybe they didn't feel that way."

"Or maybe they did, and it's just weird shadows and echoey sounds and us having nerves on edge cause Lita and Jakyr can't stop pickin' at each other," he countered, pitching his voice low again, since she was starting to look a little frightened.

"Mags!" called Lita at that moment. "Come over here where the light is good and look at this."

Obediently, he got up and moved over to the warm place near the kitchen stove, where Lita had set up her favorite lantern, one that used some clever glass balls to magnify the amount of light the candle put out. Lita was holding one of the stone bits he'd found into the light. She'd been rubbing the dirt away with a moistened cloth and had finally gotten it clean. "Does this look familiar to you?" She held it flat on the palm of her hand so he could see it clearly.

He stared at it in astonishment. He hadn't thought anything of finding what looked like a dirt-caked agate pendant, because it was smaller than the piece he remembered all too well. But now that he saw it clean, he realized this was a miniature version of the amulets that his kidnappers, and the men who had taken Amily, had all worn around their necks. Amulets that he *knew* had some sort of nasty spirit in them, one that could completely take over a person. One that could kill!

He wanted to shout at Lita and slap the thing out of her hands—but Dallen and Jermayan were still dozing quietly in the corner, and hadn't reacted to it, and he himself wasn't feeling the angry, sullen presence he had always sensed around those talismans. So though it looked the same, maybe it wasn't the same. Cautiously he touched it with one finger.

It was only stone. There was no presence, no spirit. There was, however, a crack running right through it. Maybe when it was broken, whatever had been in it had gotten out.

"It looks exactly like the things Levor and Kan-Li had around their necks," he said, furrowing his brows. "The men that kidnapped Amily had them, too. There was something bad in those, but—" he shook his head. "I can't feel anything from this. It's just a stone."

"I thought it looked like the ones we took from those corpses," Lita replied. "I didn't get a real good look at them, because they got whisked away for the Archivists to try to match up with drawings in the records. You say this one is dead, though? You're sure?"

:Dallen?: he called, instead of answering.

:I'm following. It's just a bit of agate. Nothing special about it except that it is rather pretty, and the carving is exceptionally well executed.:

"Dallen says it's harmless," he reported.

"It's a very handsome piece, and the carving is exceptional," mused Lita, echoing Dallen's words. "If this is a piece from the hands of your blood relatives, they are remarkable craftsmen."

"Well, I wish they'd use that skill for somethin' else," he said dryly.

"I'd like it eventually if you don't want it," Lita told him, "But I think you should keep it for now. It might unlock some more memories for you."

She handed it and a bit of cloth to him; he wrapped it in the cloth and thrust it in a pocket. She might be right, but he wanted to be absolutely certain that what seemed inert wasn't actually sleeping before he mucked about with it. Or that it wasn't going to form some sort of channel that a bad spirit could come through.

On the other hand, the only way this piece could have come here was through his parents. So at long last, he really, truly, had something of *theirs.*

"I can understand if you decide you want to keep it," Lita continued, and smiled at him. "It's the first thing you've ever gotten that was from your parents. If you only want to lend it to me so I can have it copied, that would be fine."

"Aye," he said, slowly. "I think that's what I'd like to do."

"Can I see that?" Jakyr had come up behind him while they spoke. Lita frowned fiercely and looked as if she would like to tell him to go away, but Mags handed him the bit of agate. Jakyr turned it this way and that, studying it. "I can copy it now, if you like. The carving, at least. I'll do some rubbings and some wet-paper pouncings. That would be quite clear, and it would be easy for you to study. If that is acceptable."

He spoke stiffly, as if there were something behind his words that he was absolutely adamant about not saying aloud. Lita eyed him and slowly lifted an eyebrow. Mags was afraid she was going to say something sharp, but instead she said "That would be most helpful, thank you."

"Mags?" Jakyr asked.

Mags shrugged. "Go ahead."

The Herald took the bit of stone off to the van, where most of the supplies for writing were kept. Mags tilted his head to one side and gave Lita an inquiring look. She was twisting a strand of hair around one finger.

"Well," she said, finally, "stiff-necked bastard that he is, that's the closest I'm going to get to an apology from him, so I expect I had better take it."

". . . and I coulda sworn someone was watching me," Mags concluded, as they all dined on smoked-venison soup and flat-bread. "I ain't never gotten that kinda feeling afore, except way back when . . . when that half-crazed assassin turned up in the blizzard, only we didn't know he was at the Collegium at all. And when there was something just watching me, down at the pawnshop. But the thing at the pawnshop never moved from where it was, and this moves all the time. Sometimes it's there when I'm alone in the back caves here, and sometimes it's over at the treasury cave."

"It might be just that you associated the blizzard with a feeling of being watched, so since there's a blizzard, you feel like you're being watched," Lita said reasonably. Then she frowned. "Except . . ."

"Except what?" Mags asked, sharply.

"Except I've gotten that feeling myself, recently," she admitted reluctantly. "Under the same circumstances, when I am alone in the back caves. I almost wish now that talisman you found *did* have some trace of a spirit in it, because then I could put it all down to the presence of that."

"Well, it's not just like the feeling I had at the Collegium," Mags amended. "None of them talisman spirits *liked* me. At all. This don't give me any feeling of bein' hated. Just . . . watchin'."

"Well . . ." Bear flushed a little. "Make that me, too. Only when I'm alone. I just put it down to that I'd rather not be living in a cave. But . . . aye. Never when we're out of here, only when we're in here. It's been going on for a while for me, since before the snow—more than once when I was walking around in the valley getting some air. And one night before the snow came, I could have sworn I saw someone off across the valley when I went out for a good look at the moon to reckon the phase. But I figured it was just a trick of the shadows. It was night, it was dark, and it was over near one of those little groves."

Jakyr sighed. For a moment, Mags was dead certain he was going to scoff at all of them. "Much as I hate to add my name to the company of the haunted, I've been getting the same skin-crawling, someone-is-watching feeling myself. Only when alone. And just about *every* time I have been alone, whether it was in the caves or in the valley. Jermayan says he can't sense anything and hasn't smelled anything, and *never* have I wished so much for a good hound in my life."

:I have nothing for you,: said Dallen. *:I have noticed you get that sensation when you are alone. You are never somewhere I can come. Perhaps it* is *a spirit.:*

"Dallen says the same," he reported. "I dunno what to say. Except the last time I got the *feeling watched* feeling without any nastiness attached, remember, I ended up getting kidnapped."

Jakyr chewed that over. "I fail to see what anyone would want with all six of us, nor how they would manage to hold us without an army, nor how they would get us *out* of a snowbound valley at all, but I'll take that under advisement," he replied. "So everyone be cautious." He glanced at Mags. "I'd like to ask you not to go to that treasure cave, but that doesn't seem fair, and it isn't as if Dallen couldn't get to you in a heartbeat if something happened."

"The time I got kidnapped, though," Mags added, "The feeling was always in the same place. Like there was some kinda invisible eye over me. An' this—it's all over, like I said. And it ain't just me."

"Forewarned is forearmed," Jakyr said. "And speaking of which—until this goes away or we figure out what it is, everyone go armed."

Mags had no argument with that. "Yessir," he said, as the others nodded.

───────────

As if talking about it had dispelled the watcher, the next morning Mags went out to the "treasury" cave and felt absolutely nothing, even though he had the talisman—if that was what it was—in his pocket.

He went back to sifting through the dirt, wondering if there really was a watcher, and now it was gone, if it had understood it was being talked about and decided to withdraw, if it was some sort of haunt and only needed to be acknowledged—

—or if it had never existed in the first place, and was the product of people with a great deal of imagination and nerves on edge from being confined so closely together.

On the other hand, maybe the point had been for him to *find* that talisman in the first place. It might have been the spirit of one or another of his parents, wanting him to find this little piece of his heritage. Why not? Spirits never lingered unless they wanted something. Maybe as long as the bit of stone had remained lost, they couldn't rest, but now that he had it, they were ready to go on to whatever reward they were bound for.

And maybe I can come up with about a hundred stories if I keep thinking about it, he admitted to himself. That was the danger of having too good an imagination. He could all too easily remember all the horror stories he had told himself about devils and monsters in the mine, ready to take him away. Even now, those memories made him shiver.

And that was when a blast of frigid air from the cave mouth nearly blew out the fire *and* knocked him off balance.

He jumped to his feet, but that was no inimical spirit that was screaming around the mouth of the cave. That was a very real and very bitter wind, and it was driving ice and snow right in here, past the turning of the tunnel and deep into the cave.

His first thought was to fight his way back to the living cave. But Dallen stopped him in his tracks before he got more than two paces toward the door.

:Don't. This is worse than the last storm; this time the hills aren't protecting the valley. Jakyr just went to the mouth of our cave with Jermayan; the wind nearly bowled him over, and it's completely white out there. You can't see a thing. You'd be lost in a moment.:

As if to underscore that, another blast of icy air slammed into the treasury cave, bringing with it a thick skein of snow.

:All right. I'm gonna go in deeper, the wind's getting me

here. Looks like it's a damn good thing Amily talked me into bringing stuff with me.:

He moved the fire, first thing; he got a pot and gathered as much of the wood and coals as he could from the struggling blaze. Then he picked up the lantern and moved on, going far into a twisting passage that effectively foiled the wind, to a place where the air grew warmer, warm compared to a cave's usual temperature. Looking around, it seemed he had found what might have been the bandit chief's own "quarters." It was a wider spot in the tunnel. There was a blackened spot on the floor that showed where fires had been built before, and there were four of the sleeping nooks spaced around the walls.

This was as good a spot to set up as any, and better than out where he had planned on camping. He left the pot on the blackened spot and dragged the rest of the pots in their box down to set beside it. He moved all of the firewood that would fit into one of the "sleeping nooks," then brought the hay and blankets down to build himself a bed in another, and gradually got things roughly arranged into a comfortable living space. He tried to ignore the fact that there was yet more unexplored passage beyond this, though the dark tunnel did bother him a bit. He didn't much like being exposed on two sides, even though one of those sides was now pretty effectively blocked by the king of all blizzards.

Once he was set up, he'd dumped out the pot of coals and gotten a respectable fire going; then he ventured down that unexplored passage a bit farther. It narrowed, then widened again, and a sort of small side cave budded off it. There he was rewarded by a single-hole latrine nook. And this one had a basin that was served by a trickle of water from the rock above, a tiny spring, perhaps coming from the source of their water in the living cave. He tasted it cautiously, and it seemed sweet and good. So he wouldn't have to melt snow for water.

That's an improvement, he thought dryly. *All the comforts of home.*

There was still more passage beyond the latrine, but at the moment, he was disinclined to go farther. He had a lot to do.

When everything was set up, his fire was warming the small space pretty well, and he had done all that he could, he surveyed the space that was going to be his home for the next couple of days with resignation. He was going to get rather tired of meat and vegetable pies . . . but there were worse things to have had with him. These would be easy to heat on a rock at the side of his fire. He could make hot tea. He had a book. It wasn't a total disaster.

And I ain't gonna be there if Lita and Jakyr go at each other again, he reminded himself. *That . . . that might be worth a couple days of samey-same food an' no Amily.*

At least the feeling of being watched was still gone.

Maybe it don't like snow any more than I do.

He woke to tend his fire—he knew he would have to be very careful with the fire in such a confined space. He was sleeping on very flammable hay, after all. One jumping coal and he would awaken in a very bad situation. He also was the only one here, and if he let the fire go out, he'd have to get it started again with a firestriker in the black dark. Then he went back to sleep.

He woke a second time. He could still hear the wind howling, faint and far, raging at the entrance. He poked at Dallen and got the equivalent of a sleepy grunt, so evidently everyone else was sleeping too. He made himself a cup of tea and went back to sleep again.

The third time he woke, he knew he wouldn't be able to go back to sleep again, so he ventured back toward the front of the cave, wrapped tightly in his cloak. There was some pale light reflecting off the back wall of the cave ahead, so he knew it must be daylight. But the wind was still raging out there, and Dallen didn't give him any indication that he should try to fight his way back, so he went back to his warmer den, already feeling chilled.

More tea, a sketchy attempt at cleaning himself up, a meat pie, and he was left contemplating several hours of wakefulness and nothing much to fill them with. If it hadn't been so cold in the treasury cave, he might have gone back to sifting through the sand for more fragments, but that wind would cut you to the bone, even that far inside the cave entrance. He deeply pitied anyone who had been caught out in that and hoped no one had. He was not tempted to use his Gift to try to find out, for what could he do to help anyone he found?

As he sat back down in his bed nest, he felt something in his pocket poke at his leg. The talisman, of course. He wondered if Lita had been right, if it could help him unlock more of those memories.

:I don't see any harm in you trying,: Dallen said in unprompted response to the thought. *:I'll guard you from here from anything nasty you wake up, assuming that you do. You really aren't any farther away from me than if you were in your stable room and I was out in the Field.:*

Well, why not? And if nothing else, he could use the practice at meditation.

He got the talisman out of his pocket, put it where he could see it in the firelight, made himself comfortable, and let his eyes rest on it while he unfocused his thoughts. If he had it right, things were not going to come to him if he forced them. He had to relax to let them through.

The problem was, this was very boring.

Other things kept intruding. A stem of hay was tickling one wrist. There seemed to be a harder spot under one buttock. The cave smelled dank. The howling wind was unnerving. And—

"So, at last we meet!" said a soft voice that sounded uncannily familiar—but not in Valdemaran! He looked up in shock.

A figure stepped out of the passage that went deeper into the hill. "I will bless rather than curse this wretched storm. It has been impossible to get you alone until now—Cousin Meric!"

Mags froze and looked up at the face that stared down at him, lit by the flickering firelight.

A face that was as familiar to him as his own.

Because it *was* his own.

Mags was paralyzed with fear and shock, as paralyzed as if he had drunk another dose of that potion that the assassin Levor had brewed for him. His heart pounded, and his chest felt tight. It was very hard to breathe. The stranger dropped down on his heels and regarded him curiously, with his head tilted a little to one side. He seemed entirely at ease. The firelight lit up one side of his face. It was a jarring experience, seeing what he usually saw in a mirror.

No wonder all the assassins who had "recognized" Mags had been so startled. The likeness between them was unnerving. Why, they even wore their hair about the same length, he and the stranger!.

Mags decided that staying very still was the best thing he could do right now. This, clearly, was the young man he had been mistaken for by all those assassins. Which meant he *came* from that clan of assassins. Which meant he probably was a highly trained assassin himself. No move was a good move right now. Any move could be interpreted as an attack, and . . . well, he didn't much want to think about the conse-quences.

:Look at his posture. He doesn't mean any harm,: Dallen said instantly into his mind. He wondered how on earth Dallen could even think that! Just because the young man was relaxed didn't mean he wasn't about to do something awful. He could merely be so confident of his own abilities that he considered Mags no threat at all.

"I don't mean you any harm," the young man said, echoing what Dallen had told Mags. He smiled a little, and it seemed to be a perfectly genuine smile. "Really, I could have murdered all of you a hundred times over before this, if I'd cared to. I've been studying you for quite some time now. Don't feel bad, though; you've never had to deal with someone who has been trained from the cradle to do what I do."

"Uh . . ." Mags swallowed, his mouth very dry. "I . . . uh . . ."

:He's completely blocked my Mind-magic. How in the seven hells did he do that?: Dallen was shocked to the core.

Startled, Mags used his own Gift, only to realize with a start that so far as his Gift was concerned . . . there was no one in front of him. No one, and nothing. Was it possible that the stranger *wasn't* there at all, that he was an illusion, or a spirit, or . . . wasn't there supposed to be a Gift that let your spirit walk about while your body remained at home?

"You're not some sorta . . . Sending. Are you?" he managed. "Because . . . so far as me and Dallen are concerned, you aren't here."

The young man laughed. "No, it's this." He reached into his shirt and pulled out a talisman identical to the one Mags had found. "If you were to put that one on and let it warm to your body, you would vanish from the Senses of the Mind yourself. Yes, even broken as it is. But it needs to be on your body for some time, to grow accustomed to you. We, those of us at the head of the House, don't wear the common ancestor-spirit talismans. These talismans are reserved for those of our blood, the direct bloodline. We are . . . privileged. But we wear these to keep us from being detected in the course of our missions."

Mags swallowed again. This was a very surreal conversation. He kept expecting Jakyr to burst in here at any moment, regardless of the blizzard. Realistically, he knew that Jakyr would be lost in moments if he tried. "What do you mean, *our blood?*" he asked. " 'Cause . . . you called me cousin. And we damn sure look alike. And . . . I reckon you know about two fellers called Levor and Kan-li, and they pretty much out and said that I was kin to them. But I don't know just what I'm supposed to be kin to."

"May I sit?" the young man asked. At Mags' stiff nod, he did so, crossing his legs and sitting near enough to touch Mags on the shoulder. He didn't appear to be the least uncomfortable sitting on the bare stone. He was as graceful as a cat, supple as a serpent. Mags had to think for a moment about what the stranger had said—that he'd been trained from the cradle. It fit in with those memories he'd gotten from one of the previous assassins.

His clothing was . . . odd. Something like Kan-li and Levor had worn, but the fabric was thicker and looked softer. It wasn't a single color, either; it was a mottled gray, and Mags realized after a moment that this would have allowed the young man to blend in just about anywhere the stone of the hills showed through. Which was to say, virtually everywhere in these caves and the valley.

"As I said, be at peace. I could have killed you too many times to count, my cousin," he said. "Watch."

He was only *just* within reach of Mags, but a moment later, he had Mags' knife in his hands. Then in the next instant, before Mags could even blink, the knife was back in the sheath at his side.

"You're one of—that bunch of killers," Mags managed. He tried very hard not to sound accusing. The last thing he wanted to do was set this man off on a rampage.

"Correct." The young man nodded, not taking offense in the least. "That is what we do. The House of the Sleepgivers. That is the name we give ourselves. Of course, the true Sleepgivers are only those who are trained to the peak of perfection. The others of the House are . . . less able." He wrinkled his nose. "Very much less able, in the case of those who first encountered you and your adopted kin. Truly, we should never have given in to venality and taken the commission in the first place. For that, my apologies." And he gave a little bow. "But I was not in command of the situation of *you*. And although we are taught to master our emotions, in the case of my father and my other relations, their emotions, sadly, mastered them."

"You know, what you're saying sounds real pretty, but it's not making any sense to me," Mags responded, with a touch of irritation, which he quickly covered. *Don't make him mad, stupid. Never make the trained killer mad.* "Who are you, why're you here, and—"

As he looked at the young man, he could see subtle differences from his own face. His was a trifle thinner, the cheekbones more prominent. His hair had a bit of a wave to it, this young man's was straighter. He thought perhaps that he was shorter than the other, too, although until they stood side by side, he wouldn't be able to tell. There was no doubt that they were related, and closely, and they could certainly pull off convincing masquerades of each other. But they were not twins.

In a way that was comforting. He didn't want to be anyone's twin. Especially not the twin of a trained killer.

"Again, my pardon, and I shall begin at the beginning. I am your cousin Beshat." He smiled, broadly. He had very good teeth, even, strong, and white. Nicer than Mags' teeth. "Call me Bey. And although the name you were born to was Meric, as it always is for the first son of the line, I shall call you by the one you have here. Mags."

Mags began to feel a hint, just a hint, of friendliness to

this—Bey. Because Bey wasn't forcing a name that wasn't his any longer onto him. Unlike Levor and Kan-li, who insisted on calling him "Meric."

"And so, Mags, this is a tale, a tale long in the making and long in telling. Your tale and mine. A tale of twins who married twins, and two cousins, one the elder—" he nodded at Mags "—and one the younger, by a mere moon. And I know it is a tale you will want to hear."

Jakyr must have been having fits by now. *:Have you told Jakyr about this?:* he asked Dallen. And got a surprising answer.

:No.: Dallen was very firm on that. *:It won't do any good. He'll die if he tries to get to you. This Bey fellow—let's try something. Ask him to take off the talisman to prove his good will.:*

Mags looked the young man straight in the eyes. They were disconcertingly direct and honest and didn't seem to belong to a hired killer. "You say you could'a killed me and didn't, but it's pretty obvious from everything that's been goin' on that your people want me alive fer some reason. So prove yourself. Take off that talisman, so me an' Dallen can look at your mind."

"Dallen, yes! That is the horse-that-is-not-a-horse! And you can speak with him all the way to the next cave!" The young man chuckled with what seemed to be delight. "I will certainly oblige you. Unlike the men my father sent, I have taken pains to study you, you *Heralds.* I know you will not harm me unless and until I prove I intend to harm you." And with that, he lifted the leather cord that held the talisman around his neck over his head and set it to one side. He looked at Mags expectantly, almost as if he thought Mags would react in some way.

As the stone cooled, the young man became *present* in Mags' mind. And Mags did react, not by startling, but by narrowing his eyes. "That's one helluva trick," he muttered, and skimmed the young man's surface thoughts for anything nasty.

Nothing. This young man was *nothing* like any of the others of "his kind" that Mags had encountered. Mags would never have known what he did—or claimed he did—just from the fairly cheerful tenor of his mind.

Of course, there are killers who like to kill. They're probably pretty cheerful about it, if it comes to that.

:*I went deeper than you, and I got nothing either,*: Dallen admitted. :*I think we should hear him out. He's . . . very different.*:

Shadow and light played around Bey from the fire behind him. He should have seemed sinister, but his completely relaxed posture and half-smile made him the opposite. "I have been following you since you crossed the Karsite Border," Bey said. "I studied you and the Heralds from afar while you were at the Throne Hall and Place of Studies. I was very, very careful. I left no trace of my passage. It was a good test of my skills, I think. Oh, my father does not know I have done this. Officially I am on my 'wild year,' when I am permitted to go anywhere I please and do anything I want, so that I will become jaded with the world and content to return to the House of Sleepgivers and take up my duties." He laughed at that, as if it was some sort of joke. If it was, Mags didn't get it. "I simply did not tell him that I did not trust the competence of those he sent after you. And it seems I was correct in my estimation." He made a *tsk*ing sound, and shook his head. "To call them fools is to do perfectly respectable fools an injustice. But . . . all right, I am getting ahead of myself. Let me first tell you of your kin."

"It's only fair to warn you I got no love for 'em," Mags said dryly. This conversation was taking on a distinctly surreal quality. The howl of the blizzard in the distance, the warmth and crackle of the fire, the assassin acting as if he'd been invited for tea and a meat pie . . .

"Nor do I blame you in the least," Bey replied. "Here is the meat of the matter. The House of Sleepgivers is all that is left of a great clan. And yet, in another fashion, it is the culmination of a great clan. Or—would you rather I *showed* you?"

"What do you mean?" Mags asked, warily.

"You have the same Blessing as your father and your mother, so I have learned from following you, and so I would have assumed from your lineage," Bey said, quite casually. "You are a Mindwalker. You can read thoughts as a scribe reads a scroll." He spread his empty hands wide in an expansive gesture of welcome and acceptance. "So read mine."

Well, if that wasn't a potential trap in the making, Mags didn't know one. Mags shook his head. "And have you cosh me while I'm doin' it, and—I dunno, cart me off like the last time. No." He narrowed his eyes. "But my Companion can."

:Oh. I like that. Jermayan can guard me from any treachery. I can rely on him; he is very good defensively.:

That meant Dallen was going to tell Jermayan at least. Mags wondered how long Jermayan could keep this a secret from Jakyr.

Possibly a long time. Jakyr isn't all that good at Mindspeaking.

Bey nodded, as if he found this completely understandable. "Wise, and I cannot blame you in the least. Let it be so."

Bey closed his eyes and relaxed . . . and Mags scooted back in his bed to put a good bit more distance between them, and took his knife in his hand.

The story unrolled in Mags' mind as Dallen got it from Bey. The House of the Sleepgivers had once been a clan so large as to be considered a nation. They were famed for their single warriors, rather than for their army. Their home was, not unlike parts of Valdemar, an insalubrious place to live; but unlike Valdemar it was hot, dry, mountainous desert. Their warriors were all they had to sell, so sell them, they did. They sold the warriors' services, and literally sold the warriors in some cases, when the warrior's family was in great need or great debt.

Mags watched as Dallen sent him the images he got from Bey's mind. If there was a spot not unlike hell, this desert was surely it. Furlongs of sand and scrub interrupted by barren mountains, hot and dry in summer, cold and dry in winter. The only water came from infrequent rains and deep, deep wells, wells that were guarded with the lives of those who possessed them.

The only two ways to live in this desert were by herding and by fighting. Only those families that controlled a well could herd, however. So the clan became very, very good at fighting. Now, under most circumstances, "fighting" would turn to "raiding" as they stole the property of their more prosperous, and better-watered, neighbors. But they were too poor to afford decent weapons, and a cadre of fierce fighters armed only with what they could make with wood and stone could not prevail against those armed with steel. They turned to another sort of fighting and raiding—making it the passage into adulthood for a young boy to kill a fully armed warrior of the "fatlands" and steal all his weapons. Thus, they became incredibly efficient and incredibly stealthy murdering machines.

Once an adult, such training did not suit going into an army or even a mercenary corps; but as a bodyguard, or even a gladiator, they were second to none. So they sold their young men, and their young men commanded the highest prices.

So . . . they prospered. But when you sell your young men, soon your numbers begin to dwindle. And that is what happened. So the Shadao—the great lord of the clan—had decided that there was only one solution.

Sell death itself.

Death that came on silent feet, came by night or day, at any hour, struck without warning, and was gone.

:It's interesting though,: said Dallen as Mags watched Bey's

quiet face. *:At one point they were very careful, almost ethical, in what jobs they took. They saw themselves as the hand of the gods. They destroyed those whom the gods should have. But after a while the money just got too good, and they took any job at all.:* Dallen paused. *:Bey is . . . he wants to go back to the old ways. He* hates *that the House of the Sleepgivers has given up what he considers "honorable work" in favor of "highest bidder." He also hates what the House has become in terms of the Sleepgivers themselves.:*

Once the Sleepgivers had never released a man to do their work unless he had reached the pinnacle of his "profession"—which essentially meant, someone like Bey. But they discovered . . . something . . .

Mags couldn't quite make out what it was; it seemed that even Dallen's thoughts were foggy on the subject. It had to do with the talismans and the drugs. There was some transference of memory involved, as he knew. The talismans held a coercive spirit of some sort. Dallen seemed to almost understand it all, but he just couldn't quite grasp what it all was and how it all worked.

:Don't worry about it. It's nasty and it's brutal. That's all you need to know.:

Maybe it worked like the Karsite demons. There was probably more than one kind of those.

So now, instead of being carefully taught and nurtured, inculcated with philosophy and ethics as well as the deadly arts, the House of Sleepgivers was turning out . . . killing machines. As soon as a boy could walk, he was taken from his parents. He was put into training, a sort of training where friendships were discouraged and cutthroat competition encouraged. Then, at adolescence, the trainees were tested and divided into three sorts. The first were the expendable ones, who were led to believe that good performance would lead to a rise in the ranks. This was not true. This would never be true. They were well trained, yes, but they would never be

missed if they were killed in their commissions. Those were
the sort that had been sent north in the initial contract with
Karse—because the Shadao felt that the House might as well
have someone else pay for the expenses of the search for his
missing heir and wife. If they were caught, their talismans
would kill them, and they were allowed to be aware of this, as
incentive not to get caught.

The second rank was of those who were like Levor and
Kan-li. They were very, very good and very, very skilled. They
knew the secrets of the herbs and the talismans. They were
entrusted with many things. But they were not the best of the
best.

Those were very few indeed, and Bey was one. They never
used the herbs. They were never given *those* talismans, only
another sort that hid them from Mind-magic and—other
magic?

Mags couldn't quite grasp that.

:Doesn't matter,: Dallen insisted, and he trusted Dallen.
*Things was all fuzzy when we talked about the Truth Spell,
and the stuff that guards Valdemar and drove that first fellow
mad. Maybe it's part of all that.*

All right then.

The ones like Bey, the best of the best, the young ones at
least, had grown restless since the old Shadao died, and the
new one, Bey's father, had come into power. They longed for
the old days of real honor and ethics, when they served as the
hand of the gods. They scorned the expendables as corrupt
and the second rankers as those without vision. They wanted
elite to truly mean *elite*.

Bey wanted the old ways back. He wanted to know that
when his knife brought the sleep of forever, it would be to one
who *deserved* it, not to one who was merely inconvenient to
someone else. On one level, Mags could almost agree with
that. Almost. But it was still killing people, and it was one
thing to kill someone when he was trying to kill you, and an-

other thing entirely to go and kill him in cold blood, in stealth, and in full knowledge that you planned his death.

But if it really was someone who deserved it? If he had a chance to kill the leader of the Karsites, or even one of those priests that summoned demons, would he? Could he?

Just as he began pursuing that train of thought, Bey started to droop . . . then got pale.

Dallen reacted instantly. *:We need to stop now. This is beginning to hurt him. He's not used to being examined with Mind-magic so intensely.:*

"Dallen says we should stop," Mags said aloud, "I guess we are taking a good bit out of you with this." And Bey breathed a sigh of relief.

"Thank you, my cousin," he said, and opened his eyes, then swayed a little. "I see now why we wear the talismans," he continued, with a dry chuckle. "It is not only to hide ourselves from your magic, it is to *protect* ourselves from your magic. It is very powerful. You may not be my equal in arms, my cousin, but you are my superior in this. It seems there are warriors of the mind as well as warriors of the knife." He bowed a little and swayed again, catching himself with one hand on the floor. "I believe . . . I should go and lie down now."

He got up, slowly and carefully, and staggered a pace or two until he could get one hand on the wall. As he leaned against the wall and took slow, deep breaths, clearly trying to find some strength, Mags was torn—should he go and help the young assassin? But that would put Mags right within easy striking range of a killer who could have been feigning all of this. How easy it would be to lure him on and on, then pretend weakness, so that he could get Mags close enough to do anything he wanted to.

"Stay where you are, my cousin," Bey said, waving at him. "A momentary weakness will not harm me. I will go to my rest place. I will return at dawn, I think. This time I will warn you." He toed the talisman toward Mags. "Or rather, your familiar will warn you. I will leave this with you so that you may know I am honest. Sleep well, my cousin. We will resume this talk soon."

With that, he slipped into the darkness, and in a moment he was gone. But now Mags could sense him, moving deeper into the caves. Deeper than Mags would dare to go with a lantern, and he was walking in total darkness.

:He got here when we did, following us. All the time we've been out, he's been exploring. And he's used to caves and tunnels; the House of Sleepgivers is one giant warren under a mountain. He's probably got a map of every little bit of cave in this valley in his head.:

Mags felt a bit weak himself after all that. *:Have you and Jermayan told Jakyr yet?:* Surely by now Dallen had said *something.* He was afraid of what would happen when they found out. Even if Bey was gone now, Jakyr would barge right out into the teeth of the blizzard without a cloak and—

:No, and we aren't going to,: Dallen said. Mags felt—well, he wasn't certain what he felt. Shock, relief, both together? He *wanted* to believe Bey. Bey was giving him virtually everything he had been craving all his life. Kin. Answers. Sympathy. Even admiration . . .

And this could all be poison wrapped in a delicious crust. Bey was a killer, and killers are trained to use all sorts of weapons, especially those that can get them close to their target, get their target to trust them, so the murder is easy and escape sure. Even if Bey didn't intend to kill him, he could still get Mags close enough to incapacitate him. And all he had to do was keep Mags unconscious with that talisman around his neck, and his friends would not be able to find him even if he was hidden right under their noses.

:Now that he's taken that talisman off, we can have him down before he can blink,: Dallen said. Not only was this unexpected, Mags was . . . shocked. Because when Dallen said *down* what Dallen meant was *dead.* He'd never, ever heard of

a Companion stating calmly that he could kill with Mind-magic.

It wasn't that Companions didn't kill—because they did. They were fierce fighters in battle and had no trouble caving in an enemy's head with their wicked hoofs. But—

:We don't do this lightly. Or often. Maybe once in a generation at most. But this is extraordinary, and we must take extraordinary risks and be prepared to take extraordinary actions. We've never had an opportunity like this, to change an entire nation with just a single encounter. These people could go back to being a force for good, Mags.:

:If it's true,: Mags reminded him. There was always that. If it all was true. Bey could be lying. It was very, very hard to lie with your thoughts, but it was possible; or, more accurately, it was possible to keep only what you wanted someone to know on the surface and conceal the things you did not want him to know deeper.

:If it's true. But the deeper he lets us go, the more we can be certain of what is true and what isn't. Are you willing to take the risk?: Dallen's Mindvoice hardened. *:If you're not, and you are prepared to take partial responsibility for it, I'll kill him now, and only you will ever know he was here. Jermayan and I will do that for you. We can go on with the plan of having you declared dead, only now, it will be with a great deal more information about the Sleepgivers to make it more believable to them.:*

Mags had to think about that, very, very hard. There was so much at stake here, far more than just him, because these were people who had done their level best to fulfill a contract with Karse that meant destabilizing the government of Valdemar at *best,* and assassinating one or more of the Royal Family at worst. And this, allegedly, was one of the highest-ranking people in that organization. So . . . could, should he trust his feelings and trust what Bey told him? Take a chance on one man he didn't know, and hadn't even met until a couple of candlemarks ago? Based only on what he and two Companions felt? When there could be something dark and dangerous lurking under that affable exterior?

Or should they snuff him out like a candle and discard him, the way any of these Sleepgivers themselves would eliminate anyone who was in his way. Coldly, calmly, assassinate Bey. And—then what? What would happen then? Bey said that his father did not know he was here—could that be trusted? What if this ignited some sort of blood feud between Valdemar and the Sleepgivers? What if he made things far worse by killing Bey than they already were?

Logic said to allow Dallen to kill him. He was pretty sure that Bey had not been lying when he said the Shadao didn't know where he was. And even if the Shadao guessed, how would he find a body rotting away in the depths of some obscure caves in an obscure part of Valdemar?

His gut said, logic be damned. His gut said that this young man could be trusted. That they weren't so different, he and Mags. That the difference was mainly in how they saw the world and what they were willing to do. Bey was willing, if he could change the Sleepgivers back to what they were, to assume the gods knew what they were doing when the Sleepgivers were assigned a target that "deserved" to die. Mags was not. But . . . Mags could also not swear he would not find *himself* in a position one day that would require that he kill in cold blood.

And after all, hadn't Dallen and Jermayan just offered to do that for *him?*

:For now, we trust him,: Mags said. *:We can always change our minds later. I don't fancy killing anyone in cold blood, not even if he deserves it. And how the hell do I know if he deserves it?:*

:And there are three of us,: Dallen reminded him. *:You are the one in the most physical danger from him. You have to sleep some time. Maybe—probably—he can get into our cav-*

ern, but one of us will stay awake at all times, and he'll never do it without us noticing.:

Mags felt a chill of alarm. If all the tunnels were connected—and they *must* be, since the others had had that same feeling of being watched—he could get to Amily!

:If he comes near us, he's dead,: Dallen said flatly. *:I promise you. And I think he's smart enough to have figured that out. What's more, if Jermayan and I keep a close watch on him, I am near certain we can stop him before he can get to you. There's always a chance he has a second of those talismans hidden somewhere, but if he vanishes from our minds, we'll alert you.:*

Mags took a deep, steadying breath. *:All right then,:* he said again. *:We trust him. For now.:*

"Cousin," came a distant, echoing call, sounding as if it originated from a place very deep under the hill. "I come." Mags wondered how far away Bey was—and how he managed to navigate in pitch-black tunnels seemingly without fear. Had he done all his exploring with one of their lamps while they had been gone? He must have; surely he hadn't brought any such thing with him. Mags wished now that they had been more systematic about marking off what supplies they had used. They were probably missing quite a bit—bedding, lanterns, rope, food . . .

On the one hand, it was terribly clever of Bey to have figured out they were not going to keep strict track of their supplies. On the other hand, if they had kept strict track of their supplies and found things missing they would have *known,* from the beginning, that there was someone in the caverns besides them.

We prolly would have thought it was a hermit or a bandit or something, but we would have been looking for him.

Would they have found Bey, though? Mags thought not.

Bey was just too good at hiding his presence. And they were nowhere near as adept at finding someone who had that talisman and was determined they not find him.

Shoot, all he needed to do was to move to the other side of the valley until we stopped looking.

Bey must have worked his way across Valdemar in the same way, stealing what he needed as he followed Mags. When had he first begun? Right after Mags crossed the Karsite border, he said, and Mags had no reason to doubt him. He'd said he was on a "wild year;" if he had already been in Valdemar for a time before he picked up Mags, he'd have had plenty of time to study Heralds and the culture of Valdemar.

If you were going to be a successful assassin, you had to learn how to assimilate quickly so you could fit in seamlessly. And Bey was the best of the best. He probably couldn't pass as a Valdemaran, but he surely knew enough not to stand out, and there were plenty of foreigners in Valdemar. *I'd give a lot to know exactly what he knows.*

Mags had not been idle in the time that Bey had gone. He'd taken the talismans—both of them—and locked them in the pot box, then piled all of the rest of the firewood on top of the box. He'd folded one of the blankets into a pad and positioned it out of arm's reach of his bed. He had every knife that he had brought over to this cave with him, out and ready to throw or stab with. He had the lantern positioned so that it would glare into Bey's eyes but gave him a perfect and unimpeded view of Bey.

When Bey appeared in the doorway, he seemed delighted at these preparations. "Very well done, my cousin!" he said with high approval, and sat down on the folded blanket. "Ah, that is much more comfortable, and my thanks for the courtesy. I trust you have done your practice at this distance?"

"Seriously? You ask that? You'd be annoyed with me if I hadn't," Mags retorted.

"So I would. I expect much of you, cousin. Even as I expect much of myself. Well, have you fully absorbed the tale of the

Sleepgivers?" Bey asked, tilting his head slightly, and wearing an inquisitive expression.

"I didn't think about much else," Mags admitted.

"And did you find a flaw in it?" Bey smiled. It was a curiously disarming smile. Charming. But charm could be as powerful a weapon as anything with a point or an edge.

"We couldn't, and we tried." Right this minute, Mags realized that there was one thing that he did *not* know. And it was important. He didn't know anything at all about Bey's motives.

"Just what do you expect to get from me anyway?" he asked, leveling a very hard look at this purported cousin. "You say you've studied Heralds, so you've got to know there isn't a chance I'd do anything to hurt my friends, my King, or my Kingdom."

Bey shrugged a little and said slowly. "You, my cousin. What I want, is you. Not for the reason that Kan-li did, because he was ordered to bring you. And not for the reason you think. It would be easier, much easier, to return the House to the old ways with two of us. In no small part because for at least a time, no one but the Shadao would be aware there were two of us. Nor would anyone be aware that you had that great and powerful Blessing. It would appear that the gods had bestowed the Blessing on *me*—and also, on me, the ability to be in two places at once. Such a thing would make me feared, which I may need to be before I am obeyed. And that is but one reason why I wish to have you at my side."

Mags shook his head. "You are not going to get me," he said flatly. "You can call me kin and talk about blood calling to blood all you like, but I'm Valdemaran, and I'm a Herald, and that's that."

Again Bey shrugged. Mags' words did not seem to disturb him in the least. "That remains to be seen. And if I do not persuade you, I still will have knowledge. Knowledge is power. You know this. If I can bring back the old ways, perhaps one day your King will wish to be rid of those demon-summoners. The Sleepgivers could be of service there. This is a rich land, and you could pay well . . ." He smiled again. "But I have not yet given up on having you."

:He's very certain he can persuade you,: Dallen said, pretty much cementing what Mags already thought. Bey was a very stubborn person—and also very certain of his own powers of persuasion.

:He don't know how stubborn I am.: After all, Mags had managed to ride out that session of drugs, which by all rights and expectations should have turned him into—well, someone else. He didn't think that mere words were likely to change him. "All right," he said aloud. "So what's next?"

"Now I tell you the tale of the four twins and the two cousins, and I think that might persuade you, Blessed One," Bey replied with a slight smile, and closed his eyes serenely and waited for Dallen to enter his thoughts.

Mags waited for Dallen to begin.

This time the images were clearer. Four portraits, done in a severe and stylistic manner. Two young men, one in gray, one in brown. Two young women, one in red, one in blue. All four of the young people were dark-haired, dark-eyed, and lean, just as he was. It was hard to say if there was any more resemblance to him, since all four faces were much alike. Mags got the feeling that "portraits" in this culture were less personal and more ideal images. *:His parents and yours,:* Dallen said. *:The one in gray was supposed to marry the one in red, but the one in brown had Mind-magic, Mindspeech, and Empathy, and the girl in red did, too. That's what he means by Blessed, because it's almost unheard of for men to have Gifts, and when they do, it's considered to be a miracle of the gods. Well, the first thing that happened was that the two with Mind-magic fell in love.:*

There were some more stylized images, as if all of this had come from an illustrated story. *:It did,:* Dallen confirmed. *:It's* *something like the stuff in the Archives, only they make an art form out of historical records. He's studied this manuscript many times. I think he was a little obsessed with the cousin he'd never met.:* Dallen's images became clearer, revealing that this was, in fact, an illuminated manuscript, or the memory of one. And there were a lot of illuminations. The boy and girl meeting on a bridge in what was clearly a cavern, sitting on a bench under a rocky overhang, walking together on a cliff overlooking the desert.

This was kind of curious. If this was the story of a pair of runaways, why was it so lovingly detailed?

:Because the Shadao never gave up on the idea of bringing them back, I think. And the next Shadao—Bey's father—was the same. I get the feeling this was supposed to be something like a child's storybook, with the moral at the end being "and one day you must bring the missing ones home.":

Well, that made a kind of odd sense. So instead of erasing the runaways from history, as plenty of other rulers would have, the Shadao turned finding them into a quest.

Given that the insane Sleepbringer—and the half-insane one—and Ice and Stone—and Levor and Kan-li had all been very much aware of this obsession, Bey wasn't the only one who'd grown up with the story and the quest as a part of his training.

:The parents were still determined that the betrothed pairs wed. But at the wedding, all four conspired against that, and since all four were wedded at the same ceremony, and all four wore the same costumes, they switched partners and no one knew until the ceremony was over.:

An image of the young man and young woman standing defiantly against the railing of other, older people. For all that the little painting was stylized, it demonstrated rather graphically that the elders were not at all pleased that their careful plans had been upset.

:Your parents were the Gifted ones, of course. And you can

imagine how someone with Empathy and Mindspeech both felt about—the family business.:

Mags could, indeed. It had been torture to kill someone who was trying to kill *him,* and that was only with Mindspeech. With Empathy, he could not begin to imagine how hard it would be.

:Impossible, really. So after about a year of marriage, and after everyone had more or less settled down and accepted the fait accompli, *the two decided to run away, and their siblings decided to help them.:* Dallen paused, and Mags waited patiently, figuring that Dallen was interpreting something he had found in Bey's memory. *:Ah, now I have their names. Meric-an and Li-Inaken. You were named for your father, as the first in the line. This is something Bey's father told him, not in the storybook. This all came to a head when they knew they were going to have a child. They had heard of a place where the talismans and the Power of the Shadao could not follow. They told their siblings that was where they were going to go, because Meric could no longer bear the pain of killing others. It seems every time he did his duty, he got sicker, and his brother was afraid that he would either die of it or slay himself.:*

Mags snorted. How could his grandfather *ever* have expected otherwise? Knowing his father was Gifted and still expecting him to be an assassin was worse than ridiculous, it was insanity. What they *should* have done was to—make him a scholar or something. Although, you never knew, for all Mags knew, the mere proximity to all those other cold-blooded killers might have been eating away at his soul, too.

: They were heading for Valdemar, obviously.: Dallen pointed out. *:He must have been talking to anyone he could, searching every record he could find, to locate a place where his father wouldn't be able to touch him—or you. You saw for yourself what happened to the Sleepgivers that tried using their powers in our borders. Madness. The talismans turning on them.:*

That certainly made Valdemar a logical place to flee to.

Mags even had to wonder if they hadn't just been so desperate that they ran on a mere rumor. "There's a place in the north where it's said magic doesn't work. We'll be safe forever there!" He could see two lovestruck people striking out in that way. After all, that was what made romantic tragedy.

:And it was quite a feat of legerdemain, because the pair that was staying undertook to impersonate the pair that was fleeing. Your parents stole a talisman for Meric and took both girls' jewelry—quite a lot of it—and fled. Bey's parents managed, by moving around the palace and changing clothing a lot, to hide the fact that they were gone for three days, giving them a good head start.:

Now Mags understood some of the things he'd seen when drugged. The young couple on the run, the birth of the baby—which was him.

:I'm not sure how you managed to see those things, Mags. I'm not sure if they're real, or someone's—Levor or Kan-li's—ideas of what happened. I'd be more inclined to think the latter.: That wouldn't have been in that storybook, of course, nor the cruder versions which the young second-rank Sleepgivers would have seen. No one would have known what had happened to the pair. But Dallen thought that Levor and Kan-li had good enough imaginations to patch something into their own memories, since they knew about Mags.

Mags agreed. There had been a sort of vague blurriness about those sequences that made them stand out from some of the others. And since his own Mind-magic had been coming back at the time he took the drugs, he could easily have picked that up from the two Sleepgivers.

:And there the tale ends. Bey's parents would have been in a lot more trouble if the Shadao hadn't been trying to find his fleeing son. And when it was obvious that your parents had escaped successfully, the Shadao was too overcome with grief at losing his eldest to punish them. And then, right when the grief faded and the anger began, Bey's mother was pregnant,

thus giving the Shadao the heir he desperately desired.: Dallen sighed. *:I will say this, Bey's father has a fine sense of the melodramatic. According to Bey's recollection, he made quite a production out of his attempt at placating his father. He went to the Shadao and offered to kill himself in reparation. He got as far as slicing a wrist when the old man forgave him. He became such a model Sleepgiver that the old man completely relented and bequeathed the title of Shadao on him at his own death.:*

"You know, Bey, all this sounds like a bad play," Mags said aloud. "Lovers fleeing, twins impersonating each other, and capping it all off with an attempted suicide and a reconciliation . . . it smacks of being awfully contrived."

Bey opened his eyes, and smiled slightly. "That is because there was a great deal more machination, politics, and secret maneuvering on the part of my father, the Shadao, in order to restore himself to the good graces of his father." Bey even chuckled. "He set things up perfectly, and my grandfather was very fond of drama. He knew it for the tool that it was."

"Sounds like a clever old goat," Mags responded, dryly.

"As for the entire melodrama with your parents and mine . . . knowing my father and my mother, I believe that he only went along with the charade to please her and in hopes of winning her love at last."

"Oh?" Mags gestured to him to continue. Bey seemed happy enough to oblige.

"My father is a hard man, a very hard man. But *your* father was not the only one who fell in love—inappropriately. He was not at all pleased with the twin that shrank from him. Frankly, he thought her weak-willed and preferred her sister. So from his perspective, the switch in spouses was ideal. My mother, at first was not enamored of either son and yielded to her beloved sister's pleas that they secretly exchange on the eve of their marriage in order to make her happy."

"Well, that starts to make a lot of sense," Mags said

thoughtfully. "One of the Gifts—what you call Blessings—that they had was something that our Healers generally have. That Blessing makes it hard for Healers to really want to be with a spouse that doesn't want it too."

"Oh? Interesting. This explains a great deal." Bey brooded a bit. "Well, as to my mother, she was contented enough to have a husband who was good to her and the position of the heir's wife. Indeed, I sometimes wonder if she didn't conspire with her sister's flight in order to have that position for herself. Only after, indeed, only after she was with child, did she come to adore her husband as he adored her. So in the end, perhaps, the gods spoke. Who can tell?"

"Well, what about how your father scraped out?" Mags persisted.

"He was always the political one. He had made important allies, he had taken *very* important commissions—in fact one of those was one your father was supposed to have taken, and he—again!—took your father's place. And the Shadao was fond of extravagant gestures. The spilling of blood on the Council table appealed to him. The stains are still there," Bey ended, thoughtfully. Then turned a bit green. "Your Blessing does not agree with me, my cousin. I shall withdraw—"

"No." Mags got up, and went to Bey, offering him a hand. When Bey took it, he helped the other young man to his feet, and guided him to the bed. "You lie down there a bit. I'm gonna talk to Dallen. We aren't going to have much more time, I doubt this blizzard has another day in it, and then my friends are going to come looking for me. We have to settle this today. I'll get you some tea."

He took all the knives with him, of course. No point in leaving extra weapons where Bey could get to them. But then he made some of that tea that Bear had given him so long ago, when his Gift started giving him problems, and brought it over to the Sleepgiver. Bey accepted it, made a face over the taste, but drank it down.

"Ehu. That is better. Let me steady my head for a little."
Bey lay flat on the blankets, his gaze fixed on Mags.

"Why are you here, *really,* Bey?" Mags asked. "Not the
answer you gave me. Your own reason."

Bey pondered that for a moment. "Choice. And family. You
were given the Ancient Memories potion, and yet, here you
are, still persisting in remaining. I want to know why you are
making this choice. You're my blood, and blood should be
calling to blood so strongly you will not be able to resist. That's
the main reason. I told you the other, it's partly selfish. It will
be much easier to reign with you at my side. The Shadao, my
father, is sickly and will probably die within a year, and if I
brought you back to him, even though you are the elder, he
would not hesitate to give me the throne. I want someone at
my side I can trust, someone who understands my vision of
bringing honor back to the Sleepgivers. And here is cold, hard
truth. When you come back with me, you will know no one in
the House. You will depend on, and be loyal, to me. I need not
fear you are machinating plans behind my back. I *will* be able
to trust you, you *will* be able to trust me because of your
Blessing. Because of your Blessing, I will be able to *know*,
without doubt, who is my friend and who is my foe and who
is vacillating and how to push them. And I will have the strong
arm at my side and the brother at my back to ensure no one
can come against me."

He took a long, shuddering breath, and put one hand on
his stomach, as if to comfort it.

That was a very long speech for someone with a queasy
stomach. Mags let him wait for it to settle. "That's not going
to happen," he said, a little sadly.

"I wouldn't be so sure. Haven't you longed all your life for
a family?" Bey smiled a little, as he saw that hit home. "Well,
what did you have in mind for the settling of our . . . conundrum?"

"I have in mind that we stop going through a third party,"

Mags said, not betraying any of his uncertainty. "I want you to open your mind completely to me, and I'll open mine to you."

"This may be more dangerous to you than it is to me," Bey warned him, his eyes going bright with eagerness, his nausea forgotten.

"We'll see," said Mags. "We'll see."

They sat facing each other, cross-legged, knees touching. Bey had brought with him the herbs for the Ancient Memories potion; he seemed sure that it would open his mind completely to Mags. Mags elected to forgo the potion, Bey didn't seem to mind. He drank the nasty stuff down with a smile; when he lost the smile, and his eyes seemed to fog over, Mags knew that the time had come.

He reached for Bey's mind; the Sleepgiver's few protections fell away like shreds of wet paper. Then, he was in . . . and he opened himself to Bey.

Under the influence of the drugs, Bey could not have held secrets from Mags if he'd been a practiced Mindspeaker, which, of course, he wasn't. Dallen had been right. Everything Bey had told him was true. Of course there were many things Bey hadn't told him. That Bey was a true scion of his father, as ruthless a politician, and as adept at plot and counterplot. That Bey intended to put Mags on something of a pedestal once he had gotten the title of Shadao, showing off the Blessed One to a very select audience, the living proof that the gods favored him. And that he intended to *keep* Mags on that pedestal, regardless of what Mags wanted. But he really did intend the best for Mags, and being at Bey's side would be . . . a rather luxurious life. Bey was never going to do what had been done to his uncle, Mags' father. Bey was never, ever, going to tell him to kill, and he was going to do his best to shelter Mags from that part of the Sleepgivers' lives.

And Bey meant every word about wanting to restore honor to the Sleepgivers. He intended to use Mags' Gifts to make that possible. It was a very reasonable idea, and probably would work, and work very well. Mags could covertly implant Bey's ideas in anyone who didn't possess a talisman against Mind-magic; he could easily manipulate people to Bey's way of thinking, if he chose.

And although it would be violating the ethics he had been taught as a Herald . . . how much good would he be doing?

Quite a lot.

But it would be violating the ethics he had been taught as a Herald. . . .

And so he opened *his* mind to Bey's, and flooded him with everything it meant to be Chosen, and a Valdemaran, the good right along with the bad. The incredible bond he shared with Dallen—how it meant that he had someone with whom he had a deeper bond even than family. His love for Amily, how here you could find someone who was your friend, your lover, your partner, and your equal. What it *meant* to be a Herald; how you were never weak, because there was always someone strong to prop you, as you would prop someone weaker than you. How it felt to make peoples' lives better, every day, even when they didn't know you were doing it. How, in the end, blood was unimportant; it was the bond of brothers and sisters of the spirit that made you more whole than mere relations ever could. At the last, he stopped showing, stopped telling, stopped even images. He just *was,* and flooded Bey with the deep and certain joy of that simple being.

Then he opened his eyes. A moment later, Bey opened his. And sighed.

"You win, cousin," he said, a little sadly. "You win."

Mags unearthed the talisman and gave it back to Bey, who put it on. They clasped arms in the manner of the Sleepgivers, and Mags felt a deep pang of sorrow. Not at what he was giving up—but at what Bey was losing.

"Put on that talisman when you decide to 'die.'" Bey told him. "It will take about a day to come to life. No one will be able to find you while you wear it."

"What about you?" Mags asked a little anxiously. "Are you going to be all right?"

"I will manage." Bey grinned crookedly. "As you saw, I am a schemer. I can always manage. I will not be put off by a little setback from achieving my goal."

And then he was gone. And not long after he left, the blizzard blew itself out. Mags broke out of the cave and slogged his way to where his friends were waiting, only now being told of what had happened by Dallen and Jermayan.

And that was when the real storm began.

"I don't know whether I think you're insane, or just incredibly stupid," Jakyr said, arms crossed tightly over his chest. "Or both. What in the hell were you thinking, trusting that man?"

"Dallen said it was worth it. So did Jermayan. Just ask him," Mags said wearily. The recriminations had gone on all day and well into the evening. Eventually Amily had come over to his side, but no one else had. Bear had railed at him until he was hoarse, and then he stamped off into the caravan, taking Lena with him. Lita had called him every variation on stupid and reckless that her inventive mind could come up with, and she was a Bard, so she came up with quite a lot. Jakyr had just hammered at him for candlemarks, until he felt just about as miserable as he had felt good as Bey left.

"What gave you the right to risk all of us?" Jakyr asked again. "Risk your own life with a member of a *known assassin tribe,* fine; you can do whatever stupid thing you want with your own life. But you were risking all of us! What if he'd come over here and began picking us off one by one? What if he'd taken us hostage? Or killed all of us and taken Amily?" The cavern echoed as he shouted.

"Dallen and Jermayan said if he made one false move, they'd take him down," Mags repeated wearily. "If you can't trust your Companion, who can you trust?"

"Right at the moment, I'm not sure I can trust *anyone!*" Jakyr shouted, and glared down at Mags. "And that's a pretty fine pass for a Herald to come to!"

Mags could not have agreed with him more. He was absolutely miserable. He'd have been even more miserable if it hadn't been for Dallen quietly supporting him—literally standing next to where he was sitting—on one side, and Amily on the other.

"You keep telling him to trust his instincts, Jakyr," she finally said. "And now you're telling him his instincts, *and* Dallen's, *and* Jermayan's can't be trusted."

Jakyr glared at her, and so did Lita. "You are neither Herald nor Trainee, Amily," he said coldly. "I suggest you stay out of this. Being besotted is no excuse for being a fool."

"I am my father's daughter, Jakyr," she replied stiffly, looking him right back squarely in the eyes. "Never forget that."

If Jakyr's glare had been a storm, Amily would have been a statue of ice at that moment. But she held up under it, raising her chin and never dropping her gaze. "I have been among Heralds all my life. I have assisted my father. I have watched him train Mags. I watched him train *you.* If this were Mags' judgment alone you doubted, I would agree. But it wasn't, and by his account it was Dallen *and* Jermayan who persuaded him to do this, not the other way around. And besides that," she persisted, "he participated in a *full* mind-share with this Bey person. You *know* no one can lie in a full mind-share!"

"This is some foreign murderer with talismans and magic we don't understand!" Jakyr exclaimed, throwing up his hands. "I don't know anything anymore! For all *I* know, he was able to somehow enthrall the Companions as well!"

Dallen gave such a snort of disgust that he left a wet spot on the shoulder of Mags' tunic—and to underscore how he felt, he deliberately turned his hindquarters to Jakyr.

The message could not have been plainer. With a wordless growl, Jakyr stalked off toward the front of the cave. "I'm going to shovel snow!" he snarled. "At least I can count on *one* thing doing what it's supposed to around here!"

Lita followed, pausing only long enough to call back over her shoulder, "This isn't over, young man."

———

Jakyr and Lita returned, tired, snow-caked, and still angry with Mags.

By this point, Mags was exhausted and nearly beside himself. *:What do I do?:* he wailed inwardly to Dallen. *:It's not like I can take it all back!:*

:Leave them alone,: Dallen advised. *:Sooner or later it will dawn on them that no one is dead, no one is drugged, or possessed by an evil spirit, or otherwise compromised. Or else Jermayan and I will finally get through to Rolan, and Rolan will—well, I am not sure what he will do, but he'll do something.:*

And until then, it seemed, Mags was just going to have to put up with being treated like the clodhopper who tracked stable muck into the Healers' room. During a plague.

Amily went off to the entrance, probably to get away from all the hostility. Mags didn't blame her. But he wasn't going to back down on this, and the only way to make that plain was to stay there and take it. Jakyr and Lita finished eating, skewering Mags with accusing glares the entire time. They got up—

And that was when Amily screamed from the front of the cave.

Mags had no idea how he got from the rug to the entrance in what seemed to have been a single leap. He only knew that at one moment, he was standing, hangdog, waiting for another tirade to erupt, and the next he was pulling Amily away from the opening, away from the huge spear that was quivering in the snow not more than a couple of arm lengths away from where she had been standing, looking out.

"Everybody get back!" Jakyr shouted, unnecessarily. Mags was already pulling Amily away, and no one else was inclined to put themselves in the line of fire.

The spear stopped quivering. It was . . . large. The size of a boar spear, and whoever had thrown it had managed to get it over the snow parapet and well into the cave-mouth. Mags' heart practically stopped when he thought about what that wicked point would have done had it hit Amily. There was something wrapped around the end of it and secured with a piece of bright red string or yarn. A message?

Jakyr went back into the cave, and returned with the lid of their biggest pot. Crouching low and getting as much of himself as he could behind its shelter, he should have looked ridiculous. But he didn't. He looked impossibly brave.

He crept up crouching crabwise on the spear; he got his hand on the shaft just behind the head and, with a yank, pulled it free of the floor. Then he slid it behind him as hard as he could, and retreated. He didn't stand up until he was well clear of any place projectiles could possibly land.

Bear got hold of the spear. He was wearing gloves as he handled it. "Don't nobody touch this thing till I get a chance to wash it down," he said shortly, and he glared at Jakyr. "And *you* go wash your hands five times. The gods only know what kind of poison they might have put on the shaft. I don't want to see you back here until they're red from scrubbing."

Jakyr ducked his head guiltily and left for the sink.

Mags ran for bows and arrows and returned with three sets, handing two to Lita and Amily and keeping one for himself. Meanwhile Bear had cut the string holding what looked like paper wrapped around the shaft. It unwound; it was either paper or very stiff fabric of some kind. And there was writing on it.

Jakyr returned as Bear gingerly spread out the long scroll on the floor. "It's in Valdemaran!" he said in surprise.

"Yes," Lena agreed, "But it was never written by anyone born and raised in Valdemar." Slowly, she began to read the words aloud as Mags, Lita and Amily watched the entrance, arrows nocked and ready.

"To you within the cave. You have among you Meric Aket Inaken, son of the son of the Shadao Meric Beket Inaken. Too long have you held this one of the House of Sleepgivers. We call upon you to tell him to come to his people. Our blood calls to him. He has seen the Ancient Memories. He must return to

be made whole. We know he holds himself to be of honor. We honor the pledge we made not to harm your Shadao, your King, and his family. But we made no such promise regarding the low-caste of your land, who have such favor in your eyes. If he does not give himself over to us, we will gather up the low-caste, of whom we made no promises, and we shall give them unto Sleep."

Mags stared stonily at the entrance, although he no longer expected anything to come in *that* way. There probably weren't too many of the Sleepgivers out there—not like an army—but there were more than enough to pick them off one at a time, and *far* more than enough to keep them penned in with arrows and other projectiles. Probably there were not enough for a frontal assault. Then again, a frontal assault was not their way. And maybe there were more than he thought.

"Well, you're the expert in these people, Mags," Jakyr said, bitter and angry. "I assume that means what I think it means?"

"It does," Mags replied, his heart turning cold. "It means unless I give myself up and let them take me off with them, they're gonna start rounding up villagers and killing 'em. They'll do it, too. If I make a run for it, they ain't gonna chase me, they're gonna start killin' villagers or you. Or both. Goin' to 'em is the only way I can make it stop."

Jakyr set his chin stubbornly. "That's not going to happen. And you aren't going to give yourself up. I'm going for help."

No one tried to talk Jakyr out of his plan, because it was obvious he wasn't in any state to be talked out of it. Instead, they all hunted for anything in the supplies that they could make armor out of. Mags and Jakyr both had their own armor, with them, but it was light armor, made to guard against glancing sword strokes and broad-headed arrows. If the Sleepgivers were going to start flinging spears the size of the one they had put their message on at him, he was going to need a lot more.

So they put Mags' armor on him first, to be worn under his own. It didn't fit, of course, and they laced it on with thongs, leaving gaps, but it would serve as reinforcement. Then they made a sort of horse armor of leather, canvas, and more leather, for Jermayan. It looked horrible, but it gave some protection for his most vulnerable spots.

"The one advantage I have is that they're going to be no better in the snow than I am," Jakyr said grimly, as they laced some padding over the top of his armor.

"Worse," said Mags. "They're from a desert. They ain't never seen snow afore, much less fought in this much."

Jakyr stopped for a moment and stared off into space. *Jermayan's talkin' to him,* Mags surmised. The guess was confirmed when Jakyr's eyes focused again, and he looked straight at Mags—this time without hostility.

"Jermayan and Dallen have been assessing our foes, and it seems we have . . . quite a lot," he said, quietly. "About a dozen, and all with those rather nasty talismans, rather than the one your . . . cousin . . . wore."

Mags didn't ask about Bey. But he rather thought that if Bey had joined the rest, or had brought them there, Jakyr would have used that as further ammunition, so he just kept quiet.

"I don't think this is a good idea, Jak," Lita said, harshly. Her face looked as if she were struggling between rage and tears. Her hands were clenched at her sides, and Mags wondered if she was actually thinking of trying to knock Jakyr cold to keep him from riding out. "I don't think this is any kind of a good idea. A dozen, with spears that we know of, probably bows and arrows too, and you floundering through chest-high snow—you'll just be an easy target. We should let Jermayan and Dallen see if they can reach another Companion that can get his Herald to the Guardpost. We can wait it out."

"And if we wait it out, they start killing villagers!" Jakyr snapped. "Do you want to be responsible for that? I don't!" Mags finished lacing the last of the padding onto Jermayan, and the Companion trotted over to the Herald, waiting for him to mount. "If I can get as far as the cleft, we'll be fine. It's not that far. They're up on the tops of the hills." He turned and put one foot in the stirrup.

"So they have clean shots at you, brilliant!" she snarled right back. "I—oh *damn* you!" She grabbed his head and kissed him, hard. "If you get killed I'll—I'll kill you all over again!"

He said nothing, just mounted without looking at her, and backed Jermayan all the way to the back of the cave so they could get a running start. They paused for just a moment, then with a clatter of hoofs on stone, they were off.

Mags had a sickening feeling as soon as they reached the cave entrance; Dallen responded to it by galloping toward him, and he grabbed mane and hauled himself on bareback as they had practiced so many times at the Collegium. Dallen skidded around and launched himself in Jakyr's wake, just as the Herald and Jermayan went down in a hail of arrows right where the deep snow began.

Mags saw it all from Dallen's back, and somehow Dallen put on some more speed. They burst out into the light.

Jermayan and Jakyr were within easy reach of the cave, and already Jakyr's makeshift armor was reddening in a dozen places. From the way Jakyr was bleeding, he wasn't going to last long. Those arrows had all been aimed at his back and they had gone through the cobbled-together armor as if it had been paper. Only one of them had hit Jermayan, but it had been the shoulder, causing him to fall before he even cleared the snow parapet.

Mags and Dallen leaped into the snow beside the downed Companion and interposed themselves between Jakyr and the archers. Mags stared up at the Sleepgivers, daring them to hit him, forcing them to concentrate on him, and not Jakyr.

He could see their faces clearly—dark hair, dark eyes, deeply suntanned skin, features not unlike his own. He wasn't wearing his cloak, and they could see *him* clearly. They had to know who he was.

And they knew he wasn't to be killed. It was a standoff. No matter how accurate they were with those bows, there was always the chance they'd hit Mags instead of Jakyr. They wouldn't take that chance.

He had been afraid he'd see Bey's face up there, but his cousin wasn't anywhere in sight. *If Bey was with 'em, he wouldn't hide.* So Bey wasn't part of this. It was a small crumb of comfort in the middle of disaster.

So he and the Sleepgivers stared back at each other as Lita and Lena and Bear and Amily ran behind him to get to Jakyr and pull him into the cave, and as Jermayan struggled to his feet and limped inside himself, leaving red splotches in the churned-up snow. He didn't dare look behind himself even to see how terribly wounded Jakyr was. He had to keep the attention of the Sleepgivers riveted on him. If he lost their concentration for even a moment, they could easily decide to start taking shots at everyone but Mags.

Mags said nothing, did nothing; he and Dallen were as still as a statue. This wasn't the time to escalate things. When Jermayan was clear, the others were finally under cover again, and Jakyr was deep in the cave, he signaled Dallen, and they backed, one slow step after another, until they were in the cleared entrance . . . and then under the rock. . . .and then, at last, safely deep inside.

Then he threw himself off Dallen and ran for his friend and mentor.

Amily was tending Jermayan, using all the skill she had acquired as Bear's assistant. The arrow was out, and fortunately it had hit at a shallow angle along the shoulder, the head just skimming under the skin and cutting the muscle. Like a knife wound along the shoulder. Painful, and laming, but no major blood vessels had been hit, and Amily could bandage it up unaided.

Jakyr was another story.

He was face down on the floor with his head in Lita's lap; the wounds were all in his back. They were cutting him out of the armor and his clothing and taking the arrows off with the armor. These were arrows meant *specifically* to piece armor, with heads hardly bigger than the shafts, so they came out easily. A little too easily; when they came out, the wounds started gushing blood before Bear could get pressure on them. And many of them had gone deep.

"What can I do?" Mags asked, falling to his knees beside them, feeling that familiar sickness in his gut. The sight of all the blood, of the wounds, the exposed flesh—it made him want to flee. But Bear needed all the help he could get.

"Put pressure here—" Bear pointed. Mags obeyed, trying not to look at the blood. He tried not to think that Jakyr could die. Bear couldn't do any more than this—take out the arrows, try to stop the bleeding, hope nothing vital had been hit, watch for infection. He wasn't a Gifted Healer. He couldn't mend the wounds or *make* the bleeding stop.

And he knew it, and tears were running down his face, his expression a scowl of desperate concentration. "I can't save him," he said, half snarling, half sobbing. "I can't! He's bleeding inside, and he's losing blood too fast!" The Herald breathed raggedly, in gasps, his skin pale as wax, and he was completely unconscious. Blood oozed from wounds that Mags, Lena, Lita, and Bear were putting pressure on and pulsed out of more that they weren't.

:Mags,: said Dallen. *:I might be able to do something.:*

The Companion rested his muzzle on Jakyr's leg, about the only part of him that wasn't wounded. *:Become the link between me and Bear. Tell Bear to think hard about what he would do if he were Gifted. Quick!:*

"Dallen says think hard about what you'd do if you had a

Gift," Mags blurted out, and then dropped every shield he had, opening himself to Bear and Dallen and joining the two, as he did when he united the Mindspeakers and those who were not on the Kirball team.

And then . . . he felt as if he were somehow *containing* Bear, Dallen, and Jakyr. It wasn't as if he were forcing them together, it was more as if—as if they were three balls of soft, warm wax, and he the hands that held them, making them into a whole. He, himself, was not part of that whole; he stood apart; he *had* to stay apart, because he was providing the vessel that held them all and the pressure that held them together.

He didn't understand *anything* of what went through him, and he didn't try. He only knew that strength was flowing out of him as fast as the blood was flowing out of Jakyr, and that this was a good thing. Because that strength had to be going somewhere, it wasn't going into Dallen, so it had to be going to the Herald.

Mindspeaking Heralds can aid Healers, if they are strong enough. That was something—from Dallen's memory? It must have been—Dallen had taught him all he knew about Mindspeaking. But Bear wasn't Gifted—

No, but in the attempt to somehow make him Gifted, Bear's father and brothers had described, over and over, what it was like for Gifted Healers to Heal. They had told him, shown him, day and night for over a year. He knew what should be done, just as someone who is not a dancer knows what the moves of a dance should look like. He just couldn't do it himself.

And Dallen didn't know what to do . . . but had the power to do it anyway, under guidance?

Mags started to feel dizzy, but he fought it back. He opened his eyes a moment to snatch a glance at Jakyr. The Herald wasn't quite so pale, and the worst of the bleeding had stopped. The wound under his hands in Jakyr's back stopped making that strange sucking sound, and the Herald wasn't struggling to breathe anymore.

But he could only spare that moment. When he took his attention off it, the bridge between Bear and Dallen wavered, the wall that held all three, Jakyr, Bear and Dallen, began to fade, and he had to get himself centered on it again. He closed his eyes and concentrated hard on holding, as if he were climbing a wall and fighting for every handhold.

Then, just when he thought he was going to pass out himself, Dallen said, *:Enough.:*

Mags let go of both ends of his bridge, dropped the containment that held them all, sagged back on his heels, and caught himself with one hand on the floor as he started to fall over sideways.

But as he opened his eyes, he realized with a sob of relief that Jakyr was going to live.

He was—perhaps—half-healed. Nothing like what a fully Gifted Healer could do under the same circumstances. Actually, half-healed was being generous. Bear—who did not seem to have suffered the same sort of exhaustion that Mags had— was cleaning out the punctures, tamping in powder of some sort, and moving on while Amily and Lita applied clean bandages. But the punctures themselves had stopped bleeding, the wounds into the lungs weren't making that sucking noise, and . . . somehow Jakyr had gotten—some blood back? He certainly didn't look as pale and waxen.

Dallen slowly sank to his knees and then started to lay himself down on the floor of the cave. Amily scrambled to her feet. *"Don't do that!"* she snapped at the Companion, who looked up at her in startled weariness. "The rock will just suck heat out of you! That's the last thing you need, as exhausted as you are! Come on, get up!" She urged Dallen back to his feet and slowly walked him over to the area where the Companions normally slept. There, she allowed him to sink down onto the thick layer of straw that served them as a bed, got his blankets, and bundled him up.

"What—happened?" Mags asked thickly.

"You told me to think of what I'd do if I had a Gift, so I did. It was daft, but I did it. Then everything started healing. Like I had a Gift, only it wasn't coming from me. I know what it was supposed to feel like if I was the one doing the Healing, the gods know my father drummed it into me for a year or more, thinking if he just told me enough times, I'd somehow sprout a Gift." Bear finished the last of the wounds and sat back on his heels. "I can't figure it out. It wasn't *me.*"

"It—was Dallen," Mags replied, and sagged a little more. "An' me too, I guess. I kinda bridged you two t'gether. Smushed you an' Dallen an' Jakyr into a big ball, and Dallen was able to fix some things."

"From the look of you, you did more than that," Bear said skeptically.

"Heralds with Mindspeech can feed energy to Healers so they can do more," Amily said, as she led Jermayan, limping, to the straw. She came back as soon as she had him settled. "Father's done it once or twice, when the Healer started to fail. It happens more often in the Field, I suppose, especially if there's only one Healer and a lot of sick or wounded. Dallen must have been able to take what Bear knew, and energy from himself and Mags, and somehow make it all work. I guess among the three of you, Bear, Mags, and Dallen, you make half a real Healer. Which is pretty amazing if you ask me. We need to get Jakyr off the floor too."

"Right." Bear got to his feet, and so did Lena. Jakyr was starting to come around again. He opened his eyes and realized his head was in Lita's lap. Face down.

"I'm dead," he said, voice muffled in her leg. "Because if I'm here, she's going to kill me."

"Shut up, you idiot. Or I'll tell your village where to find you." She leaned down and kissed his cheek. "Can you stand?"

"Not without a lot of help." He made an effort to move. "Not without somebody else hauling me to my feet."

Together they managed to get him up and get his arms draped around Bear's neck and Lita's. Bear and Lita more or less carried him that way, as he could barely set one foot in front of the other. They got him to Lita's bed, which was the nearest, and put him in it, with a couple of hot stones. He passed out.

Amily helped Mags get up, and he slumped over to the firepit and half collapsed there on the rugs. Lena bustled about, getting food warmed and making tea with plenty of honey in it. Mags felt as drained as could be.

"How did we do that?" he wondered aloud.

"Your Gift," Amily repeated. "I told you already. It's very strong. I suppose Dallen can Heal, but can't see how to do it. Bear knows what to do, but can't Heal. You bridged them and made up the difference in energy."

That's what I thought. But it still don't seem possible. He thought he should feel triumphant, but instead he only felt horrible. This wouldn't have happened if it hadn't been for him. They wouldn't even *be* here if it weren't for him. . . .

He was pretty darn sure of at least one thing. This wasn't Bey's doing. Bey hadn't been up there with the others. Bey probably didn't even realize the other Sleepgivers were there; he'd gotten the feeling that Bey hadn't left the caves in the entire time that he'd been here, so he wouldn't necessarily know when his countrymen turned up. Or even *that* they had turned up.

Well, he knows now.

Maliciously, Mags wished that another storm would come and turn them all into frozen lumps, but if the last one hadn't, they'd probably survive another. *There must be some sort of shelter up there,* he thought. *Maybe other caves, ones that don't connect with the ones down here.* That last storm might have done them an actual favor, scouring most of the snow from the heights so they could move around. Damn them!

How long had *they* been following him? Probably since his

return to Haven. He thought that if they'd been following earlier, Bey would certainly have noticed and would probably
have joined with them.

Or maybe not; Bey seemed to want to handle this himself.
He did have a lot of contempt for the second-rankers. Some of
them, at least.

His thoughts circled around and around, restlessly, and he
knew what he was trying to avoid. The obvious. He had to
give himself up. There was no other answer. He couldn't allow
his friends to be cut down, and he couldn't allow innocent
villagers to be murdered. And this time there would be no
reprieve—

Would Dallen come with him?

:I'll follow you to the ends of the earth,: came the exhausted
reply. *:Do what you must, Chosen. You will still be a Herald of
Valdemar no matter where you go or what else you are. If you
must turn yourself over to them, tell them at once that you are
Bey's prisoner and that he said not to meddle with you. So
long as we can keep those spirits out of your head, you will
remain yourself, and this will be somewhat on your own
terms.:*

Somewhat, Dallen said. And Dallen was right, he could
never do this completely on his own terms, even at the best
interpretation. All Bey had to do was make a veiled threat
about what the Sleepgivers would do to people he cared about,
back in Haven, and Mags would give in and do whatever he
asked. Really, all he had to do was threaten *anyone* in Valdemar, and Mags would yield. Mags liked Bey and trusted what
he said, and he believed that, on his own terms and in his own
way, he was honest. But Bey was also a ruthless killer and
saw no reason why threatened death could not be used as a
lever to move Mags.

He looked over at Amily and dreaded telling her. She
couldn't come with him; that was impossible. Bey wouldn't
allow it, and neither would her father. Or if Bey allowed it, it

would only be so he had another hold over Mags. Sure, they would be together, but they would be miserable, what with him knowing Bey just had to hint he'd hurt her to get his way, and her knowing that she was the reason he'd be doing things that weren't right. She sipped tea and smiled tremulously at him. Did she guess?

"I'm gonna check on Jakyr," he said, lurching to his feet. He trudged toward Lita's sleeping nook; Amily seemed to understand he needed to be alone and remained where she was.

Or maybe she realized what he had to do, and she was wrestling with the implications, too. Maybe he had made her sad that he hadn't asked her to come with him, and she hadn't yet figured out she would be the weapon against Mags in Bey's hands. Or maybe she *had* realized that, and that was making her sad. In any case, what could he say to her? He seemed to be fumbling everything at the moment.

Lita had left a lantern burning on the hook she had made above the bed area. Jakyr was awake and staring at the ceiling of the nook when Mags peeked around the canvas curtain. Before Mags could say anything, he spoke. "This was why I fought with Lita and drove her away from me, you know," he said quietly, as if he and Mags were resuming some conversation that Mags had somehow forgotten. "This was why I decided that I didn't have the right to have any close ties with anyone."

"What was?" Mags asked, sitting heavily on the rock lip of the bedding area.

"There was an ambush," Jakyr said, still staring at the ceiling. "Karsites, of course, it always seems to be Karsites and those damned demons of theirs. A nighttime ambush, and I was the only one to get out. Some people in the Guard we both knew, another Herald, my former mentor, and his new Trainee—all dead, and me mauled and left for dead. That was when I knew. Lita and I were—well, everyone thought it was going to happen, we were going to settle down together. But I knew then, a Herald's life isn't his own. That I was going to end up the same as my mentor one day. And meanwhile, everyone knew that Lita was going to be a great Bard, an important Bard, that if she stayed at Haven for just a little while longer, she'd be made an instructor and resident performer at the Palace. Except she wouldn't do that if she spent all her time worrying whether I was going to be the cause for the Death Bell every time I went out. So she'd try to follow me, and that might get her killed, and it certainly would cost her the chance at greatness. I couldn't do that to Lita. I couldn't let her waste her life, and all that talent."

He sighed heavily. And Mags thought of Amily. What would she do if he gave himself up? Cry for a long while, surely—but eventually she would get over him, she'd find something wonderful to do with her life, or someone else, or both. She was a Herald's daughter, and if anyone knew the risks, she did. She'd know better than anyone not to look back, but forward.

"So?" Mags asked.

"So she wouldn't listen. Kept trying to tell me ways we could make it all work. That's when I fought with her. Said unforgivable things. Deliberately set out to make her hate me." He closed his eyes. "I guess it didn't work as well as I thought."

Mags thought that Jakyr was asleep, but a few moments later the Herald sighed. "Don't fight with Amily; obviously I proved that doesn't work. She's her father's daughter. She knows what you have to do as well as you do, and she's probably laying it all out in her own head right this minute. She might want to be alone to cry about it; leave her alone. The sooner you can make a clean break with her, the better. Go in the morning before she wakes up. Goodbyes won't do anything but make both of you sick and sorry."

That seemed to take all of the little energy that the Herald had. Jakyr closed his eyes, looking utterly spent. A moment later, and Jakyr was asleep. Mags shuffled back out to the firepit, but Amily was already gone.

So were Lita, Lena, and Bear.

He felt too heavy with sorrow to sleep—and Jakyr was right; if he went to Amily now, they'd both cry, and try to make love, and it would ruin all the good times they'd had together; and in the end, nothing would be accomplished except to make more misery. He resolved to stay out by the firepit, wait out this last night alone, and go out in the dawn and give himself up. At least this time he knew he wouldn't have his *self* crushed and swallowed up, or distorted beyond recognition, by the evil spirits in those talismans. Bey could protect him from that much.

And Dallen would follow him; he wouldn't be all alone in a strange land. When Bey tried to get him to do things, Dallen would help him find ways to give Bey what he wanted without compromising himself too much. Dallen was right, no matter where he was, he would still be a Herald of Valdemar. Nothing that the Sleepgivers could do would take that away from him. Bey wouldn't force him to do anything he really didn't want to do; Bey needed his Gift too much, and he probably knew enough about Mind-magic to know that if you forced someone to do things against their will too often, the Gift often died within them.

If only it all didn't hurt so much . . .

He curled up around the aching in his heart and the opening wound in his soul and wept silently until he ran out of tears.

———————

"Wake up, cousin. That looks like a painful way to sleep." The soft voice jolted through his dreams.

Mags came awake all at once, thinking that the voice he had just heard was *surely* part of the dark dream he had been struggling through. But when he glanced up through gummy eyes, a handsome set of gleaming white teeth smiled down at him out of the shadow-shape looming over him.

There was no mistaking those teeth.

An irrelevant thought intruded through all his unhappiness. *Why does he have to be handsomer than me?*

"Bey!" he exclaimed, trying to scramble to his feet and nearly falling down because his left hand and leg had gone numb.

"Ehu! Not so fast, cousin!" the Sleepgiver laughed softly, catching him before he fell and steadying him. "There, sit yourself back down again. We have a great deal to discuss."

The cavern was almost completely dark; the fire had burned down to low flames over coals. Bey tossed a couple of logs on the coals; the bark caught and flared, giving a little more light. Mags could see Dallen and Jermayan, heads up, watching them. No one else seemed to have awakened.

But Bey's words only reminded Mags of what he was going to have to do at dawn. "Not much to discuss," he said, dully, sitting back down again and rubbing his leg and hand to get the prickles out. "I gotta give myself up. You know that, I know that, and there's not much anybody can do about it. Well, I'd appreciate it if you'd come with me so you can keep 'em from trying to hang one of those spirit-holders around my neck. But—"

"Not so fast, my cousin," Bey interrupted, with a gesture of negation. He sat down next to Mags. "Speak quietly. I would not like to waken your friends until we have a plan, you and I. I said, we have a great deal to discuss. I am *certainly* not going to let you walk out to those . . . toads. They would not heed me, for I am not the heir yet, and they would most *certainly* hang one of the Ancestor Stones about your neck, aye, and dose you with the herbs until you purged yourself of everything useful to me!" He scowled. "You will do me no good if your Blessing is destroyed by such handling. So I am here to keep you out of their hands."

"Wh—what?" Mags could hardly believe what he was hearing.

"When I left you, I went outside of the caves for the first time since I arrived here. I was not pleased to see my countrymen on the heights above, and particularly not pleased to see *those* countrymen. The only thing that pleased me—" the teeth shone again "—was to know how miserable the last storm had made them. So! I crept about their camp, less than a shadow, and I learned much. I watched them send their message and— I am sorry I could not prevent this—I saw them strike down your friend."

"But—what do you think I can do?" Mags asked.

"You and I have shared minds. Therefore, you have knowledge of my training. You are not *quite* the equal of me, but you are ten times the Sleepgiver of any of those dogs outside." Bey's tone was arrogant, but Mags was not about to argue with him, not with hope unlooked-for in his hands. "Your friend, who became nearly a spitted fowl—how fares he?"

"He's hurt, but he'll live," Mags said. Bey nodded.

"That is well. He is rash. If he is hurt, we can put him with the others of your friends who are no help to us. The most secure place is that cave wherein you bathe in steam. A good custom that; I adopted it, and I think I shall take it with me. We should put them there and pile wood before it to act as a bulwark. They can fire over that at need." Bey held up a finger. "Your mate. She is useful. I have seen her shoot." He held up another. "The doctor-of-herbs. He is also useful. *His* mate and the old singer, they are not. They shall be with your wounded friend, while you and I dispose of those inconvenient dogs outside, and your mate and the doctor stand ready."

Mags gaped at him. After all of the emphasis the Sleepgivers had put on blood relations—he could scarcely believe the words coming out of Bey's mouth. "But—those are your kinsmen!" he stammered.

Bey made a little motion with his hands, as if he was

brushing away a bug. "Not that close. Cousins of cousins of cousins of cousins, and probably born of slave women. Idiots. And they follow a faction that would keep to the old, bad ways. This is as good a way as any to be rid of them."

Mags felt a tiny chill down his back at the casual way that Bey had just dismissed the murder of his own countrymen . . . but he couldn't let that stop him. Nevertheless, it was . . . telling. Bey was, in his own way, just as ruthless as any other of the Sleepgivers. When something was going to get in his way, he removed it. If he had to remove it permanently, he obviously didn't let little things like kinship stop him.

That reminded Mags of the way the young Sleepgivers were first taught; make no friendships, allow no ties of affection. Compete, or fail, and become—what? Probably slaves, or servants no better than slaves, if you were lucky. If you were not, you died as a result of your failure. Bey had never gone through that training, since it was becoming clear to Mags that even as there were three tiers of rank within the Sleepgivers themselves, there were obviously two tiers, at least, of training. But Bey was the product of the culture that had produced that training. No matter how charming and likable he could be, *that* culture was what had formed him.

"So, what do we do?" Mags asked, anxiously. "You don't want me to give myself up, but I can't let them slaughter helpless people!"

Bey smiled a little. "That is not an issue at the moment. It is not a hollow threat, I do assure you, but at the moment, they are as trapped here by your wretched *snow*"—he used the Valdemaran word, because presumably the Sleepgivers didn't have a word for snow—"as we are. They cannot go and cull some hapless woodcutter for days yet. I have seen, when I discovered them and went up to spy upon them. The snow is chest-deep around about here, and as high as a house in places. It will be long before they could even attempt to make good on their threat."

Mags heaved a sigh of relief. So they had—well, probably several days at least before they had to worry about innocents getting caught up in this.

"They have been here since just before the first great storm," Bey continued. "They followed you from the city of the Crown, a little behind me, it seems." He scowled. "It is ir- ritating to admit, but they are better trackers than I. They easily uncovered all your ruses to throw them off the trail. This vexes me. I had not thought that my tracking skills were inferior to anyone." Then he shook his head. "Never mind. They thought to take you at a town, using the folk there to force you, but they thought better of that plan when they saw how chaotic your towns are. The people are not of one mind, there are dwellings spread all about, and while it would be the work of a child to simply strike at will and fade away, the tak- ing of a hostage is more difficult work than that. There was no good place or time when they could have taken hostages, and you would certainly have fought and maybe been hurt, and the Shadao specifically forbid you being injured."

"Thank the Shadao for me," Mags said dryly.

Bey looked at him in astonishment, then barked a laugh. "Ha! Almost a Sleepgiver joke! Are you still so sure you do not wish to come with me?" Before Mags could answer, he waved his hand. "Nay the answer is on your face. So, so, so, they came here. They came up over the hills, where I came in the cleft. They found the high caves where I found the low. They provisioned themselves just in time before the storm struck. They are not, however, nearly so well provisioned as you. They are cold, they are impatient, they begin to hunger, and we may use that to our advantage."

Now *that* was more like it. "You have a plan?" Mags asked, eagerly.

Bey smiled. "I have many, many plans, and they are all superior, oh my cousin. I am a Sleepgiver. I am of the best of the best of the Sleepgivers. All my plans are superior. We only need to consult and determine which is the *most* superior."

Then he looked around a little. "Meanwhile . . . I hunger. And after your distress, and sleeping all awry, I expect you hunger as well. Where are those delectable morsels of meat-in-crust? I so enjoyed the ones I stole!"

Of all of the things that Mags had imagined happening this morning, standing beside his cousin as Lita, Lena, Bear, and Amily came out at the sound of voices and saying, "Everyone, this is my cousin Bey," had not been one of them. He had imagined sneaking off at first light so no one saw him go. He had thought someone might emerge before he could, and there would be tears, or recriminations, or just silent misery. But this was almost a triumph.

The looks on their faces as Bey swept a sort of bow that included an elaborate flourish of his right hand was worth any amount of money.

The explanation took surprisingly little time. As he had suspected, although he and Bey had been using the language of the Sleepgivers all this time, Bey spoke passable Valdemaran, and he switched to it except when he didn't have a word for something. That wasn't very often. It was the Sleepgiver tongue that lacked Valdemaran words, usually, not the other way around.

Bey exerted a formidable charm and managed to win all of them over so fast that Mags would have suspected Mind-magic if he hadn't known Bey didn't have any. Even Lita was caught in his charisma. Or so he thought, anyway.

The Bard was not as enraptured as she seemed. But she also was well aware that their options were limited to Bey's plans and Mags giving up.

"I thought you said I was an idiot," Mags whispered to her, as Bey queried Bear earnestly about various supplies.

"What choice to we have?" she whispered back. "We've got no guarantee that even if you *do* turn yourself over to these Sleepgivers, they won't turn around and slaughter us anyway! They've already killed Jak, as far as they know. They won't hesitate to do the rest of us, considering they plan on wiping your mind clean of *you* anyway."

Mags nodded soberly. That was a very real possibility, and one that he and Bey had discussed, albeit briefly. Now that he knew that these Sleepgivers didn't give a toss about what Bey told them . . . once they had him in their clutches, they had no incentive to be merciful and plenty of incentive to make sure there was no one to sound an alarm until it was too late and they were back across the border.

Well, this way, if I go down, I go down on my own terms, and ain't no Ancestor-thing going to be walking around in my body, after.

They'd all settled in and around Lita's sleeping nook. The fires were being allowed to die out. Jakyr was sitting up with help from cushions, looking alert but clearly in pain.

"So this is our plan, friend-of-my-cousin," Bey said cheerfully. "We have made inventory of our options, and they are better than I had thought. The Sleepgivers above are in a worse position than we. Their food is only what they can catch on the hills above; they are reduced to shooting those thin little black birds that flock to sleep in the trees at night. They will not be able to break a path to a village to threaten anyone for some time, and they have a dilemma. They can break the path and chance us escaping, *or* they can lay siege to us and hope that we break. Also, they do not know I am with you. They are hungry and cold. They like this snow no better than I, which is to say, not at all. So, they think they have killed one of you. I think *they* think that you are not well provisioned either. If I were a fool like they, I would say *lay siege, they will come out and we shall kill them one by one except for Meric.* So. We give them something they do not expect."

"What's that?" Jakyr asked.

Bey smiled, but it was Mags that answered. "Silence. Now, that means we're gonna be a mite uncomfortable here ourselves. We let the fires burn out, so there's no more smoke above, where they can see it, and no light comin' outa the cave mouth at night. All of you pull back into that dead end where the steam bath is, even the horses an' the Companions. You'll all have blankets and the food'll be cold, but we gotta make 'em think that we run outa provisions, we all died, or maybe we got sick, or somehow we escaped. And they won't know which, till they come down to look the situation over. We make 'em come to us."

Bey took it up from there. "They will not *all* come. And they are not all of one mind, which will do us good. Some are loyal to the Shadao entirely, others favor a nephew that might be made heir were I not to be. They will send three of mixed faction, which will mean they do not fight with one mind, but singly, each hoping to be the one to say *I am the one that took Meric.* We will kill them, Mags and I, silently, and with no sign, for Mags has shared my memories and, thus, my skills. We will take the bodies off and conceal them and all signs that they were slain. And then we will wait. When the first three do not return, another three will come. We will do the same.

Now their numbers will be halved; they will send no more, and we will have to consider another strategy." Bey waited, with an air that he expected them all to agree that this was a brilliant plan. Into the silence came a distant drip of water.

"You make it sound so easy," Jakyr said dryly, after a very long pause. One eyebrow rose, slightly, and he pressed his hand to one of his wounds.

"For a true Sleepgiver, it will be," Bey said with easy arrogance. "Ehu, we will see, which are the true Sleepgivers and which the inferior. But! Some may slip by us. They might find a way down from the upper caves and come in behind Mags and me. You must be quiet, and you must also be alert to defend yourselves—which is why we will put you in a place with no second entrance. Most of a Sleepgiver's advantages are gone if he must confront a prepared target, yet they will still be formidable. Inferior Sleepgivers though they be, they are still of the House." His eyes glittered in the light. "And those of the House, as you have found, are not to be dismissed." The vanners pawed their straw, then went back to dozing.

"I don't like it," Jakyr said flatly, then sighed. "But I don't see a choice."

Bey clapped his hands, startling the vanners, who snorted. "Well said! Now, I shall go and gather what we need, the Healer and his mate will commence to move the beasts while we have light and will settle them in a place in that dead end where they can see before we leave them in darkness so that they are content once the darkness closes in, and will sleep. Elder Singer, do you keep companionship with this one, while Mags and his mate make for you all a place that is warm as may be and gather there food enough for two or three days."

Bey sprang to his feet and trotted off. Bear and Lena headed for the vanners. Before Amily and Mags could move, Lita looked sternly at Jakyr. "Why?" she asked him harshly.

Mags and Amily froze. The Herald and the Bard were intent on each other and oblivious to their presence.

Jakyr did not ask her what she meant. "Lit', I nearly died back at Carnavon Grove. I saw what happened to Tully's wife, and Kal's girl after. I didn't think you would be able to handle burying me. And I didn't think you should sacrifice a shot at becoming one of the instructors at Bardic just to follow me around and *then* end up burying me. So I . . . said what I said to drive you away. I just picked the cruelest things I could, even if I knew there wasn't a grain of truth in them. And you saw what happened here, was I wrong?"

"Damn right, you were wrong," she snapped. "And what's more, it wasn't your damn decision to make! Now you listen here, you damn fool—"

She bent over him and muted her voice to an angry whisper. Mags and Amily decided that was a good time to make themselves absent, because it sounded like Lita's idea of "companionship" was going to involve a lot of things they probably shouldn't be overhearing.

––––––––––––

The horses were asleep, the Companions with them, back behind the others. The whole tunnel had been covered with a thick layer of straw to muffle noise and keep things warm. Then firewood had been piled up to chest height across the tunnel to serve as a bulwark—not that anyone back there could see anything in the cave dark. But the ones who would be hiding behind that bulwark all knew exactly where the food and water were, and with all the bedding piled in a heap on the floor they could huddle together for warmth as the cave chilled to its normal temperature. There was a lantern they could kindle if they heard anything, and the disadvantage of being silhouetted against the light was, in Bey's estimation, outweighed by the fact they would have the light at their back and nothing glaring into their eyes.

Mags and Bey were both wearing their talismans, so that

they would be invisible to the talismans worn by the other Sleepgivers.

The fires had been allowed to die in the main cave, and Bey and Mags' preparations were complete. Now it was a matter of waiting, and they already knew they would have to wait through the night until morning. First the Sleepgivers would have to notice that there was no light coming from the cave. They might venture down out of the heights to peer in at the entrance, but they would be cautious, and Bey was of the opinion that the conditions would not be in his and Mags' favor to attack them in the relative open. No, they would have to wait until the first set of three actually set foot in the cave.

The two of them settled themselves as comfortably as possible on the straw beside the caravan, and Bey rehearsed Mags in the use of a weapon that was new to him. It wasn't a nice weapon. It was purely an assassin's weapon. He didn't think it likely that the Weaponsmaster would ever teach *anyone* the use of this thing. But it was one that was going to give them the maximum chance of silent kills.

"Throw again," Bey murmured, holding up his fist, with a hat on it, to make it the size of a man's head. Mags could barely see it against the moonlit snow outside, but that was just about as much light as he was going to when he finally used this thing.

Mags threw the braided wire loop over Bey's fist without touching hat or skin, and yanked on the wooden handle. Gently, because if he yanked at full strength he could seriously damage Bey's wrist.

"And then the knife to the kidney, which I know you know how to do. Remember, if you need to take a second blow, only to strike *below* the ribs. Do not try anything clever, like cutting the spine, or striking for the heart. A strike that hits bone does you no favors. Good. Again."

Mags was discovering that Bey's memories were actually working to improve his own muscle-memory to an extent that was a little terrifying. That time, he hadn't even had to think at all about the toss. He'd just done it. A few more times—

"A few more times, and you will be almost my equal," said Bey, echoing his thoughts. "Again."

———————

Sure enough, there were at least two Sleepgivers peering into the blackness of the cave. Mags didn't think they realized how easy they were to see against the snow. He actually spotted them first, and touched Bey to alert him to their presence. Both of them froze completely still, as only a Sleepgiver could, so that not even a single straw rustled. They breathed slowly, meditatively, through their noses, as the Sleepgivers cautiously moved their heads into the cave entrance and attempted to make out anything, anything at all. The only sound was that intermittent dripping somewhere deep in the caves. The only smell was stale, dead smoke and cave-damp.

Mags and Bey had already removed everything to the storage caves. Only the caravan remained, and that was because it was too hard to move anywhere else.

It wasn't where it would catch the light, anyway.

The Sleepgivers peered and listened, peered and listened, and got nothing for their pains. Eventually, the heads vanished, and Mags thought he might be hearing the sound of someone climbing the cliff with a rope.

"And so, they fulfill my first prophecy," Bey breathed. "Let us hope that they continue to do so."

———————

At the first light, Mags elbowed Bey when he thought he heard a whisper of noise outside the cave. Then he crouched low, and with one hand on the floor to keep himself steady, scuttled to the other side of the cave and felt his way along the wall until he came to a place where the cave made a turn to his left. This was not a way he had run before. It was a strange sort of "running" that had him skimming or gliding his feet barely above the surface of the rock to avoid making a footfall— something he had not known how to do until he had shared Bey's memories.

That turning gave him an obtuse "corner" to hide behind that would still allow him to see the entrance. Bey wasn't nearly as lucky, since on his side, the wall stayed more or less straight—except that Bey had the caravan to hide behind.

He knew what Bey was doing: setting himself up on the opposite side behind the caravan. He couldn't hear a thing, though. Bey was just that much better than he was, able to walk across straw without making a single stalk break or rustle.

Now he definitely heard something out there, and once again, there were heads showing against the dim light and the white snow, two on Bey's side of the cave, one on his. That was a piece of luck. He would only need to deal with one target.

They waited out there a very long time. Long enough for the scrap of sky he could see to lighten to blue from gray. The Sleepgivers must have decided it was more risky to be out than in, because at that point, they all three slipped into the cave, bodies pressed against the rock.

Another piece of luck. He kept his eyes narrowed against the growing light at the entrance and concentrated on the one on his side. Bey had said that he didn't think the Sleepgivers were all that familiar with the layout, even of the outer part of the cave. *"They have peered in, but not gone inside, I think. They will have to feel their way, or show a light, and they will not show a light. They will rely on the light coming from the entrance."*

All Mags needed was to be able to see the bit of movement along the cave wall that would tell him where the Sleepgiver was. And if he had been relying on his own experience, he would have been certain that the man wasn't moving at all—

or had somehow gotten out of his line of sight. But he wasn't relying on his own experience. He had Bey's experience in his head. So he was able to track the torturously slow progress toward the ambush point.

When he was certain the man wasn't going to step any farther toward the middle of the cave, he backed up a pace or two, and out into the open, away from the wall, but still in the shadow where no light from the entrance would fall on him—moving just as slowly as his quarry was. Then he waited, because there would be a brief, very brief, moment of opportunity when his quarry encountered the turning. At that point, he would be away from the receding wall, he would be creeping his hand along the turn to find it, and he would be thinking about that and nothing else.

So Bey said. *"And if he keeps himself tight to the wall, you will just have to find an opportunity to strike without an advantage, my cousin."* Not much comfort, but there were several options in Bey's memories, and he had Dallen, who was sifting through those memories and getting ready to give him the best one if that happened.

Bey sure seems nice for a killer . . .

:Actually, Chosen,: Dallen said, matter-of-factly, *:most of those memories seem to be of training. I don't think he's killed more than a dozen people himself.:*

:Well, that's comforting,: Mags said with heavy irony.

:Oh, he's still a hardened killer,: Dallen replied. *:And all that training and practice was pretty harrowing. I'll show you sometime. When we have time.:*

A hand appeared at the edge of the turning. Mags stilled his breathing. The hand inched its way around the turning, and the man stepped away from the wall, uncertain now. He had no memory of this, he *could* have no memory of this, and he couldn't know what the footing was like around this turn. There might be outcroppings he could trip on. There might be gravel. There might be a drop-off. He had to walk where he could at least dimly see, until he was certain that the cave floor didn't descend abruptly. His training was telling him to continue inching along the wall, but his instincts screamed at him not to go into the full dark. *"I would heed my training. He will heed his instincts. That is why he will fail."*

He heeded his instincts. After all, no one had shot at him and the other two Sleepgivers when they first appeared in the entrance. There was no sound except that irritating, distant dripping of water. There was no light coming from inside the cave. There was no sight, sound, smell or feeling to tell him that there was anyone or anything in this part of the cave. He would be trying to think like his quarry, and given that one of their number had been killed, his quarry would do what frightened things always did—try to find a place to hide.

The man slid one foot after the other, warily, silently, inching deeper into the cave, heading for the one goal he knew— the back of this part of the entrance, where presumably he would meet the other two, and they would decide what to do from here.

"Strike a light and make traps, that is what they will think. If there were less snow, they would go to the chimney and try to smoke you out. Instead, they will wait for you to think they have gone, and step into their traps."

The man was now almost within perfect striking reach. His arms were down at his sides, since he was no longer feeling his way along a wall. He had seen that past the turning, there was still no light. His plan remained the same.

So had Mags'. *His* nerves might have screamed with impatience, but he had Bey's memories now. And Bey remained perfectly calm in situations like this. Poised, like a snake, waiting for exactly the right moment—

His muscles moved before his mind did. The loop of braided wire lofted over the man's head. Two steps and Mags was behind him, just as the garrote touched his shoulders. Hard *yank*, with knee braced in the small of the man's back, pulling him over backward and tightening the wire so quickly he was unable to get his fingers under it, so tightly his breath was choked off immediately and he couldn't make a sound. Quick knife to the kidney to paralyze him, twist, remove, wipe and resheath. Then softly lowering him to the cave floor, garrote still choking off any possibility of breath. Holding the wire tight, one foot on the man's shoulders, as the body quivered and stilled.

"*Tsk,*" Bey said in his ear. "I heard his feet drumming on the stone. You must learn to do better than that."

"I'd just as soon not, thanks," Mags whispered back, letting go of the end of the garrote, which had a wooden handle so he didn't destroy his fingers while choking a man to death. "Good job on those two, I didn't hear a thing."

"I would have been devastated if you had." Bey bent and got the wire off the cooling corpse's neck. "Take this and go back to the caravan. I will dispose of this offal."

––––––––––––

Bey must have been incredibly strong; he had picked up the body and thrown it over his shoulder as if it were a sack of grain. Then again, Bey hadn't been starved for most of his life, and he *had* been training physically for most of his life.

Mags felt both unclean and conflicted. On the one hand, since he had Bey's memories, it felt satisfying to have pulled off such a clean kill. A job well done, like a good Kirball goal—

On the other hand, he had just murdered a man in cold blood, and he felt unclean.

Bey was not being cautious on his return; there was no need. Mags saw him moving across the cave floor, and he settled in next to Mags on the straw with a sigh.

"What happens to the talismans when the Sleepgivers die?" he whispered.

"The talismans die with them, and the Ancestor Spirits are

released." Bey paused. "Mind, I cannot swear that the spirits imprisoned in the talismans are actually the Spirits of our Ancestors." He paused again. "In fact . . . the more I think about it, the less likely that seems. Because if they *were* the Spirits of our Ancestors, one would think they would inform each other when a talisman-bearer falls. And yet, they do not."

"Sounds more like a Karsite demon to me," Mags said, after a while.

"All the more reason to cease this practice," said Bey, firmly. "But, I think I will leave this until I am Shadao. There is no sense in making trouble for myself until I am in power."

"Well, now what happens?" Mags asked.

"Now . . . ehu, I am torn." Bey sighed in the darkness. Then there was a rustling of straw, Bey picked up one of his hands and put a familiar shape into it. "Please to eat of this apple while I think." The sounds of someone biting into a crisp fruit told him Bey was taking his own advice. Mags realized that his throat and mouth were very dry, and did the same. "Well . . . if I were to order you, I would tell you to remove your talisman and send your mind up above, among the Sleepgivers, to see what you might find."

"Not certain I'd find anything," Mags offered. "The last couple of times I tried that, back in Haven, the talismans of the Sleepgivers saw me and shut me out."

"But they did not warn their bearers?" Bey bit, and chewed. The clean scent of apple wafted around both of them. Bey, like Mags, had the habit of eating his apples seeds and all. A desert dweller's habit, in Bey's case, and the habit of a boy who had mostly starved in Mags'.

There was a frown in Bey's voice when he spoke again. "I cannot imagine a Spirit of one of my Ancestors not warning me when the Blessed were sniffing about my mind. And the Spirits in the Talismans are supposed to be the Spirits of the greatest of the Sleepgivers. So, so, so. Either they are very stupid Spirits, or they do not think kindly enough of their bearers to protect them in that way. Something to think on. Well, then . . . are you brave enough, oh, my cousin, to send your mind aloft?"

Mags didn't even have to think about it twice. They needed information, and that was a fact. And he'd rather be doing this, than choking a man to death.

"I can do this . . . passively, if that makes any sense. Let things come to me. That's less likely to alert them." He took his talisman off, finished his apple and settled himself.

It was a matter of expanding shields, he knew now, rather than dropping them. He could safely ignore his friends, huddled in the dead-end tunnel . . . and he was glad he was not an Empath. Their thoughts were hard enough to bear; he didn't think he'd be able to take their actual fear and Jakyr's pain. If this was bad for him, it was much worse for them, in the dark and cold and with NO idea what was going on—

Oh, wait . . .

:Amily. First part went fine. Waiting on the second part.:

He caught her start of surprise, then left her mind as she whispered his news to the others. All right. The Sleepgivers weren't within that area, so, he had to expand . . .

He knew immediately when he had found them, which was . . . mere heartbeats after moving his shields a little more outward. There they were, overhead, and their talismans were like sullen pools of stagnant water. But they weren't doing anything to guard the thoughts of their bearers.

"I got them. They don't know I'm watching," he breathed, as if the mere act of speaking might alert them.

"Good." Bey sighed. "Oh, cousin—"

"Don't start," Mags said, cutting him off. "Try finding yourself a nice Blessed girl and raising your own. Or teach her to be like Amily, so she's your partner instead of something you keep in the women's quarters all the time."

". . . what an interesting idea," Bey replied, after a long pause. "It is one I shall definitely consider."

Mags had settled into being as passive and receptive as he could manage—and with all the practice he'd had of late, he evidently made no more impression on the talismans than if he'd been a rook in a nearby tree. Once again, having shared Bey's thoughts had taught him a level of patience he'd never had before. He was able to . . . to relax, if that was the right word. To enter into a state where it didn't matter how long it took for something to happen, because he knew it would, and he only had to wait for it. It might have been harder if he'd been hungry, thirsty, or uncomfortable, but he was none of these things.

It was possible, however, to track the passing of time by the changing light outside the cave. So it was, he thought, about noon—the sun was *glaring* down on the snow out there— when the Sleepgivers finally started to get restless, cautiously looking over the edge of the drop, and muttering to each other.

"They're getting uneasy, Bey," Mags reported. The thoughts he picked up were a mix of concern and exasperation— although the *concern* was more along the lines of *why haven't they reported back,* than *I hope nothing has happened to them.* There were also touches of the same contempt for each other that Bey had for them.

"Huh. No love lost there," he said aloud.

Bey snorted. "It is as I told you. We do not foster bonds among each other, only the bond that a man has to the House, and to the Shadao. Are they considering sending another lot?"

"They're starting to talk about it." It was hard waiting for thoughts to become urgent enough to pass over to him from behind the barriers that even people who were not Mindspeakers had. "They seem to think there was an accident. They're talking like they think the first three fell down a hole and broke something."

"Oho!" There was malicious humor in Bey's voice now. "Well, then, that changes my plan, a trifle. I am going to the chimney to see if I can convince the others there has been an accident. Wait, and worry not when you hear sounds."

:Amily, Bey's trying something. Don't you folks be worried if you hear noises.:

He turned his attention back to the Sleepgivers just in time for Bey to start moaning at the chimney, and babbling words in his own tongue.

It took them a while to hear it; it took them a while longer to realize it was coming from the same place that smoke and cooking smells had been coming from. But when they figured it out and gathered around the spot to listen, their contempt was the one thing that united them. Mags wished he could Mindspeak with Bey the way he could with Amily, but the talisman *he* wore made that impossible.

After a while, the sounds faded, as if the "victim" had lapsed into unconsciousness. Bey returned from out of the darkness. "Well?" he asked.

"It worked. They're sending down more. Something else, Bey; the reason there's so many of them is that's *four* separate groups, all figuring on getting me and impressing the Shadao. One group's under the Shadao's orders direct, two are from factions, and one's your followers."

"My followers! Interesting! Before I left, I had carefully shown no interest in you. I wonder why they think . . . ah, I have it." He sighed, but did not elaborate. "Pity I will have to kill them."

"You already did, two of the three," Mags told him. "Or you and I did."

Bey gripped his arm, and Mags stopped talking. This time the Sleepgivers were making no effort at all to hide their activities. Down came the men on the ropes that were already there. Once they all had gathered, they pulled something out of their belts, and there was a flare of fire. Mags scuttled across the cave to his place, as Bey took up his, and they waited.

Except this time there were four of them. And the flare of fire meant that they came with crude torches.

Well, that's a complication. It was a complication they were prepared for, but this could end their ability to mount ambushes. *Oh, well. We knew it was going to come to a straight fight sooner or later.*

He backed up, deeper into the shadow, and farther around the corner. There was a niche . . . he backed along the wall, feeling for it, until he found it, and pressed himself back into it. This was going to be tricky. And it wouldn't be silent. With luck . . .

Bey began to whimper and call in a thin voice that sounded uncannily distant. *I have got to learn that trick!* Mags thought, as the man nearest him turned away from him, and held out his torch in the direction of the sounds. Mags knew that was the only chance he was going to get.

He launched himself at the man, and let Bey's memory take over, because this was certainly *nothing* he had ever done in his life. But somehow . . . it worked. Somehow he managed to land a blow to the back of the man's neck that stunned him, caught him, twisted his head viciously and broke his neck, and lowered him to the floor.

All in the space of about a heartbeat.

But the torch clattered to the ground, and the noise attracted the other three, who spun and saw him crouching over their fallen comrade. Without thinking, Mags whipped out his knife and threw it while he had a good and clear target. It slammed into the left eye of the one nearest him, and the assassin fell with a gurgle, while Mags was already sprinting for cover.

He got out of reach of the torchlight and abruptly changed direction just in time to avoid the two knives thrown at *him*. One came close enough to graze his ear.

Then he shoulder-rolled and avoided a third knife that clattered into the darkness next to him. He sprang up and onto his feet, reaching for his own knives. But there wasn't anyone for him to hit; just four torches burning on the floor, and four bodies, one of which Bey was standing over.

"Oh, my cousin," Bey sighed softly into the sudden silence. "What a Sleepgiver you would make!"

———————————

Bey was disposing of the bodies again. The next assault would be a frontal one. As far as Mags could tell, none of the noise they'd made in the second ambush had gotten up to the top of the hill to warn the others, but after losing two teams, the Sleepgivers *had* to understand they'd been ambushed. There were now five of them, versus the five the Sleepgivers were aware of in the cave—but three of the five were women, and they knew that, and in their land, women were never taught to fight. So they would only expect resistance from Mags and Bear. And they wouldn't expect a Companion.

Mags took one of the torches to light his way to the others and met them at the barrier to explain all of this in person. Jakyr was lying on the bedding in the straw; the vanners were at the very back of the tunnel behind him. The rest came up to the barrier, huddled against it, eyes dark and solemn and in the case of Bear and Lena, a little frightened. Lita looked angry. Amily looked determined.

"This is where we finish this," he said. "Bey's settin' up the main cave for it. We can't afford for any of 'em to get away." He looked at Lita. "How's your shootin'?"

"In a cave by firelight? I'll hit one of you," she said with regret. "I was never that good when I was young, and my eyes are older now."

"Then you stay here and shoot anything that comes at the barrier that ain't us." Bear, he already knew was of no use, because of his weak eyes. Lena was no good with a bow. "Let's get the firewood down and Dallen and Amily out."

He led the two of them back out into the main cave, where Bey was waiting. It was very nice to have Dallen at his back again. "Where you want us?" he asked.

"Amily, I know from my cousin's memory that you are deadly with your bow," Bey said with a little bow. "Please to take a place inside the caravan. You will be safest there. If you see any of the Sleepgivers with bows—and I expect this—drop them, please. There are five left; I expect three in the front, two behind with bows."

She nodded and went straight to the caravan. From inside, she opened the window; the shutters were already opened. You couldn't tell she was even in there. Bey turned to Dallen. "I do not expect them to attack until after dark. So, is it possible for you to slip out when the sun sets and hide yourself against the snow? You will be our last guard to prevent any from escaping."

Dallen nodded.

Mags went to stand where he had stood the first two times, and Bey extinguished the torch.

Now . . . it was waiting. Waiting as the light outside waned and finally died. Waiting as Mags watched the thoughts of those above grow first confused, then angry, as they realized that they had somehow been duped. It was with relief that Mags saw they were convinced that Mags had been the one who had made the cries of distress. If they'd had a guess that Bey was working with them, one of their number would almost certainly have left at that moment, to find a way across country and back to the House of Sleepgivers to alert them to the existence of a traitor. *Probably* having Dallen Mindspeak to other distant Companions and alert the countryside would take care of that problem, but . . . these were Sleepgivers, and they had managed to elude the best of the Heralds before this.

If they hadn't been wearing their talismans, he would have taken a chance and pushed the idea into their minds that he was the one who had duped them. But he didn't dare.

The light in the valley went to dusk and then full dark. Mags never saw or heard Dallen move, but at some point after the darkness fell he heard *:I'm up to my chest in snow and laying my head and neck along it. Just behind the parapet. I* *think I am pretty adequately concealed from above as long as I keep my eyes closed.:*

"Dallen's ready," he whispered, keeping constant watch over the thoughts of the remaining five Sleepgivers.

Their anger was a burning, sullen furnace. They could not believe they had been *duped* by a lot of people they considered to be weak and soft and not terribly crafty. They barely assuaged their outrage by deciding that it was all Mags' doing. After all, he was of the House! They had learned in Valdemar from tale and rumor that Mags had partaken of the herbs that should have given him his proper memories. *That must have been it,* their angry thoughts went, so angry, that they easily projected into Mags' mind. *He remembers what he is, but not who he should be.* Finally they were all united in their rage and determination. Mags was not going to be allowed to escape them. He would take the herbs and the talisman, and finally he would join them. He would prove himself by killing these people he thought were friends, and they would all return triumphant to the Shadao.

"They're coming," he said softly into the icy dark, and not long after he warned the others, there came soft *thumps* as five men on the three ropes dropped down at the entrance to the cave. They were not even trying to be stealthy. Mags wished rather desperately that there could have been some way to bring up some light behind them, because they would have been easy targets for a volley of arrows.

But there wasn't—not without exposing themselves.

A fire-arrow suddenly arced across the dark cave, slammed into the back wall, and fell, still burning. Another joined it, and another, until the whole back wall was lit up. *Clever move.* Now if any of them came from out of cover, they'd be clearly silhouetted.

Mags heard five sets of footsteps coming down out of the dark entrance. He remained pressed against the rock. Now his heart was pounding the way it usually did before a fight. There was nothing like this in Bey's memories, for Bey had never dealt with a straight-up fight in his life. The words of the Weaponsmaster came to him first. *Get in the first blow from a distance. Even a wound makes a weakness, and a weakness will give you an opening for a kill.*

He listened with every fiber, and tried to hear their thoughts, but the talismans were all awake and concealing everything. He didn't *think* he'd betrayed himself—

:It was me. They sensed me,: Dallen said with chagrin.

:Hell. Well, at least they didn't tell the Sleepgivers.:

He couldn't see them from where he was, not without exposing himself. But the arrows were burning out . . . and their eyes were more blinded by the light than the defenders' were.

Take the risk and take a shot with a throwing knife, and chance getting an arrow? Amily was handicapped by a limited field of fire from that tiny window in the caravan . . . she might not be able to pick them off before the last fire-arrow burned out, and—

Suddenly he heard it—the unmistakable sound of two arrows fired off in quick succession—which was immediately followed by the sound of a scream and a gurgle and two bodies hitting the ground.

He jumped out of hiding and threw at the first thing he could see.

And then the entire cavern filled with light as the pile of oil-soaked wood in the firepit went up with a roar. Bey had set off the fire, probably by tossing one of those arrows into it.

"To me, cousin!" shouted Bey, and Mags raced across the space between them, putting his back to Bey's back.

A glance at the archers showed him that the two archers weren't dead yet; Amily was still shooting, keeping them from getting to the bows they had dropped. Then the three Sleepgiver swordsmen were on them, and he and Bey were fighting for their lives.

As contemptuous as Bey had been of these Sleepgivers,

Mags didn't see anything to hold in contempt, and from the grim determination he sensed in his cousin . . . neither did Bey.

But they fell into a rhythm as if they had been fighting together all their lives. Mags' world narrowed to the three swords flashing in and out of range, his hunt for a target, and the need to keep his back to Bey's. If either of them failed to cover the other, the Sleepgivers would surely see to it that was the last mistake they made.

This was dirty, brutal fighting, nothing pretty about it; if they hadn't been fighting on bare rock all five of them would have been kicking or throwing dirt in each others' faces. Nothing was off-target and there was no such thing as an illegal blow. If you could get it, you took it; a rush parried turned into a bash with the hilt to the face. Moments in, and Mags had a gash on his leg, a cut over his bicep and a bruised cheekbone.

But their opponents were in no better shape. One of them had a black eye that was rapidly swelling shut thanks to Mags; another had a slash across the forehead that was bleeding freely; Mags didn't know if that was his work or Bey's. The third had had to switch hands; his left was useless, thanks to Bey's work.

Then it all came undone.

Bey slipped in a splat of blood and went down on one knee. The Sleepgivers all converged on him. Mags whirled and slapped away the blade of the first, and rushed the second, but the third had Bey wide open and Mags was not going to get there in time—

And then the third simply wasn't there anymore, as a raging Dallen ran right over the top of him, turned in a flash, and pulped the head of the second.

Mags saw the opening, and took it, ramming his sword to the hilt in the first one's chest.

Then he went to his knees next to Bey.

It was over.

EPILOGUE

"Of all the things about you people, I am going to miss these the most," said Bey, holding up a meat pie and gazing at it fondly.

The cave had been put back to rights. Everything was in its proper place, and all evidence of the fight was gone. The vanners dozed in their corner, having slept through all of the drama. There was a great fire in the firepit, and all of them were lounging around it on the cushions and rugs. Amily had warmed up some meat pies, since Jakyr was in no kind of shape to cook, and Lena had made everyone tea with honey.

Lita (to the surprise of both Mags and Bey) had helped Mags and Bey dispose of the bodies. They'd taken them to a spot where the cave floor opened into a black hole about as big across as a man was tall, so deep that the lantern didn't even show the bottom, and a pebble tossed in took a very long time to fall. "I nearly fell in myself," Bey had said, regarding the pit with an unreadable expression. "But now it's proving useful."

Poor Amily had been very sick, after apologizing about a

337

hundred times that when she'd realized she was shooting at living human beings instead of a target, she'd flinched. Mags had just held her hair out of the way, wiped her face, given her water to take the taste out of her mouth, and said simply, "So did I."

She would cry later, and he would hold her. She would never be the same. And yet, he was certain that in the end, she would be all right.

"I hope you do not mind that you are putting up with my presence until your Guard comes to free you," Bey continued, after biting off a corner of crust and closing his eyes in pleasure.

"Mind that we're sharing our living space with a multiple murderer?" Lita asked, dryly. "Of course not. You're *our* multiple murderer."

"Oh, Elder Singer, you say the *kindest* things," crooned Bey. "Perhaps I should take *you* back with me. You would make the hair on the head of the Shadao himself stand on end."

Lita just smirked.

"I'll go den up in my own little lair when they arrive," Bey continued. "You can take credit for taking out all the Sleepgivers yourselves. In fact, I think you should. Publicly. And, of course, this fight is where my cousin will have died. It's as good a venue as any, and he's been wearing the talisman since it ended."

Jakyr and Lita nodded, and Amily held very tight to his hand. "Do you think there is any chance at all that the Shadao will think this is a ruse and send more Sleepgivers?" Amily asked anxiously.

"I would never say never, for only a fool would do that," Bey replied, after a long moment of deep thinking. "But I think it highly unlikely. He has lost twelve of the high second-rank Sleepgivers on this venture. You people, whom we thought so soft, have proven to be anything but soft. There are a limited number of us, and losing twelve, plus the four he had already lost, means he has also lost revenue. We do not kill for pleasure, we kill because we are paid very well to do so, and it will be hard to replace sixteen Sleepgivers of the second rank. I think he will accept the ruse, even if he thinks it *is* a ruse, because he must."

Silence reigned after that. It was very hard for all of them to find Bey charming, even admirable, and yet hear him say things about being a paid killer so casually. Only Lita seemed undisturbed.

"But, my friends, you should be deciding what you are going to do now," Bey continued.

"Well, first of all, the Guard has a great many roads to clear, and a Herald on Circuit is not exactly on a schedule," Jakyr pointed out. "We may end up waiting until a thaw. It's not as if we don't have supplies enough to last until then."

"And we can hunt for fresh meat," said Mags. "I wouldn't mind doing that."

"I would relish a chance to hunt for meat." Bey's eyes gleamed at the thought. "Could we do so tomorrow, do you think?"

"Dunno why not." Now that was interesting; Bey was positively nonchalant about using his skills to kill humans, but got excited at the idea of *hunting.* Maybe all that nonchalance was a mask . . .

:Don't count on it,: Dallen warned. *:I know, it's hard. I like him too. But he is what he is. And fortunately, once he goes home, he is no longer our problem.:*

"I think we all need peace and quiet and rest," Jakyr said, with a long look deep into the fire. He and Lita were sitting together, quite close together, although he didn't actually have an arm around her. Yet. Mags wasn't at all sure about how that was going to turn out. They had at least made up their decades-long quarrel and were friends again. Would they ever be anything else?

He didn't know. He wasn't about to predict. And it wasn't

his business, it was theirs. Some things not even a Herald was meant to meddle in. Not the loves of other Heralds. Not the morality of assassins.

"I would like that. I would not mind being snowed in here for a month," Lita sighed. "Bey knows the caves. If we get tired of each others' company we can go off exploring on our own."

"I know the caves on this side of the valley, at least," Bey replied. "And without false modesty, I can say I know them very well indeed. They are all interconnected, provided you don't mind leaping or bridging a few holes to nowhere." He ate another bite of his meat pie, and sighed. "They are quite fascinating. It looks as if—something—lived down here, and lived very well."

"In fact, several somethings," Jakyr said, brightening, and proceeded to explain the Hawkbrothers, their lizard servants, and some of the other creatures that lived in and around their Vales. For once Bey didn't act as if he knew everything; his eyes were wide and guileless, and he asked dozens of questions. And when Jakyr was done, he sighed happily. "It is like tales I found in the ancient scrolls, only you have seen these things with your own eyes! It pleases me to know such things exist in the real world, though I will never see them."

"You might," Mags began, but the young Sleepgiver only shook his head.

"There will be no time. First, as soon as I return home, I must make sure to tell the Shadao some entirely true and truly evil tales of the demon-summoners of Karse. This will ensure we have no commerce with them while he lives. And it might mean he will take a closer look at those who make our talismans. And then I must find a Blessed maiden who has spirit and marry her and ... huh ..." His face took on a most thoughtful expression.

"What?" Mags asked.

"I believe I know just the maiden. She will not have wed in

the time I was gone, for she is strong of face and spirit, rather than comely and pliant. Like you, Elder Singer," he said slyly, with a little bow. Lita threw a pillow at him. "I like her, I just had never even considered wedding her, since . . . well . . . what young fool does *not* prefer comely and pliant until he grows to know better?" He nodded, as if satisfied with his plan. "This, I shall do. It is a good match. We like each other, and know each other, which is more than most who wed can say. I shall tell her of you, oh, my cousin, only you shall not be my cousin in the tale, but only a Blessed friend who helped me on my travels. Then I shall help her to become the partner that you, alas, will not." He grinned broadly. "Thus, all my problems are solved! The Shadao will see that I have settled into responsibility and will call me heir. My wife shall be the treasure of my house and the guardian of my back. And perhaps we shall have Blessed children to also train! The Shadao will likely die soon after he names me heir, because he is sick and weary. And my wife and I shall guide the House of the Sleepgivers back to the old ways."

Once again, Mags was starkly reminded that the ways of the Sleepgivers were nothing like the ways of Valdemar. The Shadao, who Bey lightly said was like to die soon . . . was his father. His father who Bey said had loved his mother. And yet the son spoke of him as someone he respected but scarcely knew.

"You make it sound very simple," Lita said dryly.

He stretched, like a well-satisfied cat. "It is simple. The maid is like never to marry, unless I were to take her, or she were to marry beneath her, which she will never do. And as for returning the House to the old ways—not so simple, but neither is it difficult. It is not as if there are not many evil men in the world, and those who wish to see them gone and will pay well."

"He has a point," Lita told Jakyr, who was making a bit of a sour face.

"I don't have to like it," Jakyr retorted.

Bey laughed; apparently he found this very funny.

"Well, I can use a damn rest too," Mags said. "Jakyr, we need t'get some help up here with these people. If the rest of the Circuit goes like this first part has, it's pretty damn obvious to me that we need three Heralds comin' one after the other to remind folks they're part of this Kingdom. Maybe if they hadn't been left alone so much, they wouldn't be like this."

"That's entirely possible," said Jakyr, with a speculative look on his face. "I think that's a good idea. I think we should pass that on as soon as we can."

Which means, "You and Dallen pass it on." Mags was pleased rather than otherwise. Why shouldn't he be? This was Jakyr giving him responsibility.

But then Jakyr went further. "I have a profound apology to make to you, Mags. I berated you for trusting Bey, when Dallen and Jermayan backed you. I should apologize to Jermayan and Dallen as well," he added, looking at the two Companions on the other side of the cave. Jermayan just gave his Chosen a long, withering look. Dallen gave the Herald a long, withering look *and* snorted.

"I give you both permission in the future to do whatever you feel you need to if I do that again," Jakyr said, shamefaced. "I should have known better. I *did* know better. I let a great many things rule me when I should have been using my head."

"Aye," Mags said slowly. "Ye should have. I had t'learn the hard way t'use mine, reckon you had to do the same." He shrugged. "When it comes down t'cases, there's allus one thing. If ye can't trust yer Companion, there ain't nothin' ye can trust."

"You are going to make an excellent Herald, my cousin," Bey said sadly. "Such a loss to me!" Then he brightened. "Still! There are *days* of excellent company and meat pies ahead of us! I shall enjoy them while I can!"